*Jwh
11/28/92*

RUNAWAY TRAIN.

"I swear we're going even faster now," said the railroad dick with a puzzled frown. The train was doing close to a mile a minute when he declared, "There's a flag stop coming and I don't see how they'd stop this high balling combo no matter *what* anyone waved at her!"

Longarm stared out across the back-lit tops of the high chaparral to decide, "Someone's afraid of the dark. They're trying to make the far end of the line this side of sundown and, you know what? At this rate they likely will!"

The railroad dick said, "I noticed, and we don't have no way to signal either end from this infernal box car. This is surely one hell of a way to run a railroad if you're out to catch train robbers!"

Longarm couldn't have agreed more. The only way anyone could stop them this side of that jerkwater stop at the Kern River sounded awesomely uncomfortable. He drew his dangling legs up to hook his boot heels on the bottom slide rail of the door in hopes of landing somewhere out yonder with both legs attached if and when this son of a bitching car left the tracks. Cars tended to do that when somebody who just hated railroads yanked some spikes just down the line. . . .

*   *   *

TABOR EVANS

LONGARM

AND THE SAN JOAQUIN WAR

JOVE BOOKS, NEW YORK

LONGARM AND THE SAN JOAQUIN WAR

A Jove Book / published by arrangement with
the author

PRINTING HISTORY
Jove edition / August 1992

ISBN: 0-515-10897-9

Jove Books are published by The Berkley Publishing Group,
200 Madison Avenue, New York, New York 10016.
The name "JOVE" and the "J" logo
are trademarks belonging to Jove Publications, Inc.

PRINTED IN THE UNITED STATES OF AMERICA

10 9 8 7 6 5 4 3 2 1

Chapter 1

The trail town of South Fork was unhandy to the railroad stop at Cheyenne Wells, so Longarm hired a pair of livery mounts where you had to get off near the Colorado-Kansas line.

He wasn't headed out across the rolling prairie far enough to be packing supplies. The second pony was constitutional. He'd been sent to fetch a captured federal felon for the Denver District Court, and while hanging was doubtless too good for such a murderous son of a bitch, the constitution Longarm was sworn to uphold forbade such cruel and unusual punishments as marching another human a good thirty miles in high-heeled vaquero boots.

It was a crisp dry Indian summer day, with the summerkilt grass the color and condition of a straw welcome mat overdo for a good beating out back. For once the high plains had been dried out entire by the cloudless skies and mummy-breath winds of late summer, the resulting mustard-colored dust, fine as a lady's face powder, got into and over most everything west of say longitude 100 degrees.

By the time Longarm rode into South Fork, along about noon, his telescoped Stetson, tobacco brown duds, and both bay ponies were all the same shade of dry 'dobe. His lungs would have doubtless contained more gritty mud if he hadn't covered his nose and mouth with a kerchief he'd wisely wet with canteen water every mile or so. He still hawked a couple of bodacious goobers of shit-colored phlegm as he dismounted out front of the municipal corral and bet the Arapaho breed in charge a quarter they didn't have enough water, oats, and shade for his two dusty pals.

1

He lost, as he'd hoped he might, and, first things coming first, headed for the nearby town lockup as he beat his dusty tweeds like a rug with his already battered hat.

A town the size of South Fork hardly rated an elaborate lockup, so it didn't have one. Longarm was mildly surprised, however, as he entered, to find nobody there but a kid deputy wearing faded denims and a tarnished pewter star. The kid was seated at a banged-up desk with his back to the three empty cells along the back wall of the glorified line shack. He wasn't polite enough to stand up, but at least he had the decency to reach in a drawer for a bottle as he chuckled and said, "I can see you've been enjoying a dust bath with the rest of the sparrow birds, whether you'd be that Denver boy or not. Wet your poor whistle with some of this and see if it restores your voice."

Longarm reached for the brown bottle and gargled some before he swallowed. He preferred Maryland rye but bourbon took as much mud off a man's teeth and tongue, so what the hell.

Chasing the first muddy lava with a jolt of cleaner liquid fire, Longarm handed the bottle back with a sincere smile of thanks, which faded some as, once he'd told the town law who he was and what he'd come for, he heard the son of a bitch reply, "He ain't here. We ain't had him since just after breakfast. That's when we handed him over to that other deputy from Fort Smith, Arkansas. Said he was part Seminole. Looked part nigger, to me. He still packed a federal warrant, signed by that hot-tempered Judge Isaac Parker they say it's best not to cross, so . . ."

"You've never heard *my* boss, Marshal Billy Vail, cuss a deputy high and low for falling down on the job!" Longarm cut in, reaching for his pocket watch as he added, in a worried tone, "A man can only try, but you say that other deputy and my prisoner have at least a four hour lead on me?"

To which the local lawman cheerfully replied, "More like six. We eat early out this way, like the honest country boys we be. My boss said you'd likely get your bowels in an uproar once you got here only to find that bank-robbing Texican bound for the gallows in Fort Smith instead of Denver. That's likely why he left me in charge, here. I know I'm young and they keep telling me how much I got to learn but I sure wish someone would inform me what infernal difference it makes where you hang a bank robber, as long as you hang the bastard some damned where."

2

Longarm's mouth felt wet enough to smoke, now, so he reached in his vest and fumbled out a couple of three-for-a-nickel cheroots as he explained, "Nobody aims to hang Texas Slim for robbing banks. He qualified his fool self for the rope dance by gunning two tellers and half a dozen innocent bystanders in the course of robbing less than a dozen damned banks. Now that you mention it I do recall from his yellow sheets he shot an Osage mother and child as he was passing through the Indian Nation that time. For a judge with such a mean rep, old Isaac Parker does protect his Indian wards so . . . Damn, I made the usual courtesy call on the sheriff when I got off down in Cheyenne Wells and you'd have thought they'd have had the courtesy to save me all them dusty hours in the saddle on a fool's errand!"

As Longarm handed one of the smokes to the younger lawman the South Fork deputy explained, "That's easy. That darky from Arkansas never got off at Cheyenne Wells."

Longarm almost asked a dumb question. Then he lit his cheroot with a nod at his mental map of eastern Colorado and decided, "Anyone coming by rail from Fort Smith would get off at that prairie flag stop ten or twelve miles to the east of Cheyenne Wells to save a good five miles out of his way, for the same reasons I got off from the west a few miles further west."

He reached for the railroad timetable he'd picked up that morning at the Denver Union Depot as he continued, "I feel better about the boys in Cheyenne Wells than I do about you-all, here. Would it have hurt to send my office a collect telegram, seeing you'd already let another federal court have old Texas Slim?"

The kid from South Fork said they had, adding, "Denver wired back you'd already boarded the eastbound and that there was no way to get in touch with you afore you got off at Cheyenne Wells."

Longarm was scanning the timetable as he grumbled, "Serves me right for not stopping by the Western Union there, in my hurry to get here. Now the damned railroad's telling me there's no way I can ride back to Cheyenne Wells in time to catch the next eastbound and the one after that don't stop for water this side of bedtime!"

The kid said he'd never catch up with that darker deputy and Texas Slim by rail no matter where or when he started, now.

To which Longarm could only reply, "I noticed. I ain't sure Billy Vail wants me gunning any of old Isaac Parker's deputies

3

in any case and there's hardly any other way to take a prisoner away from one of his hardcased cusses. So maybe I'd best settle for pistol-whipping that traitor to Colorado you ride for."

The Colorado kid smiled uncertainly. "I'm sure my boss got called out of town on personal business with that very concern on his mind, Longarm. But surely your own boss ought to be able to see none or this was your fault? I mean, you was aboard that train, headed here in good faith, about the time that other deputy showed up with a warrant signed earlier to—"

"Make me look dumb," Longarm finished grimly. But even as he blew smoke out both nostrils like a bob-wired bull, he knew he was apt to make an even bigger fool of himself by sounding off ferocious over spilt milk. His own crusty boss was more reasonable, deep down inside all that lard, than he liked to let on. So the fussing and cussing Longarm was in for when he returned empty-handed wouldn't really appear on his record, and no matter how often Billy Vail swore he was going to dock a deputy's travel expenses he hardly ever did. Old Billy had even settled for splitting the difference that time a fool hotel clerk had billed the Justice Department for a honeymoon suite at double occupancy rates.

Longarm put the timetable back in a side pocket of his frock coat as somewhere in the distance a clock striking noon was answered by a couple of muffled gunshots.

Neither lawmen commented. In a time and place where any twelve-year-old without his own hunting rifle was considered underprivileged, a lawman who got excited every time he heard a gun go off was fixing to die young with jangled nerves. Longarm checked his pocket watch against the distant church bell, decided it was better to be three minutes fast than the other way, and said, "Well, it's hot outside and there's no sense pushing my livery nags past common sense when I could just as easily be ordering a good noon dinner and mayhaps enough coffee to get me back to Cheyenne Wells in time for that westbound, jerking water along about moonrise. Where would you suggest I try for, say, fried eggs over chili con carne and a slab of mince pie washed down with real Arbuckle?"

The younger lawman said he knew just the place and allowed he hadn't eaten since breakfast, either. So he got to his feet and the two of them were halfway out the door when an older gent in a straw hat and bib overalls came running at them along the plank

4

walk, all red-faced and bleating more like a sheep than a mortal man as he announced, "Highway robbery and murder most foul! Up to Ma Boyer's! They got away with at least a hundred dollars and left that nigger working yonder deader than a turd in a milk bucket!"

So the town lawman commenced running, and, despite the dry heat and the distinctly local flavor, Longarm ran after them. As luck would have it, they ran out of plank walk long before he ran out of breath.

Ma Boyer's was a general store, down the other side of the municipal corral. As Longarm followed the town law inside he doubted the place could do this much business as a rule. Like the rest of the dinky trail town, there was little about the dinky frame building to impress one. The interior layout was familiar, time-tested by small merchants on the western plains. A potbelly stove, cold at this time of the year, shared the center of the main room with the usual cracker and pickle barrels, along with a couple of chairs and a checkerboard atop an upturned soap box. Counters ran the length of the chamber to the north and south, with dry goods, tools and such along the south wall and canned goods, seeds and such to the north, where the sun was less able to bake through the pine siding. The front doors and windows to the east faced the bank of mail boxes and post office counter built into the west wall, where no windows let in the ferocious western sun of summer or the howling west winds of winter out this way.

Most of the folk inside were crowded about a gentleman of color sprawled on the sawdust between the stove and post office counter. A fat and ugly but sort of motherly white lady was holding the dead boy's head in her lap, sobbing fit to bust. A more sensible sounding woman hovering over them told the town deputy, "Ma's darky tried to clean the bandit's plow with a pick handle as he was reaching in the till with one hand and covering Ma with the other. As you see, he was faster than poor Hiram there."

A cowhand who'd just helped himself to a cracker opined, "The boy was brave as hell, for a nigger. I say we catch the rascal and hang him high. It can't be right to gun a man who's only trying to help his boss lady, no matter what his color might have been!"

Another man in the group growled, "Damned A. Murder is murder as long as you're not talking about Sioux and I ain't sure it'd be right to gun a Sioux under these exact conditions."

5

Longarm was halfway out the front by this time. The younger local lawman ran after him, bleating, "Hold on, Uncle Sam. I know a shitty little cow town killing ain't as important to you as it is to me, but my boss is off somewheres, like I said, and to tell the pure truth I ain't never investigated a case this serious afore!"

Longarm said, "I noticed, no offense. Go back inside and see if you can get us some sort of description to work with as I fetch us some riding stock. You may as well ride the spare pony I hired down in Cheyenne Wells, seeing it's already saddled and bridled as well as fresh-watered and fed."

The kid brightened and gushed, "Hot damn! You mean you're willing to tag along and back my play, Longarm?"

To which the more experienced lawman replied with a thin smile, "Not hardly. I just offered to let *you* tag along and back *mine*. The asshole or assholes I'm after just held up a U.S. Post Office, in case you failed to notice."

The kid must have. "Aw, come on. We're talking about a general store that sells stamps and keeps a few mailboxes in the back for customers to use."

Longarm shook his head firmly and insisted, "Anywhere you send or receive the U.S. Mail is a post office, and the killing of a human being on the premises of the same constitutes murder in the first, federal. So get cracking and I'll meet you here in five minutes with them ponies, hear?"

Chapter 2

Longarm hadn't suggested they posse up, but he was neither too surprised nor upset by the score or more of others ready to go by the time he returned to the scene of the crime, mounted on the bay gelding and leading the matching mare.

The kid deputy had helped himself inside to a Remington repeater. As he forked aboard the mare Longarm heard one of the others address him as Spud, which sounded reasonable enough.

Spud said they were looking for a lone wolf villain around seven feet tall and weighing mayhaps three hundred pounds, which didn't sound reasonable.

It developed nobody but the storekeeper cum postmistress inside had actually seen the killer and she'd been under the disadvantage of having to guess more than a few details, thanks to a rucksack mask, dim light filled with gunsmoke, and hysteria occasioned by sincere fondness for a willing worker shot down like a dog right in front of her.

A somewhat brighter looking cowhand in the crowd opined Ma Boyer knew most everyone in town who'd ever stolen a licorice whip, so it seemed safe to surmise the masked menace had been a stranger.

Another hand who looked as if he'd stolen his share of licorice whips in the past chimed in, "A stranger with shit for brains, you mean. Nobody else would expect to find more than a few dollars at a time in Ma Boyer's till. She always puts the extra bills under her counter as soon as they add up to more than she'd need for change."

There came a general rumble of agreement. Longarm nodded

silently, satisfied that anyone who'd known the old postmistress better would have cleaned her out instead of simply riding off with less than a hundred after killing a man for it.

He called out, "We'll ask the rascal about the finer details of this mystery once we catch him. He can't have an hour's lead on us no matter what he looks like. We know we'll be seeking a stranger to these parts across open prairie in broad ass daylight. So now I want someone who knows this country better than me to suggest his best escape route."

More than one man there seemed to feel he could evade at least the U.S. Cav on range he knew so much better. It was young Spud who threw cold water on the notion by demanding, "Hold on, if the cuss we're after is a *stranger*, how come we already got him riding *smart* across country he knows so damned well?"

A lot there seemed to feel Spud was right. So Longarm called out, "I said it was better to just catch him and *ask* him, dammit. Meanwhile, it's been my experience few owlhoot riders hit in strange surroundings without scouting some in advance. Had this one come to town the usual way, up or down the usual trail, someone else aside from his victims would be describing him way better, right?"

When he saw they were following him that far he continued, "*Bueno*, he circled in across the rolling sea of grass all about, likely off the skyline, sneaking zig-zag through the deep, however gentle draws."

A rider a mite older than Longarm agreed, "That's the way that son of a bitch, Roman Nose, led his Crooked Lance Cheyenne all over creation back in Indian-fighting times."

Another proclaimed, "Led a thousand infernal Cheyenne smack into the Julesburg city limits back in '65 and nary a soul seen 'em coming 'til white folk was getting scalped in their backyard shit houses! Do you reckon the cuss as kilt that nigger could be an Injun?"

Longarm grimaced and said, "It's best not to picture a man you're hunting when you don't know what he looks like. I could tell you a tale of lawmen on the trail of a cuss called Billy the Kid being fooled by a sort of sissy-looking little squirt and their own pictures of a mighty dangerous gunslick, but Billy the Kid ain't robbed anyone this far north of New Mexico Territory. So I'm fixing to ride south 'til I'm well clear of your average rabbit hunter and then I mean to circle 'til I spy some sign. You boys

8

can come along or stay here, if you like. Just make sure you don't tear off in all directions to mess up the one damn trail I'm interested in."

Nobody seemed anxious to do anything but tag along after Longarm and Spud as they headed south along the wagon trace leading off that way. As they rode, Spud warned the wagon trace forked about five miles on and added, "I doubt we'll spy much of a trail in any case. Anyone with eyes can see the grass all about is overgrazed straw stubble, with the 'dobe it's rooted in baked hard as plaster."

Longarm nodded but pointed out, "The whole shebang's right dusty as well. When I left Cheyenne Wells this morning the dust was kicking up clean over my head. Time I got to your fair city it was only hanging stirrup high and now the wind's died total."

Spud was slower to follow his drift than a nearby older hand who observed, "Morning breeze hardly ever blows past noon and . . . Do Jesus! The range critters won't be stirring much in all this heat and ain't nobody but us and that outlaw been riding worth mention out here since the wind died!"

Spud brightened and declared, "I see the light and remind me never to cut across fresh-dusted stubble with a posse on my ass!"

Longarm didn't answer. He'd heeled his mount into a mile-eating but ball-busting trot and the stock saddle he'd hired in Cheyenne Wells made talking at a trot even worse than if he'd been bouncing in the personal McClellan he'd failed to bring along on the cut and dried mission he'd been sent on.

The wagon trace they were following had been dust-powdered by the same morning breezes, of course, but whilst the dust lay even thicker in the ruts, the baked 'dobe ridges between got to go on baking bare as ever in the glaresome sunlight. So the first sign at all, a mile and a half down the road, consisted of a half dozen hover flies swirling above a patch of fresh mud.

Longarm figured hover flies were disguised by Mother Nature as half-ass honey bees to keep fly-catching critters away from 'em. He was still working on why they hovered like that. But since he was a lawman rather than an entomologist he just reined in and stood taller in his stirrups as he gazed about, declaring, "Someone paused to piss here and . . . Yep, over to the west."

Spud grinned wolfishly as he took in the dotted line of barely darker patches of less dusty grass. He declared, "I follow your drift. He streaked this far along the road to town, trusting to the sun-baked center, 'til he stopped to take a leak and had a grander notion."

Another rider who'd doubtless tracked more cows than men in his time opined, "Knowing we got us a telly-grafted wire to both rail stops to the south he decided he'd best head somewhere's else, and will you just look at the clear as crystal trail he's left us to follow!"

Longarm didn't answer, he was already riding west northwest along the faint dotted line, squinting against the afternoon glare as he calculated the pace of the fugitive's pony from the spaces between the patches of less dusty stubble. The cuss had been walking his mount, cautious, near the wagon trace. Further out he'd been loping. Loping that far from the scene of his crime meant a rider more worried about his own comfort than that of his saddle brute. Longarm, like the others with him at the moment, knew enough to trot their mounts with the sun so hot and nobody knowing how far they had to travel by sundown.

They'd ridden close to two miles in an ever increasing swing to the north before Spud decided, "The son of a bitch must be trying to double back on his trail!"

To which another local replied, "Trying hell, he's *doing* so. But there goes our grand notion about him being a total stranger in these parts. For where in thunder could a stranger hope to hide out in a town the size of South Fork?"

Longarm reined in near yet another patch of pissy mud and stared down soberly for some time before he decided, "Friend or foe, he's a pissing wonder. Only this time the mud's had longer to dry."

Spud pointed at other disturbances in the dusty stubble as he opined, "He dismounted yonder to do so. Looks as if he reined in from a lope, first, as if the urge to piss came sudden."

Longarm lit a thoughtful smoke as another posse rider recalled, "My grandfather used to piss like that. Poor old cuss had to get up ever' hour or so, all through the night. One night he didn't. Next morning he was found stone dead in his bed with a serene expression on his face and the mattress wet clean through."

A middle-aged rider sighed and said, "Men do piss more often as they get older. I sure wish that wasn't so, but there you are and don't that mean we're looking for a cuss at least as old as the woman he just robbed?"

Longarm blew smoke out his nostrils and announced, "I mean to ask his date and place of birth for my officious report, once I catch the sneaky bastard. We've been going the wrong way, gents. Nobody honest spied him coming to town in that dust storm. He tethered his mount behind that general store. Then he circled afoot to kill a man and scare an old lady half to death for a modest sum. Nobody out front along your main street saw him when he just whipped back around to the back and beelined off across the prairie for the nearest draw."

Longarm swung his own mount around as he added, "We've been on his back trail, not the way he's really headed, which is likely one railroad stop or another to the south."

Then Longarm was riding back the way they'd just come, trending more to the south to hit the wagon trace closer to somewhere more important than that swarm of hover flies.

Spud was supposed to be second in command. It still took one of the older riders to disconfuse him by explaining, "That puddle of piss back yonder would be fresher than the first one if our killer was riding back to the scene of his crime. I didn't think a drifter who'd gun old Hiram for peanuts could be a college professor. He just lit out lucky, like Longarm said, then cut over to the only road he knew in these parts before he could get his pissing self lost, see?"

Spud nodded and growled, "I do, now. We're looking for a mean old saddle tramp who seen a chance and took it. I'm glad I won't have to arrest anyone I know, after all."

Then he was riding too hard, after Longarm, to jaw all that much about their hard-riding but possibly senile quarry.

Yet they hadn't ridden a full hour before Longarm reined in where, sure enough, the damned wagon trace forked to offer two whole ways to get to the railroad further south.

Spud reined in beside Longarm to explain, "East fork takes you down to the flag stop at Arapahoe Crossing. West fork, as you must have noticed, coming up it, leads to Cheyenne Wells. Don't ask me which fork I'd pick if I was him."

Longarm said, "Don't have to. There's no way he can hope to board a westbound train this side of sundown and he must have noticed the telegraph lines over yonder by now. On the other hand he might just catch the afternoon eastbound if he hurries."

Longarm started down the fork that lead to Arapahoe Crossing. The rest of them naturally followed. It was easier to think than it

11

was to talk at a jarring trot, so when Longarm reined in again, after quite some trotting, Spud declared, "You figure he'd want to shave hisself a few safe minutes by catching the eastbound further east. But what are you staring down at, here and now? No offense, but I don't see nothing."

Longarm growled, "Neither do I, and that killer was pissing sort of regular, before."

Spud suggested the cuss was all pissed out for now. Longarm shrugged and said, "You could be right. Or we could be playing chess with a two-bit bandit who's never mastered checkers. You all chase him down this road if you like. I'm cutting over to the other one, and if I'm wrong, I can still board the eastbound at Cheyenne Wells with a chance of grabbing him as he boards further east."

Then he was cutting across the rolling prairie before anyone could ask what he'd do if he failed to catch that afternoon train. From the way he was riding, his answer seemed obvious enough.

Shortly after they were back on the other wagon trace, one answer and an even bigger herd of hover flies above a fresher patch of mud told Longarm he was heading the right way for certain. His only worry now was getting to Cheyenne Wells before that afternoon eastbound.

They made it with time to spare, pulling in near the railroad stop under an awesome thunderhead of 'dobe and dried horseshit dust. The dramatic arrival of so many armed and dangerous-looking riders naturally brought the local law running, despite the dry heat.

Cheyenne Wells being the county seat as well as the most important railroad stop for miles, said local law got to sport more impressive badges than young Spud. A more impressive county deputy recognized Spud and some of his riders, so he put his own .44-40 away as he declared, "We heard. We been watching for sinister strangers tearing down the trace from South Fork. Ain't seen none, so far."

Longarm waited until he'd dismounted and shook friendly with the local senior deputy before he declared, "We may have rid in wilder, with less to hide from you gents. The killer we're after seems to make a habit of slipping in and out of towns more discreet."

Spud said, "He pisses a lot, too. Following him this far, we could see he'd stopped to take a leak about once an hour or more.

12

So he studies to look older and more harmless than your average desperado."

The county law in command started to say they didn't have any old coots like so in town. Then one of his junior deputies chimed in with, "Yes we might, Tom. I just now talked with a gray haired stranger over to the saloon. Said he was there to catch the next train east after visiting with kin out to the Slash Bar Slash."

One of the hands who'd ridden in with Longarm told him, "Half a day's ride off to the southwest. They're all right."

The senior sheriff's deputy was at least as suspicious as Longarm. He asked if anyone had seen this elderly stranger arrive from any damned direction to lurk in dank dark saloons where nobody else was likely to notice him.

When the junior deputy protested he'd already checked the old cuss out his superior growled, "He'd hardly be anxious to make a public confession after gunning that colored boy up to South Fork and like Longarm, here, just said, there's ways to arrive in town open and then there's way to come in sneaksome. Let's go have us a word with that sneaky old cuss."

Longarm tethered his hired mount and tagged along after them. Nobody had far to go. The saloon had been built handy to the rail stop with waiting for trains in mind. There was a dusty paint cow pony tethered in front of the saloon. Longarm softly asked a nearby hand from South Fork if it seemed familiar. The answer was, "Nope. We'd have heard had anyone stole a horse as well as Ma Boyer's hard-earned money. Why do you ask?"

Longarm frowned uncertainly and replied, "Something familiar, yonder, if only I could get my damn brain to work right in all this thirsty heat."

They went inside to find the sheriff's senior deputy already talking to a man old enough to be his father and piss at least three times as often. After that the older man looked more like a nervous retired professor than an owlhoot rider. His summer-weight seersucker suit was dusty enough for him to have ridden that dusty pony out front many a mile. But when asked about that he protested his daughter and new son-in-law had driven him in from the Slash Bar Slash in their buckboard.

The South Fork rider who'd said he knew the outfit quietly asked for some names. When the old timer insisted his daughter, Clara, had married up with a ranch foreman named Colechester,

13

the local rider nodded and said, "He's got that right. Pronto Colechester's the ramrod of the Slash Bar Slash and I do think his young wife's name would be Clara. She coffee and caked me last roundup when I was over their way after some stock. Bakes a mighty fine marble cake and she's pretty, too."

The old man thanked him. The deputy sheriff shrugged and said, "I could say I was kin to a pretty gal from other parts, now that I know where she lives and what she cooks like. Tell us about that pinto out front, old man."

The old man almost sobbed as he declared, "I can't tell you anything about it. I never saw it before. I just told you Clara and her man drove me in to catch my damned train back home to Missouri!"

"It's my pony," another voice cut in politely. So everyone turned to see a young cuss of sixteen to twenty, dressed cow and wearing his Colt .36 conversion cross-draw. Longarm could tell right off he was a stranger to the locals as well. But he made a way better impression as he continued, "Name's Folsom. My friends call me Peewee on account all my brothers wound up taller. I got laid off at the Rocking X over on the Kansas side of the line and heard they might be hiring at that very Slash Bar Slash you all been jawing about. Had I known this old gent was related to their ramrod's wife you'd have found us drinking together when you come in."

Nobody answered. Peewee Folsom nodded and said, "You'll want to look through my saddlebags for running irons and I've no objection."

Young Spud said, cautiously, "We're hunting a cuss who robbed an old lady and gunned her hired help with a rucksack over his sneaky head. We figure he left town with close to a hundred dishonestly earned dollars on him as well."

The younger of the two strangers unbuckled his gun rig and gravely placed it atop the bar as he replied, "You can search me as well as my pony, if you so desire. You'll find no mask and do you find more than twenty whole dollars on me I sure wish you'd tell me where I've been packing it since I got laid off. They gave me a full month's pay as I was handed the shovel at the end of last month, but . . ."

"It's as easy to hide money as it is to hide rucksacking," the local senior deputy cut in, adding, "I mean to check both your tales out before either of you leave town." Then he turned to the older man to demand, "How much money might you have on you at the moment, old-timer?"

"A little over a hundred," sighed the otherwise more harmless-looking suspect, adding, "I left home with twice that much and would have spent more had not my new son-in-law insisted on paying, no matter how much I protested."

Spud nudged Longarm to murmur, "He's got the money and he's got the eldersome bladder we made note of, trailing him. So what do you say?"

Longarm said, "As a rule I'd say we ought to wait until we could confirm or disrepute their sensible-sounding stories. But I got me a train of my own to catch and by sheer good fortune there's that one clue you forgot, old son. Don't you recall that lady who described the killer for us mentioning all them gold fillings in his teeth?"

Spud looked blank, then replied in a sincerely puzzled tone, "I recall her saying he was seven or eight feet tall with his whole damned head shoved up inside a rucksack. I'll be switched with snakes if I recall her mentioning gold teeth or, for that matter, how she'd have noticed."

Longarm chuckled fondly at the younger lawman and said, not too unkindly, "You got to learn to pay attention, even when a witness may sound sort of silly."

Turning back to the sheriff's deputy he added, "I ain't no dentist, but I can surely spot gold bridgework as good as any scared old lady and unless we're dealing with two walking and talking gold mines . . ."

"You gents best let the man examine your damn teeth," the local deputy sheriff cut in as Longarm took the older suspect by one arm to gently swing him toward the light. The old man started to object, then laughed, put a hand to his old gray face, and took out his full set of false choppers to hold out to Longarm, saying, "Be my guest. Solid porcelain, every one."

That left the younger stranger smiling back at a heap of hard eyes until he laughed lightly and invited Longarm to examine away. Anyone could see, as he opened wide, he needed more fillings than he had. There wasn't a trace of gold in his mouth. Longarm still peered closer than anyone else as the deputy sheriff decided, "The witness that described that killer never described neither of these gents. We'd still best wait 'til we can check out their stories."

Then he asked, "How come you're doing that, Uncle Sam?" as he watched Longarm whirl young Folsom around, slam him against the bar, and twist both wrists behind him to slap federal handcuffs on the same.

Folsom seemed as surprised, but that was doubtless an act as well as Longarm explained, "I fibbed. The lady this little shit robbed never mentioned his teeth and had him down as a seven-foot giant. I only wanted the chance to sniff some. I told you I can't spare the time to check out both their stories. You lawmen better sniff this one's breath while you have the chance. You may learn something you'll be able to use another time."

The youth called Folsom knew what Longarm was talking about. So he would have held his breath when Spud stepped closer, had not he been punched so firmly in the ribs by Longarm.

As he exhaled in Spud's face the younger lawman said, "I smell it. What in tarnation has this old boy been eating?"

To which Longarm replied, "Nothing much. They last longer if they eat less. That's likely why he's so puny as well as so pissy. He's suffering sugar diabetes. The smell of a diabetic's breath is a bitch to describe but, once you've smelt it . . ."

"Sickly sweet, like honey mixed with paint thinner." The sheriff's deputy decided, once he'd jabbed the prisoner on the gut and had a whiff as well.

Longarm said, "Don't poke him no more, gents. He may be sick as hell and we don't want him dying on us before we get to hang him."

The handcuffed youth said a dreadful thing about Longarm's dear old mother. Longarm softly replied, "It won't work. I'm a professional who aims to bring you back alive no matter how you try to change my mind."

Then he glanced at the wall clock behind the bar, grinned, and declared, "The first round's on me, gents. For I've plenty of time to settle up at the livery and buy this poor cuss a healthy supper before we catch that evening train back to Denver."

Nobody objected to the drinks but the sheriff's deputy must have felt obliged to point out the prisoner had committed his one known robbery and murder in the jurisdiction of Cheyenne County, Colorado.

Longarm nodded but flatly replied, "There were United States postage stamps in the till he was robbing and the boy he shot

16

was working for a part-time postmistress, making him a federal employee and don't fuck with me. Marshal Billy Vail sent me all the way from Denver to bring back a federal prisoner and, come hell or high water I mean to bring one back with me!"

Chapter 3

Longarm got to know his prisoner better than he really wanted to as they spent that good five hours together on the night train to Denver. The kid turned out a born slicker smart enough to season his lies with as much truth as possible. So he really had been laid off by that Kansas spread as he'd advertised, albeit as a sickly hand who hadn't been able to pull his weight. They'd confirmed him as a worthless but otherwise innocent cuss they knew as Peewee Folsom. Longarm finally got him to sheepishly admit they'd called him Peewee more for his constant pissing than bigger brothers they'd have never seen. Folsom seemed to feel Longarm owed him some pity for having come down in his teens with sugar diabetes. Longarm said he'd read it was a fatal illness with no known cure, but added, "I'm sorry you got to die young, one way or the other, but that colored boy back in South Fork never asked to die young, neither, and you murdered him for less'n a hundred dollars. What did you do with the rest of the money you robbed, by the way?"

The doomed prisoner didn't answer for a time as the steel wheels rumbled under them to keep their conversation at one end of the half-empty car fairly private. He stared out at the darkness and licked his pale lips before he cautiously asked, "What kind of a break can you offer me for telling you all sorts of things you may not know, you smartass?"

Longarm chuckled dryly and replied, "There's always a few loose strings dangling by the time we dangle the average killer from some nice new Manila. I tidied up some as you were pissing in the county jail whilst I sent telegrams, settled up at the town

18

livery and such. I don't need to produce the stolen money to prove you rid off with it. Some kids up to South Fork have already established there was a paint cow pony tied up behind Ma Boyer's as that dust storm died down this morning. They told me over to the livery, when I asked if said pony went with the same brand of saddle they'd hired out to me, they had in fact hired that very saddle aboard that very pony to a rider describing hisself as a Folsom. You told 'em you was looking for work and needed transporting. You come up with the yarn about applying at the Slash Bar Slash when you heard that nice stranger describe the place."

Longarm got out two smokes and offered one to his prisoner. "Let's see, now, what have I left out? I doubt even a federal prosecutor will want samples of all them mud pies you made with your sugarsome piss as I trailed you all the way from the scene of the crime with a posse of witnesses, but as you likely know, any chemist worthy of the title can test piss, wet or dry, good enough to prove it come from the only diabetic within miles."

The sickly youth let Longarm light his cheroot for him before he shrugged and said, "Fuck you. I know you got enough to hang me. I'd just like to get out of dying that way if it's all the same with you."

Before Longarm could say it wasn't, Folsom insisted, "The sawbones who told me why I was pissing so much and feeling so odd said I had mayhaps three to six years ahead of me, if I watched what I et and avoided hard likker. He told me this better than two years back, so any time they give me will amount to a life sentence, see?"

Longarm did. He nodded soberly and replied, "They might give you life at hard. There's this professor back east who swears he's about to invent a flying machine as well. But look on the bright side, old son. Hanging can't hurt any worse than the lingersome death your condition promises you no matter what I do or say."

Folsom shook his head and said, "I'm used to feeling sick. I watched 'em hang a man one time and it gave me bad dreams for months. I know that if you or better yet your boss put in a word for me the judge'd let me die dignified, in a prison hospital."

Longarm cocked a brow to reply, "That well may be, but you don't know me or Marshal Billy Vail too well if you expect us to plead for a pissy little polecat for no good reason!"

Folsom asked, "What if I gave you a good reason?"

Longarm had expected he might. Men staring up those thirteen steps in that back courtyard were inclined to offer all sorts of deals. Some of them worth considering. So Longarm leaned back, his cheroot gripped at a thoughtful angle between his wolfishly bared teeth, and just waited.

Folsom glanced about, as if he feared even one of the other sleepy passengers in the middle distance gave a damn, before he confided, "You're bound to find out sooner or later, I ain't always been Peewee Folsom. Afore I was punching cows as him in Kansas I was doing time in Yuma on this here robbery charge."

Longarm sighed. "You'd think in time an old boy would either get it right or give it up, but we know about habitual criminals. That's how come we call 'em habitual. How much time did you serve, under what name, in Yuma Prison?"

The youth now calling himself Folsom said, "That ain't what I got to sell. A rose by any other name escaped in the company of a really bad hombre you and your whole government want way more than me. You ever hear tell of Tomas Ortega Baker, better known as the Fresno Kid?"

Longarm had. So he laughed and said, "Nice try but no cigar. The murderous Californio of whom you speak may be wanted for everything but leprosy, a heap of it federal. But you see, we keep yellow sheets on such yellow shits and I read 'em regular. So I can tell you that aside from never doing time in Yuma Prison with you or anyone else, he was killed by the Mex *rurales* in Nogales a month or so back."

He took a lazy drag on his smoke before adding, "As a rule I don't admire *los rurales* and their corrupt government all that much, but fair is fair and sometimes they do gun a gringo who deserves it. I hear tell the Fresno Kid was as Mexican as he might have been Anglo in any case."

His prisoner insisted, "He can pass for either if he has to. He told me his daddy was a German immigrant who's real name commenced as Bäcker. His mamma was a high-born señorita with Spanish kith and kin in high places, all over."

Longarm repressed a yawn as he felt forced to agree, "The Ortega clan is well known and considered quality, out California way. Meanwhile, like I said, we got nothing on her wayward child doing time in Yuma but *los rurales* put in for a heap of gringo bounty money once they shot the liver and lights out of him that time, like I said."

Folsom insisted, "Like *they* said, you mean. Baker told me, as we was fixing to escape with the help of some Mex vaqueros down Yuma way, how his *rurale* pals could hide us out in Old Mexico and even make it look like we'd been kilt, down yonder, afore we come back north."

Longarm blew a thoughtful smoke ring before he decided, grudgingly, "Men have been known to give false names when picked up for lesser crimes and you just heard me say what I thought of the current Mexican government, so keep talking."

"That's as much as you get until you tell me what I want to hear in return," his prisoner replied, as if he meant it.

Longarm didn't answer for a long unwinking time. When at last he did he said, "If I believed you, which would be dumb to begin with, my boss has threatened to fire me the next time I traipse down Mexico way after anyone we want on any charge. Old Billy says, and I have to allow he's right, the biggest crook and meanest bastard in all Mexico is *running* the place. So it hardly seems fair to risk another war with Mexico just to arrest less disgusting hombres than El Presidente Porfirio Diaz."

His prisoner said, "Tom Baker, the Fresno Kid, said Diaz is an utter bastard, too. Being half Mex, Tom ought to know. But that ain't where he's hiding out right now. Like me, he crossed back to these here United States once the heat died down and the fucking greasers started demanding ever more dinero."

"You had that kind of money, after escaping from prison?" Longarm demanded dryly.

Folsom explained, "Tom's Mex pals, or mayhaps cousins, had some pocket jingle as well as a change of duds for us when we met 'em in the cactus just outside the walls. He sent for more, by wire, once we were across the border. Do you want to pester me about such petty details or do you want me to tell you where the Fresno Kid can be found right now, on this damned side of the damned border?"

Longarm said he did. But when Folsom repeated his demand for a less dramatic death than he deserved Longarm had to shake his head and say, "You first. If your story makes a lick of sense I'll be proud to tell Judge Dickerson you tried to atone for past misdeeds by peaching on an even worse young killer. He might decide it could serve the cause of justice just as well to let you die natural of a sort of grim condition."

21

Folsom said that wasn't good enough and decided he'd wait and see whether Marshal Vail, in the flesh, wanted to deal. Longarm spent the rest of the tedious train ride trying to talk him out of that. He knew that unlike himself Billy Vail would be likely to promise most anything for a crack at an owlhoot rider wanted as bad as the one and original Fresno Kid. Worse yet, old Billy would be likely to keep his word. Marshal Vail was one of those old-fashioned lawmen who stuck to the letter of the law and just hated to bend even the more foolish rules.

Longarm never busted his own word, outright, if he could help it. So he rephrased his own suggestions a dozen ways or more before his prisoner agreed he'd settle for Longarm's written promise to act as a character witness for the defense.

Longarm got out his notebook and stub pencil to commit himself to that before anyone could ask him to sign it in blood. Then he tore the sheet out, handed it over, and poised his pencil tip over a blank sheet, growling, "I'm waiting."

Folsom hesitated, read their compact over a second time, and said, "He's gone home, to the San Joaquin Valley where he grew up. He told me I could come with him, if I liked. I didn't because it's one thing for a California rider to pass for an innocent local boy out yonder, whilst I got this Midwest way of talking and rope tiedown from a double rig saddle."

Longarm hadn't written that last part down. He snorted and said, "The San Joaquin Valley takes in a heap of territory, as well you knew when you decided to slicker me."

Folsom smiled thinly and replied, "They call him the Fresno Kid because he started out robbing that bank in Fresno that time, right?"

Longarm looked disgusted and said, "He ain't from Fresno. He was born on one of them Spanish *rancheros* further up the San Joaquin or down the big valley to the south, since that particular river runs north as I recall. I think I read somewhere he went to school, to the sorrow of his teachers, in Tulare County, unless it was Kern. I'll have to look it up. I doubt my boss will give a shit. They got their own U.S. marshals out California way and just betwixt you and me, I think you're full of it. How could a famous killer wanted by the federal government hide out on his own home range? You just now said the asshole commenced his wild career by robbing a bank just down the valley from where he raped at least one of his schoolmarms!"

22

Folsom chuckled and said, "He told me she wanted it. He was big for his age. As to his being able to hide that close to home, now, he's learned to act less boisterous in public after more than one close call, such as being sent to Yuma for a crime he didn't commit lest they discover where he really was, doing what, the night they had him stopping that stage more civilized."

Longarm grimaced and decided, "We'll pass it on to the U.S. marshal in Fresno, but I don't know, Kid. Seems to me a well-known want, hiding out close to home, would never get away with it unless he had a lot of friends in high places, including the very federal lawmen we'll be wiring."

Folsom shrugged and asked, "How do you know Tom ain't got deputies pretty as you doing just that very thing for him?"

Longarm growled. "It ain't pretty for any lawman to cover for a wanted man. It gets even uglier when you accuse a federal deputy of such disgusting habits, hear?"

Folsom shrugged and said, "I never. It was old Tom as told me he had the whole San Joaquin Valley in his hip pocket, federal, state, and county law included."

Chapter 4

Miss Morgana Floyd, head matron at the Arvada Orphan Asylum, was only one of the Denver belles cursed with mixed feelings about U.S. Deputy Custis Long, as they preferred to introduce him to their friends, landladies, and such.

Longarm had saved the petite brunette's life one time, and she'd found it mighty pleasant as well as only fair to reward his gallantry in the manner most young healthy men preferred.

On the other hand, Longarm had rescued many another damsel in distress and after learning about that sloe-eyed hussy he'd saved during the Chinese Riots a spell back Morgana had warned him never to darken her door again, on pain of a chamber pot, recently used, slopped over his two-timing head.

But this particular Saturday night, as the clocks all over Denver were fixing to strike twelve times, the hot-tempered and warm natured Morgana had just gone to bed, alone, to strum her own banjo in the lonely darkness of her downtown Denver room when, just as she was fixing to come, she heard someone twisting the nickel-plated handle of her doorbell out front.

She wasn't surprised as she let on to find Longarm standing there with a sack of malted milk balls and a sheepish grin. Longarm had his own sources of information and wouldn't have been there had he heard she'd found someone else, permanent.

"Custis Long!" Morgana began, wrapping her kimono of tan pongee more modestly across her otherwise bare breasts, "This is a fine time to come calling on a respectable young lady, even if she hadn't told you never to tip your hat to her on the street again! What's the matter with you? Has a certain young widow woman up on Capitol Hill heard about you and that china doll, too? Or did you have a falling out with that redhead at the Black Cat Saloon over your notorious affair with those Indian girls down by Cherry Creek. *Both* of them, I understand!"

Before she could get really wound up, Longarm cut in with, "You got me wrong about them innocent Arapaho twins, Miss Morgana. I swear on the U.S. flag and constitution that I've been pledged to uphold and defend that I have yet to so much as hold hands with both them sweet young things!"

This was the pure truth since, so far, the deer-shy Betty Buffalo Tail had refused to get in bed with him and her bolder sister, Kate, albeit she sure liked to watch and it seemed only a question of time.

Before Morgana could ask which sister, if not both, he'd been at that noisy night along Cherry Creek, Longarm handed her the sweets he knew she couldn't resist, and whipped out his notebook, saying, "I know you don't want my loving and I can't say I blame you. But I just come from the morgue of the *Rocky Mountain News* after depositing a prisoner in the Federal House of Detention closer to the depot."

As he'd hoped, the spunky little gal's curiosity was almost as strong as her love of malted milk balls and some of life's other pleasures. So she demanded, "What on earth are you blabbering about, you big goof? What interest could I possibly have in one of those disgusting criminals you associate with or, for that matter, you?"

Longarm waved his notebook at her as he explained, "Our office over at the federal building is closed for the night and won't open this side of Monday morn. Meanwhile I got important officious reports to hand in, hardly anyone seems to be able to read my hand when I'm writing aboard a writing table instead of a moving train and, seeing you keep that swell little upper and lower case grasshopper here on the premises."

"You want to use my *typewriter*, at *this* hour!" She demanded with an uncertain smile, managing not to laugh outright as she added, "Why Custis Long, whatever might the neighbors think?"

"That somebody has something important to type up?" he answered, innocently, as he handed her the notebook.

She handed it back, saying, "You know I can't read your penciled scribbles in this light, or come to think of it, by broad day. Come inside before someone hears us jabbering in an open

25

doorway at this hour and I'll warm us some coffee in the kitchen while I hear you out. I warn you this had better be good and you can just forget about the bedroom or even the sofa in my front parlor, you brute."

Life was too short to spend more of the same than need be arguing with women. So he just trailed after her as she led the way back to the kitchen he recalled as well as her bedroom, if not quite so fondly.

There, she lit an oil lamp above her pine kitchen table and sat him under it as she poked up the banked coals in her kitchen range and shoved in a few fresh lengths of stove wood. She had a time keeping the front of her kimono modest amid all this activity but they both knew it served him right to catch an occasional glimpse of what he just wasn't going to get, ever again, from a woman who felt wronged.

As she warmed up the coffee and cut heroic slices of chocolate cake to go with his malted milk balls, Longarm brought her up to date on the capture of Peewee Folsom and the prisoner's information on a much worse killer. She agreed the U.S. marshal out California way rated a detailed warning about such a mad dog as the Fresno Kid, whether the story was true or not. But Morgana knew her erstwhile lover as only a woman who'd shared pillow conversations with him about many another case could, so even as she poured, once she'd heard him out, Morgana said, "I'm missing something, here, Custis. You want to turn in a neat but thorough update on the Fresno Kid and then . . ."

"I told you I just pawed through recent press reports about him over to the *Rocky Mountain News*," Longarm cut in, adding, "There really was a jailbreak such as Peewee described, down Yuma way last winter. Neither short-time trustee who lit out into the desert so unfair answered to Folsom or Baker, but Peewee told me they were both doing less penance than either deserved, under made-up names."

Morgana sat across from him, shoving coffee and cake his way as she insisted, "I got that part. I said it seemed only right to warn your opposite numbers at the Fresno office that death by gunfire in Nogales could have been staged by a spoiled rich kid with a homicidal streak. It's that elaborate plea for the life of his treacherous pal I don't understand, Custis. Wasn't it you who seemed so pleased that time you promised those outlaws from the Indian Nation they'd never be sentenced to death by the Denver

District Court if only they'd give you some information on more important criminals?"

Longarm chuckled fondly and recalled, "Yep, they said they could put me on the trail of Jethro Markham, a famous train robber. We call that dealing, in my line of work."

She finished one of the malted milk balls she seemed to be hogging on her side of the table and sipped some oversweetened coffee before she nodded and said, "I know. You told me all about it after you'd come back from the Front Range, feeling good about the men and Lord knows how many women you'd abused up yonder."

He started to protest. She said, "I'm talking. That time you said you'd plead for the lives of those killers from the Indian Nation you knew all the time the Cherokee Police and the draconian Fort Smith Federal District had first dibs on them, didn't you?"

Longarm washed down a morsel of her too-sweet cake with strong black coffee to reply, "Well sure I did. The murdersome rascals deserved to hang and we all knew it, which is why they offered to deal and, say what you like, nobody can say I failed to keep my end of the bargain. I did tell Billy Vail I'd sworn I'd hand in my badge before I'd see the Denver District Court hang 'em. Was it my fault old Billy and Judge Dickerson agreed to let Judge Isaac Parker over to Fort Smith try 'em?"

He dug in for more chocolate cake as he soberly continued, "It ain't fair to call the Fort Smith proceedings notorious, by the way. Judge Parker and his boys are trying to keep the peace in a mighty ferocious part of the country, with red, white, and black illiterates swilling moonshine mixed by-guess-and-by-God and gunning one another for no sensible reasons a rabid coyote could offer."

He swallowed more black coffee, grimaced, and warned, "Some sob sister reporters from back East say Judge Parker seems too stern by half. There's even foolish talk about an income tax like they got in England, the closing down of even the well-run saloons, and doing away with the death penalty entire! But you mark my words, girl. The day you tell illiterate trash and halfwits they won't hang no matter what they do will be the day you see honest folk gunned down like dogs for the change in their pockets or for no good reason at all! I just now locked up a murdersome moron who killed an honest working man for less than a hundred whole dollars and Peewee Folsom *knew* you could still get hung for that!"

27

Morgana demurely demolished another malted milk ball, discovered just in time how the front of her kimono was commencing to gape, and insisted, "You're not making sense. He gave you all he had on his former friend, the Fresno Kid. So what's all this nonsense about three page letters to the statehouse as well as your federal superiors? Don't you *want* to see the wicked thing die on the gallows?"

Longarm shook his head and said, "Not hardly, and Judge Dickerson is sure to save himself a thankless chore by tossing the tedious child to Colorado and Colorado's more likely to hang him high, public, in an election year. So I'm hoping to get the state to spare him as a potental material witness by feeding all this guff about the Fresno Kid to all concerned."

He saw she still didn't follow his drift. He reached across to pat her free wrist, as long as it was there, and explained, "There's deals and then there's deals. I enjoy a rep for dealing tricky as well as keeping my word, to the fine print. So if I work sincere to save this particular punk's neck the word is sure to get around and you know what they say about bread on the water."

She did. She shrugged and said, "It's for you to say, but you sure seem to be getting mellow. I've never heard of you giving in to a crook's desires before."

He shrugged and replied, "There's desires and then there's desires. I read somewhere about this ancient Oriental warning his followers to be careful what they wished for, lest they get exactly what they thought they wanted."

"I'm sure you know more about Oriental philosophy than me!" she sniffed, before popping a malted milk ball in her mouth and crunching down hard.

He pretended not to notice as he continued, "Someday they might have a treatment for sugar diabetes. I surely hope so. As of now they don't know what causes it and there's nothing much they can do for anyone who's caught it."

Morgana looked away as she said, "They brought a diabetic foundling out to the orphan asylum a year or so back. All we could do was feed and change the poor little thing until she died. She seemed thirsty no matter how many bottles of milk or water we gave her and she wet her poor little bottom every few minutes until . . ."

"It figures to be worse for Peewee Folsom," he cut in, adding, "I seen red as well as white folk die from it. For some reason

Papagos down along the Gila catch sugar diabetes a heap as soon as they get to drawing Indian Agency rations. But this nurse down to the Papago Agency told me it ain't simply the eating of too much sweet stuff as causes sugar diabetes. The poor cusses seem to make the sugar in their blood out of wheat bread, rice, and even beer. Papago take dying more manly than most. But they've been known to bawl some, towards the end."

He polished off his chocolate cake and washed it down before he continued, "Seeing we're at the table I won't go into the exact symptoms of advanced and untreatable sugar diabetes. Suffice it to say Peewee Folsom has only been suffering the early warning signs. He allowed he'd rather die in a prison hospital. I mean to let him, wishing they'd hung him, in a few short minutes, as various parts of him commence to tingle and burn afore they turn black and have to be cut off lest they stink the whole ward up."

Morgana gagged on her own coffee and said, "Remind me never to ask about medical symptoms when we're not at the table. I've always suspected you had a mean streak, you mean thing. Was that nurse you no doubt trifled with at the Pima Agency prettier than me, Custis?"

He laughed easily and soothed, "Way older and a good deal fatter," without adding she'd been one hell of a lay as well.

It seemed to work. The petite young brunette across the table shrugged and decided, "Well, far be it from me to see Colorado hang a murderer when he can just as easily die in agony. But I can't let you pound my typewriter up here at this hour, Custis. I do have those neighbors to consider and it's not as if either those state or federal officials will be opening any mail on the Sabbath. So what if you were to type all you like, at this very table, after church tomorrow, when nobody is as apt to notice?"

He needed to study on that notion before he answered. So he did and she must have taken his silence for refusal. She wasn't any more used to refusal than your average raving beauty, so she patted his wrist, this time, as she insisted, "Come on, you'll have a whole lazy Sunday to work on your old reports, with me keeping your cup and cake saucer filled and, if you're very good, I may even let you take me to supper, afterwards."

He said that sounded easier on the neighbors than hunting and pecking after midnight. So, the coffee being drunk, the chocolate cake and malted milk balls being et, and the fire box on her kitchen range smouldering low enough to leave unsupervised,

29

they got up from the table and headed back for where he'd hung his hat by her front door.

He never put it on, once they got there, of course. There was a chance she'd expected him to, judging from the mouselike squeak she gave when Longarm swept her up off her bare feet.

She knew the way to her bedroom as well as he could have. So he asked her not to ask such dumb questions when she demanded to know where he thought he was taking her.

As they entered the inviting darkness of her lavender-scented sleeping chamber he added, "It was your own grand notion I should start all that typing tomorrow morning, bless your hospitable little hide. Don't you want to get any sleep at all, tonight?"

She protested, "I was already in bed, planning on sleeping chaste and pure, you tobacco-scented brute! I only said you could use my typewriter, not my poor body, you mean thing! What kind of a girl do you think I am? Put me down this instant!"

He knew exactly what kind of a gal she was and, seeing they'd made it far as her four-poster, he put her down, as per request, and flopped across the bedding beside her to haul her in for some down home spit swapping and a friendly feel.

She bit his tongue, albeit not enough to make him take it out, and tried to cross her naked thighs as his questing hand found its way inside her open kimono. Her struggles seemed sincere enough at first and he might have taken her more seriously when she twisted her lips from his and moaned, "Are you really going to rape me, you animal?" if he hadn't already been down this trail a time or more with the awfully pretty but mighty possessive young spinster.

But he had. So once he had two love-slicked fingers rocking the little man in the squirming boat for her she relaxed in his arms and spread her legs, sobbing, "If I forgive you just this once will you promise me you'll stay away from that Chinese waitress and her opium den?"

He swore she had his sacred word to that, the Oriental lady in question no longer working at that Chop Suey joint and never having owned any opium den to begin with. So Morgana giggled and began to play with his buckles and buttons as he went on playing with her.

By the time she had him half undressed in the now sort of musky darkness she was pleading, "Oh, hurry, darling, hurry! I'm about to come and I want you in me, deep, when I do!"

30

But Longarm really felt a mite guilty about the way he'd been neglecting the pretty young matron of late, that widow with the light brown hair up on Capitol Hill serving a better breakfast even if she didn't have such a swell typewriter, so to make up for having let her down a mite of late, Longarm concentrated more on her needs and desires than his own as he nibbled a turgid nipple and went on stroking with skilled fingers until, sure enough, she grabbed the back of his wrist with both her hands to go all stiff and shuddery, sobbing, "Oh, Jesus! You're driving me crazy and if you want any of this you'd better stick it in, deep, now!"

But he never. He knew she meant if he wanted to share that particular orgasm with her, just as he knew how it could break the spell if he changed the way he was making her come as she was coming. So he brought her to full climax with his hand, knowing just how single gals who had to jerk off a lot liked to be handled. Then, feeling mighty inspired in his own right by all this fooling with willing female flesh, Longarm cocked his bare right leg over her flushed thigh, got both his knees well planted between her own, and thrust his enormously engorged shaft up into her still twitching depths, deep as he could, with her raising her welcoming and grinding pelvis as high as she could.

As he locked an elbow under each of her knees to help she sobbed, "I can't believe it, I'm coming again, or did I ever stop coming at all? You're killing me with your loving, you loving man! Right now I don't care who you fuck as long as you never, never, never stop fucking me and . . . Yes! Now! Give it to me, lover man!"

So he did. It was easy. Stopping before he came in her some more would have been the hard part. She gasped, "Oh, dear, is all that meant for little me? I heard those Chinese pals you sneak off to see have all sorts of secret herbs, snake venoms, and such they use to whip up love potions. Is that what you're using to stay so hard in me, a durned old love potion you got from that other woman?"

He told her not to talk dirty about ladies she didn't know and had no call to feel surly about. He was too busy getting into her to get into the stupid superstitions rabble-rousers repeated about harmless Sons of Han imported mostly to build railroads for less pay than a more sensible freed slave was asking.

He did say he'd never found any chemicals more inspiring to a gent's old sweaty privates than the natural juices of an empassioned natural she-male, preferably human. She laughed like hell and asked if she got to feel jealous about other critters as well as other women. He said neither horses nor cows seemed practical, dogs bit, and none of the old boys he'd ridden the range with in his cow punching days thought much of sheep.

She said she'd heard mighty wild things about sheep and the boys who spent whole summers alone with them in the high country. When she asked if it was true a ewe in heat felt exactly like a woman taking it dog style he repeated he was in no position to say for certain.

So she suggested they get in that dog style position so's he could find out what it felt like to ravage a sheep.

As he had her that way they both agreed it hardly seemed fair to sentence a wayward sheepherder to twenty at hard for doing this very thing to a critter who likely didn't mind.

Morgana allowed it felt good to her and that any ewe who felt ravaged could likely just walk away. As he made sure she never, by gripping her hip bones firmly as he thrust in and out of her, Longarm said, "I caught a sheepherder doing this one time. On federal range. I still figured it was no never mind of Uncle Sam. But the poor cuss was sure embarrassed."

Morgana moaned, "Oooh, I couldn't stop, now, if we were doing this out on the capitol grounds with half of Denver watching!"

He doubted that, having been caught in the act a time or two. But he took it as the compliment it had been meant and pounded her all the way to glory as she opined that treating a critter this hot this way could hardly be described as cruelty to animals.

He shot his wad where she wanted him to before he felt up to explaining, "The old prunes as write laws suspect anyone having a good time must be doing something awful."

He started to mention the several states where a lawfully married-up couple could be sent to prison for trying things they might have noticed on French postcards. But he'd found it sort of stupid to talk about lawfully married-up couples with a lady he was on more casual terms with.

But she brought up the odd moral notions of their times again as they cuddled to share an afterglow smoke. He said as a man paid to enforce the laws passed by others, wise and foolish, he'd gotten over trying to figure sensible reasons, as long as they were on the books.

Placing the cheroot between her lush lips and blowing out the drag he'd just enjoyed, Longarm mused, "I read somewhere about the legislation of morals out to them Sandwich Islands, way west of the California sunset. They call laws tabby boos or something out yonder."

She asked if he meant those cannibal folk who ran around naked and danced the Holy Holy.

He nodded and said, "In grass skirts, with nary a stitch on above the belly button. Like you said, they eat missionaries on occasion and said missionaries complain they screw casual, albeit more often, than we might howdy a lady we know on the street."

She snuggled closer and decided, "It sounds less stuffy than Denver, provided a lady gets to refuse the less appealing gents."

He took another drag and declared, "I ain't sure gals do, out yonder. They say you can barely pass a bush some couple ain't playing slap and tickle in, with many a couple oddly matched indeed. Old men and women with bitty girls and boys, ugly coots with pretty young things, and vice versa, and they say it's even jake on some islands for a man to mess with his sister or daughter. Opinion remains divided on who does it with his mother, how often. I reckon even a bare-ass cannibal feels silly asking *her*."

Morgana said, "I should think so. I thought you just said they had *laws* out yonder, dear."

He nodded. "Strict ones. They don't mess with drunk tanks and chain gangs in them Sandwich Islands. They kill you outright and likely eat you, do you break one of their tabby boos."

She perked up to ask what on earth could be forbidden to a naked man eater allowed to hump most anybody he could get at. So Longarm explained, "Mostly parts of the island you can't go, some few folk you can't even cast your shadow on and, naturally, certain tasty things you ain't supposed to eat."

She said it sounded silly to forbid a man allowed to screw his sister the right of flinging his fool shadow about and demanded to hear what a cannibal might consider forbidden fruit.

He chuckled and said, "We got them high places the Lord forbade decent folk to go and I've often wondered why Mother Eve got us all in so much trouble just by picking fruit off that one tree the Lord could have fenced in or growed somewhere else, with the earth entire at His disposal, if He couldn't spare a mighty country gal even one."

Morgana began to fondle his privates as she demurely replied, "That's different. The Lord grew that one tree in The Garden to teach mankind self-control. For example, I'm sure it's only natural for me to pluck this one banana while, on the other hand, there must be any number of such bananas in town it would be sinful or stupid for me to mess with."

He got rid of a smouldering cheroot that only figured to set the bedding on fire, at this rate, as he said, "That's my point about our need to make up rules and regulations, even on cannibal isles."

She didn't answer. She couldn't with her mouth so full. So he just shut up and let her have her wicked way with him, reflecting on how fortunate it was he rode for the federal government and didn't have to arrest her for such flagrant violation of the Denver Municipal Code regarding "crimes against nature."

He found it only natural to finish off right, albeit with her on top this time, the frolicsome little thing, and, afterwards, when she shyly asked if he thought she was wicked to get such sudden urges, he assured her he'd make her stop if she ever got wild enough to endanger anyone's health.

Then just before she fell asleep in his arms, Morgana asked how long he meant to stay with her, this time, dammit.

So he studied on that before he answered, having got in a whole lot of trouble in the past by promising more than he had to when a lovely critter had him in her power.

That other lovely critter up on Capitol Hill was social as well as rich enough to own that tub they could both fit into at the same time. So there was just no telling how long she'd have to go on entertaining those rich relations of her late husband, and anyone could see how awkward even a young and healthy widow woman could find it to explain anything uncouth as him in her fancy bathroom. She'd like to shit that time the dowagers from the D.A.R. had shown up downstairs as she was inviting him to lick all that fancy Rooshin caviar off her bare tits.

He finally decided, "Well, it won't take more than five or six hours to type up my reports and such. After I take you to Sunday dinner at Romano's we might take in that vaudeville review at the Apollo Hall and we'll still have more time for screwing than we had tonight."

She sighed and said that sounded swell. Then she asked about the next night, and the one after that. He'd been afraid she might. The widow woman up on Capitol Hill had said her blamed in-laws would be headed back East no later than Tuesday, and that fool Frenchman who'd said all cats were gray in the dark was likely as unable to tell steamer beer from Saint Lou lager.

Hugging the petite brunette closer as he anticipated the more Junoesque curves of another brand entire, Longarm warned, "Don't get piggy. You know how uncertain my future is, thanks to a boss who sends me out in the field for indefinite periods after all sorts of lawbreakers."

She murmured, "I know why they call you Longarm, Custis. I know who you spent the night with that time you told me you had to go question some Mexican about something."

He didn't answer. He doubted she'd be amused by his pointing out he had indeed had to question a Mexican about something that particular night. He'd have never gone to bed with little Rosita if she hadn't assured him she was older than she looked.

His discreet silence paid off when Morgana pleaded, "Promise me you won't sneak off to be with that flamenco dancer or any of those other honky-tonk hussies you know along Larimer Street?"

To which he was proud to reply, "You have my words as an enlisted man and gentleman, little darling."

For that widow woman with the light brown hair lived way up the hill, on Sherman Street, bless both their sweet hides.

Chapter 5

Miss Morgana Floyd took her job herding orphans seriously. So she got Longarm to work earlier than usual on Monday morning, but he didn't care. It gave him the chance to drop off the letter he'd typed up for the state prosecutor, out of his way to the Federal Building or not.

He left a similar plea for the life of Peewee Folsom down the hall with Judge Dickerson's pretty secretary, who didn't put out, as far as he could tell, and still had time to surprise Henry, their office clerk, by reporting in earlier than they were used to seeing him of a Monday morn.

The prissy-looking Henry told him their boss was in the back, which hardly surprised Longarm. But when he aimed himself that way their clerk-typist said, "I have your assignment right here. Marshal Vail said to just send you on your way and not pester him when and if you ever showed up this morning."

Longarm took the all too familiar-looking wad of folded bond paper Henry handed across the desk to him, hoping against hope it was an arrest warrant. When he unfolded the eviction notice to see he'd guessed right, he sighed and said, "I see why the cruel old fart was ashamed to face a white man saddled with a chickenshit detail such as this one!"

Henry shrugged and said, "Marshal Vail said it was shitty, too. The Bureau of Land Management still insisted on our serving it. The nester involved ran the BLM boys off his property at gunpoint and seeing you're so tough as well as diplomatic . . ."

"I know how to take back homesteads improperly improved," snapped Longarm, adding, "All in all, I'd as soon herd virgin farm girls aboard an unregistered schooner bound for Shanghai. You say the poor cuss I'm supposed to serve this on already expects someone like me to darken his door?"

Henry nodded and said, "Marshal Vail said you could have anyone but Smiley and Dutch to back you if you're worried about gunplay."

Longarm knew why their boss didn't want deputies as proddy as those two tagging along. He said, "I'd best ride out alone. Looks less like a declaration of war when you see a lone rider crossing your property line."

Henry had read their own copy of the eviction before filing it. So he smugly pointed out, "That's not the property line of the Hensens you'll be crossing. The dumb Swedes had no right to sell it to those other immigrants squatting on it now. The rules of the Homestead Act of 1862 are spelled out quite clearly, in simple English, and you don't get full title to the claim until . . ."

"I know how to read the damned rules," Longarm cut in, growling, "Maybe them other Swedes they want us to send packing don't. I'll go see. Meanwhile, next time you see our boss, tell him I said he was a cruel-hearted son of a bitch!"

He doubted Henry would. The poor squatters they wanted him to treat so cruel were said to be keeping bacon hogs, laying hens and milch cows on a quarter section they thought they owned, up Cherry Creek an hour's ride south of the Denver city limits. He could see why Farmer Oland, who likely knew more about butter and eggs than the English language and U.S. federal law, might have felt upset when the BLM told him he and his family had to get off the hundred and sixty acres he thought he'd paid for fair and square.

Knowing the disputed property lay on gently rolling but otherwise wide-open prairie, guarded by a testy cuss with a Spencer repeater flinging .52 caliber, Longarm stopped off at his furnished digs on the unfashionable side of Cherry Creek to pick up his own Winchester .44-40 and, as long as he was there, his old army saddle.

Leaving the stock saddle from the livery near the Federal Building in his room, Longarm rode the nag he'd hired as far up Cherry Creek as the Diamond K spread, where some old pals were proud to loan him a real pony and offer a more informed opinion on that proddy Swede nester further south.

As he helped Longarm put his saddle on the frisky roan mare he'd selected, the Diamond K wrangler—an old cowhand called Righty because he'd lost his left hand, the riding one, to a mortified wire cut—said Gus Oland seemed a tolerable cuss, for a fucking sodbuster who barely spoke American.

Righty said the Olands kept their own stock from straying, held their yard dog to their own damn property, and knew enough to coffee-and-cake cowhands stopping by at roundup time.

Then Righty spoiled it all by adding, "Miss Greta, Oland's young wife, is pretty as a picture and friendly besides. But nobody with a lick of sense even smiles her way in front of old Gus. Porky Winslow, over to the Rocking Eleven, made that mistake at a grange dance when the Olands first moved in. He sure smiles comical these days, missing them front teeth."

Longarm allowed with a weary sigh he'd met up with such simple possessive souls in the past. He asked how many other innocent bystanders he'd have to worry about out to the disputed homestead.

Righty didn't cheer him much by saying the Olands had four kids, a boy, and three girls, all too young to 'tend school or put up much of a fight. For babies bawling at him made Longarm more uncomfortable than gun muzzles aimed his way.

He knew he was in for some weeping and wailing even if he managed to evict the poor souls without having to kill either parent. He was tempted to turn back, more than once, as he rode up the shallow braided stream to treat folk shitty. But he knew that even if he went back to hurl his badge in Billy Vail's face they'd just send someone else and at least he was good at holding his tongue when women fussed at him.

That could be mighty important in serving folk unwelcome writs, he knew. Many such errands had turned out needlessly nasty when citizens being served had taken a lawman just doing his job for a personal enemy, or a lawman less understanding of human nature had taken a desperate man's accusation of cocksucking personal. Any lawman serving warrants and worse had to be a good sport about being called a cocksucker and worse.

Reading this particular eviction notice as he rode, Longarm saw it was about as mean a one as they swore out at the BLM. The Olands had already been served a show-cause notice, which they'd never replied to, assuming they'd understood it at all. So their undefended case had been lost by automatic forfeiture in federal court, which was bad enough. Then they'd failed to respond to the first eviction notice, giving them plenty of time to appeal or pack up, which had been worse.

Farmer Oland still might have won some more time, at least, had he behaved more polite when those BLM boys rode out to serve him personal after they hadn't heard from him by mail: Blowing that one old boy's hat off and not even letting him stay long enough to pick it up had sort of exhausted all of Farmer Oland's legal options, and this was about the last good weather they'd have to work with, ready or not.

He hoped they'd at least got their last harvest in as, topping a rise, he spied the windmill Righty had told him about.

But as he rode down into the sheltered but well-drained draw to the southwest of Cherry Creek he saw they still had a good five acres of cabbage uncut, well-weeded, and straw-mulched so's they could sell it fresh in town well after the first November frosts. Cabbage could take Colorado this side of Christmas, mulched in such a swell draw with the lower streambed to the northeast draining the bitter morning air before it could bite deeper than the outside leaves of all them cabbage heads.

As Longarm approached the tin mailbox near their wire gate a chained up redbone hound commenced to cuss him and his pony along with all their possible kin on all four sides. So Longarm wasn't surprised to see a big red-bearded cuss, wearing a seaman's cap and Spencer rifle, but otherwise dressed plowboy, drifting out to meet him from that low-slung soddy closer to the windmill, outbuildings, and such. It was hard to say, from the gate, whether that woman staring his way from the open doorway with them bitty kids clinging to her gingham skirts was pretty or not. She sure was staring ashen-faced and owl-eyed.

Longarm dismounted, leaving his saddle gun in its boot, polite, but letting his frock coat hang open to expose the cross-draw grips of his double-action .44-40 as he hauled out a couple of cheroots.

When Oland joined him on the far side of the bob wire, aiming his own gun at the dust between them, for now, Longarm held out the spare smoke, saying, "Howdy. I'd be U.S. Deputy Custis Long and if you'd be Gustaf Oland you likely know why I'm here."

The big Swede ignored the offered smoke but didn't do anything outwardly unkind with his gun muzzle as he growled, with a thick but understandable accent, "Ja, I understand why they sent you out here and, as I told them others, I got four human beings along with a whole lot of livestock to feed with winter coming on, even if I don't eat nothing, myself."

Longarm put the refused cheroot away and lit one for himself before he quietly replied, "I know how tough this is going to be on you all, old son. But, no offense, you've nobody to blame but your very own self. You should have tried to come by this land legal. It ain't that tough. The BLM will sell you government-owned land outright for little more than you paid that homesteader. Or they'll allow you to file a homestead claim in your own name, whether you're a full citizen yet or not. So why in thunder did you pay good money for a farm with clouded title and, once you'd done that, why didn't you at least get yourself a lawyer when they sent you that first show-cause, way back in May, for Gawd's sake?"

"I was busy," the Swede answered, simply, starting in to add more about the uncertain springtime of the High Plains than Longarm really had to be told.

He cut in with, "I know about the late blizzards and muddy roads of a Colorado greenup. So I feel for you, but I still can't reach you, old son. You've had plenty of time to work things out less drastic since you finished your spring planting and, save for them cabbages, your fall harvest. What were you growing on that forty acres of stubble, barley for the breweries in Denver?"

When Oland said wheat, Longarm started to tell he'd do better drilling in barley, next time. But, reflecting there wasn't going to be any next time for the poor cuss, he said, "Tough to turn a profit on less than a full section of wheat in such dry country. But let's talk about how soon you and your family, along with all your chattel goods, can be off this property. The government's a good sport about furniture, tools, livestock, and such."

Gustaf Oland flatly stated, "This land is mine. I paid good money for it. I paid almost all the rest I had getting out here with my family and, like you say, furniture. Everything else you see came with the farm the Hensens sold us, lock, stock, and box!"

Longarm said, "I think you mean lock, stock, and barrel. I see how you were slickered, now. The original homestead claimer, Hensen, put in pretty good improvements out here as he waited out the five years occupancy they require as well. The act, as passed in '62, says you have to stake out, build up, and occupy the same quarter section for five years before it's your'n to do with as you so desire. If Hensen put up that swell soddy, sunk

40

that tube well, and even stocked and fenced this place afore he sold it to you all, he must have had some reason for deserting his claim, right?"

Oland grumbled, "My friend, Hensen, didn't desert this place. He sold it to me, at a fair price, because he needed the money to go home to Malmo. His sister's man, Cousin Thorbjorn, died suddenly in his prime, leaving a widow so young and six small children to manage as well as that shipyard, so . . ."

Longarm hushed him with, "I can see why your old pal Hensen would swap a marginal unproven homestead for a going shipyard back in Sweden. I pity his poor sister almost as much as I pity you. But you'd be the sucker I'm stuck with. So, as we were saying, I can give you a reasonable time to vacate this gold brick you bought, provided we get cracking soon. I'll even help in any way I can. I know folk in these parts who might loan you extra wagons and even give you a place to stay with all your chattels 'til you figure something better out."

The Swede managed to look amazingly Indian as he scowled across the gate at Longarm to say, stubbornly, "This land is mine. If you try to take it from me I'll have to kill you!"

Longarm sighed. "You mean you can try. You might even do it. I never said I was immortal. But before we get silly I'd like you to consider what comes after killing me. A gent called Red Cloud had much the same attitude about land he called Paha Supa but we called the Black Hills. He said he'd kill any Wasichu, meaning us, who tried to take his people's land and, no offense, they had a better claim to the Paha Supa than you have to this unproven homestead."

He took a drag on his cheroot to let that sink in before he went on, "Red Cloud made good on his brag, as far as the first white civilians and even soldiers who trespassed on his claim. Then more came, followed by still more. So now Red Cloud's living on the reservation Washington assigned him to, and a heap of his followers, great and small, lie buried, if they was lucky, all over the High Plains to the north. You don't hold land the U.S. Government claims by tough talk or even brave deeds, old son. You gain title to it lawsome or you just don't get it at all. Killing me or the next dozen deputies they send out to evict you won't get you more than a pauper's funeral on federal land in the end. They'll likely bury you over to Camp Weld, with them dead Indians, if your family can't afford nothing better."

The Swede looked more defeated as well as more desperate. Longarm couldn't even look at the woman and children across the yard as he gripped his smoke between his teeth and insisted, "I wish there was some other way. I know you don't buy this, but my boss sent me because he knew I liked kids. It was that Hensen as slickered you and, wait a minute, was that sister of Hensen's possible kin to you, even by marriage?"

Oland didn't see how important it might be as he scratched the back of his neck, considering, "By marriage, ja, I think maybe. My friend, Hensen, was no relation of mine, so neither was his sister. But she was married to Thorbjorn Andersen, my second cousin on my own mother's side, and . . . Why are we talking about distant relatives in Malmo, Deputy Long?"

Longarm grinned like a fox invited to guard the hen house as he replied, "Loophole. Mighty small one but better than nothing. The fine print of that homestead act you should have read before you bought a homestead off a slicker with no right to sell it reads the original claimant or a *relative* by blood or marriage has to occupy the claim continuous for five years, albeit they let you go off it on honest business for up to anything less than half a given year."

Oland sighed and said, "Those other government told me that before I ran them off. Hensen sold us this farm over a year ago and so even if he was a relative . . ."

"Pay attention," Longarm cut in, insisting, "You *are* related to Hensen, by marriage, as soon as you study on it a tad past common sense. Law courts don't operate by the rules of common sense. They go by nits, so see if you can follow my nitpicking."

He had to go over it twice before Oland suddenly laughed like a loon and said, "Ja, if my cousin Thorbjorn was brother-in-law to all the Hensens, and he left us to hold his claim because he had to go back to Malmo . . ." Then he was yelling in Swedish to his woman and as Greta Oland came running their way with all their bitty kids trailing after, Longarm saw she was really pretty as they said.

She looked even prettier at him as her man explained in their own singsong lingo. So in the end Longarm got to have coffee and cake out there without having to gun a one of 'em.

Chapter 6

The clocks were striking three and other kids were escaping from the grammar school east of the civic center by the time Longarm made it back to downtown Denver on the original stock saddle and livery nag he'd started out on. He knew that if he timed it right he could make it back to the office too late for even Billy Vail to stick him with any more chores for the day, and Miss Morgana Floyd had said she meant to knock off early that afternoon as well.

But he hurried on back to the Federal Building, once he'd settled up at the nearby livery. He had things to settle at the land office as well and he'd promised Gus Oland he'd mention his woes to a slick lawyer who knew his way around the federal courts.

The boys at the BLM laughed like hell but allowed they'd rather fight the dumb Swede in court than out on what he considered his own range, now that Oland had at least a shaky leg to stand on.

When he got back to his own office Henry told him to go right on back and take his medicine like a little man. Longarm frowned innocently and muttered, "What the hell have I done wrong?" as he ambled on back to Marshal William Vail's inner sanctum.

He found his boss lurking like a grumpy cuttlefish in a thick blue cloud of cigar smoke. It was a good thing he already knew what his older, shorter, and stumpier superior looked like, or that he'd already memorized the layout of the oak-paneled office. He managed to grope his way to the horsehair-padded leather chair on his own side of Vail's cluttered desk and light a cheroot in self-defense as he sat himself down, observing, "I see you're smoking

43

the same brand of piss-soaked jimson weed, cured in a henhouse."

Vail snapped, "Never mind what I'm smoking and watch where you flick your own damned ashes! I swear if I sent you to fetch a pail of water you'd come back with a bucket of shit! Have you forgotten this is an election year, or how the average voter and all of the opposition newspapers feel about U.S. marshals enforcing unpopular court orders?"

Longarm snapped back, "I never volunteered and, at the risk of sounding boastful, I'd say I handled it better than some might have. I just now talked to lawyer Sprague and he says even if they lose in the end he can keep a roof over their heads until next summer, what with one appeal and another."

He took a drag on his own smoke, it helped a mite, and continued, "There's a good chance the BLM will let 'em stay, thanks to the way I twisted the homestead act instead of a homesteader in front of his wife and kids."

Vail blew some of the smoke out of the way with a manila folder from his desk, as if to make sure that was Longarm he was talking to as he asked, less savagely, "Deputy Long, what in hell are we talking about?"

Longarm stared back as bemused to demand, "Was there any doubt? You sent me out this morning to evict a whole family of Swedes and, like I just said, we worked it out civilized with nobody hurt and a good chance all concerned will be satisfied in the end."

Interested despite himself, Marshal Vail had Longarm bring him up to date on his visit to the Olands and other federal officials down the hall. When he'd finished the pudgy Vail was almost smiling. Then he remembered himself and growled, "That wasn't what I was talking about. I was talking about the so-called massacre of Mussel Slough, out California way. You know what happened there, just a short spell back, don't you?"

Longarm blew a thoughtful smoke ring before he nodded just a mite and said, "Secondhand, since I wasn't there, praise the Lord. Some of our boys were ordered to back the play of some gunslicks hired by the railroad to run settlers out of their way. Nobody can say for certain who fired the shot heard 'round the West, but as the smoke cleared five settlers and two deputies lay dead or dying, right?"

Vail shook his head and said, "You been reading the opposition papers. What really happened was raw enough. In the beginning, back in the Grant Administration, the railroads got overly generous land grants from the government to encourage 'em, lest they lay their fool rails across Africa or even Asia. The railroads in turn got to lure plenty of passengers and freight along their rights-of-way by selling the land they got from the government to land-hungry greenhorns from other parts."

Longarm took an impatient puff on his cheroot and said, "I just got back from scaring some greenhorns, boss. Some folk will insist on thinking they can settle any damn where they want out here, stubborn as Mr. Lo, the poor Indian. Them squatters at Mussel Slough nested on land already granted to the railroad as a right-of-way, right?"

Vail shook his bullet head and said, "Wrong. They wouldn't be calling it a massacre and hinting the Democrats could have handled things better if the case had been that simple. Our boys out in the county of Tulare were caught in one of them real binds a lawman hates, such as enforcing a restraining order on a wife-beater whose wife secretly admires him."

Longarm thought harder, shrugged, and decided to just listen as Vail continued, "That stink Union Pacific caused with their Credit Mobilier scandal of '72 froze railroad land grants in place and clouded title for quite a spell as Congress tried to tidy up. With even Vice President Colfax trying to cover his own crooked ass, the land office wasn't about to close title one on any land deed smelling of railroad smoke."

Longarm couldn't help observing, "The Credit Mobilier mess and resulting depression of the '70's had to be sort of ancient history by the time guns blazed at Mussel Slough so recent, boss."

Vail nodded but said, "Damned A it was recent, you silly cuss. But to get back to the roots of the matter, no railroad promoter worth his salt ever let a little detail like the truth get in his way when he was out to promote his railroad. So as they went on laying track down the Big Valley from the California gold fields they advertised prime bottomland alongside the track for as low as $2.60 an acre."

Longarm whistled and said, "That's cheap for marginal grazing range. I'll bet they got plenty of takers."

Vail said, "They did indeed. Settlers lured by full-color posters and low railroad rates flocked in to fence in land, lay out irrigation works, and plant flowers from back home as, meanwhile, the railroad went on trying to secure its federal title to the same."

45

Vail tossed his folder aside, sighed, and said, "In '78 they did. President Hayes was even ready to forgive the South and what the hell, we've even named a fine avenue here in Denver after that old thief, Schuyler Colfax. Having spent a heap of dinero securing its own title to all that land, the railroad proceeded to sell it off. It granted first offer to the nesters already squatting on it, asking from seventeen dollars to forty dollars an acre."

Longarm whistled softly and opined, "Seventeen dollars sounds reasonable for prime bottomland. Forty dollars seems a mite steep when you consider the folks as settled it was expecting to pay $2.60."

Vail nodded and said, "That's the way it struck the settlers of Mussel Slough. They told the railroad to go to hell. So the railroad cussed right back and sold their claims out from under them to outsiders at $25 an acre. Are you with me so far?"

Longarm grimaced and said, "I may be ahead of you. But why in hell would any U.S. marshal want to tangle his deputies in a tar pit like that? What was the matter with the sheriff of Tulare County?"

Vail said, "He didn't aim to lose the very next election neither and, lest we forget, railroad grants are federal, not state or local. The corpses described as hired guns or U.S. deputies by various sources were neither. They were outside land speculators who got a federal judge to issue them apparently proper eviction notices. Since the settler's singled them out as targets in the resulting showdown, it's up for grabs whether they were acting on their own or secretly working for the railroad, as some say."

Longarm mused, "The other side lost more in the fight, didn't it?"

Vail nodded and said, "Five settlers killed outright and a dozen or more arrested on murder charges. No judge with a lick of sense is about to hang 'em or let 'em go this side of the next election and, meanwhile, Congress has ordered a full investigation of the charges and countercharges, with most everyone along the San Joaquin taking sides and in some cases threatening to take up arms."

The penny dropped. Longarm still tried to sound innocent as he said, "Oh, are we talking about that prisoner I brung in yesterday, and what he said about his pal, the Fresno Kid, going to ground out in the San Joaquin Valley?"

46

Vail said, "We are, you asshole, and they want him captured almost as much as they want to win the coming election!"

Longarm shrugged and said, defensively, "Well, shit, I wired our Fresno office all I had on the mean cuss and asked both the state and federal courts here in Denver to keep Peewee Folsom alive just in case he might help in any other way. What's to stop anyone who wants the Fresno Kid from capturing him if there's anything at all to Peewee's story?"

Vail snapped, "Mussel Slough and a whole damned valley up in arms about it, damn your interfering eyes! I sent you to Cheyenne County, Colorado, repeat, Colorado, to pick up another prisoner entire! But did you bring back the man you were sent to bring back? You did not! You brung back a bucket of shit, like I said!"

He saw Longarm seemed sincerely confused. So he forced himself to continue in a more reasonable tone, "Look, the U.S. marshal and all his deputies out to Fresno are under investigation with most everyone but the railroad robber barons out yonder accusing them of being guns for hire. In point of fact they did the job they'd been ordered to do by the federal courts, finding for a couple of jaspers who, like it or not, held lawful title to the land in question."

"I don't see what any of that had to do with the capture of a wanted outlaw called Tomas Ortega Baker!" Longarm insisted.

To which Vail replied, "His mamma being an Ortega, he's got at least a few friends in high places along the San Joaquin. After that it gets worse. The Mussel Slough incident took place on or about the disputed homestead of a nester called Brewer, a so-called ringleader of the outraged farmers or trash squatters, depending on which papers you subscribe to. Whether the first one to fire was in cahoots with the railroad or an honest landlord trying to take possession of his own property, seven men lay dead and seventeen voting citizens wound up behind bars as the gunsmoke cleared."

"You told me all this, Billy," Longarm cut in, or tried to.

Vail snapped, "Shut up and pay heed to your elders, you wiseass whippersnapper! As I was about to say, the Fresno Kid, if he's out yonder at all, ain't the only outlaw running loose, popular as hell with an outraged local populace. Brewer's brother-in-law, Kit Evans, and another dispossessed nester named Sontag, Johnny Sontag, have took to stopping trains regular up and down the

San Joaquin, and I ain't talking about 'em asking to ride in the caboose."

Longarm sighed and said, "I wish old boys would cut that out. Frank and Jesse still have heaps of country folk convinced they're half-ass Robin Hoods, stopping trains to help the poor."

Vail said, "Evans and Sontag have really been sharing with homeless folk run off by the railroad and other land grabbers. Lord knows how they'll ever find a jury to convict 'em, once they're caught. So my opposite number out Fresno Way ain't too anxious to catch 'em, or even stick his nose outside the Fresno Federal Building 'til the stink of Mussel Slough dies down."

Longarm started to say something dumb. But he had a sinking feeling he knew what was coming next, as Billy Vail rummaged through the papers on his desk, found the Western Union form he was looking for, said, "Read it and weep," and handed it across to his own deputy.

Longarm managed to say dreadful things with a cheroot gripped between bared teeth as he scanned the assistance request from the Fresno District Court. He didn't ask why him. He said, "Shit, I wouldn't know the Fresno Kid if I woke up in bed with him."

Vail smiled sweetly and said, "Cheer up, you diplomatic cuss. Did I fail to mention the Californios or old Spanish settlers inspired to raise Ned by all that infighting amongst the hated Americanos, or the Yokut Indians, who've jumped the Tule River Reservation amid all the confusion?"

Longarm sighed, flicked cheroot ash on Billy Vail's rug, and observed, "Oh, well, I've been worried about woman trouble late in this very week in any case. May as well go tangle with wanted killers, pissed off Chicanos, and wild Indians while I got the chance."

Chapter 7

A U.S. deputy marshal was allowed six cents a mile on a lone field mission. So naturally old Henry had typed up travel orders more suited to an infernal *bee* than anyone more interested in riding trains than transferring from one to another.

Longarm missed the early evening train they'd picked for him in any case, what with one thing or the other and saying adios proper to a teary-eyed Morgana Floyd. So he hopped a freight up to Cheyenne, reflecting that whether he collected on the beeline west or circled some, free, with railroading pals, the accounting office was likely to insist there had to be shorter route than a string-straight line drawn from Denver to Fresno.

He got into Cheyenne late that night, facing a close to eight-hour layover, so, having been warned about gambling a night away at that Cheyenne Social Club, Longarm looked up an old pal he knew to be a sure thing.

She fed him breakfast in bed sort of wistful, too, before he caught the westbound U.P. Flier, free, as long as he didn't want a lie down in a Pullman bunk or even fancier compartment up ahead of the coach seats and club car.

He feared he might, by the time they made her all the way out to California, averaging forty miles an hour. Meanwhile, it seemed mighty wasteful to spring for lie downs you hired by the mile when a man had an observation platform to relax on, free, sipping suds and smoking as he admired the receding railroad ties and telegraph poles.

Leaving Cheyenne, the transcontinental tracks swung north at Tie Siding, about an hour out of town, to avoid the Medicine Bow

49

Range of the somewhat jumbled Rockies. Well before noon you were rolling west again through the Great Divide Basin, a patch of what looked like rolling prairie way up in the middle of the air. Folk who seemed to know about such matters had written the best route through or over the Rocky Mountains was a heap like the grassy interior plains of Tibet. Longarm had to take their word for that, never having been sent to Tibet by Billy Vail, yet.

Most of the time, you didn't notice you were all that high in the sky, crossing the Great Divide Basin betwixt, say, the Sweetwater running east off the South Pass and the Savery running west off the Medicine Bows. But this late in autumn, with the leaves just starting to turn down in Denver, there was a dry taste of snow in the thin morning air despite the bright sunlight.

Longarm had a rain slicker lashed to his saddle in the baggage car up forward. But he wasn't more than a mite goosebumped back here, thanks to the bulkhead at his back and the morning sun aimed his way from the east.

He figured he'd be tired of the view over the back rail by the time the sun rose too much higher. Neither the interior plains of Tibet nor the tawny swells of the Great Divide Basin were considered all that dramatic. Now and again they'd pass a few range cows or a curious pronghorn. But he'd have been way more astounded by an elephant, or even one of those long-haired cows they herded in Tibet. A man who'd come west as a boy, right after the war, and ridden drag for Captain Goodnight and others 'til he'd mastered the skills of a top hand tended to find your average cow, or pronghorn, sort of tedious.

All the beef stock on this range was longhorn scrub, he noticed. That reminded him Kim Stover had said something, that time, about breeding her own herd fancier with a registered white-face he-brute. That reminded him the beautiful blond widow woman raised beef, plain or fancy, not too far north of Bitter Creek, where they'd stop to jerk engine water in a while.

That reminded him to quit reminding his fool self about Kim Stover and a couple of other gals as rich and tempting. He knew that did he get off at Bitter Creek and drop by to see if old Kim Stover could use an extra hand around her home spread, she'd likely find plenty for him to do, despite that promise she'd made him make her, the last time he'd said he had to get it on down the road.

Then some welcome distraction came out on the platform to join him, sitting down in the one other wicker chair before asking him demurely if it was spoken for.

Her accent was foreign, likely German, as well as demure. He'd already noticed it, and the tall willowy figure and auburn hair as went with it, when she'd ordered tonic water with no gin from the colored waiter inside. He'd decided anyone who'd drink anything that bitter without a jigger of booze to cut the taste was likely one of them tormented souls who ran on and on about women's rights and free love 'til some poor simp tried to take 'em up on it. The secret of success with the ladies was mostly knowing which ones not to try and succeed with. There was always some poor lonesome gal about who pined for some slap and tickle. But how was the man of her dreams to help her out if he was wasting his talents, time, and hard-earned cash on some pretty young thing who just plain didn't want him?

Judging by this one's outfit, she was either the property of or in hot pursuit of at least a prince of the blood. Sizing her up out one corner of his eye as he gazed off across the rolling prairie, he estimated the silly summer boater atop her pinned-up hair had cost her, or somebody, more than he made in a week. He didn't want to consider the cost of the emerald velvet dress with silk brocade bodice she wore under that open, expensive, black poplin travel duster. Hardly any dust clung to the shiny material she'd put on to protect her velvet and brocade. Poplin that good cost a bundle as well. She likely found your average bank president sort of country.

Longarm knew a train didn't have to run all the way to California to be stopped by would-be Robin Hoods, but as the one they were on began to slow and the snooty but mighty pretty foreign gal asked him why, in a worried tone, Longarm quietly explained, "Flag stop called Wamsutter, ma'am. Somebody wants to get on or get off, unless there's stock on the track ahead."

She wrinkled her pert nose as if someone had farted and allowed that in her country trains didn't run so casual.

He asked where her country might be and she sounded mighty proud as she replied, "Prussia, East Prussia, *natürlich*. My maternal uncle is the Graf Von Wolfstein but here in Amerika I prefer to be known as simply Erna Drachenfeld, without the Von."

He didn't answer. For by then their train had rolled almost to a dead stop and a cuss-dressed cow with a red bandana over most

51

of his face and a Schofield .45 filling most of his right hand was coming over the back rail at them, shouting, "This is just what it looks like and nobody will get hurt if you do just what I say."

So Erna Drachenfeld planted one of her high heels in his eye socket as Longarm shot him just above the belt buckle, aiming low as he saw her high button shoe in his original line of fire.

Then, as that one back-flipped to the tracks, Longarm rolled out of his seat to haul her to the deck beside him as, sure enough, a bullet spanged through the sliding door from inside the club car to shower them both with shattered glass.

The German gal sobbed, "*Ach, Herr Gott*! We are by your Jesse James about to be murdered, *nich wahr*?"

He told her to keep her fool head down and stay put as he slid the door open a crack with his free hand for a crack at anyone inside who required it.

Nobody seemed to. Another roughly clad cuss with half his fool face masked lay sprawled on the club car decking near a smoking sixgun. Their colored barkeep stood over him with a sawed-off baseball bat and a self-satisfied expression. As he spied Longarm peering through the slot at them he called out, "I got him whilst he was paying more mind to you all, Deputy Long. That'll learn him to scare this child almost pale enough to pass!"

Longarm laughed but warned, "You'd best hunker down, pard. There could be more of 'em, you know."

The barkeep shook his head and replied, "Not now, suh. I seen 'em mounting up and riding out to the south just now. Reckon all that unexpected gunplay spooked 'em."

As if to prove that point the older and stockier conductor came back to the club car, his own antique but lethal LeMat still smoking, to ask if anyone back there was hurt.

Longarm got to his feet and helped the German girl up as he slid the door on open, announcing, "Got another one spawled on the U.P. right of way, Saul. You can see for yourself what your barkeep served that other."

As the conductor was congratulating the barkeep Longarm turned back to the German girl to explain, "Couldn't have been the James-Younger gang or even semiprofessionals less famous. Likely some laid-off cow pokes who'd already spent the last of their roundup pay and have a winter to get through one way or the other."

By now he and Erna had joined the conductor and barkeep over the moaning loser at their feet. So when some Wamsutter natives hailed them from outside Longarm stuck his head back out the door to call down, "In here. Some old boys just tried to rob this train. We could use some help figuring out who they were."

A wiry old gent with a mail order badge stuck to the front of his sheepskin jacket called up from where he stood near the body on the tracks, "No mystery about this boy. He was Josh Webber in life. Rode for the Rocking K 'til they caught him going into business for himself with Rocking K calves he sort of forgot to brand for his boss."

Longarm helped the Wamsutter law aboard where, over free drinks on the U.P. line to help everybody think clearer, they established the one with the likely fatal skull fracture as a saddle tramp, new to the local range, who'd been seen here and about with the late Josh Webber. The conductor said he had another one down up forward and added he had a durned timetable to keep, so them ambled that way and there was no telling how far that fool German gal might have gone with 'em had not Longarm stopped her, a few cars up, to warn, "You don't want anyone pestering you for names, addresses, and such if you're bound for anywhere important, Miss Erna. Sweetwater County, which is where we're at right now, will doubtless hold a formal coroner's hearing, sooner or later, and you could be tied up here later than sooner. So why don't you just let the U.P. line settle up with that town constable. It's a railroad town to begin with and . . ."

"I can't afford to get in trouble with the American authorities, and even in America there must be some rules!" she protested.

To which he replied with a sober nod, "I'm an American authority and I just now explained some rules. You didn't do nothing wrong. They erred in picking the wrong train to rob and, like I said, the railroad company and the dinky railroad towns living off it have their own less bothersome ways of sweeping up after the horses. So let's just go find some place to set discreet and we ought to be on our way in no time."

She said her private compartment was one car ahead and that she was more anxious to get to San Francisco than she was to see the sights of Sweetwater County with the first snows of fall due any time, now. But even as she led him into her perfumed Pullman parlor she seemed to feel obliged to mention that bullet Longarm had put in the one back on the roadbed.

53

He removed his hat but remained standing in the modest space there was as he explained, "Them railroad employees ought to be more than happy to take credit for outlaws they missed entire, Miss Erna. Mr. Harriman of the U.P. Line gives handsome bonuses to railroaders who discourage railroad robbing. That conductor will doubtless offer a share to the town law in exchange for our moving on before we get too far behind the officious time of arrival in Utah Territory."

As if to back his brag the car began to move under them again. The gal smiled, albeit sort of severely, as he added, "There you go. They sure got the outlaws off and the sawdust spread quick and neat. Do you mind if I set down, ma'am, or would you rather I just leave you to settle your thoughts in private?"

She blinked as if surprised and flustered, "*Ach, bitte nehmen Sie Platz* and forgive my rude manners! As I said, I am not used to your wilder ways. In East Prussia we are, forgive me, much more civilized!"

They both sat down, her taking up more space despite her slimmer form, with all them petticoats and Lord knew what under her velvet skirts and poplin duster.

He wedged himself down in what was left on the darker green Pullman plush and though he was able to remain polite about the fresh smoke he longed for, he couldn't help saying, dryly, "I've noticed how civilized you Prussian folk act. You licked the Austrians in seven weeks back in '66 and skunked Louis Napoleon in just under seven months in '70-'71."

She shrugged and primly replied, "In both cases they could have avoided bloodshed by simply allowing us to have our way. If we must from time to time stand up for our rights to a place in the sun, at least our trains run on time and nobody would dare to even consider robbing one!"

Longarm said he seldom rode Prussian trains before he innocently asked if Sontag might not be a German name.

She said, "Of course. It means Sunday, in my native language. Why do you ask?"

He said, "Just wondering. There's this cuss called Johnny Sontag robbing trains out to California where we both seem headed. There's this other German or part German boy called the Fresno Kid. He doubtless learned our kind of robbing from his Spanish-speaking mamma, seeing your kind's too refined to rob anything smaller than a whole country at a time."

She didn't get sore. She chuckled and said, "Touché! Tell me all about my wicked *Landsmannschaft* while I discover where that stupid Lilo packed my schnapps."

So he did as she slid off the window seat cum bunk bed to her knees in order to rummage through a Saratoga trunk there really wasn't room for if one wanted to get at the built-in sink and commode wedged between the seating and the inner bulkhead.

She seemed impressed by them sending him all the way out to Fresno after unruly peasants, as she described the angry settlers along the San Joaquin.

As he was explaining nobody wanted him messing with any of the Mussel Slough squatters, if it could be avoided, she impressed him with the schnapps she poured for both of them in bitty fold-up Prussian Army cups of German silver, which was more a convincing alloy than any sort of real silver. For her schnapps was real brandy, four stars or more and likely priced accordingly if he was any judge. He wheezed, "Lord, that's sure swell applejack," before he pleaded, "Might you have any water, or at least some battery acid to chase it down, ma'am?"

She said there was a water tap above yonder tin washbasin, if it worked. She didn't offer, even though she was seated closer, so it was her own fault he had to sort of lean across her fancy bodice with his rougher tweeds to cut the schnapps she'd poured him with half a cup of tepid water.

She didn't seem to mind. When he asked if she'd like him to water her cup she said Prussians fell off horses without losing their monocles, drunk or sober, too. So he admitted he was a sissy who'd rather drink in his shirtsleeves than full dress in such a warm and stuffy compartment if it was all the same with her.

She seemed to think that sounded civilized as running trains on time and drinking schnapps neat. So he got rid of his frock coat, unbuttoned his vest, and loosened his shoe strong tie as long as he was at it.

She giggled and asked if he always wore his .44-40 to bed. So he unbuckled his gun rig and hung it up as well, even though it seemed a mite early for bed, or even discussing the same.

She, in turn, had him hold her empty cup as she peeled out of her duster, unpinned her summer hat, and sat down less formal, with her hair all adangle, to pour herself another heroic drink.

He said he was set, for now, and warned, "We ain't had our noon dinners yet and despite the scenery outside we're way above sea level, where you're doubtless more used to drinking this stuff."

She swallowed most of her drink, stared owlishly at him and said, soberly, "A most economical way to *sich betrinken, nicht wahr?*"

Then she swallowed the last of it, adding, "How do you in English say *hurra?*"

He said that was close enough and insisted, "We're way in the sky where water boils cool enough to bathe in and a body can get blind drunk on a modest amount of draft beer, Miss Erna."

She yawned, started to unbutton her bodice, and fell forward across him with her pretty face buried in his lap. That made him glad he'd taken a shower with that waitress in Cheyenne and changed his underwear as well.

It figured to give him a raging erection either way, and there was much to be said for enjoying one with a lady who'd worked that hard to get them both drunk and partway undressed.

But he still slid out from under the unconscious Prussian beauty, if she was really out and not asking for it, coy, as he gently told her, "I'm likely fixing to make us both mighty disgusted with me, Miss Erna, but I don't jacklight deer or dynamite trout, neither."

She yawned and said something in German. It sounded dreamy and dirty. He rolled her into a more dignified position and picked up her trim but modestly shod ankles to place her feet at the foot of her unmade bunk bed. She suddenly drew her knees up, exposing more of her lower limbs than he'd meant to peek at. Those sheer silk stockings they made in Paris, France, sure made a lady's legs look naked. He knew he'd be able to see even more if he lifted that hem of her velvet skirts and flouncy petticoats just a tad. But he never. It was none of his beeswax and doubtless it would be easier on his nerves if he didn't try to find out whether she wore underdrawers or not. It hadn't done him a lick of good that time that French dancer touring with Madame Sarah had let him stare right up her ring-dang-do like that. Knowing what a lady might or might not have on under her skirts only mattered when it really mattered.

So he put both fold-up cups aside, rose to his considerable full height, and put on his gun rig, frock coat, and Stetson before he let himself out and ambled forward to see when and if they ever meant to serve some damned grub in their damned old dining car.

They were. Halfway there he encountered a black kid in a white jacket going the other way with the dulcet dinner chimes they had him beat on instead of simply yelling that the soup was on. So Longarm beat most of the stampede forward and wound up seated with his back to the front bulkhead, facing a young Mormon gal and two of her damned kids. The third one, a towheaded boy of six or seven, got to sit next to Longarm on his side, there being no other seats and the Mormon gal looking so harrassed when she'd sent a waiter ahead to ask, polite.

Longarm explained that whilst he respected all religions he just had to have some coffee with his flapjacks and sausages because he hadn't had much sleep the night before.

The Mormon mother graciously nodded and said something about being in Rome, no matter what it looked like out yonder. It was her sweet little daughter of eight or nine who said she could tell he'd been drinking gentile whiskey as well.

The young mother kicked the brat under the table. But Longarm just smiled and said, "You're wrong, little miss, it was German brandy, called schnapps, and that's another good reason to order coffee, strong and black, at this altitude."

The boy beside him said folk like him who defiled their bodies with coffee and worse were doomed for all eternity.

The young mother kicked Longarm under the table whilst aiming for her brat. So Longarm winced and said, "I wish you'd let me handle this, ma'am. I know my kind is doomed for all eternity whether we indulge in coffee, tea, tobacco, and so on or not. So I figure I may as well get through the rest of this long day as best I can and, meanwhile, as anyone but a smarty-pants ought to know, there's always that loophole Brother Joseph left us poor Gentiles."

The young Mormon gal blinked in surprise, smiled uncertainly, and allowed he didn't strike her as a Latter Day Saint.

He nodded and said, "I ain't, ma'am, but, like I said, I keep an open mind and, for all I really know, Wakan Tanka may have the last laugh on us all in that Happy Hunting Ground. Meanwhile, as I was explaining to your boy, here, Brother Joseph Smith's, ah, translation of the Book Of Mormon says right out that any Latter Day Saint as wants to can pray unenlightened kith and kin into your church, whether they've asked to join or just gone on swilling coffee and worse 'til the Angel Moroni took 'em off to the Great Beyond, right?"

The Mormon gal tried not to laugh as she asked him, sort of schoolmarmly, whether he was mocking her and her kind.

He smiled back easily and said, "No, ma'am, just your boy, here. It's all right to talk that smug along your Mormon Delta, I reckon. But do you ride the U.P. line out of Utah Territory often, it's best to sound less rude to one's elders."

The young mother flushed beet red. The kid whined that he was never rude to real elders, of the Latter Day Saints. So Longarm advised him never to join the U.S. Army or Navy, and then the waiter was there to take their orders, so Longarm changed the subject by ordering some lemon slices even though he didn't want any tea and showed the kids how to make sudden lemon drops out of dining car sugar cubes.

The young mother said she was afraid they'd wind up with toothaches. Longarm was too polite to say he surely hoped so. Then he'd polished off his meal along with three cups of black coffee and felt more able to stand up some more. So he settled with the waiter and headed back for the club car again.

Partway there he bumped into that same conductor, who allowed the railroad and Wyoming Territory seemed satisfied with the way he'd tidied up back yonder. Longarm said he was glad and added, "I don't suppose you had a spare compartment a gent could deposit a mighty weary head, free? I didn't get as much sleep last night as I might have and don't never drink schnapps at this altitude, even you've had plenty of rest."

The conductor chuckled and said, "I was sort of wondering what you'd just had with your noon meal. They don't serve nothing that powerful up forward. I reckon we can fix you up with a lie down, seeing you just helped save this train a robbery. I never charge a real pal for a compartment nobody wants to hire in the first place. But need I add I'll expect you up and out of there on the double if we need it for paying passengers?"

Longarm said that sounded fair and the conductor led him back the way he'd just come, as far as one end of the Pullman car forward. As he slid the door open for Longarm the conductor said, "I doubt we'll need to disturb you this side of Reno unless we get a stampede at Ogden. We got eight other empties to book first and there ain't half as many rich folk in Utah Territory as Nevada."

As Longarm thanked him and edged around him the conductor added, "I thought you was traveling west with that Miss Dragging

Something, no offense. Reckon I'll have to keep an eye on her all by myself."

Longarm frowned thoughtfully and asked who'd asked anyone to keep anything on Miss Erna Drachenfeld, who looked to be at least twenty-one as well as free and white to him.

The conductor explained, "Got a wire from our West Coast affiliate, seeing U.P. would be switching this combination to the W.P. tracks and another crew this side of the Great Salt Desert. Some big shots out by Frisco Bay seem concerned she gets there safe and sound as well as on time. I never wired back about that attempted train robbery. Western Pacific says her fancy pals are inclined to rant and rave as it is."

Longarm shrugged and said, "Well, she did mention kin as put Vons in front of their names and poor Louis Napoleon just found out what a temper that Von Bismark cuss seems to have. She was sleeping off, ah, some altitude when last we parted, friendly but chaste. So she's all their'n, to rant or rave as they might choose."

Then he ducked inside, shut the door, pulled down the stiff green canvas window shades, and stripped to the buff as soon as he'd made up the bunk bed. Thanks to old George Pullman, they all made up about the same simple way.

As he lay full length to haul the crisp sheet and thin but warm brown blankets over his weary naked flesh, two wide awake and weasel-eyed men he was unaware of were very aware of the time and place as they lurked in a dark corner of the Last Chance in Evanston, just the other side of the Aspen Tunnel betwixt the drainage of the Bear and Green rivers. The saloon had been dubbed the Last Chance because the next railroad stop lay in Mormon territory on the Utah side of the line and everyone knew how the Latter Day Saints felt about snakebite medication.

The two guns for hire weren't as worried about snakebites as they were a westbound combination due in around three that afternoon. When one suggested another round of nerve medication his more experienced pard growled, "Not at this altitude with less'n two hours to go. They say Longarm moves like spit on a hot stove and I don't want him taking this child with him, even backshot, because some drunk-ass stumblebum gave him the split-second extra a really determined cuss needs."

The one who wanted a drink protested, "Aw, not even Hickok had much to say that time Cockeyed Jack McCall got the drop on him from behind, did he?"

The older and obviously wiser one shook his head and said, "Some say Longarm's faster than Hickok was. I don't aim to find out. When his train rolls in we get aboard, cold sober and innocent-looking as the dudes we took these duds off. Then we spot where he's riding, sit down sweetly ahint him, and blow his nosy brains out the front of his fucking face!"

Chapter 8

Longarm had been seated in that big Mormon Tabernacle in Salt Lake City some time, listening to that big pipe organ as he tried to figure out how he'd wound up in the middle of the services naked as a jay, or how come nobody in the congregation all about seemed to care.

It seemed painsomely obvious none of 'em had noticed, yet. Lord only knew what folk who didn't hold with sipping tea or dipping snuff were likely to say as soon as they detected a naked Gentile with a full erection hunkered betwixt two angelic young gals wearing nothing but that curious underwear the Mormons issued Latter Day Saints of both genders.

One of them had hold of his old ring-dang-do as they went on singing "Bringing In the Sheaves," and he just knew he was fixing to kiss her, at least, if she didn't stop. So, since he couldn't seem to stop her and wasn't about to be stomped by a whole congregation of singing saints, he decided he'd best wake up.

Once he had, it took him a second or more to get his bearings in a more rational world. He was still naked, but lying down under some bedding, praise the Lord, and that was his own hand gripping his old ring-dang-do, which was just as hard as he'd dreamed. So he let it go with an awkward grin, hoping the lady seated on the narrow bunk bed with him hadn't noticed. Erna Drachenfeld looked awkward in her own right, blushing bashfully and apparently unable to meet his eye as he asked her to what he might owe this honor.

She still had all her duds on, and it was socially acceptable for a young lady to have her hair down, indoors, in the company of a gent she knew to talk to.

She said, "One of the porters was kind enough to direct me to this compartment, and even let me in when you failed to answer my discreet tapping and the calling out of your name."

He didn't ask how much she'd tipped the porter as he made a mental note to use the infernal inside bolt, next time. He covered a yawn with his palm and replied, "You'd have to tap some to be heard above the tapping of the trucks right below my fool head, ma'am. As for your calling, I rendered it to dulcet singing in my dream, just now. Some say dreams are meant to tell us secrets about ourselves. But I hold with the notion they're meant to keep us asleep as long as possible. Have you ever noticed how you dream it's showing when you've kicked the covers off or you get an invite to a formal supper you can't sit down to just yet, when you've overslept breakfast after going to bed a mite hungry?"

She blushed pinker as she admitted unsatisfied appetites had led her into some odd corners of dreamland in her time, so, right, she'd caught him jerking off in his sleep. But it wasn't as if he'd invited her to watch, so he asked what in thunder she wanted as he felt his own ears burning awkwardly.

She said, "I wanted to thank you. When I came back to my senses to find myself sprawled helplessly with my skirts up around my hips and my, ah, unmentionables in damp disarray, my first impression was not, I fear, at all charitable to you."

He said her schnapps, combined with thin mountain air, had left them both sort of helpless. It would have been rude to suggest she'd likely pissed herself a mite. So he simply added, "Your ankles was crossed and your skirting was sedate as I left you to sleep it off, ma'am. I figured you was safe enough to leave in that condition with a spring latch on your own compartment door. Unless you suspect that porter with his pass key, I'd suggest you got into less dignified positions on your own, in your sleep."

She sighed and said, "In my drunken stupor, you mean. I've never had a mere three drinks effect me so and I have certainly learned a good lesson."

He said he still didn't see what she wanted him to do about it, now that things had turned out all right. She stammered, "I came to apologize. When I first came to my senses in my own car my first thought was that you'd, you know, while I was too drunk to resist. I know you'll find this hard to believe, but a Prussian

62

officer and gentleman I'd been taught to trust once had his wicked way with a younger, more trusting maiden who'd allowed him to introduce her to pink champagne."

Longarm said he'd heard that bubble juice could sneak up on one, even when it wasn't pink. He felt no call to say that other rascal's sneaky seduction didn't surprise him all that much. It might have sounded like bragging to say he didn't stoop to such methods.

He didn't have to say it. Erna placed a gentle hand on what she likely took for his wrist, under the bedding, as she halfway sobbed, "A lot of other men might have thought I was asking for it after I'd invited them in and gotten so drunk with them. I thought of that after it was a little late to repair the damage, even before I'd taken steps to repair any damage to my own future and discovered, to my astonishment, nobody had really, ah, invaded my privacy."

He sat up on one bare elbow, the shades were down, after all, so he could shake his head to clear it and then, when that didn't work, ask her what damage they could be talking about.

She said, "To you, not to me. I just told you I was able to tell you hadn't had carnal knowlege of me as first I'd feared."

He grimaced, rubbed his tongue over his sleep-gummed teeth, and asked her to hand him the vest hanging yonder as he said he still had to be missing something. As she handed him his vest so's he could get at a smoke and his waterproof matches he said, "There was no way I could damage me without I damaged you, that way, and to tell the pure truth I've about recovered from the last time I got damaged that way by anyone."

She repressed a titter and demurely replied, "I assumed as much from the way you seemed to be . . . dreaming, just now. But as I said, I thought worse of you when we stopped back there to take on more water."

He muttered he must have slept through any recent flag stops or water jerks. She said, "I know. I was so afraid I'd see you there when I dashed across the platform to send a telegram to, well, I suppose you should call him my fiancée, in San Francisco. I am not certain he will be waiting to meet me by the San Francisco Bay. He is almost certainly going to wish to meet you, however. He is a military attaché at our San Francisco Consulate and, I fear, a notorious duelist as well."

Longarm forgot all about the cheroot he'd just stuck between

63

his mouth as he stared at her thundergasted to demand, "Jesus H. Christ, you just wired a Prussian officer with diplomatic immunity as well as a poker up his ass, most likely, that I'd poked his intended piece of ass with my innocent American dick?"

She looked as if she was fixing to cry. So he lit the damned smoke and shook out the match as he said, "Forgive my manners, ma'am. I get challenged to duels over ladies about as often as I use strong lingo in front of 'em. What's to stop you from wiring your Prussian bully boy it was all a mistake, soon as we get in to, let's say, Evanston? I should think he'd be cheered by the news another man didn't lay you, after all. I know I would, if I was him."

She sighed and said, "To tell the truth I've only spoken to Franz a few times, long ago at court in our own country. I know how hard it must be for an American commoner to understand, but marriages among a higher class of society are arranged more delicately."

He blew smoke out both nostrils and replied, "I know how delicate you high-toned European lords and ladies keep your stud books. I never figured that pretty Princess Alexandra of Denmark married that fat and foppish Prince Edward of Wales because she admired his looks, or his brains. How do we get me out of a shoot-out with the brainless fop you've been fixing to breed with, Miss Erna? It hardly seems fair to shove a poor boy into a fight he just can't win against a cuss with two whole governments backing him when we both know he never did the dirty deed he's accused of!"

She sobbed, "I know. I told you I'd examined myself as I was, ah, taking certain precautions. What if you were to get off the train before it got there? That would give me time to talk to Franz and, ah, convince him of my faithfulness to him."

Longarm shrugged his bare shoulder and said, "I wasn't planning on riding all the way to the Oakland yards with you to begin with. I'll be getting off at the state capital of Sacramento to catch the valley line down to . . . Never mind where to. You've got me worried enough about fighting duels over she-males I've never even kissed, dang your pretty hide."

So she gravely removed the cheroot from his mouth and leaned in to plant a warm wet kiss flush on his lips, and, once they'd come up for air, ask him if that made up for the trouble she'd caused him.

He took the lit cheroot back to get it safely out of the way as he hauled her in for another, closer, and when his questing free hand somehow found itself exploring under her velvet skirts and silk petticoats she shifted her hips and raised one knee to help it find its way, which it did, about where he'd expected she might have something that nice, the way she'd hooked one heel on the rail of the bunk bed to open wide and say "Ahhhhhh!"

She'd gotten rid of the underdrawers she'd dampened with no earlier help from him. It was tough to tell how much of the dampness in and about her welcoming mat was passion or preparation. She'd said she knew how to take care of such matters and this time they were both wide awake and knew just what they were doing.

So he rolled her across him as he got rid of the bedding between them and she raised her bare rump from the mattress to meet him as he did it to her that way, at first.

He probably found her emerald velvet skirting up around her bare hips and silk brocaded breasts more exciting than she did, inside 'em. So she pleaded with him to let her get on top and, once he had, she put on a mighty interesting show in the tricky light, peeling herself to the green-shaded buff save for her sheer stockings and high button shoes, as the wheels clicked under them and she rode up and down his shaft like a mighty well-built child on a merry-go-round steed.

They were still going at it, standing up with one of her shoes in the tin sink, as their train slowed down for Evanston. She pleaded, "Not when the train is standing in a station! What will the others on board think of us?"

Longarm figured most of the train crew knew damn well, menfolk being at least as prone to gossip as some women, while the other passengers had no call to suspect others of being in bed in broad ass daylight. But he still moved her over to the bunk and lay them both down without taking it out. She found that flattering if her internal throbbings meant a thing. He was throbbing some in his own right as he peeked out the slit betwixt the shade and windowsill to see where they might be.

When he saw by a platform sign they'd made Evanston he got into a more comfortable pose atop her and said, "We've about made up the time we lost to them train robbers this morning. By suppertime we ought to be admiring the Great Salt Lake out the dining car windows to our north."

She raised her silk-clad thighs to lock her high buttons across his bare behind as she shyly asked if he could move just a little without letting anyone in the corridor outside suspect anything.

He could. By the time the train was moving again she was moaning and groaning and moving pretty good in her own right.

Meanwhile, back in the club car, the gunslick who'd just passed the secret site of their daylight passion rejoined his comrade in crime to declare, as he sat down as well, "He don't seem to be on board. I been as far forward as they let you go and there ain't much ahint us but a mess of empty roadbed. Undertaking Sam must have made a mistake."

Their self-appointed leader shook his head and softly replied, "Undertaking Sam don't make mistakes. That's how come they pay him so well for undertaking jobs like this. He wired us from Cheyenne after this train pulled out. He said Longarm was aboard, riding coach but likely sipping and smoking back here, the way he's prone to travel."

His younger sidekick shot a casual glance around the less than half-filled club car as he murmured, "I'll bet you my share of the bounty on the bastard he ain't back here, now. So that's one thing Undertaking Sam guessed wrong about. Who's to say the sneaky lawman didn't get off somewheres betwixt Cheyenne and that last stop?"

The older killer, who managed to get older by thinking more than some killers, pondered his young pard's point before he decided it made no sense, explaining, "I ain't certain why Undertaking Sam's, ah, client, wants Longarm stopped. But he does want him stopped before he can get out California way. So they have to be concerned about why Longarm's headed that far west. If he was working on something in the high country of Wyoming Territory, nobody would be worried about him doing it in California, see?"

Most anyone could have. The junior member of the team suggested, "If he's anywhere on board that McClellan and Winchester he brung up from Denver ought to be riding in the baggage car. I could see, next stop, were I to stroll up the platform and ask casual about our own baggage, right?"

His more experienced mentor snorted, "Wrong. We boarded back yonder without no baggage and porters notice things like that, the tip-hungry coons. You go jawing about baggage the train crew knows we don't have and they'll have us arrested as possible train robbers before we get to shoot anybody, hear?"

The younger one grumbled, "You got to see your target to shoot at it. He ain't in the dining car or any of the men's rooms up ahead. He ain't in any of the day coaches or seated on any of the Pullman plush. Of course, that still leaves the Pullman bunks, daylight or not."

His mentor frowned and pointed out, "You just said you checked all the Pullman seats. They don't unfold 'em into bunk beds and drape all them curtains across 'em this side of nine or later, tonight."

The younger one grinned smugly and declared, "A lot you know. They got some of them newer Pullman palace cars up forward. Mostly foldout, like you just said, but they got these bitty private compartments betwixt the shit houses and platforms at either end. No way to see if Longarm or anyone else could be sitting, private, in one of them."

His mentor glanced out the nearby window at the passing sunlit rocks and trees to object, "Mighty fancy for a lawman traveling by day with no prisoners. Of course, he might have run into a pal who makes more money and having him hid out in a private compartment makes more sense than assuming Undertaking Sam's gone blind on us."

The younger and hence more eager killer grinned wolfishly and said, "Hot damn. What say we start working out way forward, knocking on doors and saying we're porters with telegraph messages for Deputy Custis Long?"

The more thoughtful one considered before he decided, "Might be a smoother way. This side of suppertime we'll be moving down the east slope of the Wasatch Range and the tight-knit spreads of the Mormon Delta. I don't know about you but I'd sure hate to dodge Mormon posses, on foot, on their own range, should something go wrong."

The younger and hence bolder one frowned and declared, "This seems a piss poor time to have second thoughts, Raymond. Undertaking Sam is likely to feel mighty vexed with the both of us if you crawfish out of the deal at this late date!"

The older Raymond shook his head and said, "I ain't suggesting we crawfish. I'm suggesting we execute the son of a bitch foolproof. By supper time we'll have passed through the thicker settled parts of Mormon country and, better yet, Longarm ought to want his supper, in that dining car, no matter where on board he might be lurking at the moment."

The younger one grinned wider and said, "Hot damn! That's when we blow his brains smack in his soup, right?"

Raymond said, "Wrong again. Backshooting a famous gent amid a crowd of witnesses can be injurious to one's health, as Jack McCall found out at the Number Ten Saloon in Deadwood. Backshooting Hickok was the least of his problems. Getting away after he done it was his real problem and, as we all know, he never. So this child ain't about to gun no lawman in the dining car and go diving into the Great Salt Lake, which would be the only cover for miles."

"Where *do* we kill him, then?" his younger pard pleaded, eager as a coon hound pup under a hunter's moon.

The more experienced killer said, "Where it's safer to get off and fade into the crowd, of course. So listen tight. Do we spot him in the dining car we only have to act innocent and find out where he holes up the rest of the time. By that time we'll have made the last water stop for a spell and ought to be rolling lickety split across the Great Salt Desert, flat and white as a table cloth for many a mile."

"Hot damn, that where we shoot him and dump him in the desert?"

"Not hardly. I'd as soon run afoot from Mormon posses in these mountains than try to get away across salt crusts spreading clean to the horizon no matter which way I run. So we wait 'til this train rolls into Elko, Nevada, along about midnight. *Then* we empty our guns into the rascal and scamper off down the dimly lit but crowded main street of a considerable cow town. I know a hotel lobby there we can get our winds back in these business suits whilst everyone else mourns the passing of the famous Longarm. So let's order some drinks to his memory, long as we got plenty of time."

Chapter 9

There were limits to how many positions any couple could come in before they got sort of interested in other natural appetites. Erna pointed out and Longarm had to agree that having their suppers served in bed could involve as much bother, and certainly more lewd comments in the kitchen, than just getting dressed again and eating natural.

Hence the hired guns moving forward to the dining car in response to the serving gong got a break they didn't deserve when Longarm and his hungry pal from Prussia popped out into the narrow corridor just ahead of them.

Longarm glanced casually at what seemed a pair of dudes who'd been aboard long enough to need shaves. When neither harmless-looking strangers made any suspicious moves he waved them both on ahead of himself and Erna, knowing the backs of two apparently law-abiding citizens were safer from him than his might be to anyone he didn't have to turn his fool back on.

The two killers didn't let on they'd followed his drift as they strode up the train ahead of him and Erna. The one called Raymond had already memorized the car and compartment number for later. To make certain, he wrote it down as soon as he and his younger sidekick were seated several tables away from their intended victim, and, since it couldn't be helped, she-victim.

Erna didn't know she was slated to be murdered in bed that evening. As her handsome if hardly distinguished escort had promised, they were coasting along the south shore of the Great Salt Lake as they waited for their grub. Erna said the passing dunes and white-capped waves clean to the hazy northern horizon, save for the barren mountainous mass of Antelope Island off to one side, reminded her of that Baltic Sea back where she'd got engaged to old Franz.

He said, "It's tough to tell a big lake from the main ocean from its shore instead of a map. When old Jim Bridger discovered this one back around '25 and tasted the water he was certain he'd forged his way to the Pacific Ocean."

Their waiter brought their black bean soup, made fancy with slices of lemon floating in each bowl. The Harrimans were inclined to put on airs, back East. Longarm got the fool lemon slice out of his otherwise substantial soup as he went on, "Jim Bridger was inclined to jump to hasty conclusions. He once bet Brother Brigham Young a silver dollar for every ear of sweet corn anyone would ever harvest at this altitude. It was a good thing Brother Brigham didn't hold with sporting wagers. The clear bright days out here make up for the somewhat shorter growing seasons, given all that irrigation works the Latter Day Saints got right to work on whilst old Jim and the other mountain men was still laughing at 'em."

Erna seemed to think you were supposed to squeeze lemon juice into your black bean soup. As she did so she demurely asked whether it was true Brother Brigham had married a hundred women.

Longarm smiled thinly and said, "More like twenty-seven and he got on tolerable with most. They say one was a real shrew who low-rated him in public and of course that was that last one some saints say he never wed at all. It was after he died in '77, from a ruptured appendix, not overwork in or out of bed, that this one gal commenced to publish all sorts of guff about dirty old Mormons keeping harems of white slaves and such.

"I think I read a magazine article by the lapsed Morman girl you must mean," said Erna, adding, "She did make it all seem very sordid."

Longarm shrugged and lowered his voice a mite to reply, "Heaps of things folk do look unseemly, or even downright silly, to others not sharing in the enjoyment. I'll allow there's folk of every religion who ought to be ashamed of themselves. We'll soon be crossing some salt flats where Mormon fanatics tried to do me dirty a spell back and I reckon some few gals, or even boys, have been converted to all faiths against their will.

But fair is fair and I have to say most Mormons I've dealt with have treated me decent enough."

"Including the ones with extra wives?" she demanded, archly.

He smiled innocently and explained, "They don't approve of sharing their wives with others any more than other Christians do, whether they have extra ones or not. I'd say Mormon wives fool around on their men about as often as Calvinist or Papist wives, no more, no less. But why are you so interested, honey? Was you planning on marrying up with a Latter Day Saint in the near future?"

She sighed and said almost anyone but a Prussian Lutheran with a jealous streak had to be an improvement. He didn't answer, since he seemed one of the improvements she'd just mentioned and you'd think even a flighty furriner would make up her pretty head before she'd head across oceans and continents to either marry gents or get 'em into duels.

It was after dessert, herding her back to his compartment, he got her to admit, shamefaced, she might have wired she'd been spoiled for her Franz before she'd learned to like the poor soul she'd accused. He said he felt honored she'd decided she liked him better alive, but suggested, "Can't you get out of it by telling your intended you got laid in say Elko or Reno by some fictitious tinhorn who promised to make you an opera star or something? I mean, I can deliver you mussed up and screwed silly, if you so desire."

She laughed like a mean little kid and confided in the privacy of the corridor she just loved to be screwed silly but preferred to get off trains as properly groomed and dressed as she got on.

He allowed that would be tough for Queen Victoria after a cross-continental trip behind steam-driven and coal-fired locomotives.

As they approached the compartment they'd been using as a love nest she sighed and said, "I know. But I have, ah, sanitary supplies as well as my cosmetics and more than one change of unmentionables back in my own compartment and we shall have more than this one night ahead of us, *nicht wahr*?"

He sighed. "Not hardly. Sunrise ought to see us well the other side of Carson's Sink, if not in the Sierra foothills already. So I fear you'll be getting off in one sort of underpants or another before this late in the day, tomorrow."

71

She said in that case they'd best go to bed again in her compartment so's she could get up more prim and proper, in the morning.

He felt no call to argue. He'd tidied up the spare compartment they'd let him use before taking Erna to supper. All the belongings he didn't have on him at the moment were riding up forward in the baggage car, no matter where he put down the rest. So they just kept going 'til they got back to her more cluttered quarters, and it was fun sitting on her big leather trunk while she got undressed again with some of him inside her.

But as the sunset turned the salt flats outside to peach cake frosting and he banged her dog style in the romantic light, her mood turned mighty indigo, as women's moods were inclined to turn after the first full flush of strange stuff began to fade.

She asked him, mighty casually, considering, whether he'd ever noticed that no matter what one was up to, good or bad, it seemed no time at all before one was up to something else entire?

He allowed they called that phenomena the passage of time and got it in her a tad deeper as he soothed, "Time might get tedious as hell if it stayed stuck in one place. Imagine spending all eternity having the same hangover, or even doing this. I mean, no offense, but even this could get to start feeling like work instead of pleasure if we just kept doing it, without knowing we'd be coming again, sooner or later."

She arched her spine to croon, "Oooh, *ja, hart und tief, aber* can't you see that no matter how good it feels and how long we try to make it last it will all be over, *we* will all be over, in what will seem in the end the blinking of a star!"

He said she sure screwed morose as he went on enjoying the end of her that didn't sound so gloomy. Most men in his position would have. Her shapely upthrust derriere sure looked inviting in the orange and purple gloaming. Tearing as they were across uninhabited salt flats there were no inhibitions involving window blinds and he could see for miles as he thrust in and out of her four or five inches.

Somewhere out yonder, he knew, lay the likely still-visible tracks of that wind wagon he'd used to escape those Danites, or Avenging Angels, of the Mormon persuasion that time. Ruts carved in the salt by the '49ers were still visible some places out yonder, and it did seem only yesterday he'd been saving that other pretty gal from death and, forget about fates worse than death, sweating bullets and sure he'd never see another sunrise.

Yet here he was, many a sunrise later with another pretty gal in the very act, and he had to wonder what that other him would have thought had a voice from the future called out, "Don't worry, old son, you'll get out of that fix alive and in no time at all you'll be passing close by aboard a Pullman car with plenty of food and drink and a gal taking it dog style besides!"

Erna asked what he was laughing about. He doubted she wanted to hear the whole tale. So he said, "You're right. I can already see us up forward again having breakfast, even though we just et supper. Reminds me of this pal of mine as married up with a Lakota gal one time. She enjoyed everything about living white but keeping house. She allowed she was blamed if she'd sweep any damned floor that only figured to need sweeping again before the week was out. You see, her folk had raised her on the move and you don't have to sweep a teepee much before you get to shake it out and pitch it somewheres else."

She said she was almost there and begged him to finish in her sweeter. So they did, and then she commenced to cry, sobbing she could see stars out yonder, now, and just knew that tedious officer she despised would be in her like this, before she knew it.

He didn't suggest such a naturally warm-natured young thing might wind up begging that other cuss to make it last. He suspected things would work out as well as they usually did. That pretty young Princess Alexandra had doubtless had similar second thoughts on her way to wed the fat dumb Prince of Wales. But, last he'd heard, they'd had a mess of royal brats, so she must have gotten used to the notion by now.

It was this gal's more dramatic solutions to her sudden changes of heart a man had to study on. Being a mite older and doubtless way more experienced with changes of heart, Longarm knew she'd have felt guilty about setting gents up for a duel even if they hadn't wound up such good friends. He knew it was just as likely she'd get unpredictable again if she rolled into the arms of that hot-tempered Prussian feeling frustrated. So even though she said she felt like dozing off for a spell before they did it some more, he remounted her as soon as he could manage, growling. "Powder River and let her buck, little darling!"

To which she could only protest, "*Ach, wieder?*" and then, "*Ja, wieder immer wieder!*" as she proceeded to respond in kind with hard thrusts of her trim hips. She'd said they rode horseback a heap, back where she came from. He suspected she jumped fences, swell, astride, the sassy little thing.

But Longarm was bigger, stronger, and, more importantly, he had a plan. So long before midnight he had her begging for mercy, complaining she was commencing to get sore and, dammit, had another horny brute she hadn't seen for over a year waiting for her poor bruised body by the Frisco Bay.

Hence, she was sound asleep with her bruised body mighty sated before their train slowed down along the banks of the Humbolt River, a braided desert wetwash this time of the year.

As Longarm quietly dressed in the dark he felt sort of bruised and well-sated, himself, and he'd heard Red Robin might be playing at the Sage Grouse Saloon in Elko, too.

It seemed safer to just sneak his saddle and possibles off there and catch that later night freight. That way he'd be safe from both Red Robin and anyone a jealous Prussian officer might send after him. For the sweetly snoring gal by the window could hardly tell anyone which train to meet in Sacramento if she didn't know where in blue blazes he was when she woke up.

Putting his hat on last, Longarm loomed to full height and adjusted his gun rig under his frock coat before he eased out into the deserted corridor. Up ahead the main part of the car was even darker, what with the curtains of dark green tent canvas screening the other sleeping passengers and leaving just the narrow aisle to navigate.

As he passed one canvas-draped Pullman bunk he heard a she-male voice protest, "Not in *there*, you ninny! You promised you wouldn't do me that way once I let you have your way with French rubbers."

Longarm smiled wistfully and forged on, aiming to hole up in that empty they'd loaned him and maybe even find those damned matches he seemed to be missing. In the field or back in town he preferred to pack waterproof matches, that Mex brand with the wax stems being about the best and not every tobacco stand selling such lights.

Thus it came to pass that just before midnight, as the train hissed to a full stop along the Elko platform, the two hired guns were in the process of kicking in the door of that forward compartment, guns drawn and commencing to blaze, even as Longarm came through the rear door of that car, going for his own gun as he came.

The older one grasped the horrible mistake they'd just made a split second too late to correct it. Longarm's first round parted his front teeth to spray a Christ-awful mess all over the suit of his younger sidekick as the latter went right on blazing away at the fortunately vacant interior of the dark compartment. Then Longarm's second round caught him smack on one staring eye as he swung his own head and gun to meet his fate.

There was no call to shoot head-shot as well as failed assassins again. So Longarm didn't as he stepped gingerly over both to crawfish into the open doorway of the shot-up compartment and start reloading.

As he'd expected, the corridor filled in no time with confused men and women in various stages of undress, saying various dumb things, such as, "What happened? It sounded like gunshots!"

Or, "Good heavens, what a mess! Are they going to be all right?"

Several pilgrims called for any doctors aboard to come forward. Before any did, a Western Pacific conductor Longarm fortunately knew from earlier trips elbowed his way through, bitching, "Out of my way, Gawd damn you one and all! I got me a timetable to keep and, aw, hell, who done this?"

Longarm moved out into the light with his gun held polite and his federal badge aloft for assurance as he modestly confessed, "I cannot tell a lie, Pete. From where I was standing as I fired it appeared they were out to assassinate me or someone as nice."

Old Pete Collins nodded soberly and said, "Heard you was aboard, Longarm. Reckon that'll learn 'em to send boys to do a man's job. But who do you reckon sent 'em, for what reason?"

Longarm said, "I wish you hadn't asked that, Pete. For I'll be switched with snakes before I can even hazard an educated guess."

Chapter 10

Pete still had a timetable to worry about that didn't allow for shoot-outs in the corridors, while Longarm had been planning on switching trains at Elko in any case. So along with the town law of Elko they pitched in to deposit the two dead men and Longarm's saddle and possibles on the loading platform by the time the tender up forward had taken on enough pea coal and water to cross the more desolate stretch ahead.

As the train he'd been riding pulled out Longarm heard a familiar she-male voice call his name and, apparently, cuss him good. He didn't savvy much German. As the rumble and roar faded away to the west he noticed the tinkle of an out-of-tune or badly-played piano drifting toward the tracks from the rinky-dink end of the town. He knew Miss Red Robin was way better in bed than seated at an upright, and that she played piano professional. He still turned to the nearest Elko lawman, an older gent with a bushier mustache, for help in naming either of the head-shot sons of bitches sprawled at their feet on the splinterwood.

As luck would have it, at least half a dozen of the lawmen and curious townsmen assembled knew one or the other cadavers. For the late Raymond Bean and Fanny Gleason had been well known all up and down the Humbolt as occasional assassins and full-time stock thieves. Opinion was divided as to whether the younger Gleason had been dubbed Fanny because he would jaw on and even demonstrate his half-ass notion a grown man would want to fan a sixgun in a serious shootout or if he'd been, as some suspected, the love toy as well as follower of the older and much more serious Raymond Bean.

In any case both had been wanted, bad, by more than one Nevada county as well as the stockman's protective association based over to Carson City. So the hairy old cuss in charge of enforcing the law in Elko said he'd be proud to take care of the more tedious paperwork if Longarm meant what he said about not filing for any of the bounty money posted on such otherwise useless carrion.

A railroad dispatcher as helpful told Longarm that night freight he'd been studying on wouldn't roll in before a quarter to two A.M. So Longarm waited friendly 'til they'd put the two stiffs away for the night in a root cellar the county coroner used for such temporary storage. Then, still having plenty of time to spare, Longarm ambled over to the Elko Western Union office.

He spent the next five minutes or more writing up a storm on their yellow telegram forms. Once he'd finished, the fussy-looking old cuss on the far side of the counter pursed purple lips fussier and told him there was no way on earth Western Union could go along with him.

The clerk said, "I take your word you're a lawman working on what seems a serious federal case, ah, Deputy Long. I see what you want with the answers to some of these questions you want some of our other branch offices to answer. But our state and federal charters as well as company ethics forbid us to divulge private information about paying customers."

Longarm had heard as much from other such nitpickers in the past. One way or the other he'd usually won, in the end, but since he had that train to catch he just said, "Wire your company headquarters for clearance if you enjoy your job with Western Union. Be sure to mention my name. You'd best mention my riding for U.S. Marshal William Vail of the Denver District Court in case a new vice president in charge of shooting trouble gets it thrown his way. Once they tell you to do your damned duty to the U.S. federal government I'd be obliged if you wired all the answers to me in care of your main office in Sacramento. Lord willing and the creek don't rise I ought to be that far from here by the time you've finished this chore."

The older man sniffed and declared, "I'll inform my superiors of your implied threats. I doubt they'll be impressed with the powers of a mere deputy as you seem to feel they should be."

Longarm fished out a smoke for himself and lit it, answering a surly attitude in kind as he said, "I ain't half as impressive as the crusty old cuss I ride for. I could tell you tales as would curl your hair, if you had any, about pestifersome pettifoggers who got in the way of simple justice and ain't working where they used to work, these days. But I came in here in peace and I'll leave the same way, since I feel sure you or your replacement will forward the information I need to Sacramento."

Then he left, cheroot gripped between his grinning teeth at a jaunty angle, before the old priss could give him any more guff.

Having time to kill as well as legs in need of some stretching, Longarm strode deeper into the night life of Elko, still going strong despite the hour and modest size of the town.

Things had gone way smoother in these parts than out California way at Mussel Slough. Around Elko the railroad and settlers hadn't made half the mistakes leading up to that recent shootout. Laid out in the '70's before scandals had clouded title to railroad grant lands, Elko had been sensibly sited as an express stop along the W.P. main line and, lured by rail transport and the year-round waters of the broad if shallow Humbolt, settlers had flocked in to take advantage of the railroad's offer of town and country lots at a reasonable price or to file federal homesteads where, railroad grant or not, the water table was high and the sage good enough for scrub stock.

So now Elko was the seat of the recently incorporated county of the same name, big enough to lose some of the original thirteen states in, and when they weren't raising hell the locals who didn't work for the county or railroad raised everything from garden truck to Indian beef.

Longarm passed the saloon all that piano music seemed to be coming from. It wasn't easy, even suffering the aftereffects of Miss Erna Drachenfeld's bouncing. For he knew that despite her usually bright red hair the older, shorter and more curvesome lady they called Red Robin was a natural brunette.

He knew he was one of the few of her many admirers allowed to see that much of Red Robin, after work, and one had to admire any gal who could screw so swell, that fastidious.

On the other hand he had a mission to carry out as well as a possibly limp dick for the foreseeable future and that damned old night freight figured on getting here before he could get even Red Robin away from that piano and out of her red dress.

He knew what she might say or think of him if he just stopped by, platonic, and then caught a train out as she was just fixing to knock off early. So he turned in a good three saloons down to find a place at the dark end of the bar and order a tall schooner of suds he could nurse for a spell.

It didn't work. One of the town lawmen who'd been over at the railroad platform, before, asked a townee drinking between them to trade places so's he could jaw with an old pal.

He repeated his own handle as they shook again. Longarm hadn't paid as much attention, the first time. But this time, having way fewer details on his mind, he repeated, "Fritz Zimmermann, I remember," before he added with a thoughtful frown, "You talk American good as me and I hope you won't take this wrong, Fritz, but might you Speckle Sea Dutch, as they say in the old country?"

The German-American laughed easily and said, "Way better than you do, I'd vow. Who do you want me to talk German with, Pard?"

Longarm said the time for talking had passed but asked if Fritz could tell him what "Hill Feel" or "Not Shoot" might mean.

When Fritz said *Hilfe* meant "Help" and *Notzucht* meant "rape," Longarm said he'd been afraid they might.

Chapter 11

Somebody higher up the Western Union totem pole must have reflected on Billy Vail's seniority and how many miles of wire they had stretched across federal range within his jurisdiction, for a whole stack of telegrams lay waiting for Longarm when he dropped by the next afternoon in Sacramento.

The well-situated capital city of California lay in about the center of the big banana-shaped valley filling a good part of the second largest state west of the Big Muddy. The northern half was drained by the river Sacramento had been named for, since the cross-country railroad crossed the river there. The southern half, way drier, was drained by the less famous San Joaquin. The two rivers met southwest of Sacramento City to form a swampy delta and drain on west into Frisco Bay. So the northern reaches of the big central lowlands were called the Sacramento Valley whilst the southern parts were called the San Joaquin Valley, even though both valleys were really one, with about the same daily temperatures and generally sunny weather from one end to the other. The apparent moisture in the north and drought to the south were occasioned more by the amounts of rain in the mountains all about, with the Sierra Nevadas to the east catching way more, north or south, than the lower coastal ranges between the big valley and the wide Pacific to the west.

All Longarm really cared about all this, that afternoon, was that the day was too sunny and warm for a man wearing cotton longjohns under a three-piece tweed suit by the time he'd toted his saddle and possibles to a nearby hotel he knew of old and packed all those telegrams to the more distant federal building near the statehouse grounds. It did get cold enough to frost an occasional pumpkin this far north in California, but the sissy trees on the statehouse grounds were in full leaf and the grass was still green as grass grew in June, back in Denver. They said the Presidio at San Francisco was the only U.S. Army post that never issued summer uniform shirts or winter overcoats. It got cold enough for overcoats this far inland, though, if only for one month a damn year.

He'd been in the Sacramento federal building before. So, lest he disgrace his own outfit by sweating like a scared pig, Longarm ducked into this one room he knew off the main Court chambers and, sure enough, he found it empty, save for a chesterfield couch and some racks of dusty law books hardly anyone ever needed. So he bolted the door he'd come in after him and proceeded to shuck his gun rig and duds.

Tossing everything atop the tufted leather of the chesterfield, he soon had himself stripped down to his sweaty longjohns. He'd just peeled out of them to stand upright in no more than his socks as he neatly folded 'em, when the damned door on the far side of the dinky chamber popped open to admit a law clerk of the she-male persuasion, who just as suddenly and naturally crawfished back out the way she'd come, bleating like a lost lamb and slamming the door after her. But not before Longarm had noticed she was a pretty little thing in a light brown dress and matching hair that reminded him of a swell lay back in Denver, and not before she'd likely had as good a look at him and all he had to offer.

There was nothing he could do, now, but bar that other damn door with a sheepish grin. Then he put his damned duds back on over his somewhat barer flesh and, not having brought along a damned bag, stuffed the folded-up longjohns behind the damned chesterfield, for now.

Feeling way cooler, if not more dignified, Longarm stepped back out and found his way to the office of Billy Vail's opposite number in Sacramento.

He found himself jawing with an older and less prissy version of old Henry, instead, the boss marshal and senior deputies being out to lunch at an hour Billy Vail would have fits over.

Longarm didn't care. He was only there because it was rude if not dangerous for one lawman to enter another lawman's jurisdiction without letting him know he was there, doing what. Jawing with one of their clerks counted about as polite and the best part was that no clerk had authority to give a full deputy a hard time.

This one, who said Longarm could call him Mr. Sheffield, seemed more anxious to help than hinder, in his own sniffy way. He said he'd already heard from old Henry—there seemed to be a typewriter player's trade union—and added that as far as anyone he worked for cared Longarm was on his own.

He explained, "We have it on good authority our notorious Fresno Kid lies six feet under, down Mexico way, for as long as those fool greasers allow him. I wish someone would explain how come they dig folk up after a year or so in the ground to hang on the wall in some church cellar."

Longarm said, "I asked a friendly Mex sexton one time as I was passing through Sonora. The churches are hard-pressed for space since Mexico declared her own independence from Spain and took away a heap of churchly privileges. So in drier parts of the country where dead folk tend to mummify instead of rot they make room for the more recent dead by moving earlier ones in to pack neater in the vaults, hung up like you say, to keep 'em dry and tolerable smelling."

Mr. Sheffield made a mummy face and said, "That there Spanish Inquisition has worse things to answer for. Suffice it to say we've closed the books on Tomas Ortega Baker, alias the Fresno Kid, and you must have heard about the tragedy of Mussle Slough to the south."

When Longarm said he knew as much about it as he wanted to, the Californian still insisted on snapping, "This office had nothing at all to do with it, but will the infernal opposition papers treat us fair? They will not! To read that infernal Dennis Kearney the U.S. Justice Department takes its orders direct from the railroad barons and backed their hired guns for thirty pieces of silver!"

Longarm smiled in a noncommital way. He was still working on Dennis Kearney and his Workingman's Party. On the one hand the hot-spoken Irish agitator had achieved some worthwhile labor reform measures with his persuasive orations and torchlight processions. At the same time he'd inflamed Californians and others against the poor, already abused Chinese, caught between demands for jobs at fair wages for "Real Americans" and the desire for cheap labor on the part of the so-called robber barons.

Longarm went with, "I know you boys are braced for that congressional investigation and Lord knows what they'd find out about us in Denver if they got to going over the books all the way back to Adam and Eve. As I said when I introduced myself, just now, I don't expect anyone out here to help me hunt down a killer who might have been killed already, and what happened down to Mussel Slough is none of my beeswax, even if I could watch it all happen a second time, which of course nobody can."

He placed the stack of telegrams on the desk near the older man's typewriter, along with a couple of pages torn from his notebook, as he added, "I would like to leave this stuff with you in case your own boss has any ideas about it. I took notes for myself, for later. As my covering letter says, Western Union fed me more questions than answers when it back-checked its own recent messages betwixt Cheyenne and other parts, recent."

Mister Sheffield didn't move to read anything, so Longarm sighed and said, "A couple of hired guns from Nevada were waiting for me near the Utah-Wyoming line. So they had to know which train I was on and I'm inclined to travel impulsive."

He got out a couple of smokes and offered a cheroot to Sheffield as he continued, "By good fortune the Western Union clerk in Evanston, Wyoming, recalled two strangers answering to the descriptions I wired him of Gleason and Bean. They hadn't been sending or receiving wires under them names, of course, but once you know a wire sender's chosen alias it ain't too tough to find out he'd been chatting long distance, in code, with some cuss calling his own fool self Sam Smith, in Cheyenne. Western Union in Cheyenne was able to tell me, in turn, a Sam Smith had been sending and receiving to a T. S. Jones, care of Western Union in Denver. I don't know whether T.S. stands for Tough Shit or not, but it seems obvious the whole bunch had something tough in mind for their Cousin Custis, who has to be me, unless some other poor soul riding the same trains from Denver to Evanston got saddled with the same first name."

He lit both their smokes with the same match and said, "You'll see the various suggestions about making sure I had a good time and so on were meant as a code, tougher to break and harder to spot than any cipher. So I'm still working on some of the nits and of course there's no way to tell who Smith in Cheyenne or Jones in Denver might be before I figure out what in thunder they wanted!"

Sheffield let some smoke out and decided, "That's easy. They wanted you dead. The one in Denver wired you were headed

83

out this way and the one in Cheyenne had time to cut Bean and Gleason in on killing you for cash."

Longarm nodded but said, "That don't tell me shit 'til I figure out some infernal *motives*. I took the liberty of wiring Sam Smith, care of Cheyenne, I'd been unable to show Cousin Custis a proper time before we'd all wound up in Elko. Then I suggested old Sam send anything he had for Cousin Custis to me, Ray Watson, care of Western Union, Elko."

Sheffield started to ask a dumb question. Then he nodded and said, "I take it the late Raymond Bean had been communicating with Cheyenne as Ray Watson?"

Longarm nodded and said, "I've got pals who pack badges and owe me staked out near the Cheyenne Western Union. Don't matter what our Sam Smith sends or doesn't send a dead boy in Elko, as long as he tries. My own home office is naturally keeping an eye peeled for our T. S. Jones in Denver."

Sheffield thought before he shrugged and said, "Mebbe, if someone acts mighty dumb. Wouldn't all those mysterious Western Union customers have some prearranged signal to let 'em know a message was the real McCoy? Say one word, anywhere in the already coded message?"

Longarm said, "*I* would. On the other hand I can think up way more original names than Smith and Jones. The point of all this tedious talk is that I just told Western Union to forward any messages for me here, to your office. I'll wire you all from wherever I wind up and you can forward anything that looks important."

Sheffield asked why Western Union couldn't handle the chore just as well or better, seeing they stayed open twenty-four hours at a time.

Longarm explained, "Privacy. Like I said, I don't know how long or how far I may wander before I'm near another telegraph office and, meanwhile, anyone could say they were me and pick up anything left for me with a telegraph clerk who'd never seen me."

Sheffield nodded soberly and said he'd put what Longarm had so far on the Sacramento marshal's desk, adding, "You must think you're up against a master criminal, bold as brass!"

To which Longarm replied with a grimace of distaste, "A master criminal is a contradiction in terms. I hold that whilst some crooks may be smarter than others, they all have a screw loose somewhere or they'd see the error of their ways before I

84

had to make 'em see the error of their ways."

The older man said he'd worked for the Justice Department too long to have to have the damned wages of sin explained to him. So they shook and parted friendly.

Out in the marble corridor Longarm consulted his pocket watch and headed back to where he'd cached his cool-weather underwear. Whether he'd need it or not in sunny California he didn't make enough to throw almost new longjohns away and they'd take up little room in a saddlebag, once he snuck 'em back to his hotel as, say, a cloth-wrapped pound of his own damned beeswax.

He found the hall door locked, this time. He wasn't too surprised. That blushing she-male law clerk had doubtless bolted it on the far side once she'd come back through the judge's chambers to fetch the tome or tomes she'd been after.

Longarm tried knocking. When that failed to work he glanced about to make certain he was alone and got out his pocket knife. One fold-out blade had been reworked for him by a friendly locksmith in a way that was in clear violation of Colorado State law. So it was a good thing he was a federal lawman who sometimes had doors to open without having the time it might take for a court order.

This being one of them, and those longjohns being genuine cotton jersey, Longarm made short work of the attempt to keep him out with no more than a fool barrel bolt.

It was his turn to be embarrassed when he ducked quickly inside the dinky room to see, as he was already shutting the door behind him, what that brown-haired little thing in that light brown dress was doing by the broad light of day through the frosty glass skylight above that chesterfield.

She had her summer weight skirts up around her bare hips as she lay on the tufted cordovan leather with her bare thighs widespread and nary a stitch below the waist above the garters of her brown cotton stockings, as she covered her naked privates with the hand she'd been doing something else with as he'd first caught her.

He gulped, grinned sheepishly down at her, and said, "Well, seeing we're about even, I'll just be on my way if you'd be kind enough to reach behind that sofa and hand me my longjohns, ma'am."

She swung her high buttons to the marble floor, sitting bolt upright with her skirts no higher than mid-thigh, now, as she blushed beet-red and sobbed, "I wasn't doing what you might have thought I might be, Sir. I was only relieving a most embarrassing itch in what I thought to be total privacy when you, Sir, broke in on me like a thief in the night!"

Longarm chuckled fondly and said, "They do say attack is the best defense and, like I just said, I only wanted my own underwear. I had some private itchings of my own, as you may recall, and so I shucked it and tucked it behind that sofa you're sitting on."

She said something about men not understanding she-male problems as she went on posing primly with both hands in her lap, thighs tight together as she stared down at the cold flooring past her cotton-clad knees. She looked as red as if she was coming down with scarlet fever. So Longarm just moved over to sit sideways beside her and reach over the back of the chesterfield as she slid down to the far end, gasping, "I want to, but I'm afraid. It feels so good, but you have such a big one and your belly and chest are so hairy!"

He got the folded up wad of underwear out to show her as he soothed, "I understand and I don't mean to tell on you, ma'am. I catch boy clerks acting much the same in various parts of the Denver federal building. I tell them I understand, too."

She covered her red face with her hands and drew up her knees, exposing more than she might have thought as she hooked both heels into the tufted leather between them, sobbing, "I wish *I* could understand what comes over me almost every time I find myself alone in a locked room with something soft to lie down on! I heard you knocking on the door, before. I tried to stop. I really wanted to stop. But I thought I'd have time, if I did it faster, and then you somehow got in to catch me in the very act and . . . Were you playing with your own when I walked in on you, before?"

He chuckled kindly and said, "You caught me too soon, before the thought might have occurred to me. I read where they asked this wise Oriental sage whether he considered it a sin or not. He said nine out ten men and women did it and that he suspected the tenth one was a liar. Is it safe to assume you don't have your own private room at home?"

She peeked through her fingers at him to declare, "As a matter of fact I'm forced to share one bedchamber with two other working girls. Why do you ask?"

He said, "Just figured this might be as private a place as you could get at. I chose it to change duds in because, like yourself, I knew hardly anyone ever comes here, present company excepted."

She got it, tittered, and told him he was awfully fresh before she sobered with a repressed shudder to demand, "Do you think I've started to go crazy? They told me back home, in Sunday School, about the sin of Onan landing one in the insane asylum, but what's a poor girl to do when she's new in town and shy besides?"

He put a soothing hand on one of her exposed knees, which flinched but stayed put, getting soothed, as he assured her, "Gals don't get to sin the way Onan did in the Good Book. He was a boy. After that it don't say the Lord drove him silly. It says the Lord smote him stone cold dead."

For some reason that seemed to scare her worse. As she stared goggle-eyed and quiverlip he continued, "When you study on it, Onan had already been acting silly when the Lord took a disliking to him. I've always thought Onan's crime against nature was in taking it out of that poor hot-and-bothered widow woman at the last minute, not in jerking off, afterwards. I don't doubt they both wound up jerking off after the mean way he acted and you don't see nothing in the Good Book about *her* getting smote, do you?"

She giggled but went on blushing as she replied, "I'd never thought of that. The poor girl must have been driven to distraction by such cruel treatment."

To which he could only reply, "I only take it out at the last if a lady asks, and when I do, I have the common courtesy to satisfy her one way or another."

She allowed she'd just hate to have any man start anything with her he didn't mean to finish. But when he ran his hand down from her knee to the soft bare flesh of her inner thigh she grabbed his wrist and pleaded, "Don't you dare! I'd never be able to ask you to stop once you got my poor little clit going again!"

He said that had been the general idea. She shook her head wildly and said, "Not in here. We might get caught. Someone else might want to look something up in these old law books."

He started to argue. Then he sighed and allowed, "Well, at least two total strangers have wandered in here within the past hour or so and there do seem to be an awesome amount of law books in here to study. So what say we go to my hotel instead? I'm staying at the Wayfarer's Rest on Fifth, betwixt the railroad depot and the Sacramento Court House."

She gasped, "Oh, no young lady of quality could go up to a strange man's hotel room and even if she could I'm on duty here until quitting time."

He tried to move his hand, saw she seemed to mean it, and assured her, "I ain't so strange, little darling. I'm U.S. Deputy Custis Long and they'd booked me into Room 301 near the stairwell. I just hate to arrive in a war zone after dark, so I mean to spend the night, just the one night, here at the capital before I have to tumbleweed on."

She hesitated before she soberly replied, "You could call me Susan if I meant a thing to you. For in other words you're saying anything we did this evening at that sordid transient hotel would be no more to you than a passing sordid fancy, right?"

He said he never did anything sordid to a lady unless she asked him to and added, "I've always figured a passing fancy with a discreet stranger had the most fancy tricks with one's own hand beat by many a mile, Miss Susan. But since I find this undecided situation uncomfortable as holding a mouthful of Maryland Rye without swallowing, we'll just say no more and my underwear and me will be on our way."

She seemed surprised when he let go of her leg and rose to his feet with a wistful smile. She was likely one of those country gals who preferred to be thrown for a toss in the hayloft, saying, later, they hadn't really wanted it.

He said, "Custis Long, Room 301, and if you can make it by sundown I'll throw in supper at that fancy French place down the block."

Then he and his underwear were out the hall door and it was up to her whether she finished herself off with her hand, met him later at the Wayfarer's Rest, or both.

Chapter 12

Sundown found Longarm smoking too much and too fast in his hotel lobby. Once the wall clock and his growling stomach convinced him he'd be dining alone he did so at a Chinese joint he recalled between the depot and the steamboat landings along the Sacramento River to the west. Nobody on his pay but a total asshole ate in fancy French joints alone.

The lo mein was a mite greasy but they made it up to him with their swell ginger beef and fried rice. He didn't ask the pretty waitress how Irish women and Chinamen made tea better than anyone else. He'd asked both and never gotten a sensible answer. So he just drank more tea than usual, even knowing it was likely to keep him up when he had such a good crack at a good night's sleep, alone.

On the way back to his hotel he stocked up on fresh cheroots and some magazines to read, knowing they'd cost more at the lobby stand. Then he eased in via a side entrance so's he could case the lobby for love-starved Susans without seeming love-starved, himself.

The only thing in the lobby that didn't look way too ugly to kiss was seated in a blue Dolly Vardin dress with a frilly bodice. Her jet-black, soft, and wavy hair was pinned up under a mighty dumb hat that looked smart on her. The dead bluebird stuck to the bleached straw matched her dress in a manner indicating a keen eye, expensive shopping, or both.

She never waved him over, if she noticed him at all. So he could only sigh and sashay past her and up the stairs. As an experienced traveler he'd naturally hung on to his room key. As an experienced manhunter he'd naturally wedged a match stem under a bottom hinge as he'd left for supper. It was still in place. One had to peer close, as cheap as they were about hall lighting. There was a bitty window down at one end, but the amount of outside light, after sundown, was pitiful.

On the other hand, he reflected, he stood less chance of burning to death in bed with no lamps burning out in the hall where late night drunks could get at 'em. So he went on in to find, as he shut and bolted his door, a big hunter's moon smiling in through his east-facing window as it rose from behind the black paper cutout of the Sierra Nevada.

That inspired him to leave his shade up and not bother with his bed lamp. A man in his line had to undress in the dark or pull down the shades for the same reasons he wedged match stems in his door hinges now and again. Thanks to the bright moonlight as well as all that strong tea, he was able to hang everything neatly as he took his own good time getting down to basics.

Once he'd even shucked his socks and slid his bare ass between the crisp clean sheets, he experimented with closing his eyes. But he knew he was wide awake when, even counting backwards, he failed to be bored by an attempt to tally all the gals he'd ever had.

Like most of us, he tended to lose track past the first two or three dozen. He'd get to say that spunky tavern wench he'd met whilst celebrating his survival at Cold Harbor and suddenly recall that shy little thing in that haystack he'd had earlier. He knew he was never in this world going to tally worth a damn once he got himself and his old organ grinder West at the beginning of the postwar cattle boom. So he was fixing to light the bed lamp and see what the Police Gazette had to say about women when he had a grander notion.

There was no way that gentle tapping at his chamber door could have been a raven. He didn't know any ravens in Sacramento. So he told her he was coming and then, lest she get the impression he was already halfway there, he whipped down the shade to approach the door more modestly with his raging erection.

As he opened it to find her dark outline hesitant he hauled her in and planted a warm kiss on her soft moist lips as he pressed her thin summer dress to his naked flesh and slammed the door shut with a bare heel. She responded in kind, her hat falling off as with his free gun hand he unpinned her hair to let it fall while he moved her to the nearby bed.

As they fell across it together she gasped, "Good heavens, you don't waste time, do you, Deputy Long?"

"Call me Custis," he suggested, as he swept her skirts up out of their way to discover that, this time, she was wearing silk drawers above her frilly garters, worn mid-thigh.

Fortunately they were those scandalous French drawers Queen Victoria was said to disapprove of. So a man could get at the real thing just by moving the narrow silk crotch to one side, which was doubtless why Queen Victoria disapproved. As he started to rock the little man in her boat with two love-slicked fingers she protested, "Oooh, don't tease us. Treat me right. But first let me get out of this damned dress!"

He had enough self-control to let her. But it wasn't easy and he was really hurting by the time they were going at it like old pals with two pillows under her writhing rump and her jay naked, save for her shoes, stockings and corset. She'd agreed, panting with passion, life was simply too short to waste any of it fooling with corset laces and she sure bulged interesting above and below her tight waist-cinching.

After they'd come thrice, the last time dog style, she allowed it was getting uncomfortable. For a lady could breath deep or she could possess a wasp waist, but she couldn't do both, and one did get to gasping with a gent hitting bottom now and again. So he spread her flat on her bare tits and whaleboned belly to unlace her up the back as he chuckled down fondly and said, "I'm looking forward to starting from scratch with another build entire, once I get my second wind, I mean. I was starting to think you'd changed your mind about all this. You missed a swell supper and . . . By the way, have you et, yet? I mean, it's early and we got all night."

She laughed, face down, and thrust her bare rump up at him in fun as she protested, "Good grief, I'm not about to have you lace me back up and as a matter of fact I ate at the depot, earlier, as I was trying to decide how to approach you."

He finished unlacing her and fondled her bare rump as he laughed and said, "I noticed you seemed shy. You might have picked a better place to sup than that greasy spoon at the depot, though. I reckon you were more interested in this appetite than others, right?"

As she rolled over, out of her corset, she spread all four limbs in languid welcome, crooning, "Oh, was I ever, even though I must say you surprised me with the enthusiasm of your welcome, even after all I'd heard about you."

He swung his bare feet to the floor to grope for a cheroot and some matches in the dark as he digested that odd remark, coming from her. Then it fit. He nodded and said, "You showed a mite late because you had to discuss my offer with your roommates and at least one of the same, I fear, had heard some gossip about me and a stenographer or more I might have met the last time I passed through Sacramento?"

She said something like that. So he found the smoke and a light, swung back aboard the bed with her, and thumbnailed a match head afire to light the cheroot between his grinning teeth.

He almost dropped it, lit, on his own bare chest when he noticed he'd never been screwing Miss Susan at all. The raven-haired beauty beaming at him by matchlight had been that stranger gal from down in the lobby, all this time.

She demurely asked, "What's wrong? You look as if you've just seen a ghost, darling."

He shook out the match before it could burn his fingers, saying, "Let's see if I got it at last. Our shy little Susan went home after work all hot and bothered over an adventure I found way less exciting than she must have. She told her somewhat older and easily wiser roommates, no offense, I'd be waiting here with considerable enthusiasm and a dong she'd already sized up?"

"I'm . . . call me Maggie, and she lied," his newfound girlfriend replied, reaching down between them to fondle as she added, "She said you were only hung like a horse. This thing's sort of scary, even soft, and I swear I don't see how I took it all, hard, just now."

He took a luxurious drag on the cheroot and asked if she'd like to try that again or smoke a spell, first.

She went on stroking as she agreed the night was young and so it might be best to pace themselves. He gently placed the cheroot to her lips for a drag as he just as gently said, "We'd best study on whether you'll be having breakfast in bed with me or not, Miss Maggie. I paid single rates and as a rule you can get away with, ah, guests until the wee small hours. But if you'd like to spend the whole night I'd best go down and pay for double occupancy."

She hesitated. He pictured wheels clicking inside her pretty head as she considered what she'd tell her other roommates and, above all, that little Susan. Then she said, "A girl does need a place to stay in the wee small hours, and sneaking out of here without being noticed would be easier, no doubt, during the morning rush to work."

He said, "There you go. Unhand my dick and finish this smoke whilst I run down, tell 'em my old lady just arrived by steamer, and slip 'em an extra six bits for you."

She laughed dryly and asked, "Do you think I'm worth it?"

He took the cheroot from between her lips, kissed her, and put it back as he sat up, saying, "Don't talk bitter. It was your own sweet notion to take me up on my offer to your roommate and nobody said nothing about paying nobody for nothing."

As he spoke he was already reaching for his duds. He had his pants and boots on as Maggie suddenly rolled to her hands and knees to slide over and kiss him, warmly, in the nape of his neck. He turned to kiss her right, hauling her around into his lap so's to crush her bare breasts to his naked chest as she tried to swab his tonsils with her passionate tongue.

As they came up for air at last he said, "Woosh, and hold that thought whilst I show you how sudden I can move up and down two flights of stairs! I'd roll you over on your sweet back and do it now, if I wasn't half-dressed."

She panted, "I'd love that, Custis. Do it again before you leave. Fuck me hard and deep so I'll always remember you that way!"

He laughed and said, "You're on, as soon as I get back from the room clerk with permission to screw you silly by broad day!"

So she reluctantly let him finish dressing. He knew what some might think he'd been up to if he went down to the lobby in just shirt sleeves, or even all unbuttoned. So he made sure the shade was all the way down and struck a match to neaten up by lamplight. As he tied his fool necktie with the aid of the dressing glass the naked beauty reclining atop the bedding regarded him wistfully to declare, "My God you're good-looking, in your own rustic way, and to think you have to keep your shades drawn lest someone do you dirty. It hardly seems fair."

He shrugged and said, "Since we both work for the Justice Department we know how unfair things might get if we didn't. But at least we got each other, tonight, and I mean to treat you just swell as soon as I get back up, both ways."

She laughed as he started to slip on his frock coat and then, with a thoughtful shrug he buckled his gun rig around his hips, first.

She asked if he was planning on meeting someone in the lobby. He said, "It's happened. I know for a fact some cuss named Smith, or Jones, sent a couple of known guns for hire to do me dirty on my way to meet you. I got them, but, like you said, we live in an unfair world and I don't even know why Smith and Jones are sore at me."

As he put on his hat she sat up, demanding, "Wait! I want to hear more about . . . two hired guns, you say?"

He replied, "In a minute. I'd rather have my own duds off whilst conversing with naked ladies and we got to have something to talk about, between times."

She protested she was scared as he reached for the doorknob. He told her to bar the door after him if she liked and not to worry her pretty little head about anyone being after *her*, for Pete's sake.

Then he was out in the hall and headed down the stairs in the dark before she could fuss at him any more. He wasn't looking forward to getting shed of her, come morning and his southbound train to catch. Longarm had always found parting more a pain in the ass than a sweet sorrow, even when the gal he had to part with was trying to be a good sport. A gal rooming most nights with others, who could barely let a man out of her sight when he was coming right back, figured to be a weeper and wailer indeed in the cold gray light of the morning after.

He was suddenly struck by what that Prussian gal had been saying on that train a million years ago. It had seemed, at the time, as if time commenced at the dawn of creation and wound up where they were screwing in a railroad compartment and jawing about it feeling too good to last. Yet here he was groping his way down a dark flight of steps after just screwing another lady entire and . . . It hardly seemed worth the bother, knowing he'd be coming back up to screw her some more in no time at all.

But the tedious ticks of eternity had to be endured if one was to enjoy a few nicer ticks. So he moved on down until, more than half way to the bottom, he detected stealthy movement on the stairs below. Then he crawfished back up to the second story landing and crabbed around to flatten against a wall with a thoughtful hand on the grips of his sixgun.

He didn't draw. Whether anyone was out to do him dirt or not they could hardly be expecting to meet him on the stairs. He hadn't known, himself, he wanted to pay for double occupancy.

There were two of them, he could tell, as they kept going up the stairs. When he heard a key tag jingle and someone stifled a nervous giggle Longarm relaxed and muttered, "Great minds run in the same channels," before he went on down to the lobby.

As he crossed it from the stairwell he failed to see anyone behind the room clerk's desk. Another gal in a light brown dress was seated in the same lobby chair Maggie had sat earlier, in blue. As their eyes met, her's wide as saucers, Longarm blinked and said, "Evening, Miss Susan. No offense but this sure seems awkward."

She gulped and said, "How do you think *I* feel? I wasn't going to come at all before my roommates as much as shoved me out the door and said they'd never forgive me, either. I know what I'd be passing up. I've seen you with your pants off. But I've still been trying and trying to get up my nerve and . . ."

"Your friend, Maggie, got here ahead of you," he cut in, unable to invent a better way to put it as he started about in vain for some sign of that room clerk.

Susan rose to her feet with a puzzled frown, saying, "Maggie? Maggie who? Have you been fooling with another girl, Custis Long?"

She followed as he strode toward the desk, muttering, "Someone has surely been fooling someone around here. You don't have a roommate called Maggie, black wavy hair, a mite older-looking than you, with, ah, broader hips?"

She'd just insisted she had no idea who he was talking about when he spotted the room clerk's shiny black shoes near his overturned stool, then, craning over the desk, he could see how they'd put him on the floor. The poor boy's throat had been cut from ear to ear.

Whirling about, Longarm picked the girl up bodily and carried her to a far dark corner, where he planted her on her rump behind a potted rubber plant and snapped, "Stay here and bang the floor with your pretty face if it gets any noisier. I haven't gone loco en la cabeza. Someone just murdered the room clerk. I'll be back to protect you better as soon as I see who else might need protecting!"

Someone obviously did. He heard a muffled fusilade of gunfire as he hit the bottom steps. The shots had been fired somewhere above. He had his own gun out as he took the stairs two at a time. Doors had popped open on the second floor and the hallway was full of curious shouts, but no gunsmoke, so he kept going.

On his own third floor the air was reeking of burnt powder and he could barely make out the burly figure lighting a hall sconce. But he could tell the jasper was holding a Colt Detective Special in his gun hand, so he threw down on the son of a bitch, snapping, "Drop that gun and grab some plaster, you son of a bitch!"

The lamp lighter did as he was told, protesting, "I ain't no son of a bitch. I'm the house detective, trying to shed some light on a Gawd awesome mystery, here!"

Longarm warned him to leave his damned gun where it was, anyway, as he waded through the drifting gunsmoke to note, with a start, the two men's riding boots, spurred, jutting out into the hall over the doorjamb of room 301.

As he joined the hefty house dick there he could see a man dressed cow lay face down inside with his face in the lap of the stark naked lady who'd told Longarm to call her Maggie. She'd been shot at least five times at point blank range, judging from the little blue holes and powder burns in and about her still-tempting tits.

The house dick opined, quietly, "If it made a lick of sense I'd say they were caught by a person or persons unknown as he was eating her pussy in an open doorway, full dressed."

Longarm said, "It doesn't make a lick of sense. There's no powder burns on the back of his light-blue denim jacket. So he died some other way, fast enough to land on his knees as someone else pumped lead into her. It ain't clear whether he dropped her on her back and emptied the rest of his wheel into her or whether that other corpse kept her up, clinging to her in his own death throes. Neither way could he have passed me on the stairs a second time. Is there another way down and out, Pard?"

The house dick said, "Sure, we got fire escapes and service stairs up the back. Can I pick up my own gun, now?"

Longarm agreed that might be best and suggested they fetch the Sacramento P.D. as well, adding, "They got your room clerk, down to the lobby, too. Must have wanted his passkey. Killed him silent with a knife. Likely that Bowie I see, now, almost under the bed. Say the plan was for this dead one to knock, knife quiet, and slip away as silent as they did downstairs."

The house dick nodded grudgingly as he tried, "Say his backup was covering him with a drawn gun, in case something went wrong, and something went wrong. So, all right, how did that naked dead lady nail him and, come to study on it, who in blue blazes *is* she? Poor old Dave never said we had any possible hookers checked in up here, tonight."

Longarm dropped to one knee to roll the dead man off the dead woman as he quietly said, "I doubt she was a hooker. I'm still working on who she really was." Then he whistled as he saw how the dead man had died.

The house dick leaned over for a closer look, saying, "He ain't a check-in, neither, I'll bet. Only poor old Dave could say for sure. What's that on his upper lip. Looks as if his nose is running pearls."

Longarm said, "Hat pin. Better leave it in place for the coroner. I'm sure they'll find it a mite longer than most ladies use, and that she drove it up his nostril and into his brain with considerable skill."

As the house dick whistled in wonder Longarm explained, "There's a small but direct route to the brain without bone in the way if you know what you're doing. A Texas gal I know trained in that Japanese style of brawling says you can drive a poor soul's nose septum into his brain like a knife if you kick him or hand chop him just wrong. I'd say this lady favored her sneakier approach because, had she lasted long enough to pull that pin back out, she could have told anyone who asked that the cuss had died natural, mayhaps from too much excitement about her pussy, as you first suggested."

The house dick said, "It's likely just as well she never got away with it entire, seeing we got enough of a mystery just deciding who she was and how she wound up dead and bareass on the premises. She must have been expecting the one she killed. There's no way in Hell no gal could run a hatpin up a gent's nose on a sudden impulse. So she must have had her weapon in hand, poised to strike, as she opened the door jay naked and killed him before he could kill her and . . . You know what, this ain't going to be a simple case at all."

Longarm said, "It's a real pisser, all right. You stay here and keep anyone from moving anything whilst I go down and fetch the law for you, hear?"

The house dick said, "Much obliged, stranger. What room might you be staying in, should the copper badges want a statement from you?"

97

Longarm was already halfway gone as he called back, "I ain't in any. I was just fixing to check in, downstairs, when I spied your dead room clerk, heard those shots, and tore up here to add to the confusion."

Then he was on the stairs, calling, "Sorry about that," as he ran down them.

He found the police already there in the lobby, attracted by the sounds of gunplay. There were two of them, both beat coppers. Before either could notice the body behind the counter or the gal he'd hidden in that dark corner, Longarm yelled, "Murder most foul. Third floor. House dick already in charge at the scene."

To which one of them replied they'd just see about that as they both ran up the stairs.

Longarm tossed his room key in the pigeonhole below the one it belonged in, close enough, and tore the top sheet out of the hotel register to put away, for now, as he dashed over to Susan, scooped her up, and frog-marched her out that side entrance as he warned her, "We can't afford a public scandal no matter what we do about saving your sanity. So we'd best find another hotel and make sure we can prove we checked in together if ever we have to."

She protested that was a sin against state and city if not natural law. He soothed her as he moved them both toward the riverfront, "I don't expect we'll be called upon to prove toad squat. But it pays to drag red herrings across one's trail when you can. I can tell you, now, there was a double killing back yonder, a man and a woman."

She gasped, "Oh, dear Lord! Who were they?"

To which he could honestly reply, "Can't say. I didn't know either of 'em. We know we're innocent because we were flirting in the lobby when we both heard the gunshots she died from, up on the third floor."

She said, "Oh, the poor thing! How did her male companion die?"

He said, "Way sneakier. She doubtless thought he was her male companion when she killed him with a hat pin in the dark. Then a pal he'd brought along gunned her and now you know as much as I do. As luck would have it I left my saddle and possibles in the tack room of the livery serving the general public as well as that hotel. So I left nothing upstairs to worry about and I'll thank you to forget I once said I was staying at the Wayfarer's Rest."

98

He walked her further along the dark walk and checked the glass of a store closed for the night to make sure they weren't being tailed as he added, "Matter of fact, as I now recall, I spent the night at the Steamer Palace with this pal I was trying to cure of Onanism."

She flustered, "You're awfully fresh, and isn't this a sort of seedy part of town your taking me?"

He soothed, "You'd hardly want to be seen cheeking into a hotel with a man along Capitol Avenue and I promise clean sheets and no bugs where I'm taking you. I often check in there when I'm fixing to catch the San Francisco steamer. That other one was handier to the depot, as some sneaky folk must have figured and this time, no offense, I mean to sign us in as Romeo and Juliet Montague and let 'em work at figuring out where I'm at."

She giggled and asked where he'd come up with such wild names.

He said, "Shakespeare. I may be self-taught but I ain't ignorant. That would have been their married names, had they lived, the poor kids."

But by the time he was signing them in a man and wife, without baggage, while Susan seemed about to pee where she stood by the stairs, he'd decided to go with the names of a less famous pair he knew back home in West-By-God-Virginia. He knew he might not be the only one abroad that night with a fair education and old Maggie, whoever the hell she'd been, had spoken high toned enough to have sat through a classical play or more.

Once he had Susan upstairs she'd started to cry instead of pee. He left the lamps unlit and opened the shades to let her admire the lights on the far shore winking off the seaward flowing Sacramento. She still said she felt low down and dirty, even though, so far, he'd never even kissed her.

So he hung up his hat, coat, and gun rig to set her on the bed and kiss her. She kissed back with a skill suggesting some experience. But as he reclined them both across the counterpane and cupped one of her smaller, firmer breasts in his free hand, she sobbed, "Oh, no, I just can't! I'm sorry! I know I'm driving you mad with desire and I really want to respond, but this feels so wicked and depraved I just . . . Look, I'll give you the money you wasted paying my way in, downstairs, all right?"

He sighed and said, "I'm the last of the big time spenders. I can afford the extra six bits. Just take it easy and let things simmer

99

down, outside, and I'll be proud to take you home."

She asked in a lost little voice, "You'd still be willing to do that for me, after the way I've been acting?"

He said, "I mean to smoke at least one cheroot, first. You're right about this not being the most fashionable part of town and an unescorted she-male anywhere after dark can get whistled at. As to the way you've been acting, well, you said you'd been driving yourself loco for a spell."

She commenced to cry again, rolling on her tits and tummy to do so good and hard as he lit a smoke, propped on one elbow beside her. When he saw she didn't seem to be stopping of her own accord he patted her upthrust fanny fondly and soothed, "There, there, I never meant you were loco because you didn't want to sleep with me. I know all sorts of fine ladies who've never evinced the slightest desire to sleep with me and I'm sure most of them are sane."

That made her laugh, albeit bitterly, and tell him, "I've a good mind to give myself to you and show you just who's sane around here!"

He took a lazy drag on his smoke and allowed it was her choice entire.

She said, "I'll bet. I'm not a foolish virgin, you know, and you men are all alike when it comes to giving a poor girl any choice in the matter! You know durned well that even as we speak you're just dying to rip off all my clothes and ravage my poor little body with that big mean thing of yours!"

He yawned and confessed that at the moment her notion seemed an awesome amount of work for the likely pleasures involved. It might have unsettled her to hear he wasn't sure he could get it up, this soon, after hauling it out of the more mysterious Maggie.

Picturing himself with the fake pearl of a hat pin parting his mustache didn't inspire much lust, either. So he was thinking more about that mighty odd brunette more than he might have been a plain old case of second thoughts with brown hair as she rolled to face him in the dim light, insisting, "You can't fool me. I'll just bet you're even hotter than me, right now."

When he suggested neither one of them seemed to be acting all that hot, considering the time and place, she shyly reached out to feel the front of his tweed pants. It felt mildly interesting to him, as well, as she kneaded his limp dick like dough to marvel, "Good

100

Lord, what's wrong with you? You're not one of those queer boys who'd rather do it to a boy, are you?"

He grimaced, blew smoke out both nostrils, and replied, "Not so far. Meeting too many gals like you could convert a man to most any sins less complicated, though."

That reminded him of an old limerick that might apply. So he said,

There was this old greaser named Bruno,
   Who said about screwing I do know,
      A woman is fine, while a boy is divine,
         But my burro is numero uno!

She said that sounded disgusting and asked if it was true some men, and women, went all the way with critters. She sure was curious about the subject for such a reluctant sinner.

He said, "As a matter of fact this hotel detective I know swears women go in for more variety in their love lives than men, not because they're more wicked, but for pragmatic reasons."

She wanted to hear more. He explained, "To begin with, as any poor male can tell you, nothing she-male acts as anxious to screw as most anything male. So all a curious lady animal lover has to do is invite the animal of her choice to mount her and, being male, it likely will."

"You men are all alike." She sniffed.

He chuckled fondly and said, "And ain't your kind glad? A poor boy curious about the same subject could get killed, messing with a dog big enough to take him on, bitches being so bitchy at times."

She protested, "That's not fair. It's a man's world and even when a girl wants to cut loose and enjoy herself you mean old men don't seem to know how to treat us. Shall I tell you how I got started down the primrose path, and why I wound up so confounded about my needs and desires?"

He said he sure wished she wouldn't, but the the next thing he knew she was droning on and on about an older she-male cousin back in Ohio teaching her to pleasure herself with her fingers, candlesticks and such. He'd already surmised she liked to play with herself a lot.

She'd liked it so much, in fact, she'd given her all to another cousin, this one a he-male, at the age of thirteen, with mighty sad results, he being eleven and not knowing exactly what to do.

When Longarm suggested she might have explored further with a full-sized gent she said, "Oh, I have, more than once, and a couple of times I felt sure I was going to climax before they, you know, pulled out like that infernal Onan and just fell asleep on me."

He nodded soberly and said, "I'm commencing to see the light and you're right. Our best bet is for me to take you home and let you just strum your own banjo. For, speaking as a lawman who reads medical books on occasion, I'd say you've created your own monster in the form of a clit too mindful of stimulation and a vagina, that's the delicate word for your cunt, as expects too much of any man, after all the times it's come with daydreams."

She gasped, "Don't talk so dirty. You're making me feel all blushy wet! I know what you're saying. I once went to a doctor of female complaints, telling him I was a wedded woman who couldn't get any satisfaction. He asked right off if I'd been fooling with my you-know and I was too embarrassed to tell him the truth. He did say if I had been I should stop, and let my husband try again after I'd had time to calm down my irritated parts. That's what he called the parts I like to rub, my irritated parts, and I've tried and tried to leave them alone, Custis, but . . ."

"Don't try," he cut in, adding, "I've tried to cut out lots of bad habits. I've even managed, when they were really bad. I've found smoking too much, drinking in moderation and fornicating when and where it caused no harm more pleasant than evil, when you study logical on how long we have, no matter how logical we act."

She said she wished she could get down and dirty with him, if only.

He said, "I wasn't finished. You can't. Even if I talked you into it I'm only human. I could never screw you half as good as you can dream of screwing all alone and, what the hell, at least a gal don't have to look her best for her own friendly hand, right?"

She laughed like hell and said she'd never be able to tell anyone about half the love partners she'd made up, or half the things a girl could use, aside from her hand, to pleasure herself with.

He turned away long enough to snub out the cheroot, saying, "They say confession is good for the soul. Your soul, maybe. It's starting to give me a hard on. So I'd best get you home before we wind up jerking off side by side like a couple of silly school kids in a hayloft."

She said, "Ooh, could we? My cousin and me used to do that, back home, exciting one another with dirty talk, and as I told you before, I can't play with myself in front of my roommates, lest they take me for one of those Lester girls."

He started to demand an explanation he didn't need before he saw roommates could suggest romance with a well-endowed stranger before they'd approve mass masturbation. He said, "I think lesbian was the word you were groping for. I'm not sure jerking off together counts. But if you'd rather do so, here, before I take you home, go right ahead. It ain't as if I'd find your secret vice a new discovery."

She stammered "Good Heavens, in front of someone else? In front of a *man*?"

He asked, "Why not? You liked to jerk off in front of the older gal who taught you, right?"

She said, "I don't know. I don't think I could. Just thinking about it has me all, you know, feeling wet and silly."

He said he figured she was getting a mite hot and rolled closer to take her in his arms again as he said, "Just relax and I'll get you started."

She protested, "Wait, are you sure you're not trying to talk me into letting you rape me?"

He chuckled, assured her it couldn't be rape if anyone *let* anyone do anything and then he had his seductive hand in place, cupping her mons through her thin brown skirt, and she was already moving in response as he deftly drew the cloth up inches at a time with his massaging fingertips. She hadn't come down to that first hotel with underdrawers on, whatever in tarnation she'd had in mind, so he soon had her quivering naked crotch at the mercy of his bare hand, and he massaged it without mercy but with considerable skill until she pleaded, "Oh, Lord, I think I want to after all! Take your big old thing out and shove it up inside me, Custis! I know just what it has to feel like and I want it, want it, want it all!"

He soothed, "No you don't. I'm out to make you come, not let you down, Little Darlin'. You just go on pretending I got Don Juan's pecker, green-eyed serpents and purple corn cobs in you, all at once, as I carry you across the Jordan, East of Eden, or wherever."

Then he kissed her and wedged his fingers up inside her as he rubbed the wet web of his thumb back and forth across her over-developed clit, with explosive results indeed.

He was glad he'd been kissing her, open mouthed, when she'd screamed like that and cracked the knuckles of his friendlier hand. Knowing more about she-male needs, if not anatomy, than some Victorian doctors, he brought her down easy with continued but ever more gentle massaging until she told him, adoringly, "That was lovely. Can we do it some more?"

He said he failed to see why not and in her sated but still romantic state he was able to get them both undressed as he kissed her, played with her, and nibbled her collar bones and nipples. She agreed with a giggle it felt even nicer to lie nude against his naked body as he began to work her up again with his hand. As he'd sort of hoped she might, she soon suggested he might as well put the real thing to her. So he did. But even though she was a sport about pillows under her firm young buttocks and found it "curious" when he got her heels hooked over his own collar bones, she protested she preferred to come the other way and didn't, in fact, think she could come at all, this way.

He kissed her anyhow and said, "Don't worry about it, then. I made you come like a good sport and it didn't kill me when you got to come by yourself. So what say you let me just enjoy you, this way, and once I've come I'll play with you some more."

She said that sounded fair but added, "I thought true lovers were supposed to come together, dear."

He asked, "Where in the U.S. Constitution does it say that? The idea of . . . let's call it true friendship, is to make sure a friend has a good time. When you invite friend to dinner does it matter if you both chew the same grub and sip the wine at the same time, as long as have your fill? That romantic bull about it not feeling good unless everyone in the room comes at the same time has ruined more swell orgies, I'll bet."

She laughed, moving sweetly below the waist, and worked her legs higher as she said she understood what he meant, thought it made sense, and said, "You just go ahead and enjoy me this way all you like and I won't even worry about the way you feel inside of me for now."

So he did and, getting into the spirit of friendly fornication, Susan gave herself to him unselfishly, for perhaps the first time in her life until she suddenly found herself marveling, "It does

104

feel ever so much nicer, and even exciting, when I just relax and take it this way. You do have such a lovely tool and, oooh, Custis, what are you doing to me? It feels so grand and you've got it so deep and . . . Dear Lord, I think I'm coming again, with a man's cock in me!"

Chapter 13

So after spending such a sordid night with Longarm, Susan wanted to follow him to the ends of the earth or at least as far as Fresno.

He got her to let him go on alone by promising to treat her as selfishly on his way back and convinced her of his bad intentions by giving her some names to research for him in the federal office files, any time she wasn't strumming her old banjo, of course.

Some of the names came from that sheet he'd torn out of the hotel register, along with his own. It seemed a long shot, but Susan seemed so anxious to please and there was no saying who might or might not have business with the government before or after checking into a transient hotel near the depot.

Once he'd shed little Susan near the federal building he picked up a morning edition of the *Sacramento Daily Recorder* and scanned the same as he inhaled an extra cup of black coffee a discreet distance from the Wayfarer's Rest.

He saw to his considerable relief there was nothing about himself in it. That house dick had taken all the credit he could for almost catching the murderer in the act. The murdered folk he'd found in an open doorway still seemed almost as mysterious. The man found dead with his face in a dead woman's lap had been packing a library card and voter's registration made out to one Walter Brown of Angels Camp. Walter might have been his real first name. The sheriff's department of Calaveras County had wired back they didn't have a damned library in Angels Camp, albeit there'd been talk of starting one at the rate the town was growing, thanks to that fool fable about frogs Mister Mark Twain had made up.

The woman who'd said to call her Maggie had packed no I.D. at all amid her belongings found in the room she'd died in. Longarm didn't find that as mysterious as the *Daily Recorder* seemed to. He knew few municipal codes required a woman to show proof of identity or support, while most any night court judge would hold one over for the grand jury if she was caught packing forged official paper.

Because many a petty crook or wayward wife knew less about the law than Longarm, the fact that Maggie had, hinted at a criminal education. He'd tried over and over to work out some way she'd brain-stabbed that other jasper as she let him in in the dark because she wanted to make love some more. But no matter how he sliced it he sure felt glad he'd been fair to that hotel. Dozing off with little Susan, a known quality, had been tough as hell as he'd tried not to think about dozing off in Maggie's arms and never waking up again.

Seeing he seemed to be in the clear, and knowing he had nothing yet that might help the Sacramento P.D., Longarm left the newspaper on the counter for someone else to read and mosied on.

He was able to enter the livery out back without going near the main entrance of the Wayfarer's Rest. They still had his saddle and possibles draped over a saddle tree in their tack room. So once he'd settled up and tipped fair he toted everything back to the depot and checked it through for Fresno.

After that things got tedious for a spell. His infernal train didn't pull out for an hour and a half. Once it had, Fresno lay a six hour ride to the south across scenery that got less interesting with every mile.

The great central valley of California was better for growing food and fiber than it was for looking at. It was fifty miles or more across with the tracks running almost smack down the middle. So whilst the Sierras to the east and coast ranges to the west were possible to see from the train as hazy purple cutouts on your average sultry day, neither were much fun to look at, once you'd got used to them.

Closer in, the land lay flatter than many a ballroom floor, with monotonously laid out irrigation canals moving sluggish brown water through some stretches and big shallow puddles or acres of tule reeds breeding skeeters where no settlers had been ditching, yet.

From time to time you'd pass a shelter belt of trees, mostly popple or sycamore with here and there some of those feathery green pepper trees from South America. Low rambling houses, whitewashed frame or brick, were wider spread than even the trees. Most of the brownish gray dirt, fine as whole wheat flour, was covered with a patchwork of fenced in row crops and open range. California beef was grazed on more cheat grass and wild mustard than most.

Neither weed was native to the range. Old time Indians cussed the Spanish-speaking Californios for introducing the chest-high yellow flowering mustard, whilst the Californios said the infernal gringos had spoiled their mustard meadows by bringing cheat grass in with 'em. The only break the cows got was the longer growing season. They got to graze more hours of the year on weeds that otherwise offered less nourishment than real grass.

You saw more cows grazing as best they could out between the flag and water stops. Produce farming was more profitsome a modest wagon ride from a town or shipping point. From time to time the way straighter railroad tracks ran within sight of a river bend. The San Joaquin ran about as wide as the Sacramento to the north but not a third as deep, even this far downstream. That was how come big side-wheel steamers ran from Frisco up to the capital and beyond while only a few shallow draft stern-wheelers poked up the San Joaquin after freight, at highwater. The railroad he was riding had about monopolized all such business of late. Whether they'd keep their rates low enough to undercut the stern-wheelers was about as predictable as the death of little Eva in your average production of Uncle Tom's Cabin. Meanwhile they gave you a pretty good ride for your money.

As the rails carried you south the river got pushed clean out of mind to the west and, away from the ever wider-apart irrigation works, the range got more arid, with ominous wide patches of dusty eat-out, where the overgrazed sod gave out entire to let the sun and wind at the fine alluvial soil.

That was the trouble with replacing the native elk grass with faster growing shit. The wild mustard roots probed deep enough to hold the dirt together where it grew. But it grew in scattered clumps like the even more useless tumbleweed. The cheat grass that should have formed a half-ass sod betwixt the clumps of mustard was called cheat grass because whatever it was it couldn't be real grass. It thrived on bare dirt after any rain at all for as long as it took it to sprout in the sometimes moisture, shoot up stems that were mostly air, and go to seed so's it could just die and turn to an almost inedible fire hazard. Dead or alive it didn't hold the soil worth a damn with its weak and shallow roots.

The mountains to the east caught rain clouds that just skipped across the coast ranges and big valley, he knew. So there was plenty of runoff, year round, with the water table high under that sunbaked crust outside. Wherever they passed irrigation networks the broad flat fields were emerald green, this late in the fall, with cultivated beans, cabbages, sweet corn, and crops Longarm wasn't too certain of. Some wide patches looked to be covered with grape vines, only pruned short and stubby to grow more like shrubbery than vines. Whatever they were, they'd shed their leaves for the short coming winter and been harvested of all their grapes, currants or whatever.

The point some fortunate settlers made with those few and far between irrigation works was that irrigation was the way to go in this southern half of the big central valley. Having grown up on a hardscrabble hill farm in West-By-God-Virginia, Longarm shared the enthusiasm of most for the life of a cowman over that of a plow jockey. But he was still smart enough to tell damn-near perfect cropland from piss-poor grazing. So that tragedy to the south at Mussel Slough made more sense with every mile he traveled south.

He knew that big Miller Lux outfit grazed a hell of a herd on the even less-developed range south of Fresno. But if they had a lick of sense they'd be ditching some of their holdings and drilling in such cash crops as they could ship with their beef at as much or more of a profit. Being more a lawman than a cowman, these days, Longarm had trained himself to think more about profit and loss than fun, since money really did vie with romance as the source of prison time.

Thinking purely as a settler with mortgages and other bills to pay, he knew that stuck with a quarter section of the San Joaquin Valley to sink or swim on he'd fence it and water it and drill over half of it to salad greens and such shit while he waited for his fruit trees and vines to grow. For, bleak as it might look without irrigation, that big valley was as close as any part of North America got to those otherwise silly railroad posters, advertising a golden West of fruits and nuts, with bananas and coconuts as far north as Oregon, if you just had faith and a few mild winters.

Longarm had come West after the war before the Wedding Of The Rails had resulted in oceans of railroad grant lands to peddle and the railroads had commenced printing travel posters in full color. So he'd never expected to pick bananas whilst hunting buffalo with nubile Indian maids in grass skirts. But he knew how many greenhorns had flocked West to invest their life savings in some mighty odd opportunities. The resulting desperation accounted for a lot of the chores he and his guns were called upon to cope with.

Sensible folk spending less time in prison than the other kind, he knew he'd have to watch out for some less inclined to view the business opportunities along the San Joaquin with detachment. It seemed everywhere they sent him he met stubborn types who insisted on plowing up natural cattle country, building whole towns on natural flood plains, mining for gold in abandoned clay quarries or, as some half starved cows out the window had just remarked, tried to raise beef on semi-arid bottomland.

Folk were like that. The Indians who'd owned California first had gone on eating acorns long after the Californios had brought corn, beans and even pigs and chickens up from Old Mexico.

Now the old Californios and earlier Anglo cattle barons got sore at anyone hinting an acre of irrigated land under fruit and nuts might yield a greater profit than the same space devoted to sunbaked weeds and scrub stock. Back before they'd had the railroads, the Californio cattle barons had only shipped hides and tallow around the horn by clipper and fed the rest to their unpaid peons and those famously big California buzzard birds.

From the little he really knew about the ugly business down around Mussel Slough, Longarm suspected any U.S. deputy marshals involved had, like himself, started out sort of cow and hence held the cow trade's good natured contempt for any man who'd willingly perform stoop labor in the fields, on foot. Those sodbusting settler's putting up a real fight must have startled the shit out of 'em, accounting for the death toll. Indians were inclined to get in that sort of trouble, standing up to green army officers with orders to just move the pests somewhere less valuable.

Longarm was glad Mussel Slough wasn't his mess to clean up. He had enough on his plate, what with half the folk he talked to

110

assuring him the Fresno Kid lay dead and buried in Old Mexico while at least some of the folk he ran into seemed anxious to kill him.

He doubted anyone would be trying that hard to keep him from catching young Tomas Ortega Baker if the wild Anglo-Mex was nowhere ahead to be caught. Billy Vail hadn't sent him after anyone else out this way.

He went over all the names he had, so far, including those he'd ripped out of that hotel register along with his own. He failed to recognize any of the other signatures or even find one fishy, save for a cuss named Smith who, since he'd checked in with a Mrs. Smith, had likely had something other than assassination in mind.

It hardly seemed likely anyone out to commit anything more serious that screwing on the premises would have checked in at the desk in the first place. Neither of the killers who had been surprised by the murderous Maggie, and vice versa, had checked in proper. They'd slit the desk clerk's throat and either tried to get into 301 with his passkey or simply tried knocking with results the *Daily Recorder* had printed on their front page.

They'd been after him, not Maggie, he knew. For that had been his name, not hers, on the top page of the hotel register. So that meant Maggie had read it there first and . . . Right, asked if her old friend Deputy Long was in, been told he was out, and just waited in the lobby like a spider waiting for a fly.

He thought about the confusion when he'd let her in, upstairs, thinking she was Susan. The murderous Maggie had doubtless been amused by the way her intended prey had greeted her with open arms. He felt pretty sure she'd enjoyed that part as much as she'd let on, since she'd had many a chance to hat-pin him to death as she'd been screwing him silly. He had to credit her with coolness under fire once he'd offered her an even better plan of escape by offering to let her leave more dignified in the morning rush. Had things gone her way the maid might not have found him before checkout time, already going stiff and the gal who'd hat-pinned him clean out of town.

He could see she couldn't have been working for the same mastermind as the cruder killers who'd come calling later that same night. So that added up to at least two enemies, or sets of enemies, out to do him the same sort of dirt.

111

He was damned if he could figure a sensible motive for even one enemy that serious. The obvious notion someone was out to prevent his capture of the Fresno Kid fell apart as soon as one studied on it. A son of a bitch wiring ahead from Cheyenne to gun a lawman in Elko could have just as easily wired Tomas Ortego Baker instructions to light out from the San Joaquin Valley for a spell. Peewee's tip had only suggested the Fresno Kid had headed back to his old stomping grounds near Fresno, not that there was no place better to hide.

"I'd never single him out of the crowd if he'd just taken this same line north to Sacramento, for instance," Longarm told himself as, outside, he could tell they were coming to more serious civilization at last. Considering a federal want at large back there in Sacramento all this time opened up a whole new can of worms, which he decided to set aside, for now, at once, muttering, "Too dumb for a killer smart enough to stage his own death in Nogales and convince the law he might have gone home while, all the while, he's been somewheres else."

Longarm laughed and shook his head as if to clear it as he got all those wheels within wheels unmeshed. He'd gotten in trouble in the past by thinking too deeply about crooks dumb enough to be crooks. He called it "Playing chess when the name of the game might be checkers." For, like most lawmen, he'd found real crimes tended to be a lot more simple than one might think crimes got from reading the likes of Mr. Edgar Allan Poe.

Meanwhile, since even toothaches and train rides have to end sooner or later, he was able to solve the mystery of all that new scenery outside with the aid of his pocket watch.

The county seat and farming community of Fresno had commenced as a jerkwater for the railroad, back in '56. Since then it had grown some as the natural shipping point for cotton, grain, fruit and nuts, especially sun-dried raisins, grown closer in, along with livestock and minerals from gold to graphite gathered further out.

The Fresno Kid had gained his nickname and notoriety robbing banks and such in and about the county seat. His friends and enemies agreed he hadn't been registered to vote there. But aside from Fresno being the logical place to hire the riding stock he'd need to search more thorough for the little shit, Longarm knew protocol required he pay the usual courtesy calls on the local lawmen, especially with at least some of them on the prod over all the mean things the newspapers were saying about 'em being hired killers on the payroll of the ever-popular railroad baron, C. S Huntington, aka "the Octopus" by his friends and foes alike.

Thanks to all the irrigation ditches and trees they kept planting around Fresno, it took a spell longer than he'd expected to roll to a stop near the center of things. Hence he was standing on the steps and dropped off to stride forward to claim his baggage before the train came to a complete stop.

As he strode up the platform toward the baggage smashers, a lean and hungry-looking stranger wearing an old Army shirt and a Schofield .45 fell in beside him to remark, "I'd be Greg Mandalian, Sheriff's Department, and if you'd be a gambling man or hired gun I'd be obliged if you just got back on and kept going."

Longarm told the local law who he was and tried to tell Mandalian what he was doing there. The saturnine sheriff's deputy smiled thinly and said, "Sure you are. The Ortegas paid handsome to have the body shipped all the way from Nogales and entombed in their private tomb just so's the likes of you could arrest their black sheep on this side of the border. Are you out to nail one of your own on a malfeasance charge or help 'em cover up? Nobody federal tells us shit but it has to be one or the other with President Hayes on the personal warpath."

By this time they'd made it to the baggage car. So Longarm handed his claim check and a dime to one of the railroaders shifting stuff from the gaping car door to a waist-high baggage wagon before he turned back to Mandalian to insist, "I know President Hayes got elected on a reform platform and I know he's tidied up a heap after Grant because I've been sent to arrest more than one holdover from the bad old days. But I give you my word I wasn't sent to investigate that already stale story of Mussel Slough. You likely know more about it than I do, since it all took place just one county down."

As they tossed Longarm's McClellan and lashed on possibles to the platform instead of the handier waist-high wagon, the ungrateful shits, Mandalian said, "You must not know anything if you think I know more than you. I've talked to old boys who say they were there and you get a different story every time. The U.S. Marshal over the deputies who admit they were there swears he and old C. S Huntington ain't never smoked corn silk together but, naturally the Octopus keeps telling anyone who'll listen that

113

the evictions were a matter of total indifference to him and his railroad."

Longarm bent to pick up his load and balance it on one hip with his left hand as he indifferently remarked, "Both gents could be telling the truth, as I read the published accounts of the shoot-out."

He started into town as Mandalian made a noise halfway between a "Pshaw!" and an outright, "Bullshit!"

Longarm insisted, "Read it yourself and consider what even the shot-up squatters charge. They say two bully boys claiming to be the owners of the Brewer Claim with all improvements showed up with a bill of sale backed by a court order backed by the U.S. Marshal. I can tell you from sad experience us deputies have no say in the wording of arrest warrants, eviction notices and such."

Mandalian shrugged and said, "I've had to put widows and orphans out on the road for Fresno County. The railroad still must have paid a pretty penny to the higher ups who ordered those deputies to back those hired guns posing as outraged landlords."

Longarm paused to get out a smoke as well as his bearings. He lined up on a church spire on the far side of the Fresno Federal Courthouse near the post office and commenced to trudge that way through the blazing afternoon sunlight while the curious local lawman kept pace, asking, "How come old Huntington gets off, in your book, Uncle Sam? Ain't it a fact them disputed deeds to already settled spreads down around Mussel Slough list the Southern Pacific Railroad as the original owner?"

Longarm let some smoke out to reply, "I suspicion the original federal grant was made out to the Western Pacific and then transferred to Huntington's Southern Pacific holdings, real estate as well as rail, during the protracted court actions as finally proved title."

Mandalian insisted, "Don't cloud the issue with pestiferous lawyer talk. One way or another, by hook or by crook, the railroad got title to all that land folk had already settled on, right?"

Longarm shrugged his free shoulder and allowed, "Might have seemed that way to the squatters. They doubtless squatted where they did on account of the land being so handy to the railroad tracks. That don't mean they had a legal leg to stand on. I don't have the right to plant my spuds in your front lawn just because I admire the site."

114

Mandalian asked, "What about squatters rights? Don't the law say anyone who sets on property for seven years gets to keep it?"

Longarm shook his head and replied, "Nope. If it did, nobody with a lick of sense would ever spend good money on property deeds. The law you just cited says anyone who's held the same property as his or her own, undisputed by anyone else, can't be evicted without a proper hearing in a court of law, followed by a proper serving of a lawful writ of eviction, giving time to vacate said property nice with all one's portable chattels. So without having been there, that's what I'd say those other deputies were about at Mussel Slough when the discussion got heated. No sinister railroad interests had to send in hired killers. The railroad had already sold the land out from under them squatters. It had its money. The land speculators who'd bought prime bottomland at $25 an acre were the ones with the problem, and so, as the papers on both sides agree, they got a federal judge to order them squatters off one-time federal land."

"Then *that's* who the Octopus bribed," said Mandalian, flat out. Longarm let it go. It wasn't his beeswax.

He didn't see why Mandalian should follow him inside to accuse the Fresno federal boys of being paid assassins. So he held out his free hand and thanked the nosy cuss for helping him tote his shit this far. Mandalian looked sort of puzzled, but shook so's they could part friendly on the courthouse steps.

Inside, a uniformed bailiff directed him to the marshal's office on the top floor. When he knocked and tried the knob he found the door that was generally open to the public locked.

He put down his load and knocked some more. After some mice had scurried around on the far side for a spell someone opened the oak door a crack to say, "The marshal's over to the grange hall, talking to them jaspers from Washington. Nobody here is supposed to talk to anyone else 'til he gets back."

Then they slammed the damned door all the way shut.

Longarm pounded again and raised his voice to announce, "I don't care. Just tell him Deputy Custis Long from the Denver District Court dropped by to pay him the usual courtesy call, you discourteous son of a never-mind. Should he care at all, I'll be at the Kings River House for now. Can't say how long. We wired you all why they were sending me out your way. I don't give a shit about your problems neither."

Then he picked up his stuff some more to grump down and out and across the civic center to the affordable hotel he'd just mentioned.

He left his saddle and most of his possibles in the livery next door and strode into the lobby packing just his shaving kit and fresh underwear and socks. He considered registering under a fake name, lest he make things too easy for at least two sets of enemies. Then he considered how tough it might be for friendlier folk to find him if he got too coy. So he decided to split the difference by hiring a corner honeymoon suite overlooking the street out front and a lot to the north, overgrown with wild mustard, anise, and tar weed, all waist-high or more but offering no serious cover from his third-story vantage point.

The bellhop who showed up to the ajoining rooms and bath gave him an odd look when he allowed no Mrs. Long would be joining him up there, later, unless he got lucky. They'd made him pay in advance, down at the desk for checking in with such measly baggage. Longarm tipped the wise-ass a whole dime for packing such a load up the stairs ahead of him and then, as soon as he had the layout to himself, he proceeded to make a few changes.

They had the room you first entered fixed up as a sort of parlor where shy couples could receive visitors or eat in their bathrobes. But just in case anyone wanted to stay over they had this half-ass sofa you could make up as a single bed if you really wanted. So he took off his frock coat and draped it over the back of a nearby chair for openers. Then he found some bedding in a handy linen closet and made the bitty daybed fit for a flop, despite the hour.

He hauled a lamp table nearer and ground out a cheroot he'd about finished to make the ashtray on said table more homey. Then he ambled into the smaller and better-ventilated corner room to see they sure enough had a swell four-poster centered for sleeping or screwing amid the night breezes off the High Sierra to the east. He hauled the shades most of the way down and dropped to one knee in the gloom to check the clearance under the bed slats. He was pleased to see no fuzz balls and noticed the flowered chamber pot was clean as well as empty.

There was no commode in the next-door bath. The limited plumbing allowed for a lion's-paw tub and a corner sink you could piss in, standing, if that was your secret desire. The management expected you to shit down the hall or in the chamber pot provided. Only the very rich or very country expected the chambermaids to empty their chamber pots down the hall or out back, as a rule.

Leaving the four poster as it was, for now, Longarm flopped atop the daybed in the other room to rumple the bedding realistic. Then, leaving his coat and tie off in the unseasonable fall weather of Fresno, he picked up the earpiece of the new Bell telephone on the parlor writing table to learn they did indeed provide room service. The gal downstairs told him not to talk silly when he asked if it was possible to call the Federal Building or Sheriff's Department on the wonderous device. He hadn't noticed the spiderweb of overhead wires you saw spreading in towns like Chicago and Saint Lou since that Great Centennial Fair back east. Some sob sister had gone on and on at the time about George Armstrong Custer being massacred by Stone Age savages the same summer Alexander Graham Bell introduced his wonderous system of world-wide communication. But all Longarm could manage to communicate so far in Fresno was that he wanted an early supper and that fried spuds sounded fine if they hadn't had time to mash any, yet.

They sent his supper up within the hour on a rolling table, shoved along by that same young bellhop. As he'd hoped, the squirt commented on his odd desire to kip out on that day bed with a perfectly fine four-poster closer to the bath.

Longarm tipped him again, it hardly seemed fair, as he explained he had back trouble from a recent fall and found the softer feather mattress in the other room too soft. Then he sent the kid back down to gossip about that as he sat down to the rolling supper, took off the tin covers, and discovered he'd really been almost as hungry as he'd let on, making up excuses for the hotel help to comment on any guest dumb enough to pay for two rooms and pick the least sensible one to sleep in. Folk hardly gossiped worth mention about strangers who behaved about as expected.

He'd finished his steak and spuds—nobody but a rabbit would have bothered with the collard greens he'd never ordered—and he was almost finished with his raisin pie when he heard someone rapping on the door from the hall and went over to answer it, sixgun polite but his twin-shot derringer discreetly palmed.

The calm and friendly-looking little thing standing there in a seersucker dress and summer bonnet didn't seem to need shooting. So he asked what else he might do for her while he decided her big brown eyes went swell with her chestnut curls.

She introduced herself as Miss Sylvia Moorehead who reported for the *Fresno Observer*. Since she already knew who he might be and seemed to feel that made him newsworthy, he invited her in, knowing how her kind tended to twist your words if you simply told 'em to go fuck their fool selves.

Room service had provided plenty of coffee and he had a clean hotel tumbler to pour some into for her. She said she'd already eaten when he offered her what was left of his dessert.

He sat her in his chair and planted himself on the edge of the daybed as she complimented him on his part in the Denver Chinese Riots of yesteryear. He modestly replied, "I just hate to wash and iron my own shirts and we didn't have near the trouble in Denver you all had out this way, thanks to the railroad barons hiring and firing so fickle. I only had to pistol whup a handful of born bully boys and I'd be obliged to you and your paper if we could let her go at that. It was no big deal but, like the War, some poor losers do nurse dumb grudges beyond all common sense."

The pretty cub reporter dimpled at him and explained, "Our editorial policy is to leave the Chinese Question to the next congress. You're so right about it being a delicate subject in an election year. But, off the record, do you think they'll really pass that proposed act aimed at barring further Chinese immigration?"

He stared wistfully at the remains of his raisin pie on her side of the damned table as he replied, "Never underestimate the stupidity of a pedigreed lapdog, a tom turkey or a congressman. The Supreme Court, to its credit, keeps knocking down state laws and municipal codes aimed at inciting to riot. So I reckon congress will just bar the Sons of Han from entering the country if they can't make 'em cut off their pigtails and join a proper church, preferably Protestant."

He sipped some coffee before he added with a sigh, "I wish they wouldn't. I have to enforce federal statutes and it's already tough enough to keep Indians off the sauce and out of them Ghost Dance shirts."

She said she'd read about him nipping that one in the bud, up to the Rosebud. He grimaced and replied, "For the time being, maybe. I'm afraid the horse nations still have one good uprising left in 'em and now some dumb congressman wants to start up with four hundred million Chinamen, last count."

She tittered and asked if they could get down to business,

demanding, "Have you been sent by the federal government to replace the useless marshal across the way or do you actually expect to make some arrests in connection with the Mussel Slough murders?"

He blinked incredulously and protested, "Neither. To begin with I don't have the rank to replace any full marshal and, after that, it was my understanding everyone suspected of gunning those two land speculators has been arrested and so charged."

He could see where she and her doubtless popular local paper stood on the unpopular railroad and federal land grants as she flared, "What about the murder of those five innocent settlers, shot down in cold blood by lawless U.S. marshals?"

He took a deep breath and let half of it out lest he sound too preacher-man as he patiently replied, "I wasn't there, so I just can't say how I'd have dealt with an armed mob if I'd been sent to serve a court order signed rightly or wrongly by a federal judge. But let's define some terms, here, ma'am. By the simple rules of English grammar you can't define anyone engaged in a firefight with federal lawmen as innocent and, wait, I ain't finished, both sides agree both civilians out to evict that Brewer family wound up stone cold dead, whoever commenced shooting so cold-blooded. So if you'd like an educated guess, I'd say somebody there made a dumb as well as hostile move, leaving to a heap of confusion followed by seven men on the ground and a lot more running or reaching for the sky by the time those doubtless cowardly lawmen had a good-sized mob under control."

She insisted, "Everyone says the first man to draw was one of those troublemakers hired by the Octopus."

He soothed, "It stands to reason a would-be landlord backed by a court order would set out to murder a whole armed mob in front of federal lawmen, ma'am. Like I said, I wasn't there. Were you?"

She looked away to demurely allow, "No, but I've spoken to friends and relations of the men framed for gunning those hired guns sent by the railroad barons. Some say they were shot by those U.S. marshals as well."

He nodded soberly and said, "I always aim first at the folk my own boss sends me to back up. Suffice it to say I wasn't sent all the way out here to investigate a dispute both the state and federal governments have other gents investigating. Did you have

119

any other reasons for declaring my Fresno comrades in arms so useless?"

She nodded primly and declared, "Nobody riding for the Fresno Federal District Court has ridden far as the city limits after all the outlaws infesting the San Joaquin Valley all summer!"

Longarm had already noticed how tough it was to catch as much as a glimpse of Billy Vail's local counterpart. So he cautiously asked what official reasons the local press had been fed for such shy ways.

She made a wry face and said, "They naturally claim it's up to the various county sheriffs to posse up after crooks too petty for your high-toned federal courts."

He smiled wearily and said, "That's all too true, at times, and I rid in a war, one time, designed to test the limits of federal control over jealously guarded states rights. I ain't allowed to go after say a stock thief or even a stickup man unless he crosses a state line to avoid prosecution or gives me some excuse, such as stealing a U.S. postage stamp or whistling at an Indian lady recorded as such by the BIA. Messing with breeds is a purely local offense."

The local newspaper woman looked disappointed in him as she said, "In sum, you're not going to do anything about Black Bart, Johnny Sontag or even those Chinese hatchet men our readers are all so concerned about?"

It had been a statement rather than a question. He still replied, "I'd have to know whether any of the gents you just mentioned have outstanding federal wants on 'em before I could answer you one way or the other. I've only heard gossip about that mysterious road agent who writes such dreadful poetry. But it's my understanding he's been stopping Wells Fargo in the Redwood Country to the north for modest sums. The most he's ever made in one robbery was less'n four hundred in cash along with a silver watch and diamond ring passengers had entrusted to the strongbox of their stage. So far, Black Bart's been too slick, or too lucky, to interfere with the U.S. mails and in any case Wells Fargo wants their own Jimmy Hume to track Black Bart."

He started to sip more coffee, saw nothing but grounds in the bottom of his infernal cup, and said, "I know they say Sontag and Evans have been going after railroad trains since that incident at Mussel Slough, but . . ."

"Chris Evans is innocent!" She cut in with some heat, adding, "I can't speak for the Sontag brothers. But it was poor Chris Evans'

120

own sister they mistreated so savagely at Mussel Slough!"

Longarm hadn't heard of either side treating any women all that savage. But he let that go to assure her with a puzzled smile, "You know way more than me about Johnny Sontag if you have him down as plural, ma'am. Most versions I've heard have Kit Evans and Johnny Sontag riding against the railroad in revenge for Mussel Slough. Am I missing something?"

She hesitated, then sighed and said, "A good reporter's supposed to be objective, so, yes, Chris Evans has turned Robin Hood in what most around these parts consider a just cause. Opinion is more divided on the Sontag brothers, John and George. They went broke digging low-grade quartz down by Visalia and . . ."

"That's a good ride from Mussel Slough, right?" he cut in.

She nodded and replied, "They told us you were sharp. Some with a heap of nice things to say about Chris Evans hold the Sontag brothers weren't involved in any way with that land dispute before our Chris, who was, took to taking revenge on the railroad and they saw a much easier way of mining gold. They say John Sontag's closer to our Chris than George, who seems willing to rob anyone, far and wide. Meanwhile the lazy federal marshals who started all this trouble say they have no federal warrants on either our Chris, the Sontags or half a dozen wilder outlaws roaming up and down the San Joaquin right now while our brave sheriff, naturally, keeps insisting he's only allowed to chase outlaws within the county lines. So what are you going to do about it, Deputy Custis Long?"

Longarm smiled sheepishly and replied, "Anything I'm ordered, by a ranking federal official, ma'am. To tell the pure truth I find it unusual but not impossible no federal warrants seem to have been sworn out on such well-known train robbers. It's none of my beeswax if the railroad would rather have the Pinkertons deal with 'em. The Pinks could likely settle a local Robin Hood's hash more permanent than a jury of his admiring peers."

He saw there was no coffee in the damned pot, either, held up a cheroot for her to decide, and once she'd nodded with a Mona Lisa smile, struck a light to get it going before he continued, "Leaving Mussel Slough and its aftertaste to you and your readers, ma'am, I may as well tell you why they did send me out here. You're sure to find out sooner or later and there's an outside chance you can help me with your better grasp of these parts."

121

She opened the bitty black notebook she'd been carrying half concealed all this time, as if she expected him to say something worth her recording for the ages.

Knowing there was no saying who might read her confounded paper, he chose his words to say no more than Billy Vail might want him to as he confided, "I'm after your hopefully less popular local boy, Tomas Ortega Baker. Don't laugh. I know he'd supposed to have died like a dog down Mexico way. Another young outlaw who might have been telling the truth or stalling for time says he bribed some Mex lawmen to just say they nailed him. How do you like it so far?"

She shook her head and said, "If you're telling me and my readers the truth you've been sold a salted claim. I know all about our so-called Fresno Kid being trapped by *Los Rurales* in Nogales and going down in a blaze of glory. I covered his funeral down at his Tia Felicidad Carillo's spread along the Kern. It was an open casket Papist rite. I wish it hadn't been, but there I was and there he was, close enough to the way he'd looked in his school photograph, and about the same color, come to think of it."

Longarm grimaced and soothed, "Arsenic embalming's like that. It does keep a body from getting too rancid but some find that slate complexion a mite disturbing. Did you know the lad personal, say in school, and I thought he was an Ortega on his maternal side."

She answered, "I never went to any school with any Fresno Kid. As for his Tia Felicidad being a Carillo, she naturally married into one of the other Spanish Land Grants when she was ready to marry at all. She's still a very attractive woman, before one considers she inherited all that Ortega bottomland in her own right."

Longarm nodded thoughtfully as he thought back to some pillow conversations he'd had up to the Motherlode Country with another lady of the Old Californio persuasion. He knew no one human being could own or likely count all the scattered acres of grazing, farming, timber and such while trying to hog so much of a barely explored globe. A lot of the early Californios allowed to marry up and found dynasties had retired from California outposts of the Royal Lancers and Catalan Volunteers, a tough dragoon outfit despite their tight red breeches. Being from the north of Old Spain to begin with and marrying up with Anglos almost as often as they messed with mission Indians, the main stem Californio grandee tended to look as Americano as his poorer relations might look Mex, and Longarm had been assured that while they loved to piss and moan about el gringo moving in to steal their land and Mamma's wedding ring, a heap of the slicker Californios had hung on surprisingly well, some families such as the Alvarados, Carillos, Ortegas, Sepulvedas, Vallejos and Yorbas, to name less than half of 'em, being just as rich and if anything more snobbish than the Cabots, Lodges and such back East. He knew without looking it up that the Carillo clan held old Spanish grants, recognized by the U.S. when they made peace with Mexico that time, from the sea coast around the Santa Barbara Mission all the way inland across the chaparral to that bottomland Sylvia had just mentioned. If the Fresno Kid's maternal aunt had inherited more of the same from her own kin he'd been treated as a poor relation indeed. The ramrod of a combined spread half that size could make more stealing from his employers than by robbing your average bank!

Taking a thoughtful drag on his cheroot, Longarm decided, "They do say some young jaspers are just wild and ornery by nature. A rich aunt kind enough to ship a dead nephew all the way from Nogales, expensively embalmed, would have likely given him a pony and pocket jingle, had he asked at all polite. So I'd say he stole horses and robbed folk just to be mean. How do you know you knew him from an old photograph if you'd never seen him before you attended his fancy funeral for your paper, Miss Sylvia?"

She said, "My friends call me Sillie, but I wouldn't be dumb enough to accept the word of a doting aunt with family tintypes on display. A few others in the family chapel that grim morning remarked on how much the boy they'd known in life had been changed by death and, I suppose you'd know more than me about embalming. So I naturally went right to our newspaper morgue when I got back to Fresno, that same afternoon."

"They planted him before noon, Spanish style, so's nobody had to miss *la siesta*?" he cut in.

She nodded and said, "I don't hold with such customs, being Scotch-Irish to begin with. As I was saying, I went right back to our morgue and dug out everything we had on Tomas Ortega Baker and, as long as I was at it, his more respectable relations on both sides. We didn't have any photographs of him as the Fresno

123

Kid. He'd naturally gone to school in both Kern and Fresno Counties before he went bad. So we had this class yearbook from Fremont High and . . ."

"Hold on," Longarm cut in, "Your paper had a high school yearbook in with the newspaper clippings a halfway respectable family ought to rate?"

She laughed and said, "Don't be silly, that's *my* nick-name. As you just said, respectable folk don't get mentioned in the papers too often. But there was mention of a then younger Tomas Ortega Baker attending the wedding of his lovely Tia Felicidad Ortega to Don Carlos Carillo, better known to his friends as Chuck. I suppose one can't have too many Ortegas on tap for one society item. The same piece mentioned her nephew as a graduate of Fremont High and I did the rest with my own little brain. We naturally keep separate stacks of local historical data, such as high school yearbooks, so that part was easy. They had photographs of the whole class and . . ."

"How?" he cut in with a frown, explaining, "They just now patented that new process allowing 'em to print halftone photographs and, so far, only fairly fancy publications have even tried. My notes say the Fresno Kid would be in his middle twenties today, dead or alive, so how . . ."

"Paste," she cut in, explaining, "Sepia-tone prints developed in some quantity from the original glass plates and then pasted in place in each fairly costly yearbook. I imagine any classmate who didn't have any front money simply never got his or her copy. I know that's how they worked it when *I* graduated, a year or so later."

It was nice to know she was over the age of consent, Sillie or not, albeit he wasn't planning to do anything important about that as he insisted, "You're sure the face in that old yearbook and the one staring up out of a coffin matched exact? I mean, one corpse gone off-color looks a lot like any other while . . ."

"They've entombed the same boy they photographed seven years ago for that high school yearbook," she insisted, adding, "You don't have to tell me how seven years, two dozen Mexican bullets and a long train ride preserved with arsenic changes one. You just heard me say some friends and relations who'd known him in life had their doubts. But I'm a trained observer, paid to pay attention to details. I knew any photographs we might have in our morgue wouldn't resemble his overall appearance too closely. So I made notes of such details as his hair line, cleft chin and let's not forget the heavy eyebrows, almost meeting in the middle, or . . ."

"I've read our yellow sheets on the cuss and that sounds like him." Longarm cut in, letting some thoughtful smoke drift between them as he tried, "What if someone slick enough to stage his own death in Nogales and funeral in Kern County was to get at an old high school yearbook with some fresh paste and a print of someone else, aged artificial?"

She laughed incredulously and said, "You're on! Let's go! The library may be closed but they're holding night classes in English over at Fremont High and . . ."

Then Longarm was on his feet with a suddenness that startled her to silence. He seldom asked questions just to hear himself talk. So he helped her to her own feet and, the fall nights being cool and the day about shot, he grabbed his frock coat as she prattled on about high schools keeping old yearbooks some damned where about the premises.

The clear sky above was going pink to purple with a wishing star already winking to their east by the time they'd made the fairly impressive sandstone steps of Fremont High. They had a right to do themselves as proud with such an up-to-date edifice as a public high school, Longarm figured, wistfully. He'd run off to the war before such educational opportunities had been common in West-By-God-Virginia or, for that matter, anywhere.

He'd read somewhere the public high school had been invented back in in '21. In Boston Town, of course. They'd been considered a mite too fancy for the taxpayers in less fancy parts 'til after the war. But the famous Supreme Court finding of '74, declaring Kalamazoo had to build a damned high school if the damned Michigan constitution promised every kid a decent education, had resulted in at least half-ass tries in most towns big enough to rate a county courthouse.

There seemed to be neither a lock nor lookout on the big front door. So they just breezed in and Sillie, knowing the way, steered them for some office or other down the hall in the gathering gloom.

An open doorway ahead was spilling lamplight out across the mock marble flooring. As they passed Longarm glanced in to see grown men and women seated at desks like schoolkids as a plump young schoolmarm with her black hair pinned in a severe bun

125

seemed to be scolding hell out of 'em in a mighty odd lingo.

When he asked, Sillie explained, "Armenian. So far, knock wood, we only have a dozen or so families in the valley. I think they're some sort of Christians ruled by the Turkish sultan and they seem to think California is lot like Armenia, without the Turks."

Longarm said that reminded him of Papist Irish and asked, "How come you say knock wood? Have you plain Americanos been having a time with such unusual new neighbors?"

She shrugged and replied, "Not so far, but I doubt we'd have much trouble with Miwok or Yokuts in such modest numbers."

That reminded him of the nearby reservation jump. So he asked what she and her paper might have on that. She shrugged and said Yokuts, the word being singular or plural, hated towns so much they couldn't stand the cluster of BIA building on their foothill reservation to the southeast. He agreed it seemed logical nobody had seen the quietly sullen acorn eaters near any local settlement. He hadn't been sent to find out why they'd jumped the reserve, and it was the war department's job to round 'em up if that was what their agent wanted. Lots of time a halfway sensible Indian agent, such as old Ed Wynkoop back in Colorado, could cool things off at little or no expense to the taxpayers before anyone got hurt, serious.

Then they'd made it to the office Sillie had been searching for. There was a young assistant dean of girls on duty, lest those grown Armenians down the hall get out of hand. Sillie introduced her to Longarm as a classmate of her own school days. Longarm didn't care. Her face was tolerable but she filled her dark gingham bodice like a sack of spuds, unsorted. When Sillie told her what they wanted to look at the assistant dean picked up her desk lamp and led them into a nearby file room. Old yearbooks were on a top shelf. So Longarm held Sillie's waist lest she break her neck standing up on a chair as she rummaged about for the right one. She wasn't wearing stays under her dress after all. He admired gals who were wasp-waisted by natural inclination.

He had to unhand her when she said she'd found the right yearbook. The three of them looked down at it as Sillie turned pages 'til she found the Fresno Kid, before he'd been the Fresno Kid, staring up in sepia-tone from amid the rest of his graduating class. Sillie declared his pasted-in photograph was a duplicate of the one they had in their own files, over to the morgue of her paper.

Longarm didn't answer as he stared down soberly in the fairly decent lamplight. The nice-looking but sort of pouty face staring back at him reminded him of at least one young pool shark you saw lurking near the front where he could admire the passing ankles. The eighteen year old Fresno Kid hadn't looked all that Spanish. There were some other young faces in the book that did, albeit none had Spanish names. Longarm didn't find that surprising. Rich Californios sent their kids to fancy private schools. Poor folk, Anglo or Mex, didn't send their kids to high school when there were more important chores to concentrate on, such as milking the damned goats and never mind the color of Washington's white horse.

Longarm made mental notes on classmates who hadn't gone as wrong after school let out and told Sillie, "I'll take your word a man could age seven years, alive, shrivel some, preserved with however strong embalming juice, and still look something like the kid in this photo. After that I've seen half a dozen old pictures of Jesse James, attested to as his true likeness, and I'd still bet a month's pay they couldn't have all been posed by the same man."

She soberly asked whether he was doubting her word or her eyesight.

He said, "Eyesight. Flimflammery with one old yearbook would be duck soup simple. Gets way more complicated than simply fibbing as soon as you consider some sneak changing sepia-tones all over town."

She sounded hurt as she insisted, "I know what I saw, along with a whole chapel filled with closer kith and kin. The boy in this old photograph and the only somewhat older man in an open casket were one and the same!"

He said he was sure she was sure. Then he turned to the homely school official to say, "I got to impound this here yearbook as evidence, Ma'am. I'll see you get it back as soon as I can have a fresh copy made of this . . . Oops, never mind, for now."

They both seemed to think he was awfully smart when he pointed to the name and address of a Fresno photographer proudly printed in one corner of every page of prints with a rubber stamp. He still told 'em most photo studios kept the glass negatives of any portraits they had of local society, adding, "White kids graduating from high school stand head and shoulders above the unwashed masses of Mex and Chinese stoop labor in these parts. I'll bet I can get all the extra prints of the punk I need at less'n two bits, enlarged."

Sillie agreed but asked what good even a blown-up portrait of the late Tomas Ortega Baker would do him, repressing a shudder as she demanded, "You surely don't want to view his remains, after all this time in that stuffy tomb!"

He grimaced and replied, "Don't want to. Might have to, with or without a court order. I learned about arsenic embalming during the war. Officers on both sides and even a heap of the enlisted Union dead got sent home that way. They say Old Abe, himself, was pumped full of arsenic so's they could haul him all around by train as the weather was warming up."

He shut the old yearbook and being so much taller than either gal, managed to put it back on its shelf without having to climb up on that chair as he continued, "Folk who got a last look say Old Abe was nigh dark as the folk he'd liberated toward the end and most states have passed more recent laws against preserving bodies with arsenic. It ain't racial prejudice. It makes it impossible to tell, later on, whether a rich old gent really died natural or from the flypaper soup his loving heirs might have been feeding him to sooth his colic."

The gal who only worked there said she'd never heard of flypaper soup for the colic. Sillie proved she'd reported more on domestic strife by calmly expaining, "Flypaper's made with a mixture of sticky molasses, glycerin to keep it sticky, and arsenic to kill the flies."

The dean of girls said, "Oh." Nobody with a lick of sense had to be told how to drop a few sheets of flypaper in say tomato soup and fish just the paper out before serving.

So he continued, "Aside from darkening the complexion and making it nigh impossible to prove foul play, that simple but powersome way of embalming holds dead folk together pretty good and if that gent you saw in that box and this boy in them old sepia-tones should be one and the same, then nothing that's happened since I left Denver makes one lick of sense at all!"

128

Chapter 14

The shapeless dean of girls had to stay at the school and ride herd on those Armenians and some other ignorant immigrants taking night classes. The shapelier she-male reporter had to report in to the night desk at her newspaper before she knocked off for the night. She offered to show Longarm that other yearbook and said he could escort her home, later, if he liked. But he said he had to send some telegraph wires. So they parted friendly out front.

He was no fool. Sillie had already let it slip she roomed with other unwed ladies at a nearby she-male boarding house and he'd dig postholes before he'd let himself be shown off to a gaggle of unwed giggle-gals when he didn't figure to wind up with a kiss on the lips for his trouble.

He really had promised Billy Vail he'd try and keep in touch by wire. So he ambled over to the Western Union to send a terse outline of his adventures since leaving Sacramento. He knew his pinch-penny boss would be pissed at the vast expense of reporting nothing much at a nickel a word, so he sent his report at night letter rates. Western Union charged way less if you let 'em put your message on the wire in the wee small hours when their telegraphers had nothing much to do whether they had to stay on duty or not.

Figuring his home office would know where he was by business hours the next morning, Longarm stopped in at the taproom of his hotel to find out whether or not he might want to hang about Fresno long enough for anyone in Denver to wire back.

Hotel taprooms frequented by traveling men and locals inclined to wear neckties had small town barber shops matched neck and neck for local gossip. Knowing the best way to shut the regulars up was by asking questions with a strange voice, Longarm bellied up to the bar in the cozy redwood-paneled taproom to order Maryland rye, lest they take him for a saddle tramp, with a steamer beer chaser lest he wind up walking funny early in the evening.

As he'd hoped, the modest all-male crowd got back to the conversation they'd been having when his mysterious appearance amid them had occasioned a thoughtful lull. The topic seemed armed robbery. A mighty old or mighty recent event, since that newspaper gal and her night desk hadn't mentioned it just now.

Longarm put away his shot of whiskey and put out the fire with a gulp of steamer beer whilst resisting the temptation to ask for details. So about the time the fat bald barkeep determined he was a guest at the hotel as well as a seasoned traveler with good manners, Longarm had a better handle on the latest outrage of some ferocious Mexicans disturbing the peace along the San Joaquin.

Everyone but the courteous Longarm laughed sort of cruel at the one old-timer who opined the outlaws were led by the son if not the reincarnation of Joaquin Murieta, the Robin Hood of Spanish California.

The old-timer insisted, "My Mex cook says that's what she's heard and ain't it true that posse trailed Murieta and Three Fingered Jack to the reed swamps all about that lake a bare forty miles south of us as we wonder?"

Another gent old enough to have been out that way at the time objected, "Unless it was along Cantua Creek, up in Panoche Pass, or some other place that confirmed drunk and so-called Captain Harry Love recalled as he changed his fool story every time he told it."

There was a murmur of agreement and someone said, "I have it on good Mex authority Love's posse never captured and decapitated any real bandits at all. Nobody at the time knew what the real Murieta or Three Fingered Jack really looked like. So Love and his boys just jumped a party of vaqueros hunting mustangs down past Lake Tulare and butchered 'em for the bounties on the real gang."

The old timer who'd been laughed at snapped, "That's my point, exact. The Mexicans say nobody never killed their ferocious Joaquin and everyone agrees someone ferocious is leading a Mex

130

gang over the same old stomping grounds, stomping folk the same way, so . . ."

"Murieta and Three Fingered Jack pulled their last officious stickup back before the war and then some. Whoever Harry Love managed to kill, Love was gunned fair and square back in '68 by good old Chris Iverson."

Another older man chimed in, "Up in Santa Clara, the wife-beating bastard. I mean Harry Love, not Iverson. I understand Iverson and Love's widow got on swell, later."

The one who'd raised the issue of dates, alone, swore like a mule skinner stuck in deep sand, then insisted, "Never mind about the son of a bitch they paid for killing the sons of bitches. My point is that, dead or alive, Murieta and Three Fingered Jack quit robbing folk better than a quarter century ago. Even if either was still around, they'd be too blamed old to pester anybody."

More than one old-timer, not all of 'em gray yet, laughed boyishly when a gent who'd been silent up until then announced, "Well, now, I don't know about that, Jake. I'm about the same age Murieta would be if he was still around and I reckon I could still get it up if you'd like to bend over."

Longarm had permitted himself a wry smile at the picture. That was the cue for another regular to address him, saying, "You're entitled to an opinion, you shy young cuss. So, speaking as a stranger but a white man for all that, would you be going with a return of Joaquin Murieta or some other mean Mex entire?"

Knowing he could be in trouble either way, Longarm shrugged and opined, "Speaking as a lawman privy to wanted posters, old and new, I'd say nothing much can be said for certain about the original Garcia and Murieta. The fairly handsome head they still display for a fee, preserved in a jar, has been pretty well established as that of one Joaquin Valenzuela. His kith and kin have attested him to have been an innocent vaquero from a fine old Californio family. At any rate his head was recently moved from Stockton to a penny arcade in Frisco and nobody connected with the U.S. Justice Department cares."

Someone asked, "Who in blue blazes was Garcia?"

Another old timer muttered, "Manuel Garcia was Three Fingered Jack, you dumb dude. I'd say this young lawman knows his birds from his bees."

There was a murmur of agreement and Longarm knew he was free to ask questions about more recent events, now. But nobody

131

there thought the more recent Fresno Kid could be up and about at this late date. The old-timer who was worried about meeting Joaquin Murieta said he hadn't been there, personal, but that he'd talked to more than one local stockman who'd paid their respects to the dead rascal's maternal aunt, the beautiful Widow Carillo nee Ortega.

As Longarm lit a smoke he added, "Nobody really gave a shit about the black sheep of the family she was putting away like such a sport, poor gal. Nobody else in the family has ever gone bad and they've still had their share of tragedy, what with first her older sister, the dead boy's Mex mamma, then her husband, good old Chuck Carillo, leaving her alone with enough to cope with afore the infernal rurales blew a dozen holes in her worthless nephew."

Another old timer chimed in, "Got 'em all put away in that fancy family tomb old Don Hernan Ortega built when the world was lots younger. Looks like one of them Greek temples, only made of red sandstone, same color as dried blood."

Longarm figured another beer would just about balance the black coffee he'd had earlier, now that he had the regulars talking. They didn't pay him enough to order drinks all around and he didn't seem to be drinking with anyone in particular. So he had the barkeep put a head on his steamer and after some sipping and puffing he had the home spread he'd be heading for in a spell a mite straighter in his head.

The gents said the Fresno Kid's Tia Felicidad kept her own family holdings as field headquarters of her considerable grain and cattle operation because the sort of 'dobe castle she'd spent her girlhood at was way fancier than the Carillo grant to the southwest she'd married into. Everyone agreed that whilst the late Chuck Carillo had been a good old boy, Felicidad Ortega might have done better, and so it hardly seemed likely she'd married him for his money or sizeable but mostly marginal holdings to the southwest. Combining their joint shares of the Ortega and Carillo grants had only swollen Felicidad's about a third and that third was mostly parched cheat and dusty playa two thirds of the year.

The only one who disagreed was the old-timer who worried about the return of Joaquin Murieta. He said, "Now I don't know about that, boys. Bottomland is bottomland, even away from natural runoff, as soon as you consider how easy it might be to run irrigation ditches across all that soft dirt."

He spit pretty good at a fairly distant cuspidor and pointed out, "With or without irrigation the widow Carillo must get a pretty penny from the Octopus, seeing the railroad had to lay that one feeder line across that otherwise marginal grazing."

He spat again and added, "Lord knows what they have to pay her, but unlike them poor bastards down near Mussel Slough she holds her land in fee simple by deeds older than these United States."

"Same age," another old timer objected, explaining, "Portola led his lancers and dragoons into northern California the same year our Continental Congress was telling off the king of England back East. That must have made the king of Spain uneasy. At any rate, most of the land grants he handed out in these parts date well after 1776."

The worrywart who spit so swell shook his head and said, "Not this side of our agreement with Mexico to respect all land titles held by former Mex citizens as long as they obeyed the laws and paid the damned taxes of their new country. I doubt the jaspers who signed for our side read the fine print on them old royal grants. More than one slick Mex had tried to get around 'em and been struck down by the Mex version of our Supreme Court."

A local dressed more like a banker suddenly brightened to declare, "I see what you mean, having been stung by an ignorant greaser now and again. Spanish speaking politicos being the way they are, the kings of Spain had them royal grants drawn up tighter than a Scotchman's asshole. Both the state and federal government can condemn a regular American's property out from under him under our laws of public domain, based on the English common law we started out with to save time."

A more rustic drinker closer to Longarm asked what in blue blazes English common law had to do with Spanish land grants. So Longarm told him, "Nothing. Spain being less progressive than England at the time, they never provided for public works across private land. So did you want to run a road, a canal, a railroad or whatever through some other gent's south forty you just had to get his damned permit from him and him alone. No pals at court, or anywhere else, could make you surrender a square inch for a dime less than you damned well demanded."

The rustic whistled and complained, "I thought we was the ones who declared for life, liberty and all that shit. What do you reckon the Widow Carillo makes 'em pay her to run a train across her range?"

Longarm shrugged and said, "Can't be enough to deny them any profit on the run. I'd ask her when I drop by in a day or so if I thought it was polite, or I had a lawful reason. Since I can't think of any, I likely won't. She figures to be annoyed enough with me when I ask her for the key to that family tomb."

The one who looked like a banker said, "No she won't. She won't be there, this time of the year."

Another explained, "Spends most of her time, these days, up San Francisco way. She and old Chuck Carillo had just built themselves a swell townhouse on that Nob Hill when he up and died on her. Some who've been there say it's swell."

Not to be outdone, the fancy dresser said, "None of the big rancheros spend half as much time counting cows as they used to. Those who weren't wiped out by the big die-off during the war years have gone ever more into farming what they can water and letting the rest lie fallow for later. I think Doña Felicidad came down for the recent roundup and before that for her nephew's funeral, of course. But if you want to serve a court order on her this side of say the spring planting you're headed the wrong way."

Longarm put away some more beer and allowed he'd seldom visited a spread where someone hadn't been left in charge. He didn't feel they were old enough to hear how he handled a search warrant when there was nobody home to serve it on.

Considering how he meant to get that far, he declared, "I sort of planning to hire some riding stock here in Fresno and drift south, getting the feel of the Fresno Kid's old stomping grounds."

When someone objected the infernal Fresno Kid lay entombed by the wide but shallow Kern he sighed and replied, "That's what I mean. I might save considerable time and trouble for all concerned if I crack open the box and determine just who they put in it. So mayhaps I'd best grab another train down as far as . . . Bakersfield?"

The more rustic drinker nodded and said, "You'll still have some riding but not as much if you follow the Kern upstream."

Another warned, "Talk to someone in town as knows the Miller Lux riders. You'll be riding a good part of the way over their big uncertain holdings and there has been some stock-stealing up and down the valley this fall."

134

The one who looked as if he rode more laughed and said, "Aw, shoot, no Miller Lux riders are likely to gun a white man they meet on their range for no reason at all. There's a damned old wagon trace runs along the Kern as a post road and public right of way. I'd feel safer alone on range patrolled by honest cowhands, regular, than aboard a fool train run by them unpopular son of a bitches who think they own the whole damn valley!"

A townsman on his far side nudged him warningly as the worrywart who'd brought up Murieta said, too sincerely, "That's right. They say them Mex raiders have even taken to stopping trains, the uppity no-good greaseballs!"

Longarm smiled uncertainly and said, "Do tell? The only train robbers I've been hearing about of late, in these parts, is that Evans Sontag gang."

There came a silence once could have cut with a knife, had he been sent so far to wave knives in taprooms. He smiled sheepishly and said, "I see I seem to have put my foot in it, gents. So, save for saying I meant no insult to anyone here, how do I take it out?"

Nobody told him. It was if he wasn't there as he finished his beer, put down the stein, and simply behaved as any experienced traveler should in suddenly tense drinking establishment. He backed clear of the bar and then, seeing none of the suddenly tense drinkers were moving to stop him, strode silently for the archway leading into his hotel lobby.

It felt like at least a country mile. Then he'd made it to the darker lobby and, in case he might be missing something, flattened out against the wall, just outside, to hear some subdued growly sneers and someone, he couldn't see who, saying, "What did I tell you? They're all alike. That infernal President Hayes lets them railroad barons take turns screwing his First lady and they'll never rest 'til they hang our gallant Kit Evans like a dog!"

A milder voice soothed, "The man said he was after that far-from-gallant Fresno Kid, Curly."

So Longarm knew which bald cuss was speaking, this time, as he heard, "Bullshit. Not even the fucking government could be worried about stone-dead road agents. Can't you boys see that was all a cover up for his real mission, the political assassination of our own Kit Evans? If it was up to me, somebody would assassinate that sneaky son of a bitch from Denver first!"

Chapter 15

Longarm liked to wedge that match stem in the door jam when leaving a room locked but unoccupied in an uncertain world. But he hadn't wanted to look odd or give away trade secrets to that newspaper gal. So he entered his dark hired digs low and sudden, sixgun muzzle leading the way, and had himself wedge in one corner with the door kicked shut before he decided he hadn't been ambushed after all.

After that he bolted the door and, leaving the lamps unlit, made a few moves he'd already planned, lest he die in bed of lead poison.

He'd already let anyone who cared know he'd made up the daybed in the sitting room of the suite. So he moved next door and gently eased that four-poster into a better position, balancing it on one leg. Then, leaving the thick mattress in place, he whipped off the bedding, including a quilted counterpane that could be folded into a fair pallet atop a fairly new rug, and proceeded to make himself a sneaky trundle bed that didn't really trundle under the thicker bare mattress overhead. He figured anyone waking up down yonder with a gun handy to his head would have a clean shot through the bedroom door at the hall entrance to the whole damned suite.

After that there remained the chore of tearing a newspaper found atop the writing table into quarters so's he could scatter balls of crisp crinkly newsprint all over the rug. He'd just about finished when the jangle of that telephone from the darkness nearly jumped him out of his old Army boots.

It was for Pete's sake after ten at night and he idly wondered whether Professor Bell had considered such possible rudeness when he'd invented his wonderous machine. Then he'd picked up the ear phone and bent down to ask the contraption what it wanted, only to be treated ruder. The night owl on the other end hung up. Longarm swore and was about to do the same when the same gal he'd ordered supper from, earlier, came on the line to ask what he wanted, now.

He said, "I don't want nothing, ma'am. You just now rung my bell and, being raised polite, I answered. So now it's your turn."

The hotel operator sounded annoyed as she replied, "Neither I nor anyone else has called your room this evening, Sir."

To which he could only reply, "No offense, but somebody must have. Didn't you tell me, before, your Bell system only extends to the extended premises of this business establishment?"

She assured him, "The other guest rooms, the taproom and livery next door and of course the barber, tobacco shop and a few other ground floor conveniences closed for the night at this hour."

He agreed it was an ungodly hour to be ringing telephones at folk but demanded, "Might someone in one of them shut shops, or another hotel room, for that matter, call this room without you knowing of it, ma'am?"

She said she didn't see how, since all the telephone lines in question ran through her switchboard. So he thanked her and hung up.

Then he was back out in the hallway, sixgun drawn and smiling wolfishly as he doused the already dim wall lamp, muttering, "It ain't smart to repeat the same criminal pattern but, on the other hand, there's a heap of dumb bastards in your average jail."

He took cover at a bend of the hall that still gave him a good field of fire betwixt the stairwell and the door of the suite some tricky rascal had just telephoned, sneaky.

Like many self-educated men, Longarm was a voracious reader who liked to stretch himself on shit he found tough to savvy. Thus he'd read up enough on the modern wonders of electricity to figure more than one way to short-circuit a telephone switchboard. Knowing that hadn't been an honest wrong number gave him an edge on the slicker who'd thought to get an edge on him by phoning ahead to make sure he'd be in when they . . . What?

He silently hummed the old Calvinist hymn, "Farther Along" as in "Farther along we'll know more about it." For anyone who hadn't been laying for him in there would have to come up the stairs or out of another damned door to get at him, no matter what they planned for someone they'd just located so damned cute.

Thinking of other doors reminded him there could be any number of doors behind as well as ahead of him. So he'd just rolled his head and shoulders that way, around the corner from his own door, when all that dynamite went off, and it was a good thing he hadn't been staring when the door of his room and bits and pieces of the furnishings inside blasted every which way at buckshot speed and he got knocked on his ass by the shock of the whole shebang alone!

Then voices were screaming in the smoke-filled blackness all around as Longarm got back to his feet, yelling, "Go back inside and bar your damned doors! This is the law speaking and we got at least one homicidal maniac running loose in this hotel!"

Then he noticed the orange glow of sunrise, or worse, through the haze of nitro-scented fumes and yelled, again, "Forget what I just said and grab your socks! This hotel is on fire as well as beset by mad dogs!"

He was already up, dressed, and closer to the stairs than the flames licking the tin ceiling from the gaping doorway of his corner suite. So he'd have made it easier had not some damned brat commenced to bawl somewhere amid all the smoke and some gal hadn't tried to pass him in her shimmy shirt, yelling, "My baby! Oh my God!" and such as Longarm grabbed her by one flannel-covered arm to swing her toward the stairs instead as he assured her, "You can't. The busted glass ahead would cut your bare feet to the bone even if your flappy flannel failed to catch on fire!"

Then a man half-dressed and running full blast came their way from yet another doorway and Longarm tossed the young mother at him, yelling, "Save this lady whilst you're at it. I'll get her kid!"

Then he was forging his way through the rising smoke and falling cinders toward the sounds of that invisible but mighty noisy tyke. He knew an older kid would have been scared skinny, waking up to a bomb blast to find your mamma off to the shithouse and the strange surroundings burning down around you. In his hurry to get to the kid he'd forgotten the sixgun he still had in hand. But that was just as well when he almost bumped noses with another grown man in the thick smoke, who replied to Longarm's weary smile by gasping, "Oh, Dear Lord, it's you!" and going for his own sidearm.

Longarm shot him flat and kept going, planting a boot heel in the bastard's chest for good measure as he concentrated harder on the locale of that wailing kid than the possible reasons for that slight impediment to his progress.

The damned kid stopped crying, overcome by smoke, but not before Longarm had made it close enough for an educated guess. Most of the other doors down that way were already open. Doors wound up that way a heap in hotel fires. So when he came to one that was shut he tried the knob to find it was locked, and simply tore on through it.

He'd been right about that young mother locking up on her way to take a late night crap. Her kid was in a dresser drawer pulled out to form an improvised crib. He scooped the infant up, bedding and all, then, as long as he was there he grabbed some she-male duds off the foot of the real bed, tossing them over the baby for added shielding, and holstered his .44-40 so's he could pick up the fool woman's heavy gladstone before he told the ominously silent infant in his arms, "Here we go, Pard. If we both burn to cinders I'll never speak to you again."

They came closer to that than he'd really meant by the time he'd raced along the burning hall carpeting to the stairwell, holding his breath and hoping the kid would have the sense to do the same with its mamma's duds covering its little fool face.

But it must have, judging from the way it was coughing as he jumped over smouldering steps between blazing bannisters to make the first landing, spin through all those little spinning stars, and risk one smoky breath as they ran through the dark deserted lobby to the cheering crowd outside.

"You've saved her! You've saved her!" wailed a banshee in a flannel nightgown as she busted free of the Fresno fire department to charge Longarm and his load. That seemed to scare her baby into bawling back at her. Longarm hadn't known he was saving a baby girl. The mother he'd just saved her for didn't seem to know or care he'd hauled most of their stuff out as well. As a fireman and a motherly Fresno lady joined them just inside the fire lines to take over for him, Longarm asked the fireman if he'd handle the young mother's possibles, explaining, "I got to go back. There's a gent lying dead or wounded in the hall upstairs and I'd like to see what he or his pockets have to tell me."

The fireman took the otherwise half dressed woman's things,

having had some experience along such lines, but told Longarm, flatly, "You ain't going back in there, Mister. The boys hope to save the livery and maybe even the bar, but that hotel's a total loss at this end."

Longarm said he was a U.S. deputy, not a damned Mister, but even as he turned around he saw what the fireman meant. Through the busted-out lobby glass one could see the tin ceiling glowing like the lid of an overheated kitchen range and more inflammable furnishings were aflame from the ground floor up. He knew even if it was possible to get back to that cuss he'd just shot, and it wasn't, there's be little left to identify by now. As he was saying as much to the fireman they both heard a wet pop above the crackle of the flames. The fireman said, quietly, "Hope we only hear that once. I'd tell you what that sound means, but you wouldn't thank me."

Longarm soberly replied, "I know what it was. I was in a war one time and fought some since. Once you've heard one human skull explode that way you never forget the sound."

The fireman nodded and said, in a surprisingly cheerful tone, "Our brains are mostly water and you know how water pressure builds when there's no handy way for water to boil."

It was just as well he'd finished when that young mother, still holding her whimpersome brat, joined them to sob, "I don't know how to thank you, good sir and . . . Good heavens, is that my very bag with all our money and my humble jewels as well?"

As the fireman handed them over to her Longarm declared, "As a rule I'd warn you how dumb it can be to have all your valuables in one handy package, ma'am. But in this case we'll say no more about it and can you handle all that by yourself?"

She said she'd carried it this far from Memphis, along with her kid. By this time the motherly older gal had horned in to say she meant to take mother and child under her officious but well-meaning wing and that they'd better get cracking at the rate everything but that burning building would cool off before midnight.

Longarm and the fireman both urged them to get cracking. So they did. Another fireman joined them to say, "Well, we got the horses and tack out of the livery and the captain's posted a guard on the taproom supplies around to the side lot. Anybody here got any marshmallows?"

The fireman Longarm had been jawing with chuckled dryly and

said, "We got one turkey in the oven, topside, according to this gent, who says he's the law, by the way."

The second fireman said, "We got lucky, considering the way that son of a bitch is burning. Some other guests I just talked to say it started with some sort of explosion. Next thing anyone knew someone was yelling at 'em to run for it, just in time. She sure was a tinder box, wasn't she?"

Before Longarm could say anything modest or vain a third fireman hauled one end of a snakelike leather firehose to where they stood admiring the flames. When he said, "Captain said to see if there was any use hosing this side," the one who knew all about exploding skulls snorted in disdain and demanded, "To what end? Can't you see it's going out by itself already?"

The other one agreed, "Everything that knew how to burn has about burned away. This gent in the cowboy hat says we got smoked meat in there as well. Best to let a mess like that burn much as it can. I just hate scooping 'em out of the coals before they're nice and crisp."

The light was getting tricky as the hotel burned down to a monstrous heap of glowing coals. But Longarm was still able to recognize Greg Mandalian as the latter bulled through the crowd to see if anyone needed to be arrested. The sardonic deputy sheriff nodded at Longarm and said, "Evening. You been smoking more than usual, Uncle Sam?"

Longarm smiled thinly as they shook and said, "You don't know how close I just came to being smoked sausage meat nobody would ever be able to I.D."

He hesitated and then, since the Fresno fire department had as much right to know, he said, "The fire started in my corner suite. They planted dynamite somewhere inside whilst I was out hunting crooks, the crooked bastards. I'm pretty sure they set it off by wire with a regular blaster's battery somewhere else in the building."

Mandalian whistled and asked how come he'd lived through such a murderous blast.

Longarm said, "I never. I was out in the hall when they blew up my whole corner of the hotel, secure in the belief I'd be blown up with it because they'd just rung me up on the telephone to make sure I was there. They hung up as soon as I answered."

The same fireman who'd wanted to pump water on a dying fire asked how come he hadn't been there, after all. Mandalian was the one who growled, "Wake up or shut up, you fool kid. The

141

man just said he'd had a mysterious phone call late at night in a strange town."

But Longarm knew the firemen couldn't know he was in Fresno on the trail of at least one wanted killer. So he said, "Suffice it to say I was out in the hall, waiting to see what happened next, and you boys know as much as me about . . . Wait, I almost forgot. After the blast, in the first confusion of the fire, I ran into a stranger in the hall who seemed so surprised to see me I had to shoot him, first."

Mandalian decided, "That's what I'd have done in your place. So what did this mysterious gunslick look like, Pard?"

Longarm said, "Hard to say, in all that smoke. Dressed sort of cow. Broad hat brim, no coat, gun worn side-draw, low on his right hip. Gun ought to make it through the fire, if it ever goes out."

One of the firemen declared, "Not in shape to be much use to anyone but we'll dig it out for you once the ashes cool and . . . Then what? You want us to deliver it to Greg, here, at the county courthouse?"

The usual answer would have been no. But so far the local sheriff's department seemed more anxious to uphold a fellow lawman than those ass-covering political hacks at the federal building. So he nodded and said he'd be obliged, adding, "Ain't sure where I'm likely to be found for the next few days. Seems every time I settle on a halfway permanent address somebody comes calling to kill me."

He reached in his vest to hand smokes out all around as he added, "All in all, it sounds safer if I just give out mailing addresses and bed down somewhere's more private."

Mandalian beat Longarm to lighting a big kitchen match as he said, "That's about the way I'd want to catnap, too. You can rest assured we'll hang on to any baked evidence 'til you get around to asking for it, Uncle Sam. Doubt even a gun with serial numbers will be any use to anyone if it's been stole or hockshopped more than once. Can't you even hazard a guess as to who could be gunning for you, Uncle Sam?"

Longarm shrugged and said, "If I had suspect one I'd be arresting him, her, or it on suspicion. So far, my prime suspect has to be the cuss I was sent to bring in, and so far everyone keeps telling me the Fresno Kid lies dead as a doornail, many a weary mile from here."

Chapter 16

It was no secret the stock and tack from the half-burnt hotel livery had been split up between a couple of other such establishments in the neighborhood. Longarm tipped the old Mex in charge of just one to keep just one thing secret. Then he spread the bedroll off his own saddle in their hayloft so's to catch a few winks of undisturbed sleep.

Next morning, head way clearer and first things coming first, he strode over to the railyards and asked his way to their dispatch shed. The one-eyed but frock-coated cuss in charge seemed pleased to see Longarm's federal badge and said, "It's about time we got some help with them ferocious farmers."

When Longarm said he hadn't heard the Sontag brothers were sodbusters the dispatcher said, "Them too. Our regular railroad dicks have a sporting chance against regular train robbers. It's the other farm folk, young and old, male and she-males all along our right of way I'd like to see sent forever to a federal prison!"

Longarm said that might be tough to arrange in an election year and said, "I'm sure all but the kids will get weary of throwing rocks at passing trains once them farm boys arrested down to Mussel Slough get out of jail."

When the dispatcher said they'd be sent away for a mighty long time if his railroad had a thing to say about it Longarm shrugged and replied, "It's your railroad and your railroad glass. Something more ominous crossed my mind as I was considering travel plans in the wee small hours. You know how you lay there, wondering whether you should go back to sleep or get up and piss? Anyways, I've an errand down by the Kern at that big Ortega-Carillo spread and the directions some old boys gave me don't add up."

The dispatcher proved he knew how to run a railroad by stating without hesitation, "You take our main line south as far as Visalia. From there a passenger freight combo makes one run a day along the Blue Dog spur. She leaves the Blue Dog mines at high noon, gets into Visalia no later than two if the brakeman knows what's good for him."

He hesitated long enough to run a thumbnail through the stubble on his jaw and added, "They want their empty gondolas back at the mines. So there's a couple of hours turn around time as works out handy enough. The combo leaves Visalia every afternoon at four and gets back to Blue Dog in time for a banker's supper. Since you say you only want to ride far as the widow Carillo's you'd want to get off where they jerk water, smack on the trestle across the Kern. You could walk her, afoot, from there to the old Ortega homespread."

Longarm frowned and grumbled, "I could do better than that, seeing it's a combo hauling freight cars as well. I could hire a pony down around Visalia and ride to the damned rancho. So how come after I'd said I was the law they directed me ever so sweetly to get off way to the west in Bakersfield and ride so infernal far up the Kern?"

The railroader shrugged and said, "Some old boys feel greening the wayfaring stranger proves superhuman intelligence. That Blue Dog spur runs smack across parts of the old Carillo grant and close enough to the Ortega homespread to walk it, like I just said. You'd waste a hard day in the saddle riding east from Bakersfield."

Longarm nodded soberly and said, "Someone else had already made mention of railroad tracks across range now held by the famous widow Carillo. I got the impression some of 'em liked Kit Evans and the Sontag brothers way more than they admired your railroad. Tell me more about the way that feeder line runs, once it departs from where I damn well wanted to get off in the first place."

The dispatcher didn't have to look it up. He said, "Follows the main line south from Visalia a mite, then it veers off across the playas and mustard flats 'til, like I said, it crosses that old Spanish grant range, jerks water at the Kern, and proceeds southeast into the rolling chaparral. The Blue Dog mines are along a quartz reef where the foothills commence to climb serious and sprout real trees. Why do you ask, if you're only headed for the widow Carillo's?"

Longarm reached absently for a smoke, noticed he only had one left and, not wanting to be rude, just inhaled some dry fall air before he said, cautiously, "Ain't sure. Don't know the country as well as some of your local train robbers might. But if I was planning to stop a train on the far side of the Kern, or knew someone who did, I wouldn't worry about even a famous lawman who'd be getting off before anyone might want to stop said train."

The dispatcher blinked his one good eye and said, "Holy shit! I got to get that right on the wire! But hold on, it's just about breakfast time outside and if anyone was aiming to stop a train leaving Blue Dog at noon, why would they be worried about you or any other lawman aboard the afternoon combo when . . . Right, they're planning to stop her *this afternoon*, north of the Kern, in the high chaparral patrolled by nobody but lazy Mex vaqueros, if them, this time of the year!"

He turned from where they'd been jawing near his doorway to hunker over his telegraph set and start sending. Longarm was dying for that smoke, but he knew enough Morse to make sure the older man had it all pictured about the same way. Then, knowing they could both be wrong, he waited for a break in the transmission, called out a polite enough "Adios," and strode back toward the center of town to see about breakfast and a tobacco shop, lighting his last cheroot along the way.

He just hated to finish his breakfast coffee and dessert without a smoke. So he stopped by a corner shop and stepped inside to stock up on cheroots. They had one of his favorite brands and sold newspapers as well. There was nothing about that explosion and fire he'd just lived through, yet. But even the Fresno papers were carrying the mystery of that naked lady and the cowboy with a hat pin up his nose. So he picked up a copy of the *Fresno Observer*, seeing he had friends who worked there, and carried it along with him to peruse as he demolished some fried eggs over chili con carne over a slab of sugar-cured ham that had sure looked tempting and wasn't bad.

For some reason the pretty Mex counter gal stared awestruck back at him when he allowed he'd have some of that prune pie when he bragged on up above her in chalk. She said not many patrons ordered prune pie for breakfast, even when they hadn't already had so much breakfast. He smiled confidentially and confessed, "I'm more curious than hungry, thanks to you and that chili *autentico*. But I've never had any of your famous prune pie and *la vida es breve*, like it says in our Good Book as well."

So she fetched him a heroic slice of mighty dreadful-looking pie and refilled his coffee mug as she complimented him on his Spanish and informed him sadly, in the same, she was new in town and hardly knew a soul.

He was sorry he'd shown off like that. For life was all too short, in English as well, to pick every damned daisy along the way and she was likely a *chiflada* who wouldn't go all the way the first night to begin with.

So he didn't get to read his paper and prune pie might have tasted better if he hadn't been in such a hurry. He had more than one good reason to hurry. He had chores to finish in Fresno before he rode on and he knew himself well enough to know that if he didn't bust free of her purring kitten comments on his healthy appetites and the musky fumes of her jasmine perfume and clean young sweat he was likely to convince himself she was a suspect and, right now, he had more than enough suspects on his puzzled mind.

He left her a whole quarter extra to keep her from feeling all her efforts had been wasted on a henpecked gelding and, still packing that other gal's paper, asked directions to that Fresno photographic studio who'd bragged of their services in that yearbook.

It just wasn't his day. The young ash blonde they'd left in charge was even prettier than that Mex waitress. But at least she wasn't as flirty, so he was able to keep his mind on his mission as he showed her his I.D. and explained just what he wanted.

She proved bright and helpful as well as downright mouth-watering. She said she could already let him have an enlargement of that old sepia-tone of Tomas Ortega Baker, free, because he was hardly the first lawman who'd ever asked if they might have photographed the Fresno Kid before he'd become so famous.

As she bent over, pretty as anything, to rummage through a bottom drawer for him, Longarm obeserved, "Lots of old boys have had their pictures took before and even after they've gone wrong. Makes it a lot easier on us upholders of the law, when we're going by the right picture. But, no offense, I've seen pictures of different gents entire sold as one cuss who's authentic likeness might be worth something."

146

She straightened back up and turned primly toward him with two indentical nine-by-twelve black and whites, unmatted. Her front view was pretty as anything, above or below her frilled choke collar, as she almost snapped, "We don't charge for prints that may be useful in trapping a criminal, good sir!"

He said he hadn't meant to be uncouth and explained, "Some less ethicated photographers must, for, like I just said, they've sure spread a heap of false impressions that keep showing up to confuse the law and most likely history. I know for a fact Tashunka Witko, the gent we called Crazy Horse, never posed for one photograph because his dreams had told him it would be bad medicine. Yet now that he's gone on to live with Old Woman under the Northern Lights they have plenty of pictures of him, all different."

He studied one of the identical prints she'd just handed him as he quickly added, "I see this is the same pouty squirt staring into the future from that old yearbook, though. I'm glad. I didn't think the *Fresno Observer* and Fremont High could be in cahoots with wanted killers but it's still good to know this spoiled brat was him and nobody else but him."

She said, "Only too happy to be of service, good sir, but may I ask what use those prints will be to you, now, seeing the spoiled brat, as you so aptly describe him, has been dead for months?"

He owed her some explanations for her own courtesy so he brought her up to date on the confusion as to just whom they might have put to rest in that family tomb. She seemed to feel she was ahead of him when she cut in with, "But they must have captured this very same young man in Nogales, good sir. For the Mexican authorities wrote us for help in identifying our wicked Tomas and we sent them prints from the same negative."

She thought and added, "My employer, Dr. Campbell, could tell you more about all this. I confess I'm new here and I wouldn't want to go through his desk in the back without his permit."

He soothed, "No need to, ma'am. Not for nit-picky dates as to postmarks, leastways. We know when *los rurales* captured someone they put in for the bounty on him by pumping him full of lead. Whoever they ambushed must have walked right into it like a lamb to the slaughter, but that raises a heap of questions my boss couldn't care less about. For should it turn out true as it reads, on the face of all the evidence, I've been sent on a snipe

147

hunt by a petty crook buying time with big fibs."

He explained how the Fresno Kid's erstwhile cellmate had either played a pal false or had a heap of fun with a gullible lawman. She tried to help by soothing, "That sick former friend may have thought he was telling the truth. Tom Baker could have said something about heading back to this valley in the wake of all that greater trouble to the south, and he'd have naturally had some way to fool the law in mind, such as staging his own death and internment.

"That remains to be seen, with the help of these prints," he added soberly, putting both in a side pocket of his tweed coat as he mused half to himself, "Say the Mex *rurales* had a cadaver worth a bounty on their hands. Say even one of 'em had heard the otherwise worthless rascal had been raised gentle and afforded a good education. That would account for an otherwise awfully fancy embalming job, to give 'em time to double-check and . . . Damn, sorry about cussing, Ma'am, it would make no sense to take extra trouble preserving the features of a dead outlaw after you'd shot someone else in his place, would it?"

She said she didn't think so, either. He sighed and confided, "No matter how you slice it, I got to scout me up an exhumation order, a search warrant, or whatever it takes to get folk to open a family tomb for you."

She looked horrified and declared, "Oh, you poor man! I know some who rode down to pay their respects to the family a good three or four months ago, and we've had a very hot summer this year!"

He said, "It's my job, grim as it's inclined to get at times. While I'm still here, admiring that swell lilac sachet instead, I got another question you might be able to answer without messing in anyone's private desk. You say you know local folk who attended that funeral down by the Kern. I understand it was open casket."

She nodded but said, "I wasn't there. I understand it was ghastly. They had lots of flowers and that sweet-smelling incense the Chinee and Papists go in for, but poor Hannah Kellermann says she was sure she'd faint before they finally shut the lid over his disfigured face. She said he looked as if he'd been tanned to cordovan leather."

Longarm said, "I reckon in a way he had. Am I correct in supposing this Miss Kellermann knew the cuss, personal, before

148

they pumped him full of bullets and preservatives?"

The ash blonde nodded but hesitated before she confided, "Very well, albeit I'm sure some of it's just spiteful gossip, knowing the poor thing as I do. Hannah Kellermann sat next to Tom Baker in her senior year at Fremont High and, well, she's never denied being sweet on him, poor thing. She cried all over me the evening she got back from his funeral. She said it all seemed such a waste and how different she felt it might have gone had only he had a good woman to influence him."

Longarm smiled thinly and said, "She might know better how lucky she might have been if someone let her read the rascal's yellow sheet. Whether that's him in the box or not, he was one bad apple. Do you reckon she had an enlarged print, such as you just gave me, at hand as she viewed them discolored remains?"

The blonde blinked and said, "Of course not. I imagine she has her old yearbook at home and I just told you she went to school with the boy and had higher hopes about him."

He said he'd as soon ask the lady personal about her last hasty glimpse of an older cuss who'd been tanned to cordovan. So she got out an address book and wrote it down exact for him on a slip of foolscap. As he put it away with a nod of thanks he asked if there was any Mister Kellermann he had to study about greeting, badge in hand.

She shook her blond head and said, kindly as possible, "Our Hannah is destined to die an old maid, I fear. She got out of school seven years ago at an age my own dear mother had already married."

He didn't ask her how old she was and how come she was still single, if she was. Lots of working gals left their rings off just to confuse customers who might otherwise act more picky.

First things still coming first, he went next to the Western Union to see if Billy Vail had wired any new instructions. They did have a wire from Denver on tap for him. But all it said was that they were still pawing through the files for otherwise easygoing gals who drove hat pins up nostrils and that Peewee Folsom, bless his sticky-sweet hide, had come down with some sort of diabetic fit and been transferred to County General, under guard, of course, where the sawbones said it was a sometimes thing. Sometimes they snapped out of it for a while and sometimes they didn't. So that left Longarm muttering, as he left the telegraph office, "Where in the hell are we going, to do what? At this rate we won't have even one witness who says that Fresno Kid is alive and everyone else we talk to swears he's dead!"

Chapter 17

Miss Hannah Kellermann lived alone on the top floor of a carriage house on the respectable but not too fancy side of the tracks. That didn't surprise him. He'd been told she was a spinster gal and what she might do for a living was none of his beeswax. What did surprise him was her looks. Without thinking hard about it he'd expected a rapidly aging spinster with a German name to look somewhat plain and way more, well, German. The more funny than plain-looking little gal who opened the door at the head of the stairs in floppy Mex sandals and a paint-spattered blue smock looked more like a Gypsy fortune teller on her day off. But she was polite enough, once Longarm showed his I.D. and told her what he was after. She waved him on in—that was when he noticed the pencils and artist's brushes in her dust mop of coal black hair—and waved him to a sort of Turk's divan along one slanted wall of her queer-shaped quarters as she told him to feel right at home whilst she fetched them some refreshments.

That's what she called a jug of dry red wine, a heel of sour-dough bread, half a ball of Dutch cheese and a bunch of purple grapes, all on a prospector's gold-pan: refreshments.

As she sat down beside him, the pan in her lap as she crossed her legs like she was used to sitting so low in skirts, if that smock qualified as proper attire for a white woman, he noticed the oil painting she'd been working on, closer to her one north facing window. The easel was turned partway from him. He could still see she had some old Spanish mission about right with its baroque bell tower smiling in the California sunshine against a cloudless sky a mite more turquoise than the real sky outside. The oranges hanging from that live oak in the foreground seemed a mite orange and live oak leaves were never Kelly green but, all in all, he had to say she sure painted swell.

She said, "Thank you. I know there's nothing quite so grand in this big dusty valley but this is the picture of California that sells back in Bavaria. I've an uncle in Munich who sells my paintings on commission as fast as I can ship them to him."

She handed him some cheese on hand-busted bread and helped herself to some wine from the neck of the jug before she added, "To tell the truth I'm getting tired of that dumb old mission and those dumb old orange trees. But Fresno folk won't pay half as much for my pictures of Bavarian farmhouses and to tell the truth they take longer. Have some dago red."

He washed down some bread and cheese with the just right wine, telling himself it was no worse than kissing a hostess, French, before he declared, "I'm glad to see you're doing so well on your own, Miss Hannah. As to any plans you might have made about a future with your classmate, Tomas Ortega Baker . . ."

"He was dead, to me, long before the greasers killed him. I know I went to his funeral. I know I cried, coming and going, but what can you expect, I'm artistic, and there was a time, way back before he started raping other women, after spurning me, I might have had some foolish plans."

She took another swig of wine, he noticed she wasn't eating, and demanded, "Why not? He was an Ortega on his mother's side and handsome as sin, the redheaded son of a bitch. So sure I'd have gone all the way with him, had only he asked, but, no, he had to laugh at my monkey face and attack that much older schoolmarm down where he'd first learned to read and write, from *her*, for Gawd's sake! Have you ever?"

He said, "Nope. None of my schoolmarms tempted me that much and, back up, what was that about *red hair*, just now?"

She shrugged and said, "Well, not fire engine red. More that shade betwixt titian and . . . hold on, I'll show you."

She did, springing to her feet to run over to the window and get cracking with her oil painter's palette as he got out one of those black and white prints, muttering, "I sure wish they'd invent some way to photograph colors. The officious description I read gives his hair color as brown and from this print I had it pictured a right dark brown, almost black, to go with his sort of Spanish features."

She went on mixing paint as she told him, "He took after his mother's side and none of them looked too greaser. They were probably from the north of their old country, like lots of the Californio ranchers."

She returned to the divan with a flat mixing stick freshly painted the same shade those old masters had used for more refined-looking folk he'd still call redheads. The doubtless more artistic Hannah said, "Tom, his late mother and that snooty young aunt of his all had the same shade of hair and chocolate eyes."

Then she swallowed a real gulp of wine and demanded, "What damned difference does it make? I never even kissed him and you'd have to stand on a chair to kiss his stuck-up Tia Felicidad so why don't you kiss me, you mean thing?"

The thought had in fact occurred to him about the time he'd decided she couldn't be wearing anything under that blue artist's smock, but she did sort of remind one of a little mischievous monkey, now that she'd brought it up, and he was on duty in broad ass daylight, cuss her frisky ways.

On the other hand, he was questioning a federal witness at the moment and the standing instructions were to be considerate as possible to possibly innocent folk. So he tossed his hat aside as she got rid of that pan, and, as they met friendly with their lips, hers felt far from innocent. She sucked his tongue almost painfully as she grabbed his free hand to show him what she was wearing under that smock. Since she'd started out with her legs crossed, spreading wider as they flopped back across the artistic jumble of pillows, he didn't have to aim to get two fingers in to the knuckles, right where she seemed to want 'em, and she sure seemed a hairy little monkey.

As they came up for breath whe whimpered, "Oh, I'm so ashamed of my body and in a north light, too! Promise you won't look at me?"

He didn't get to answer before she'd slipped the smock off over her head and it was too late. She looked mighty fine to him, in her own fuzzy way, as she threw herself flat on her back, cupping her funny-looking little breasts up to him as she smiled, eyes closed, and begged, "That's it, darling, keep your eyes closed, like me."

He saw no need to as he swiftly shucked his gun rig and duds, inspired by her as well as those recent temptations in that chili joint and photography studio. The mysteriously dark and simian German gal was desirable and sort of repulsive at the same time.

But by now he had an erection he'd have shoved in most anything that didn't look like it bit. He could tell she was as inspired when he got aboard to rub bellies with her, her's being almost hairy as his, and she wrapped her agile arms and legs around him to swallow him alive with her fortunately toothless love maw.

She felt more girlish inside, so it made for a pleasure something like enjoying her dry wine and overaged cheese on sourdough bread served crude. She smelled clean and screwed she-male as some pagan fertility goddess. But he still had to bite his tongue to keep from laughing at those chest hairs sprouting from around her bright pink nipples. It was easier when he kissed her with his own eyes closed.

For she was sweetly she-male at that end as well, despite her wiry not quite womansome or even human parts squirming under him everywhere else. The contrast sure made her hungry little twat feel swell.

Meanwhile he had an early afternoon train to catch and the morning was already better than half shot. He knew it was considered rude to eat and run. It was even ruder to fuck and fly. So he tried to split the difference by pounding her to glory pronto and then spin her on his spit to keep going, dog style, without stopping, as she pounded the pillows with clenched fists and begged him not to scoff at her hairy rump.

So he didn't. At least she had no tail to wrap around his waist as they continued this odd, for him, experience. It felt much the same as humping a petite enthusiastic young lady of the human persuasion, as long as he kept his eyes closed. But by broad daylight a man could swear he was committing beastiality. She even had a streak of black fuzz up her spine and he wondered whether she shaved her monkey face. For no armies that had marched through Germany or anywhere else in any history book *he'd* read could account for the artistic little gal's hairy hide. She had to be a sport of nature, like those bearded ladies you saw in freak shows. They said the one who worked for Barnum was real, with natural she-male organs and, most likely, feelings.

He knew how cruel Comanche and school kids could tease and she'd already mentioned the no-good but good-looking schoolboy she'd been sweet on sneering at her. From his yearbook picture and later record it was safe to say Tomas Ortega Baker had sneered nasty. So as he could tell by her internal contractions she was fixing to come some more he rolled her over again to

154

finish right, and tender, with her little fuzzy body all aquiver and her innards all aflame whilst he ejaculated in her.

Later, as they drifted back down from the clouds in that rosy afterglow of a great lay, Hannah sighed and murmured, "That was just what I've been needing since a certain art dealer left town with a consignment of alpine scenes, the son of a bitch."

Longarm didn't want to know that much about another man's organ grinder where his now reposed. So he softly said, "I hope you've got over the Fresno Kid. I'd like to go over that last time you think you saw him, as they were nailing the lid on his box."

She grimaced, not a pretty sight, and said, "I think they screwed the top in place. It was one of those really fancy mahogany caskets with silver handles and all. That Felicidad Carillo thinks she's so fine, with her dramatic veil, real black silk and all. Everyone knows that in life she'd always looked down on Tom's poor mamma for wedding an Anglo of modest means. And of course, after he started getting in trouble after we all graduated from school she never spoke to him again. They say she bailed him out of jail, or had her fancy lawyer do so, after he'd . . . You know, with that old grammar school teacher he had odd urges for. But when he rode down to the Ortega homespread to thank her she refused to receive him. What would you call a kinswoman like her?"

"A lady," replied Longarm, adding, "Of the proud grandee persuasion, that is. She'd naturally put family duty above disgust and not too many aunts would feel proud of a nephew who raped schoolmarms."

He reached across Hannah's hairy naked charms for the duds piled nearby on her floor as he felt for a smoke, saying, "You mentioned it seemed odd, your ownself. There was something odd about that older woman he mistreated?"

Hannah shrugged and said, "He hardly raped anyone in front of me and the rest of the class of '73. They say she had an understanding with a top hand who worked for Miller Lux, even though she must have been at least thirty at the time. The silly woman swore she'd been a virgin when a boy she'd taught in grammar school came back at a time her true love was off on spring roundup to confess he'd always had a hankering and, when that didn't work, throw her down across a school desk and ravage her good. I'll bet she led him on, at least a little. For I used to flirt like anything with Tom and he always treated me like a lady—an ugly lady—the handsome brute."

Longarm had time to count in his head as he lit their smoke. The yellow sheets had Baker going bad enough to get arrested right after he finished school to find himself a sudden orphan with no particular future. Some said he'd been a nasty little shit, growing up. Longarm lit the cheroot, shook out the match, and mused aloud, "His Anglo dad died of some ague when he was attending that grammar school down closer to the rest of his maternal kin, his father being a first or second generation German, no offense."

She sniffed and said Baker wasn't a German name and that Tomas had always bragged on being a real Californio. He let her have a drag on their cheroot as he mused on, "Be that as it may, we can forget about paternal kin he didn't have in these parts. If his mother was the eldest sister, who'd inherited the Ortega grant, an older brother?"

She handed the cheroot back as she said, uncertainly, "We're speaking of another child when I was too young to notice, but I think old Don Ortega was still alive when Tom's mama was suddenly widowed, and they say there was an awful row. She moved up here with what her proud grandee family called her gringo bastard but I do think someone in the family must have sent her money from time to time. Tom was always well-dressed and had plenty of spending money when I went to high school with him. Why are we talking so much about a lot of dead people, darling?"

He blew a thoughtful smoke ring and replied, "Trying to make sure they're all dead. I'll take your word on Baker's parents and I have no call to argue land titles with proud grandees, as long as they haven't held up any banks or raped anybody. Alive or dead, the Fresno Kid would never wind up with all that Ortega-Carillo land if he knocked his Tia Felicidad up before he shot her."

Hannah giggled and said, "You wouldn't suggest such a risk to a man's privates if you'd seen her at Tom's funeral, the frigid bitch. I'll bet any man who could get it in her would lose his poor pecker to frostbite. I went up to her and told her I'd gone to school with her nephew and all and she just looked through her veil at me as if she'd just smelled something disgusting."

Longarm suggested, "She might have. Her nephew had been shipped a good ways in warm weather, if that was her nephew.

So now I want you to study hard and draw on your artistic skills as you picture that dead face in your mind's eye."

She said that was easy, considering how upset the sight had made her feel. But he insisted, "Dead or alive, Tom Baker had regular features. He was what you could call a type. Nice-looking folk fall into fairly regular types because as soon as our features get unusual enough we're considered ugly."

She bitterly demanded, "You mean like me?"

To which he could only reply, "You just different enough to be . . . interesting, but you're helping me make my point. If you were just a tad less . . . artistic, you'd fit into a whole herd of pretty young brunettes without standing out worth mention. If someone were to put you and a couple of others of your general type on exhibit, after even a moderate amount of taxidermy . . ."

"Glugh!" She cut in, tweeking him playfully as she insisted she still felt pretty lively and adding, "You're forgetting Tom's very unusual hair. I remember noting at the time, as a technician used to mixing colors, how close my dead classmate's hair matched the unusual shade of his snooty presiding aunt. You could see it under her veil and the goofy Spanish riding hat she'd pinned atop her fancy hairdo."

"Hair can be dyed," he pointed out.

She began to fondle him more suggestively as she repressed a yawn and said, "Well, of course she probably touches up her hair, the old bag. She has to be forty if she's a day, for all her fancy airs and frosty beauty. If she's kept her looks at all natural she owed it all to refrigeration!"

Longarm chuckled at the notion but said, "I was talking about the redhead in the box. Even a society matron would attract some comment if she changed the natural color of her hair entire. But we were told the Fresno Kid had been planning for some time to fake his own death. So what if he and his pals took their time finding some poor cuss who might pass for another with his hair dyed red and his face tanned almost black?"

She said she'd already told him how upset the sight had made her and added she'd have never felt so upset if she hadn't once considered acting this friendly with the poorly preserved rascal in question. Then she demanded he rise in the presence of a lady. It was easy, skilled as she was with her artistic right hand. So in no time at all she seemed to have gotten on top and at this rate he'd never get to Visalia in time to call on the county sheriff's department and still catch that combo leaving Visalia around four.

Hannah seemed to take it as a compliment when he rolled her on her back some more and hooked a wiry leg over each of his elbows to spread her wide and polish her off deep and sudden. She was rolling her unkempt black mob all over, Lord only knew where those pencils and such had flown by now, as he went over railroad timetables in his own head whilst pounding away, distracted enough to keep going without coming, even though it was starting to feel grand, whether he missed that fucking train or not.

Chapter 18

He almost missed the court clerk he was after when he finally made it to the federal courthouse just before the noon break. Then things picked up for a change when he saw the skinny balding cuss about to leave for lunch was a fellow federal employee he'd once met friendly up in Frisco in connection with another federal case entire.

The somewhat older clerk's handle was MacIntosh, Ewen J., but he preferred to be called Tosh. So that's what Longarm called him as they went across the way to a fair-sized saloon Tosh vouched for as a place serving lager beer and a swell free lunch at a reasonable price.

Longarm liked lager beer, steamer beer, and most any beer but that inky Irish brew even the Irish turned their noses up at when they could afford porter and such. As he and Tosh bellied up to the bar to order tall schooners, it being a mite risky to sample the free lunch in a strange saloon after ordering a mere tumbler, Longarm told the court clerk what he really wanted.

They both knew no lawman worth his salt pestered a judge for papers the court clerk could manage if he was a real pal. But Tosh smiled dubiously and said, "I dunno, Longarm. I'd be risking my ass rubber-stamping anything that likely to stir up serious litigation and I doubt any federal judge this far out of range will issue you any exhumation orders on a rich boy planted two counties off!"

Longarm sipped some suds and insisted, "The Fresno Kid, or whoever that is, wasn't buried. He's just setting there in a family tomb on private land. So I'd say a simple search warrant would be enough to just get me through a damned door and coffin lid. It's his widowed aunt who's rich and she spends most of her time up Frisco way. So we're talking about me bullshitting my way past at most her segundo and he'd likely a Californio who's learned to get along with our kind if he's still alive at this late date."

Tosh glanced uncomfortably away and said, "I see they're serving salami today. I'm new in this valley and I still know all too well who the widow Carillo is, Longarm. She's got her own opera box up in Frisco and they say when she's sitting there the soprano makes an extra effort to hit every note just right."

As they carried their schooners down that way Tosh added, "You'd do better asking Kern County for a writ. You've no idea how we feds have had to pull our horns in since that stinking mess at Mussel Slough and, in case you didn't know, Mussel Slough runs between here and that family tomb you're so casual about busting into."

Longarm reached for some sliced swiss and wrapped it around a pickled pig's foot as he replied, "The Fresno Kid was down Mexico way when you boys got carried away at Mussel Slough. I suspect he'd heard the law was walking on eggs on his old home range and so whether it worked or not he made mention of slipping back this way."

He bit into his improvised snack, washed some of it down with lager, and continued, "No county justice of the peace is about to issue me a search warrant a federal court's afraid to have me serve on a mess of household help backed by ranch hands. Even if one was, the case is federal. Kern County has no just cause to care who's been laid to rest near its southern border."

Tosh said, "I thought your man was wanted all up and down the San Joaquin?"

Longarm shook his head, swallowed, and explained, "Not in his home county. Like Frank and Jesse, the otherwise dumb shit was smart enough to raise hell anywhere but the vicinity of his dear mamma's kin. I need more details, now that there seems to be some odd she-male angle to this case that still makes my nose tingle every time I think about it. But as far as the yellow sheets I've read on the rascal show, his first serious offense took place a county north, in Tulare County."

"The same as Mussel Slough," sighed Tosh, reaching for more cold cuts as he decided, "Not for love nor money, *amigo mio*. Those fucking congressmen are bound for glory and reelection on the blood spilled at Mussel Slough. My court's not about to tangle with a powerful Californio clan as well. They say the widow Carillo has at least two state senators, one of 'em single, after her, ah, opera box as we speak."

Longarm started to go on about the Fresno Kid raping a teacher way back when, not fighting over land more recent in any damned county. But he saw he was wasting time and he'd already done that a heap, more artistically, in Hannah Kellermann's bohemian garret. So he polished off his pig's foot, made a hasty Genoa and cheese on pumpernickel for the road, and said he had to get it on down the road.

Tosh pleaded, "Don't let's part unfriendly, *amigo mio*. You know I'd be proud to, if only I could. But I just got transferred in and barely know anyone. I think the judge they assigned me to just got in from Virginia City his fool self. So . . ."

"I know how a whitewash works," Longarm cut in, adding, "I got put through one of them congressional hearings a spell back. In my case my conscience was clear and Marshal Vail was man enough to back me. So we didn't pull that shell game, transferring folk in and out of our federal district 'til nobody on earth would ever be able to rightly say what might or might not have happened."

Tosh smiled sheepishly and said, "You just described the final resolution of Mussel Slough in a nutshell game. I'll bet a hundred years from now they'll still be trying to decide who was in the wrong or in the right."

Longarm finished his beer, put down the empty schooner, and flatly declared, "Folk acted stupid on both sides. You don't fight a court order by gathering an armed mob instead of at least one good lawyer. When you find yourself facing an armed mob refusing to obey a court order you don't throw down on 'em and indulge in open warfare, however modest. That's what we've got us an army and navy to do. But what's done is done, with loss of rash blood on both sides and praise the Lord I only got to worry about other assholes entire."

Tosh walked him out front where they parted friendly and Longarm saw he still had time, if he got cracking. So he legged it back to that friendly livery where he'd stored his saddle, Winchester and such. They still had it handy in their tack room. He slipped the kid on duty a dime and stepped back out in the noonday sun with his laden McClellan braced on his left hip, just behind his cross-draw .44-40. Then Deputy Mandalian and a fancier-dressed dude he hadn't met before popped out of the saloon across the way to head him off.

Mandalian said, "Uncle Sam, this here's Mr. Marvin from Frisco, down to investigate that hotel fire you were in for his insurance outfit."

Longarm nodded friendly at the insurance dick but kept going as he explained, "I ain't trying to be rude. I'm trying to catch a train. Feel free to tag along and I'll be proud to tell you all I know, since it ain't much."

The well-dressed Marvin listened intently as Longarm told them about the funny telephone call and all the noise and confusion that followed. Marvin said, "I wish there was some way we could stick the Justice Department for the total loss that followed an obvious attempt on the life of a federal agent. But I suspect we'd lose that one in front of your average federal judge. Mandalian, here, tipped us off to sift the ashes for wires the telephone company never strung. No sale. A wire is a wire once the building it was strung through has burnt to the ground."

Mandalian said, "We found that gun, though. Schofield .45 as might have been stole from some Army post. There was some human teeth and what could have been shards of a well-baked skull nearby. You know that other gent who saved that young mother whilst you saved her jewels and baby? Well, he might have been with the one you shot a few eye blinks later. We've managed to talk to everyone else who got out last night, they all say thanks to you. But the cuss who carried that barefoot gal down the stairs, bodily, has vanished from human ken like the snows of yesteryear."

Longarm chuckled and said, "They usually run in pairs. Few hired guns have the balls to lone wolf it."

Marvin said he found it hard to buy a paid assassin saving anyone from a burning building and asked, "Why would a common criminal do a thing like that?"

Longarm said, "I asked him to. If he recognized me in all that confusion he was cooler about it than his sidekick. You may know insurance but you don't know human nature if you think it's that unusual to act decent by instinct. When I saw a pretty little gal about to go up in smoke I never told myself I ought to save her because I was an honest lawman. I just did what came natural to our species. That Professor Darwin says we're mostly descended from fairly thoughtful brutes. The brute I handed her to picked her up and carried her to safety partly because he was headed that way in any case and no doubt because he'd only been paid to murder me and she was a she-male of his species screaming for help. They say Frank and Jesse are both kind to their women and respectful to their mamma. I met a gal one time who's sure she danced with Billy The Kid down New Mexico way and she reports he tried not to step on her toes or dribble tobacco juice down the front of her party frock."

Mandalian said, "That's the way we read it. It's too bad the gal he saved was too busy weeping and wailing about her infernal kid to pay more attention to him. She says her eyes were all watersome from the smoke and that once they were outside he just set her down and walked away, cussing under his breath. She figured at the moment he was merely chagrined about losing his own baggage to the fire. Then she says she forgot about everything 'til you showed up with not only her baby but her baggage. I'd go see her and see what she meant about owing you her everything, Uncle Sam. She ain't bad looking, cleaned up, and the only other man with any claim on her, she says, is way down in Pueblo de Los Angeles."

Longarm told the sardonic Mandalian he was shocked by such a suggestion and they parted soon after at the railroad depot, just in the nick of time. The southbound local he wanted was pulling out as he caught sight of its rear car in motion and broke into a dead run to catch up, easy enough, and toss his saddle and stuff over the rail of the observation platform before he sprang aboard after it.

Nobody else was using the observation platform, so he left his load where it lay and stepped inside the club car to enjoy a sit-down with a schooner of steamer before the conductor came back to punch tickets.

Once he had, Longarm showed his I.D. and courtesy pass, which worked half the time. This being one of them, the conductor asked if Longarm was headed to join that big posse down to Visalia. When Longarm asked to be told more he was told, "We got a tip the Evans Sontag gang might be aiming to stop the Blue Dog train. If they do they'll be sorry, this time. Got us a whole heap of surprises who'll be riding in the forward boxcars, with their horses as well."

Longarm whistled and said he'd heard something about some sneaks talking odd about the Blue Dog train. When he asked whether those lawmen were Tulare or Kern County the conductor snorted, "In an election year? Surely you jest. The posse will be led by our own railroad dicks with the help of some adventurous cowhands who never liked sodbusters or mining men to begin with."

Longarm didn't ask him to elaborate. Tosh MacIntosh had already remarked on the numbers of farm folk already sore about the government picking on Kit Evans' sodbusting in-laws. Mining men closer to the Sontag brothers outnumbered cow folk better than ten to one in the big valley, now. He was almost sorry he'd been so slick about obvious admirers of the halfass Robin Hoods trying to keep him away from the scene of crimes to come. No matter how the battle went, a heap of voters were sure to piss and moan about betrayals of innocents and hired assassins in the pay of the rich. As if the owners of that Glendale train should have waved their hats in the air and raised three rousing cheers when Cole Younger, Frank and Jesse stopped it that bright moonlit night.

They were going to get Frank and Jesse, Evans, the Sontags and Billy, just as they'd already gotten the Youngers, Joaquin, Three Fingered Jack and all those other halfass Robin Hoods. And no matter how many the law caught up with, the little folk who admired 'em made up halfass ballads full of whoppers so's some other halfass could mount up to ride the owlhoot trail 'til he, in turn, turned into a legend of a gallant desperado too good for the law 'til he was betrayed by a woman or a false-hearted friend.

Meanwhile the run down to Visalia only took an hour and change. So once he'd stored his saddle and such with the stationmaster he felt free to try again for that search warrant.

Visalia, the seat of Tulare County, was named for a fancy center-fire stock saddle, or vice versa. So it was still considered a cow town despite all the recent settlers flocking in to try farming the fertile but bone-dry southern quarter of the big central valley. You still saw more stock than flat or even McClellan saddles aboard the ponies tied up along the main street, albeit in truth many a plow jockey suffered a strange sea change west of the Big Muddy and might wear wooly chaps to a grange dance if he wasn't watched close on his evenings off.

It was safe to assume many cow ponies were the real McCoy, though. For old Henry Miller and his slaughterhouse-owning pard,

Charles Lux, had a heap of hands riding the cattle empire they owned outright or controlled by way of old Hank Miller's eye for water rights and railroad sidings. It didn't much matter who might or might not run a few head on public land in competition with you when you held the water cows needed to wash down all that free but sun-dried grazing, along with most anywhere you might want to poke 'em aboard a market train.

As if to prove the gossip he'd heard clean over in Denver, a young cowhand fell in beside Longarm as he strode the streets of Visalia to murmur, "I can see by the crush of your Stetson and that gun you didn't think I could see that you ain't no farmer. But pass the word that the powers-that-be don't want us taking sides in that feud betwixt the railroad and the farmers."

He dropped back before Longarm could assure him he hadn't ridden all the way from Denver with his Colorado crush to take part in their private struggle for control of the San Joaquin Valley.

He suspected he saw why the Miller Lux interests were resisting the temptation to take sides against the ever-growing numbers of farm folk pushing the open range ever further up the big valley. Working cowhands disliked fence-stringing farmers, with good reason. But the cattle barons they worked for didn't raise cows as pets or ride around singing songs about all that wide-open range.

Open range stayed open because nobody had yet found a better use for it. Livestock could range and even thrive on land too poor, or dry, for more profitable food or fiber to be grown on.

Longarm knew some parts of the West, such as the Nebraska sand hills, would never be used for anything but grazing by anyone but optimistic assholes. He could see just as clear that the days of the cowboy and even the wheat farmer were numbered along the San Joaquin. The fertile soil and long growing season simply conspired against anyone out to compete with any neighbor able to get irrigation water to such a potential jungle.

Those who got in on the ground floor with irrigated acres would wind up with more acres as they proved Professor Darwin's notions about survival of the slick and strong against the dumb and helpless. Meanwhile old Miller and Lux were already slick and strong. They'd control ever more water and plow under ever more marginal grazing as they slowly laid off those cowhands they'd just ordered not to take sides. They'd already seen the

165

farming side would be the winning side with a powerful thirst for water as well as the political power of their voting weight.

It cost less to market water than cows if a gent could hold on to his water rights, and the Big Four of California railroading had already shown how expensive it could be to hang on to political plums with the bulk of the voters pissed at you. So there was no mystery about the biggest outfit along the San Joaquin sitting out the showdown. The remaining cattle outfits, Anglo and Californio alike, had less to gain and more to lose if their marginal range went under the plow as one big irrigated truck garden. So what they might or might not do was up for grabs and, praise the Lord, no concern of the Denver District Court.

He found the county courthouse in Visalia with no trouble, and, since he was pressed for time and doubted he'd be making many arrests in Tulare County, he asked for directions to their court clerk instead of their sheriff.

He found Tulare County's answer to Tosh MacIntosh a much older gent with specs thick enough to pass for the bottoms of two shot glasses. He'd been fussing over a pad of legal-sized foolscap with a big fat pencil, inscribing block letters big enough to read across the room if one wasn't stuck with his eyesight. He waved Longarm to a seat near his rolltop desk and accepted a cheroot with a gracious nod as he asked what he could do for his country. He said he was seldom called upon by federal lawmen.

He listened intently as Longarm brought him up to date in as few words as possible. It still took them the better part of their smokes. Then the sweet smiling old cuss, who admitted they called him Blinky said, "I'd be proud to have my girl prepare you a search warrant and there's an outside chance we could get a Tulare County J.P. to sign it for you. After that it ain't worth the paper it's written on in another county entire. Why don't you ask down in Bakersfield? That's the seat of Kern County, where they've entombed the mean young son of a bitch."

Longarm said Bakersfield was out of his way and asked Blinky the odds on any Kern County J.P. bucking the widow Carillo.

Blinky chuckled dryly and said, "You're right. She's an Ortega as well. Neither clan's main stem is centered in Kern County, of course. The top Don Carillo holds sway around Santa Barbara whilst the Ortega, too respected by the spics to be called a Don, sold off his Rancho Nuestra Senora del Refugio back in the sixties, but he reinvested the money smart and claims direct

166

descent from Cortes and gets to say who may or may not be inducted into the California Pioneers. You don't ask to join, they invite you, if they damn well feel like it."

Longarm hadn't come for a lecture on matters that only mattered to stuck-ups, as far as he could see. So he said, "No offense, but I ain't interested in how high the Fresno Kid might be on his maternal totem pole. I just want to see if he's dead or alive."

Blinky nodded, reached in a pigeonhole of his desk and banged on a sort of hotel bell as he drew out a neatly folded form of legal bond.

A buck-toothed and middle-aged gal with a great figure came in to see what they wanted. Blinky called her Mildred and asked her to fill the warrant out. Longarm had thought he'd known what the older man had been scrawling on that legal pad as they talked. He knew he'd guessed right when Blinky tore off half a sheet and handed it to his stenographer as well, saying, "Here's the property to be searched along with the probable cause. Don't type in any J.P.'s name. I'm still trying to come up with how we'll ever get it signed."

Mildred left. Blinky turned back to Longarm to confide, "I hope you know no lawyer worth his salt would let you serve that on the widow Carillo."

Longarm nodded and confided right back, "I understand she's up in Frisco at the moment. With any luck, the Californios I have to bluff won't read English as well as your average lawyer."

Blinky chuckled and said, "That's why Mildred will have your worthless writ typed up in no time. I'd really like to see that young villain caught, if he's still alive. When we heard the Mex *rurales* shot him down like a dog in Nogales a heap of folk thought he'd died way too gentle, the spitesome little shit!"

Longarm brightened and asked, "Did you know him, personal?"

So there went a bright idea when Blinky confessed, "Not in the flesh. He was too slick to stand trial in Tulare County. Coming from such fine old Californio stock, on his mamma's side, he was turned loose on low bail despite or mayhaps because of all the talk of a lynching bee. Naturally, as soon as he got loose, he run down to his rich and willsome Tia Felicidad along the Kern and, like I said, Kern County just don't arrest anyone the widow Carillo don't want arrested."

He took a thoughtful drag on his cheroot before he added in a musing tone, "Of course, Felicidad Ortega wasn't the widow

Carillo then. She married Chuck Carillo a few years later, after her worthless nephew had robbed that bank up in Fresno and proven how bad he really was, even to the likes of her."

Longarm nodded and said, "That first and apparently only offense she forgave him would have been the rape of some schoolmarm, right?"

Blinky growled, "Not some schoolmarm, a sweet little virgin gal who'd just got engaged, a mite late in life, to a promising top hand. Her name was Ruth Cooper. Don't remember his. He took to drink and got laid off by Miller Lux, afterwards. Some say it was over what Tom Baker did to his true love whilst others figure it was because she left Tulare County, never to return, once she'd made out the deposition I took down, myself. It wasn't her fault she'd been defiled by a former pupil gone rotten, we all agreed, but naturally no gal would want to stay where folk whispered ahint her back and mean little kids yelled bad words at her through fences."

Longarm asked for a description of the vanished as well as ravaged maiden, and there went another dawning notion when Blinky described a blandly pretty mouse with straw-colored hair. He couldn't make a woman wronged by the Fresno Kid as a dangerous she-male out to protect him in any case, unless, of course, she'd been driven *loco en la cabeza* by Baker's uninvited donging.

He put that aside as just too wild and allowed he was still unclear as to just where the young Tomas Ortega Baker had been, at what time, growing up so bad.

Blinky said, "That's easy without even looking it up. His mamma, the late Concepcion Ortega, her friends called her Connie, run off with a German immigrant prospector and all-around dreamer called Herman Bäcker. He changed it to Baker when he started selling mining supplies instead of mining pure sand a few years later, here in Tulare County. By then they'd had that one awful brat. So they sent him to school with Miss Ruth. Her having just started teaching over between here and the foothills. She said, later, he'd always been a cut-up but a sort of sweet little shit as far as she was concerned. Ain't it just disgusting to consider a bitty grammar school boy sitting there with a bitty hard-on for his pretty young teacher?"

Longarm nodded but urged, "He went to high school further north before he ever did anything to her, right?"

Blinky nodded and said, "She'd have likely been able to fight him off before he graduated from her one-roomer. That would have been about the time his daddy died, of drink, some say. Anyway, Connie Ortega Baker sold his halfass business and moved up to Fresno. Lord knows what she did to make ends meet up there."

Longarm said he'd heard her younger sister, Felicidad, might have sent her some money from time to time. So old Blinky nodded and decided, "Makes sense. Lord knows the sisters were fond of one another and as she later proved, Tia Felicidad just doted disgusting on her disgusting nephew. They say he sucked up to her as if he had a hard-on for her as well, the doubtless incestuous and certainly depraved young shit. Anyway, by the time his mamma had died as well, up Fresno way, his disapproving maternal grandad had died and he might have thought he had his doting aunt and the Ortega grant in the bag. But things went sour once he'd been down with her for a spell after high school. Nobody can say what, for certain, but judging from what he did to that schoolmarm almost as old as his Tia Felicidad, one can guess. The official version given out by her *segundo* at the time, Ramon Duran, was that the kid didn't know shit about working cows and didn't want to learn. At any rate his Tia Felicidad suggested he might be happier trying to sell mining supplies to his dad's old customers and even grubstaked him to his own outlet, up this way."

Blinky saw his stenographer was returning with the typed-up search warrant and finished with, "He didn't want to learn that trade, neither, and we've already talked about him revisiting his old schoolhouse. Now you know as much as I thought I'd ever want to. You'll let us know if that wasn't him they stuck in that family tomb, won't you?"

Longarm promised he would and thanked the two of them as he got to his feet and put the actually worthless but nicely made out writ away.

As he did so Mildred politely protested, "Don't you want to have some judge or J.P. sign that for you, Deputy Long? It won't be valid until it has been."

Longarm and old Blinky exchanged innocent glances. The old clerk soothed, "You let us bigger boys worry about such grown-up matters, Mildred. Deputy Long has a train to catch."

She tried, "Oh, you mean he's going to drop by another office on his way to the depot or something like that?"

To which Longarm could only reply, with a gentle smile, "Yes, ma'am, something like that."

Then he was gone. He'd have plenty of time to scout up a pen and ink along the way and any house servant or ranch hand who'd accept a Tulare County search warrant in Kern County would likely accept the promotion of the late James Butler Hickok to Justice of the Peace.

Chapter 19

Once he got back to the depot with plenty of time to spare they told him he'd have even more. They were making up the Blue Dog combination a mite late as well as unusual that afternoon.

Longarm didn't ask how come they'd be leaving closer to five from a siding on the far side of some empty stock pens. He'd been the one who'd suspected something sinister betwixt Visalia and the Kern, and most everyone knew you loaded ponies aboard a boxcar by way of cattle ramps if you had any handy.

He wasn't planning on riding after train robbers but he still took his saddle and possibles across to the Visalia Livery to hire a spunky roan gelding with Morgan lines lest he wind up lost on foot in the gloaming. They'd said the old Ortega place was close to that river crossing, not smack dab on it.

He still had heaps of time, and now, having something faster than boot heels to get around on, he trotted the roan over to the Western Union, as short a ride as that was, so's they could get to know one another before he had to ride more serious.

The roan neither bucked nor tried to eat his boot tips, so he decided it would do as he dismounted out front, tethered the handsome brute, and strode into the Western Union.

That turned out smarter than planned as well. He had nothing new to report and hadn't expected Billy Vail to chase him to Visalia at nickel-a-word day rates unless it was mighty important.

But as he tore open the telegram the motherly old gal behind the counter handed him, he saw it was. He should have known enough to cuss silent in front of a telegraph lady because she was blushing like a schoolgirl as she asked what had upset him so.

He replied, "I'm sorry I called him that, ma'am. But, you see, we had this captured killer suffering sugar diabetes, back in Denver. So they stuck him in a hospital lest he die before we could hang him."

She asked, "Did he die?"

Longarm sighed and said, "Worse than that, he escaped. My home office says he was naturally under guard but the boys on duty must have thought him sicker than he really felt, the sly cuss."

He put the fairly lengthy message away to read over, later, as he told her, "In sum, they thought I ought to know because I'm out this way after a former cellmate of the slippery cuss and they've traced his movements aboard a westbound train and out of the Ogden yards near the Great Salt Lake by the time they'd put that much together by canvassing everyone who might have noticed."

He picked up a pencil tied to the counter with a string and block-printed a terse answer on one of their pads, saying, "Best send this direct as well as collect, ma'am. My boss is doubtless having fits, and knowing I got my eye peeled for the slippery fugitive may restore his complexion some."

She naturally read his message as she counted the words for her own outfit. She proved she was smart as well as motherly when she asked how anyone might expect to find anyone in a state the size of California.

He explained, "We doubt he headed west to pan for gold in your motherlode country or even pick grapes up around Fresno. My boss wouldn't be asking I watch out for the rascal if he didn't know I was already headed for a possible hideout that same cellmate might have told him about."

She said she'd get right on it. So they parted friendly, and, not wanting to ride his hired pony around in needless circles, he went across the street afoot to restock his smoking habits. Seeing as he had the time to kill, he wet his whistle in the rinky-dink saloon next door.

Most of the regulars seemed to be sodbusters, and the topic of conversation seemed to be Indians. Those wayward Yakuts were still at large: over a dozen grown men along with thrice that many women and children. So far they hadn't killed or even burnt, but that many howling savages running loose, Lord only knew where, had everyone in these parts spooked serious. The Yakuts had lit out mounted from a reserve no more than a hard day's ride away.

Longarm might have eased their minds a mite if he'd really cared to. But he didn't have that much time to kill and it might help the poor confused Yakuts, later, if they managed to scare folk for a change.

For it was usually the other way round when it came to Miwok, Yakuts and other so-called digger Indians in these parts.

None of the many nations west of the High Sierra had been such close kin to the true diggers, mostly Paiute, of the great sagebrush deserts to the east. But the early pioneers had encountered the mild-mannered California nations after dealing with the hardly more dangerous but more pesky desert wanderers haunting the wagon trains across the Great Basin in hopes of stealing something grand as an empty flour sack or a cigar butt with a few good puffs left to it.

The Paiute did dig for roots, insect grubs, some said worms, with their hardwood wands, albeit the ones he'd shared tobacco with now and again vowed they'd much rather dine on pine nuts, rabbit or, the spirits willing, antelope. But in any case most of the California Nations had lived way nicer on sweet camus bulbs and hearty acorn grits he'd tasted and enjoyed. For the dozen or so species of oaks in these parts offered a plentiful substitute for hominy if only an industrious *muk'ela*, which was their word for squaw, took the time and trouble to prepare it right.

White folk tended to dismiss their acorn meal as bitter ground acorns, unfit for anything but hogs, and called a *muk'ela* a *mahala*, which was their word for an easy lay.

They despised the Indians for that as well, naturally. Any good old boy could tell you a woman low enough to give herself to him was mighty low. The Indians had likely figured they were being friendly. They'd been scared shitless as well as confused by the strangers, Anglo and Hispanic alike, who'd taken turns converting them to wear pants and obey the Ten Commandments or, just as often, robbed 'em blind, ravaged their women and kicked the shit out of 'em for asking what all this might have to do with Jesus, meek and mild. The famous winner of the west and pathfinder who'd kept getting lost, now Governor Fremont of Arizona Territory, had found the timid acorn-eaters a real blessing when, after a handful of Mex guerillas had scared him shitless and sent him running, he managed to "pacify" more than one Indian village by firing grapeshot through their grass huts.

Longarm finished his one beer and left the locals to argue the best way to settle the Indian question. He was awfully glad he didn't have to. For there seemed to be total assholes, red and white, who just couldn't agree the sky above 'em both might be blue.

He untethered his hired mount across the way and mounted up to walk it back to the railroad yards. As they came in sight he could see the rising smoke and car tops of that Blue Dog combination across the way. He gave the strange pony plenty of rein to let it pick its way across the ties and tracks. It did all right. Most ponies could, if you didn't treat 'em too bossy. A man with any wrists at all could usually make the ornery ones behave. He'd found it just spooked a good mount when you tried to take every step for it in advance.

On the far side of both the yards and that train he saw other riders had beaten him to the open pens and loading ramps. After that there seemed to be some confusion. For as he walked his own mount in to join the heated discussion, he saw that while some gents dressed cow were loading ponies aboard one boxcar with no apparent dispute, two ladies, mounted sidesaddle, seemed to have been barred from further progress at the foot of another ramp leading up to the car a mite closer to him.

He'd just figured out who that one in the tan whipcord habit and perky derby might be when she youhood him and waved her riding crop as if she was going down for the third time.

Longarm heeled his own mount forward, ticking the brim of his Stetson to Miss Sylvia Moorehead of the *Fresno Observer*, even as he admired the somewhat older beauty she was with. The strange gal was all in black velvet with her almost titian mop pinned up under a flat black Spanish hat. She looked as if someone had just shoved an ice-cold poker up her ass as Sillie introduced them. He was too slick to say an artistic gal had mixed that hair shade for him, almost right. He just howdied the widow Carillo the way a gent was supposed to, meeting up with at least a queen, before he asked the way friendlier newspaper gal what else he might do for her.

Sillie demanded, "You're a U.S. marshal, Custis. Make them let us load our ponies and ourselves aboard this train! They keep saying it's a special run and of course it's a special run. Madame

174

Carillo can't get home any other way and I'm covering a tip about Kit Evans and his band."

The beautiful widow, too close to forty to call young, shifted uncomfortably on her palomino Arab and murmured, "Please call me Felix, Sillie. Madame sounds so stuffy, among friends."

Longarm liked her. You couldn't help it, even when you suspected she was trying to make folk like her. That had to have trying to make folk hate you beat. So he hauled out his wallet and opened it to flash his badge at the two young and one middle-aged hands further up the ramp, afoot, to politely ask why he couldn't escort their little ladies and their ponies aboard a means of public transportation.

The middle-aged cuss opened his buckskin vest wide enough to flash the private agency badge pinned to his dark shirt as he replied in as polite a tone, "This train ain't running public this afternoon. You and your guns are welcome aboard. They'd have my you-know-what for breakfast if I put a lady related to both the Ortegas and Carillos in harm's way!"

Longarm turned back to the gals to say, "He has a good point, ladies. At the risk of giving away more than you already know, Miss Sissie, this train's leaving loaded for bear because the Merry Men of the Green Chaparral might be planning to stop it, this side of Miss Felix's stop."

Sillie insisted, "Pooh, you could bully us aboard if you put your back and real badge into it."

He nodded soberly and said, "I could. I don't aim to. I've never liked bullies to begin with and whether either of your pretty heads are important to anyone else or not I'd be derelict in my duty and downright chagrined if anyone put a bullet in either one."

He suspected Felix, despite her democratic declarations, might be fixing to cloud up and rain all over everybody. So he soothed, "I can tend to anything important down to your place, seeing it is my duty to ride that far with these other boys. Meanwhile, you'd both be safer here in town 'til we see how safe it might be to ride this particular train. Uh, don't either of you have anyone here in Visalia you might spend the night with?"

Sissie said, "Don't act so dumb. Hasn't anyone told you Madame . . . I mean my friend, Felix, owns the biggest hotel and a lot of the rest of Visalia?"

Nobody had. He smiled sheepishly and said so, meeting the widow's big brown eyes as he added, frankly, "They don't pay me

175

to poke my nose in a lady's honest affairs, ma'am. Was I correct in assuming your first withering glance might have something to do with something this newspaper gal's already told you about my awkward reasons for visiting these climes?"

Felix nodded soberly and came as close to pleading as a *señora con sangre azul* was supposed to as she asked, "When does it end? How many times is that poor confused Tomas supposed to disgrace one family?"

He said, "Once we clear up some confusion, ma'am. As I hope this other lady's already explained in more detail than I want to, they want me to make sure they can really drop the subject."

"He's dead," she said, bleakly, meeting his eyes unwinkingly as she insisted, "Did you really think I'd allow them to put some total stranger in our family tomb? My dear father and mother and only sister repose nearby in that very tomb, along with elders and ancestors back to the time we drove our herd over the coast ranges, before that annoying gringo struck gold up by Sutter's mill!"

That was the trouble with Californios. It seemed if you asked one the time you got a history lesson. He said, "I'm sure you thought you were doing the right thing by a black sheep, ma'am. Miss Sissie and others as were there say the funeral was grand and they were just as sure it was your nephew's funeral. Meanwhile, I got this search warrant just in case, but seeing we know one another, now, and . . ."

"You wouldn't dare!" she flared, gripping her riding quirt white-knuckled but holding it polite as she continued, eyes agape and lips gone pale, "I just told you almost everyone I ever held near and dear reposes with Tomas in such little dignity as death leaves us! You mustn't disturb my dead! I won't let you!"

He thought he sounded reasonable and not unkind as he softly assured her, "I've no call to disturb none of the others, Miss Felix. I don't even aim to disturb young Tomas a hair more than I have to. I just want one little peek."

She made a gagging sound and demanded, "After this much time since we closed his casket for the last time, and I mean the last time?"

Longarm didn't think she'd like to hear about some of the disinterments he'd had to take part in. He didn't like to think about them much, himself. So she never heard from him about that time they had to have another look at Honest Abe, after

176

some dishonest rascals had tried to steal his body and they had to make sure they were putting the right coffin back. If she had, she'd have heard more than anyone really needed to know about arsenic embalming. Longarm had been told the familiar face had still been recognizable after all that time, in a sort of disturbing way. Her point about death not allowing anyone all that much dignity had been well taken.

She didn't find his sweet reason so reasonable. She said his request was out of the question. It seemed a mite early as well as rude to inform her he wasn't requesting. He said, "Well, we can talk about that later, in case you'd like your own lawyer present."

Before she could tell him what she thought of that the steam whistle sounded up the line and the older railroad dick, who'd been listening goggle-eyed, yelled, "You'd best get that roan aboard if you'd like to ride with us, Deputy. The ladies and their ponies stay here, and that's that. I'd risk the displeasure of President Hayes in the flesh before I'd take on the Ortegas, Carillos, and C. S. Huntington!"

Felicidad Ortega Carillo was still arguing she was everything he feared but a Huntington as Longarm dismounted to lead his livery mount up the ramp. She hadn't said why she was in such a hurry to get home. By the time he had his roan tethered with the other four ponies facing the far side, the train seemed to be pulling out.

He moved over to the open doorway, shoving one of the younger railroad dicks out of his way as he called back, "Any messages for your *segundo* or *mayodomo*, Miss Felix?"

To which she replied in an angry soprano, "We have our own telegraph line and you'll be sorry if you disturb my dead. That is the word of a *hidalga con sangre azul* and more than a hundred guns on her payroll!"

As the train picked up speed the older railroad dick said, awestruck, "She sounded like she meant that and she was holding back on the time she entertained Lemonade Lucy, the President's wife, when they were visiting Frisco that time. But what the hell, you were bluffing about busting into her family tomb, weren't you?"

To which Longarm could only reply, "I wish I was. But they want me to find out whether her nephew is dead or not and I'll be switched with snakes if I can figure out a way half as certain as simply having a good look at the mysterious mess in that there box!"

177

Chapter 20

The scenery outside got more interesting as the Blue Dog train rolled southwest, ever closer to the south end of the big valley, where the Sierras and coastal ranges collided with the crossways Tehachapis. Long before the tracks had to climb such serious hills the dry range all around commenced to roll a mite, leaving flat patches of sometime lakes covered with tule reeds or sun-baked mud, depending on how alkaline, separated by higher ground overgrown with weeds and brush. The mustard and cheat grass gave way to chaparral as the trail rolled further and the range got bumpier.

Longarm, seated in the half-open doorway of that boxcar with the older railroad dick, agreed most any number of train robbers could be hunkered most anywhere out yonder amid the ever higher chaparral. Most of it grew no higher than halfway up a horse but some of that scrub oak topped twelve feet and of course you could hide a whole Indian town just below the skyline in what looked like open country but rolled like the swells of a lazy sea.

"I'd slow down some if I was trolling for outlaws with this train," said Longarm after judging their rate of progress with the aid of the telegraph poles whipping past.

The railroad dick replied, "We studied on that, setting up back in Visalia. Evans and the Sontags are local boys. For all we know they've rid this very combination in more tranquil times. So it's best we stick with our regular timetable and, even so, we're running late. Anyone who knows enough about railroading to rob trains ought to know a brakeman delayed in leaving a terminal would order more speed, not less, from the engine crew."

Longarm went on staring pensively out across the range to their southwest. The sun was low above the distant lavender ridges of the coastal ranges, now, and the scattered cows they passed looked contented as they stared back with mild interest, chewing their mustard-flavored cuds. It was that lazy time of the day the Hindu folk called "the hour of cow dust," just before the even nicer gloaming, when the temperature felt just right and the light made everything fall easy on the eyes and you wanted things to stay just the way they were a mite longer than they ever did.

Longarm lit another smoke, which wasn't easy at the speed they seemed to be moving now, and opined, "I'd hit anytime now, if I was out to stop a train with enough light to see by and a whole night of owlhoot riding to work with, after. But if they know the timetable this combo runs by, they must be planning to rob her going slower. I know they jerk water at the Kern, where I got to get off. How 'bout other stops along the way?"

The railroad dick said, "She only stops to jerk water that one time on this Blue Dog run. In a pinch she could run the whole eighty miles or so nonstop. But what the hell, the river Kern flows engine water, free. As to other stops, they're all flag."

Longarm didn't have to have that explained. He rode trains a heap. It was the custom along all but the mostly busy Eastern lines to just run through most dinky stops unless ones dispatches told one to pick something up there, drop something off there, or the stationmaster waved a red flag or red lantern, depending on the time of day, to say some paying customer wanted to put himself or whatever aboard.

Thinking about flagging down trains, and whether even the hot-headed Kit Evans would try anything so brassy, Longarm commenced to sing under his breath about that sassy goat who'd et its owner's red shirt and been punished accordingly. It went . . .

> There was this goat, its name was Ned,
>   It et a shirt, the shirt was red,
>   They tied Ned down, to the railroad track,
>   They never expected, to see Ned back,
>   He struggled hard, but not in vain,
>   Coughed up the shirt and flagged the train!

The railroad dick picked up just enough of the familiar ditty to chuckle and decide, "You're right. The crew's pushing this

179

combo too fast for anyone to board her rough and ready from any horse born of mortal mare. There's no timber this side of the Kern stout enough to block the tracks. They're going to have to try flagging."

"Or derailing." Longarm pointed out. He didn't have to elaborate.

The railroad dick grimaced and said, "I wish you hadn't suggested that. They say the Sontags are only in it for the money, but Evans has a personal hard-on for poor old Mister Huntington. He's sworn to shoot what he calls an octopus between the eyes after tearing off all its arms."

Longarm said, "I heard Kit Evans was a mite pissed about Mussel Slough. Some say old C. S. Huntington ordered it."

The railroad dick snorted in disgust and said, "Mister Huntington had no more to do with Mussel Slough than you or me. I know what they say about him being a greedy octopus and all but why in tarnation would even Attila the Hun order a fight betwixt folk he didn't give a shit about?"

"Then you agree with those who say the railroad had already been paid for the disputed land and had no call to horn in?" asked Longarm.

The railroad dick nodded and said, "The land speculators who bid more than the squatters thought fair, couldn't have been blood enemies of the railroad bunch. But it was their grand notion to evict them squatters over by Mussel Slough, starting with Kit Evans' in-laws, the Brewer family."

"Might you know how federal deputies wound up with such a shitty chore?" asked Longarm, knowing all too well how it felt.

The railroad dick said, "I wasn't there, but that part's easy. They couldn't have got any county sheriff who has to run for election to treat a whole heap of county voters so mean. If they asked for help from my private agency I never heard about it. We ain't angels, but we charge a handsome fee in advance when we know we can expect gunplay, and the Mussel Slough squatters had given advance warning they'd resist any attempt to deny them their squatter's rights. That's what they thought they had after they'd just moved on to a disputed land grant, squatter's rights. I wish they wouldn't sell guns to unread folk with stubborn ways and quick tempers."

He got no argument from Longarm on that. One of the things that made his job so interesting was the number of good old boys who'd dropped out of school right after the schoolmarm had taught 'em about this being the land of the free and their right to bear arms. Longarm agreed with both those notions, but he still wished folk would read some of the fine print before they marched on City Hall or Chinatown to demand egg in their beer or pie in the sky.

He let the wind of their swift passage whip some smoke away from his lips and grumbled, "I fail to see how U.S. deputies got stuck with backing that dispossession."

The railroad dick shrugged and suggested, "They say money will buy most anything but poverty."

To which Longarm grimly replied, "That's what I just said. Not the poor deputies. My gun ain't for hire even if I was willing, on my own. Those would-be landlords had to have had a federal writ to demand a federal back up. So how would you go about getting a federal judge or at least a courthouse paper pusher to issue shit about the private ownership of farmland in an incorporated county of a sovereign state?"

The railroad dick said, "Don't ask me. All I have to go by is what I read in the papers and the charges and countercharges have been flying back and forth thick as bullets must have, with more result, at Mussel Slough that fatal day. No federal official any reporter can get to recalls a thing about Mussel Slough, including the paper pusher who rubber-stamped whatever. Depending on which paper you read, any number of deputies you'd like rode on to the Brewer claim armed with a court summons, a show-cause, a dispossess or their truculent dispositions alone."

Longarm didn't answer as he studied on whether he'd have ridden out to pester that stubborn Swede near Denver with no orders on paper to show, had things gone otherwise.

The railroad dick suggested, "The boys who were actually there could tell us, I reckon. Neither the land speculators nor nesters who went down in that sudden outburst ever will."

Longarm made a wry face and decided, "Hell with it. Like the man said, they'll be arguing about Mussel Slough long after we're gone. They've shuffled the deck to cover some asses in higher places and them congressmen investigating the mess have more ways than me to get to the bottom of it, if they really want to."

The railroad dick smiled fondly and declared, "Well, now, I just wouldn't know about that, Longarm. They say you're pretty good at your job, next to your average congressman."

Longarm said, "Thanks. I am. I'm one of the ways they have to investigate with, if they really want to. They're more likely to just let things calm down natural as the one or more responsible worries about his job. Must have a fairly good position with Justice and he's doubtless sweating bullets and shitting green right now."

"I swear we're going even faster, now," said the railroad dick with a puzzled frown as Longarm tore his mind from the troubles of other federal deputies to get back to his own. The telegraph poles and some burros they spooked in passing agreed the train was doing close to a mile a minute, even before the railroad dick declared, "There's a flag stop coming and I don't see how they'd stop this high balling combo no matter what anyone waved at her!"

As some empty loading pens and a sunflower windmill whipped across their line of vision he added, dryly, "See what I mean?"

Longarm stared farther out across the backlit tops of the high chaparral to decide, "Someone's afraid of the dark. They're trying to make the far end of the line this side of sundown and, you know what? At this rate they likely will!"

The railroad dick said, "I noticed, and we don't have no way to signal either end from this infernal boxcar. This is surely one hell of a way to run a railroad if you're out to catch train robbers!"

Longarm couldn't have agreed more. The only way anyone could stop them this side of that jerkwater stop at the Kern sounded awesomely uncomfortable. He drew his dangling legs up to hook his boot heels on the bottom slide rail of the door in hopes of landing somewhere out yonder with both legs still attached if and when this son of a bitching car left the tracks. Cars tended to do that when somebody who just hated railroads yanked some spikes just down the line.

The railroad dick got to his feet to lean out the doorway, shaking his free fist at anyone who might care as he yelled, "What do you think you're doing, you frightened motherfuckers?"

Whatever it was, they didn't seem to be slowing down. Then they were rumbling out across a timber trestle and Longarm called them worse names as he stared down at the muddy width of the whole Kern River for the few eyeblinks it took to leave it behind while Longarm wailed, "That's where I meant to get off, God damn your entire profession of unprofessional assholes!"

The railroad dick said, "Bite your tongue. I ain't in charge of this combination and I'm commencing to wonder just who is! I know both the brakeman and his engineer and I've never seen either act like this before. What could have got into 'em this evening?"

Longarm got to his feet, peeling off his frock coat and getting rid of his hat as he adjusted his gun rig, saying, "Somebody had best find out, before we get to the end of the line. I just hate to run out of track going sixty miles an hour, don't you?"

The older man gasped, "Jesus! How?"

Longarm didn't answer. It was tough enough to get from the deck of a rolling boxcar to its roof, from inside, when no grab irons had been provided by this particular door.

He had to leap up and slightly out, hoping to grab the top slide rail because, otherwise, he was going to go tippy toe through the tops of all that sticker-brush until he likely busted his neck.

Then he had a double backhand grip on the greasy steel. So he swung his lower parts back in, then way back out as, behind him, the railroad dick moaned, "Oh, Sweet Jesus!"

Then, as he'd intended, he'd done a backward pullover, sideways at sixty miles an hour, to lie prone atop the swaying boxcar long enough to wipe his greasy hands reasonable with a kerchief he felt no call to hang on to, after.

As he let the wind have it he eased to a wary crouch. Then there was nothing left to do but procede along the catwalk provided along the tops of the cars for brakemen to use if they really had to. He had to, but he wasn't any damned brakeman and striding against a sixty mile wind on a swaying narrow strip of duck-walking with a Christ-awful drop whipping by on either side.

His low-heeled boots helped when an unexpected lurch threw him off the officious walk to teeter a full three paces along the sloping slicker roofing. Then he had to leap the uncertain space to grab the brake wheel on the next car and after that he sort of had the hang of it . . . 'Til he got to the two passenger coaches and baggage car up forward.

They didn't make what railroaders called varnish cars with catwalks running along their tops. So it was a good thing he'd had some catwalk practice before having to teeter-totter his way on to the coal-filled tender along three bowed roofs of gritty painted sheet metal. He almost fell between the forward coach and that baggage car. But he made it alive to the tender and then it was duck soup over the water tank and coal into the engine cab.

There was nobody else in attendance. The fireman's shovel lay on the gritty steel deck with what looked like brains and some blood for certain clinging to the sharp blade. There were ruby dots on the glass of the pressure gauge near the engineer's throttle as well. The dead man's switch that was supposed to shut off the steam if anyone let go of the throttle had been tied in place with a red print bandana. Longarm moved over to remove it and the dead man's switch proceeded to do its duty.

He had no call to apply the brakes as the combo slowed sedately on a noticeable uphill grade, this far south of the Kern. They rolled less than a full mile before they stopped natural and he applied the standing brakes to keep them from rolling backwards.

As he climbed down from the cabin in the way less noisy gloaming he saw others dropping off to head his way, even more confused. Some of the railroad dicks and cowhands threw down on him with their guns before that older railroad dick could yell at them to grow up. Longarm headed back to where he'd left his hat, coat and pony. So they met by the baggage car. Longarm said, "Evening. The reason I just stopped involves a missing engine crew. I hope they just got throwed off while the train was in motion. But at least one of 'em got to bleed some, first."

Someone else yelled, "The brake crew don't seem to be with us no more, neither!"

So the older railroad dick moaned, "Aw, come on, Lord!" as he boosted himself up to slide open the side door of the baggage car.

Nobody had bothered to toss those boys off along the way. The gray haired gent in charge lay on his side near the open safe near the front end, with his knees drawn up like a sleeping child and the back blown out of his skull.

His teenaged assistant sprawled face down across piled baggage nobody but he had cared about. They'd used a heavy caliber, likely a .51, on him as well, judging from the awesome exit wound in the back of his once-white shirt.

As Longarm and some of the others climbed up beside him the old railroad dick did a little war dance, sobbing, "Oh the tricky as well as ruthless murdersome motherfuckers! I see it all, now. They got on with us back there in Visalia and that'll learn us to hire extra posse riders in haste!"

Longarm said, "That's the way I read it. Mighty easy way to rob a train but it's sure hell on the hired help!"

There were two equally bad courses to follow, this close to sundown. The sneaks who'd signed on to chase their fool selves had obviously taken out the train crew, helped themselves to the payrolls of more than one mine up ahead, and jumped off before the train had picked up so much speed, well north of that river crossing. So backing that far and then fanning out to scout for sign, in chaparral, in the dark, promised tedious hours in the saddle for the posse and an easy lope to safe cover before sunrise for the train robbers.

Forging on to the Blue Dog end of the line meant more time before they could hope to search for any of the missing train crew, and there was an outside chance one or more of them could still be alive, needing help, Lord only knew where along at least fifty miles of track.

Longarm was the one who thought of the widow Carillo's private telegraph connection. The older railroad dick decided, "That's our best bet, then. We forge on to the way closer Blue Dog end of the line and put it all out on the wire. Doña Felicidad's vaqueros can find anyone needing help back yonder as well as we could and meanwhile we can all-points the sons of bitches by wire in hopes of 'em riding into a warm welcome no matter which way they've headed. Does anyone here have a better description than strange riders, dressed cow?"

A younger gent who fit that decription to a T said, "I'm missing a couple of friendly but unfamiliar faces I was jawing with back in the Visalia yards. Said they rode for Miller Lux at busier times of the year. That's how come I didn't know 'em. The old Triple Seven is good enough for this child."

Longarm said, "I suspect they fibbed about riding for the Miller Lux combine. I was told back in town that the big ranchers would as soon sit this one out."

A slightly older hand agreed, "I heard tell the same. I doubt old Hank Miller cares about Kit Evans one way or the other, but he'd got enough of a feud going with Big Jim Haggin. He don't need more trouble with them dad blasted sodbusters who seem to think Kit Evans walks on water!"

The railroad dick in command said, "You boys who got a good look at those fake Miller riders stick with me and Longarm, here." Then he pointed at another railroad man to add, "Melville, you take over as brakeman. Collins, didn't you used to be an engineer? Whether you were or not, see about getting us on up the line. Rest of you boys get back aboard so's we can wind up some place more sensible!"

They all did and there was even some ruddy light left as the Blue Dog train rolled on. Longarm didn't ask who the biggest cattle baron in California seemed to be at feud with. If it was at all important to his mission he'd doubtless find out and if it wasn't he didn't give doodle squat.

Chapter 21

He couldn't help learning more than he cared about the Miller Lux and Haggin feud once they got to the Blue Dog end of the line, because it ended at a sprawling brawling mining complex and because Big Jim Haggin was to mining what Miller was to cattle and Lux was to meat packing, west of the Sierra Nevadas.

He heard gents jawing about it in a smoke-filled saloon near the dispatch shed where they let him use their telegraph as well. They had way more to send than he did. So once he'd left a terse field report they said they'd patch through to Western Union later, when they had the time, he secured his hired pony and possibles with a handy establishment that provided livery, hostel, and saloon services on the same premises, handy to the railroad.

More than one other patron felt the sprawling Miller Lux outfit had to be in cahoots with outlaws, not so much because of their recent branching out into wheat and even salad greens, for Gawd's sake, as because anyone at feud with Big Jim Haggin had to be a shit-eating thief.

The disputed property each accused the other of stealing seemed to be water. Mining magnates were as interested in water rights as cattle barons, and, holding so much property in the higher mining country, Big Jim Haggin was in some position to say which way said water ran, once it left his mountains.

Miller and Lux, having so much pull up Frisco and Sacramento way, were in position to block dam building in the mountains better with lawyers than some cruder gents might manage with dynamite. A mining man Longarm bothered to ask said, so far, it seemed to be a Mexican standoff with neither side free to hog

187

all the waters of the San Joaquin Valley 'til he licked or came to some agreement with the other.

Longarm didn't ask for elaboration. He already knew how elaborate the riparian laws of these United States could get, with some states adding to the confusion by passing laws only a lunatic could make heads or tails out of.

Longarm had been mixed up in such disputes in the past, sometimes more personal, betwixt rougher players. So he knew that short of assassinating one another the would-be monopolists would just wrangle her out one way or the other. The one who could gain title to the most "prior riperian usage" as the lawyers put it, figured to win in the end. American common law, based on English common law, went back to Roman notions on who owned water running across who's private property. It was considered permissable to impound every acre you might own under a private mill pond, fish farm or whatever, but shitty to cut off anyone downstream from running water they'd enjoyed using ahead of you. That meant, contrariwise, you could leave the poor souls without a drop in their creek if you could show you'd been using it ahead of them. That was why they called such claims water rights. A deed showing prior claim to a spring or even one side of a stream could be worth way more than your land, by itself, was worth, to rich folk further down who wanted to buy out your stranglehold on their water supply.

He couldn't see how Big Jim Haggin or Miller and Lux could be interested in robbing trains or hiding either the Fresno Kid or Peewee Folsom, though. Meanwhile he hadn't et supper and the one beer he'd ordered in hopes they'd at least have some damned nuts on the bar wasn't helping. So he mosied next door to hire himself a flop for later. Then, the dingy hotel dining room looking depressing as well as deserted despite the hour, he wandered on in search of sustenance.

Passing yet another saloon in the confusing darkness of a hillside mining complex, he heard a piano being played just awful and paused for a peek through the grimy glass.

The hourglass-figured lady torturing the piano against the far wall wore a familiar dress of bright red velveteen, albeit she'd changed her hair color back to black for at least this one evening, he saw, as he marveled, "You sure do get about, Miss Red Robin. I could swear that was you on the far side of the High Sierra the other night but, what the hell, *I* made it this far, didn't I?"

He moved on, one appetite coming at a time and Red Robin seldom knocking off before midnight. He found a great-smelling hole-in-the-wall serving hashed brown spuds over steak sliced thick enough to bleed inside its sizzled crust. He ordered a side order of chili beans to balance the meal and tamped it down with apple pie and only a couple of black coffees. He was looking forward to a few hours of sincere sleep before he had to put himself and that poor livery mount through the wringer.

They'd be sending that train back north before the crack of dawn, carrying that posse and their own mounts, he knew. But even though he wouldn't be stuck up here 'til the usual noonday northbound he knew they'd expect him to posse with 'em and, damn it, Billy Vail would, too, if anyone asked him.

Longarm knew it wasn't his case or even federal, the train robbers being slick enough to leave the mail sack in that baggage car untouched. But a peace officer sworn to uphold any law code was expected to pitch in and assist another in hot pursuit. So he knew they'd expect him to at least go through the motions 'til the trail grew cold.

It had to be, at best, lukewarm by this late date. The rascals who'd signed on to trap themselves could have jumped off with their plunder most anywhere confederates had been waiting in the chaparral with getaway mounts. Given a whole night's riding, they'd have made the grid of county roads and country lanes, all of 'em well-traveled, spread for miles out from the county seat.

He knew they could be holed up in Visalia, itself, as well as any number of innocent-looking farm or ranch houses. Only a handful of Kit Evans's friends and relations had been squatting on that disputed railroad grant. Five or ten times that many had bought or homesteaded lawsome up and down the whole damn valley.

Once he'd drained his last cup and paid for his supper Longarm headed back to that hostel, wishing it was a might later. For he as well as the evening still felt too young to turn in, while the obvious alternative sounded a mite unwise for a man facing a hard day ahead in the saddle.

But as he heard the more dismal than dulcet tones of what had to be either "My Old Kentucky Home" or that bull fighter's march out of Carmen, up ahead, he knew he was fixing to just grit his teeth and take his beating like a man. For a man could pass on Red Robin once if he was really pressed for the time and opportunity.

But life was just too short to miss out on a roll in the feathers with anyone that great, and willing, when he didn't have anything better to do for Lord only knew how many hours.

The piano banging stopped as he drew near the bat wings of the rinky-dink in question. As he parted them Longarm saw the piano stool in the back stood deserted. She'd likely knocked off for the moment to give herself as well as everyone's ears a short rest. He figured as long as he had the chance he'd best go out back, himself. It was considered rude to tell a lady you had to take a leak whilst she was talking to you.

He stepped through the bead curtain screening the back exit of the barroom. He found himself in a dimly lit corridor a mite longer than he'd expected in a mining camp joint. Instead of back steps leading out to a yard that might or might not have a formal outhouse, this joint had doorways, marked ladies or gents as the case might be. So he entered the one marked gents to find a genuine flush commode and a zinc sink with running water so's you could even wash your hands, like some society swell.

He used both facilities, reflecting on how up to date they were in these parts as he dried his hands on their almost-clean roll towel. Victorian plumbing wasn't primitive, anywhere, because Victorian folk enjoyed the smell of shit and buzzing of flies or because they were ignorant. A fair flush commode had been invented for the delicate-natured Queen Elizabeth before the first Pilgrim Father had pissed on New England. After that it had been a matter of cost and, above all, a handy supply of running water.

Nobody could flush a crapper with well water. Water didn't run that way. Running tap and crap water had to start from somewhere above the places you wanted it to run. Then you needed fairly stout pipes as well as the simple but fairly expensive hardware Longarm and most of his fellow literates knew how to use. They'd said the mining magnates in these parts dabbled in the water business as well. It stood to reason an outfit anxious to peddle water would import at least some plumbing supplies to peddle as well. He knew lots of water outfits piped water to paying customers at cost so's they could charge them ever after for the water.

Making sure his tweed pants were buttoned modest, Longarm stepped back out in the gloomy corridor, just as a vision of desire stepped out of the lady's room between him and the barroom, doubtless fresh-pissed and hopefully wiped fresh under that lush red velveteen.

So he overtook her with a knowing grin and grabbed her by both velveteen covered tits from behind, knowing that was the way Red Robin liked to be greeted by old friends.

Then he noticed he wasn't holding the Red Robin he knew as she stuggled and spat, "Unhand my pure maidenly flesh, you villainous asshole! Can't you pick and shovel jockies get it through your hard-rock heads I ain't that kind of a girl?"

Longarm had already turned her loose by the time she'd finished, aiming a slap at his bemused face by way of emphasis. He caught her bare wrist, not unkindly, to soothe, "Take it easy, ma'am. I know I done wrong but I thought you were someone else. I reckon I just got redheads on my mind this evening."

The almond-eyed and black-haired beauty stared up at him bemused to demand, "Do I look like a redhead, you grabby cuss? You ought to be ashamed of yourself, getting that drunk at this hour!"

He held on to that uncertain wrist as he assured her, "I am ashamed. But I ain't drunk, ma'am. The other lady I just mistook you for has red hair, as a rule, albeit I know for a fact . . . I mean I have it on good authority she's a natural brunette, such as you."

The piano playing gal who didn't look at all like the real Red Robin, head on, said, "I think I know who you mean. This silly red get-up was my booking agent's notion. I feel my art can stand on its own merits and while we've yet to meet, some who have assure me her piano playing is just dreadful."

Longarm answered, soberly, "It is, ma'am. But you're both swell-looking and that makes up for a heap. If I let go your hand, now, will you let me live?"

She laughed—she had a nice laugh—and declared, "You're not bad-looking, either, and I may forgive you just this once."

So he let go, saying, "I'm still sorry and since I ain't ordered out front, yet. I'll say adios here and just be on my way."

She demanded, "How come? Don't you like my pianoplaying?"

"You play piano swell," he lied.

So she said, "Stick around, then. I need to think about it for a while. But if those shoulders are real and you're neither married or in league with that Miller Lux outfit, we'll talk some more when I take my next break."

191

Then she turned and parted the beaded curtain to receive a round of applause as she stode back to the upright and sat down to bang on it some more.

Nobody seemed to take much notice of Longarm as he found himself a place at one corner of the bar and admired her profile as he nursed draft lager. Her face was outlined admirable, too. He figured her for a little younger than the real Red Robin but, if anything, a mite harder.

That was going some. He'd met the one and original Red Robin over Texas way when she'd been on the run after gunning a man in Chicago.

As things had turned out, the rascal who'd had a gunning coming had lived and in the end it had been all right to kiss her instead of arresting her.

This one had already told him why she was dressed up the same way and banging out the same old tunes to remind homesick gents from the East or no-longer-callow vets of the War about other times and places. It was too bad neither could play such tunes for shit. He was still working on whether the real Red Robin mangled Dixie because she'd been too young to get the drift when the song had been so popular on the campgrounds, North and South, or whether she really missed notes she was aiming for. Red Robin had never missed anything she'd grabbed for in the dark, bless her sneaky little hands, but of course it was way easier to find a raging erection than say F Sharp, without looking.

When the barkeep drifted over to put a head on his beer Longarm murmured, in a desperately casual tone, "She's pretty good. What do they call her, Pard?"

The barkeep confided, "She's touring this season under the stage name of Aura Lee. But if the truth be known, she's really the one and original Red Robin. She made a bad contract with the Cheyenne Social Club and can't use her real name 'til it expires, see?"

Longarm pretended to. He saw her booking agent was an inspired fibber and that made him wonder whether she was being cheated as well. He decided it was none of his beeswax, unless she wanted to get way friendlier to him than she was that poor piano.

He couldn't tell what she thought she was playing. Most any lyrics went as bad with it. She hit a couple of licks closer to the bullseye and he laughed incredulously as he realized she was trying for the very one she'd named her fool self after. As she got

192

to the even sorrier parts he found himself mouthing, "The angels came down in the night, to steal my Aura Lee," and it was all he could do to keep his fool eyes from watering as his memory took him back to his troubled teens indeed, lounging 'round a dying campfire whilst that kid who'd fallen at Cold Harbor pissed and moaned about old Aura Lee on his mouth organ.

It sure beat all how sentimental old soldiers felt about made-up gals they'd never even seen a picture of. Most likely every old boy who'd felt so wistful about the sad fate of Aura Lee had swallowed many a lump just thinking about that mockingbird that sang on Sweet Hattie's grave, whoever she'd been, from the North or South. Sad songs about awful things that had never happened to gals one didn't really have to worry about were perhaps a welcome rest from thoughts about the true horrors of war, and loved ones back home who might really come down with something, or go off with someone else.

That horrible rendition of Aura Lee must have been her namesake's theme song. For she'd no sooner finished than she rose to join Longarm at the bar, confiding, "I get to take an hour's supper break about this time of the evening. Would you care to join me for a nibble, up in my quarters?"

He said he was just dying for a nibble. So she led him back through those beads and up a back stairway to the combined dressing room and flop provided by the management. She led him over to the bed along one wall, there seemed no better place to sit side by side, and they'd no sooner sat than she said, "You can stay up here 'til I get off just after midnight. I have to get back on that damned piano before any of my other customers complain. So what are you waiting for?"

He gulped and as she already seemed to be groping for the hooks and eyes up the back of her tight red bodice, he asked, "When you refer to me as one of your customers, might we be calling me a music lover or a more pathetic lover, Miss Aura?"

She turned her spine to him, saying, "Help me with these hooks and don't talk dirty. I'm an artist, not a hooker. Didn't you mean it when you grabbed me so passionately down below, you big tease?"

He chuckled fondly and remarked he'd grabbed her sort of high, as he recalled, while they got her out of her red velveteen lest they rumple it. Then he really grabbed her below and rumpled her candlelit nude charms indeed with half his own duds still on.

After that she made him pause to undress completely so they could get to know one another better. That was what she called it when she got on top in nothing but her high button shoes and striped socks, red and white—knowing one another. He figured she'd been brung up on the King James version but didn't think this the time to ask.

They bent some of the other rules in the Good Book before she refused a drag on his afterwards smoke with a sigh and asked him to help her into her outfit so she could go down and entertain others, less friendly, before anyone came up to ask what might be keeping her.

As she bent over his reclining nude form to kiss him adios she said, "Get some sleep if you like. You're going to need all your strength when I return, Lover. Nobody but me knows you're here and I'll lock up on my way out."

He didn't argue, until she'd left. Then he rolled to his bare feet and padded over to the door she'd just locked with her key to snap the barrel bolt in place. The one and original imitation of Aura Lee had just been awfully kind, but he didn't know her well enough to entrust with his life, just yet, and if she really wanted to get laid some more she could knock on the damned door when she came back.

He thought about that as he moved back to recline atop her bedding, pensively puffing his smoke. He'd been set up by more than one false-hearted woman in his time. But wasn't he starting to get a mite silly on the subject?

Aura Lee didn't need a certificate of good credit to eliminate her sweet self as a suspected assassin. He knew at least two evil minds were separately plotting something awful. But even had she been the one true love of mastermind A or B there'd been no way on earth for anyone to have baited a trap with her. Not at this place and time, leastways. He hadn't known he'd be spending the night up here in these hills to begin with. After that, while it was possible he'd been spotted by some confederate of some crook, it hadn't been possible for anyone to get to that gal ahead of him and tell her he'd be by directly to surprise her from behind as she was returning from a squat.

He blew a thoughtsome smoke ring at the candle burning on her nearby dressing table to decide, "We can trust her, at least 'til somebody gets to her with something more tempting than our old organ grinder. After that, we've been holding up one end of a bar

194

in a fairly well-lit saloon for more than one beer. If we could see in from outside or, shit, if we were already inside, acting innocent as we kept an eye peeled for someone our boss had told us to watch for . . . Yep, that door better stay bolted."

It did. After he'd finished the cheroot he was feeling a mite chilled as well as gummy-eyed. So he hauled the covers over his naked body and nested his weary head on her sweet-scented pillows to see if he could catch a few winks.

He could, but it wasn't easy, listening to her dreadful piano playing down below. Then he was dreaming about that time that player piano had gone on playing in a smoke-filled cantina with half the customers dead on the floor and most of the rest run off, and then he was wide awake again as the echoes of all that gunplay faded away amid the surrounding hills.

Downstairs, the piano had stopped as if to listen, too. Then, as it started playing again with a shrug of Aura Lee's bare shoulder he could clearly picture, he realized he hadn't dreamed that gunplay from whole cloth. Someone had been blasting, loud, likely in one of the mine shafts up the slope.

Then he heard the clanging of a horse-drawn fire engine and knew that hadn't been a late night mine blast after all. He swung his bare feet to the floor and started to reach for his duds. Then he wondered how come. Late night fires were tempting fun, but there was no saying who might or might not recognize his face in the crowd before he got to return the favor. He was pretty sure of the lusty brunette who'd left him up here out of sight and reach, knock wood. But the mystery masterminds, plural, had one hell of an advantage on him 'til he had some notion who he might be watching out for.

He'd already hung his gun rig handy over a bed post. He groped up his vest and unsnapped his double derringer from one end of his watch chain to tuck it between the end of the mattress and the headboard. For something was up, down below. Aura Lee had stopped playing and he heard boot heels thunking.

He'd just decided he'd best put on his pants, at least, when his gracious hostess tried to open the door from outside and, finding it bolted on the inside, made some ungracious remarks about it.

He rose, sixgun raised, to let her in. As he did so she glanced down to spy the .44-40 he was holding polite, and gasped, "Good grief, you don't have to hold a gun on me to get me back in bed with you! It was my idea to begin with, Stud."

He chuckled, shut the door after her, and barred it some more as he explained, "Loud noises make me uneasy. What was all that about, down yonder?"

She moved over to the bed again, pleading, "Help me out of this dumb dress. All I know is that nobody seems interested in my piano-playing right now and I've been wanting to play with you some more since last you let me."

That reminded him of how swell she looked with her duds off and so in no time at all they were going at it dog style. She found it as inspiring to watch herself getting humped like so, in her dressing table mirror. He liked to stare straight down as he enjoyed a gal that way by candlelight. She surely was a winky little thing.

They finished more romantic with her leather-clad ankles locked around the nape of his neck. Then, as he lit another smoke, she sat up to remove her shoes and socks as well, observing, "Nobody will expect me to get back on that piano with most of the camp down the street by the depot."

He lit their cheroot before he demanded, with a puzzled frown, "That explosion I heard before was somebody blowing up the depot, or mayhaps that train standing next to it?"

She grunted off the last sock as she replied, "I don't think so. The mining man who called in the doorway about bucket brigades made mention of the hostel across the way. Seems they had some sort of an explosion in one of the rooms upstairs."

Chapter 22

They sure had, Longarm saw by the dawn's early light after Aura Lee had reluctantly let him out of her bed. This time the local fire fighters had doused such flames as a good charge of 60% Nitro had set off, raising the tin roof and lobbing the brass bed he'd been planning to sleep alone in over the stable next door.

This time nobody at all had been more than seriously scared. Early risers were still watching a fireman who worked for the mining company hosing down the already soggy ashes. Longarm studied faces in the crowd as he pretended to watch the clean-up.

It didn't work. He recognized some of the posse members he'd ridden to this end of the line with, unplanned and certainly unannounced. He hadn't expected Peewee Folsom to make it this far, yet, and the Fresno Kid was supposed to be dead in that family tomb, if only they'd let him get near it.

Neither his hired mount nor his saddle and gear had been blown up by that charge they'd obviously planted under his bed—or the bed they must have been expecting him to be sleeping in that late at night when they failed to spot him elsewhere in town, bless Aura Lee and her womanly needs, as she called 'em. So he'd just settled up and led his saddled-up roan back outside when that older railroad dick caught up with him to say, "We've been looking for you and your guns. We've been ready to roll out for some time, you slugabed. Where've you been all this time?"

Longarm said, "Mostly in bed, of course. Caught some eggs over hash and my morning coffee along the way. You could have gone back down the line without me, for all I cared. I told you

197

where I was trying to get to and you know those train robbers are long gone by this time."

The older private lawman sighed and said, "We got to try. Doña Felicidad's vaqueros found the train crew by first light, the poor bastards. They wired us from a flag stop closer to where their bodies were flung from the train. They'll be waiting for us there to posse up with us."

Longarm asked, "How come? Them train robbers couldn't have got off before their victims, could they?"

The railroad dick grimaced and said, "Them vaqueros likely passed any sign they left, south of the bodies, since they barely made out the crewman wearing a white shirt in the shitty predawn light. But why are we jawing about it here? Let's gather up the rest of the boys and head back along the line to find out!"

So they did. Longarm didn't really want to, but he had to, even knowing how things were going to turn out.

The way they turned out was, after he'd recrossed the Kern River, muttering dark curses at all concerned, they detrained near one of flag stops they'd passed the afternoon before, this one about fifteen miles north of the river and, damn it, that private family tomb, where, sure enough, they found a bunch of obvious vaqueros and some Anglo riders dressed more natural, spitting and whittling along the railroad platform near the dispatch shed. The five bodies of the missing train crewmen had already been wrapped for shipping in canvas tarps and lined up neatly down at one end of the platform. A couple of toolsheds and the tar-paper houses the handful of railroaders lived in made up the rest of what looked more like a town on the map.

The local hands rose to rustle up their own mounts as the older railroad dick ordered his own boys, and Longarm, to detrain. Some of the ponies put up quite a fuss. But Longarm was pleased to see the roan he'd picked dropped off with no more than a couple of good licks from his hat.

After that things got more tedious. Everyone there agreed the gang would have ridden on at least as far south as the vaqueros had found the southernmost crew member and they'd all been scattered along the trackside south of the dispatcher and his handy telegraph set.

They rode a fair ways before one of the vaqueros pointed down with his rawhide quirt to say that scuffy patch of raw earth and

198

uprooted cheat was where the brakeman had landed, shot once, but enough.

The older railroad dick opined nobody had noticed the gunshots above the rumble and roar of a speeding train.

Longarm called out, "They got rid of the crew and got off, their ownselves, before we were really speeding. They'd have busted their fool necks jumping off at more than say thirty, after tying the deadman's switch in place."

The older railroad dick said he stood corrected and still hadn't heard the damned shots. Then he ordered everyone to press on, in English, of course, so Longarm smiled at the vaqueros closer to him and cheerfully called, *"Vamanos pa'l carajo, muchachos."*

They didn't argue, but he did detect a slight hesitancy as they seemed to mull his casual words more than what he'd just said really called for. What did a Californio say when it was time to get the hell on down the trail?

He decided he didn't much care. The boys were real Chicano with way more Aztec and such in 'em than, say, their Doña Felicidad, and he knew Spanish, like English, had different regional accents. So if they put, "Let's get the hell out of here," another way, more power to 'em. He'd just speak English to 'em, loud, if they gave him any sass about his border Mex.

They didn't seem to want to as, one by one, they indicated where they'd found the five dead crewmen. After that they all rode on a ways, ponies moving so much slower than railroad trains, until Longarm called out a suggestion—he wasn't in command—regarding both sides of the tracks.

It had been a good suggestion, they all agreed, when one of the vaqueros found some horse apples in the chaparral east of the track about the same time an Anglo spotted a swathe of flattened mustard west of the same.

The morning sun was high and bright as they circled some to all read the sign the same. The train robbers had dropped off, a couple rolling some, to be met by others holding spare mounts.

After that it got worse. The whole gang of around a dozen had lit out as if for the Sierras, only to circle south, then east, to cross the tracks a mile down the line and make for the coastal ranges, some said.

As they rested their own mounts and jawed about it, just east of the crossing, Longarm asked the older railroad dick, "Don't the

199

main line of your railroad run north and south a few short miles ahead?"

The older man nodded soberly and said, "With a choice of two flag stops betwixt here and the maze of reed swamps and frog ponds between here and the coastal ranges."

A nearby rider dressed more cow spat and said, "They might try to lose us among the tules. They might try to lose us on the rocky slopes of the brushy coast ranges. But if I was them I'd just be spitting and whittling in Famoso or mayhaps Waso by the time any posse could ride in. You know you'll never get any of them sodbusting sons of bitches to point finger one at their hero, Evans."

Longarm knew it as well. But the older railroad dick insisted on following the clear if rapidly cooling trail of the outlaws. When it developed the vaqueros sent by Doña Felicidad's *segundo* meant to ride on with the posse, Longarm had even more reason to announce he'd never been sent all this way with a federal badge to chase California fruits and nuts. Nobody shot at him when he reined in to let the rest of 'em ride on. So it was safe to say they were more interested in the Evans Sontag gang.

Longarm cut catty-corner through the high chaparral to meet up with the Blue Dog line some more than an hour's ride to the southeast. The one line of telegraph poles followed the single line of tracks to their west. But a two-rut service road or wagon trace he recalled ran in line with the tracks to their east. He crossed over to follow that, because he wasn't wearing chaps, and tweed pants had their limitations in high chaparral.

There was clearance for a buckboard team, let alone a single mount and its rider as they followed one bare rut at a ball-busting but mile-eating trot. Longarm got teased from time to time for preferring his unfashionable McClellan to a he-man high plains roper or even a center-fire Morgan. But Longarm knew what he was doing aboard such a humble rig.

His old Army saddle was of course named for the old Army man who'd designed it, the otherwise confounding General George McClellan who'd snatched a draw from the jaws of victory at Antietam and then lost to Lincoln in the election of '64.

Before all that he'd been a fair garrison soldier with time on his hands to piddle with quartermaster and ordinance details. So even though he hadn't known how to lead 'em in battle, his Army of the Potomac had been the best fed and equipped outfit on

200

either side and his men liked him way more than Honest Abe had as he'd marched and counter-marched his chocolate soldiers in heroic circles lest he lose any of 'em.

Horses would revere McClellan's memory as well, if horses savvied such matters. For the Army saddle old George had designed and ordered in swamping numbers was easy as possible on a horse no matter what it did to a rider.

Here and there he spotted sign in the dust ahead. All the hoofprints fresh enough to matter were aimed the way he'd just come. So he read 'em as the tracks of those half dozen vaqueros he'd just parted company with. That made at least half a dozen he didn't have to worry about once he reached Doña Felicidad's. He'd worry about how many were still around once he got there.

It took longer than by train but at last he spied the trees along the Kern, ahead, and not a minute too soon, with the sun so high and the two of them so thirsty, now.

He saw the ruts he'd been following were more a wagon trace than a service road when they swung away from the tracks toward a way wider clump of fruit and shade trees hiding the river and most everything else ahead.

As he rode into the sweet shady welcome of an old orchard, almonds, plums or apricots, from the leaves on the picked-off branches, some cur dogs commenced to yap at him like forest wolves at tricky pistol range. He didn't have any call to shoot any. They knew better than to get that serious with an armed stranger. Like their blond or carrot cousins around many an Indian camp, they'd been trained to give the alarm at a safe distance. Anglo or Mex riders were content to just shoot at uppity canines. Some Indians tended to have 'em for supper.

He rode a surprising distance through well-tended orchards before he came in sight of the rambling ranch house and its sprawl of outbuildings. Thanks to all that yapping an ad hoc welcoming committee was lined up along the front veranda.

They were easy to make out, despite the overhang of thick Spanish roof tiles and the sycamore shade trees all around the main house. For unlike their cousins in Old Mexico the Californio breed liked to whitewash 'dobe walls 'til they seemed to be made out of salt blocks.

Aside from being fashionable as their Anglo neighbors, the many layers of whitewash likely helped on the rare but awesome occasions it really rained out this way. South of, say, Monterey, California got more sunny days than it really needed, sometimes a whole year's worth, punctuated by tropic rains that could set unbelievers to building arks.

As Longarm reined in within easy hail of the men and women lined up in the shade of the veranda a gent around forty, dressed like an Anglo cowman but featured a mite more olive than most, stepped out into the dappled sunlight to announce, "Doña Felicidad wired us you might be coming, if you'd be Deputy Long."

When Longarm allowed they had him pegged the *mayordomo*, *segundo* or whatever continued, "I'd be Jesus Garcia, most call me Soose, and I run things here when the boss lady's up in Frisco, which is most of the time since her Don Carlos passed away. She's ordered me to extend you the usual hospitality of a civilized breed until she can get here the hard way from Visalia. Meanwhile you're not to poke your nose into her personal quarters or you know what."

Longarm wasn't sure whether the smiling but frosty-eyed cuss meant the family tomb itself or what they'd do to him if he busted into it. As he dismounted an eager kid ran over to snatch the reins from him and so there went his Winchester, along with a jaded pony who could doubtless use the shade, water, and rubdown over to yonder stables.

That left Longarm with his search warrant as well as sixgun and derringer. As he shook with Garcia and followed everyone inside he decided not to whip out any of 'em before the owner of the property to be searched arrived. Soose Garcia looked too Americanized to trick with the actually worthless writ he'd signed that very morning on Aura Lee's dressing table, and if his boss lady had already started south along that same trail, no doubt with some of her other riders, he'd do better arguing with her here than amid the confusion of a running gunfight.

Inside, the main room of the ranch house, more like a baronial hall, had walls a darker shade of old rose stucco while the ceiling was that intricate pattern of crossed carved beams and rafters they called "*rallo por queso*" or cheese grater.

After that the furnishings were that Anglo-Hispanic mix the ever-proud and oft-rich Californio admired. Antique Spanish chests and armoires of oak or chestnut shared the cavernous room with English chesterfield sofas and Queen Anne crap-doodles of mahogany or fruitwood. The possibly tamped-clay floor was covered wall-to-wall with oriental rugs. They took away his hat and sat him on yet another tufted leather chesterfield near a fireplace big enough to cast pig iron when it was going full blast, he'd have bet.

Fortunately, at this time of the year it was out, with a basket of fruit instead of logs on the hearth. There was a low-slung teak table of Chinese design betwixt his knees and the fireplace. Garcia said he had some chores to tend but that Longarm could get most any heart's desire from Simona, their housekeeper, who stood smiling down at Longarm as if she hoped he desired a blow job.

He didn't. He liked his women halfway pretty as well as willing and old Simona looked as if she might ride brooms when she wasn't ordering one of her maids to sweep up. So he told the friendly old crone he could do with something to drink if she didn't mind. When she begged him to let her feed him at least a snack as well, he recalled spending his usual lunch hour in the chaparral and allowed he could stand some cheese and crackers as long as she was headed out to the cocina in any case.

She wasn't. She clapped her hands and a pretty little thing with scared Indian eyes came in to get ordered about like Cinderella in a rapid fire Longarm couldn't follow. He'd heard border Mex was slow as Spanish got spoken and he sometimes had trouble keeping up with that.

The *moza* dashed off to do as she'd been told as the old housekeeper just stood there. It made Longarm feel awkward. He asked if she'd be kind enough to sit. She blinked as if the thought had never occurred to her. Then she perched her skinny old butt on a stool by the fireplace to tell him he was *muy gracioso y democracio*. So, his dry mouth tasting more like wild mustard than spit, he asked if she'd mind, his smoking while he waited for that drink.

She stared owlish and gasped, *"Pero supuesto*! You are the guest of Doña Felicidad! Forgive us for not offering! Would you prefer a Havana Perfecto or perhaps a milder Claro?"

He said his cheroots suited him fine and lit one while she stared at him sad as anything. As she materialized a sterling silver ashtray to place on the table in front of him she sighed and said, "In God's truth I long for the old days before *El Diluvio*. *Pero* there is much to be said for the less formal manners of Doña Felicidad's generation. I feel so ashamed when I recall how much I disliked her just a few short years ago."

Longarm didn't want to get into what they called the Deluge. He knew she meant that freak weather they'd had out this way rather than the flood of Anglo Forty Niners they'd survived easier. So he asked how come she'd disliked her boss lady a spell back. Old Felix had struck him as a mite imperious as well as pretty.

Old Simona sniffed and said, "She was not my *patrona* when first we met. My late husband and me belonged down the river on the Carillo grant. Don Carlos Carillo was almost like a son to us after we had watched him grow to manhood. So when he wed what I thought in God's truth a flighty little creature with the brains of a sheep and the pride of a queen . . ."

"I've already met Doña Felicidad," he cut in, as that *moza* came back with a silver serving tray too heavy by half for a gal to tote.

As she set it before him he saw they expected him to consume a pitcher of iced lemonade or a jug of wine or both, along with piled up rum cakes, smoked salmon, kippered herring, sugar-cured ham and salami and cheeses all the way from Frisco's north beach, if not Italy, itself. When he asked where they got the ice this late in a California year she said special schooners brought it all the way down from Alaska glaciers. He dug in and stuffed his face as she went on about her boss lady.

She said, "I was wrong. She is an angel from above as well as a direct descendant of all fourteen *soldados* who first entered *Alta California* in 1769. I found her at first, as I said, coldly correct in the manner of all Ortegas I have ever seen. I confess my husband and me said unkind things about her when Don Carlos first brought her home for to visit the additional lands and servants she would be joining with her own. I do not think she spoke ten words in a row to me in the first ten years she and Don Carlos were married. Of course, they spent most of their time here or at their even finer *casa grande* up in San Francisco. Our Don Carlos began to act more, how you say, businessman, after he wed such a well-schooled heiress. They say she went to some *universidad* back East and studied *Yanqui* business methods there."

Longarm washed down some cold cuts on rum cake with red wine and remarked, "I know how country folk feel about young gals going off to college. I noticed she talked sort of fancy. But what was that about her being an angel?"

Old Simona sighed and said, "I said terrible things about her when we heard Don Carlos had died, so young, up in San Francisco.

People who had visited his office there said he worked at his desk as many hours as a *Yanqui* and was not natural for a man so young to die from *la cardialgia*. I said it was her fault, for pressing him for to be so ambitious. I did not know, at the time, it was his own desire to surpass his Ortega in-laws and be accepted by his *Yanqui* rivals that drove him."

He silently offered her some wine, at least. She shook her head primly and continued, "It was only after both our men were dead I got to know her. She came down, all the way from San Francisco during the social season there for to pay her respects at my Roberto's funeral. That part was perhaps to be expected, she was, after all, our *patrona* and a woman of *sangre azul verdad*. But she melted my unworthy soul forever when she took me in her own arms, afterwards, for to tell me she was not only keeping me in her *patrocinio, pero* promoting me to *gobernadora de la casa grande!*"

Longarm nodded thoughtfully and said, "I can see why her help's so fond of her. Is it safe to say she closed down her late husband's homespread when she put you in charge of her fancier place, here?"

Simona nodded and said, "Neither she nor Don Carlos spent more than a few days at a time at either rancho in their last few years together. All the furnishings and even some of the roof tiles are over here, now. *Pero* sometimes our vaqueros use the old Carillo *casa* when is cold or wet on the range. Most of Doña Felicidad's combined herd grazes the original Ortega grant. In God's truth the Carillo grant offers rougher grazing, away from the river. I once heard them talking about the water running past being worth more than the land itself. They were speaking of this at the dinner table with some *Yanqui* associates. I was more interested in seeing everyone got enough for to eat and drink, of course."

Longarm nodded, polished off some of that salmon just to see if it was really Atlantic and, deciding it was, fancy as that sounded, said, "I know about water rights. I suspect I know what kept the late Chuck Carillo so busy at his desk of late as well. As stuff I've read about old Spanish grants comes back to me, I seem to recall the old Spanish kings, no offense, were inclined to grant awesome tracts of land awfully casual. I read over such down in Mexico City in connection with another case, one time. They tended to run boundary lines from something vague as a mountain side to an old tree stump a few miles off, then from there to a clump of cottonwood or a growth of prickle pear. As for water and mineral rights, they never bothered to discuss 'em at all. So it's small wonder some Californio families spent a heap of time in court, sometimes losing, when gents with sharper eyes for fine print got out this way, some feeling them old Spanish kings had been way too generous, no matter how the treaty of Guadalupe Hidalgo read."

The older housekeeper smiled toothlessly and assured him, "Not in the case of these combined holdings. As anyone can see, both grants were clearly bordered to the southeast by the Rio Kern. Is true some might dispute the other borders a hundred paces either way, *pero* what good would it do them? Is no water for vacas grazing so far from the river or water tanks within a *vera* of its northwest bank. Since *El Diluvio* nobody grazes any grant as heavily as they once might have."

Longarm ate some more ham. He followed her drift because he'd jawed about the same disasters with other Californios in the more recent past. It was curious how the golden ages of the Southern Planter and the Californio Ranchero had ended in the closing years of the War Betwixt the States, for totally different reasons.

What they called the Deluge out this way had commenced the first winter of the War back East. Tropic rains had lashed down for five straight weeks without letup, turning seasonal creeks to brawling brown rivers too big for their beds and spreading uprooted trees and bounding boulders far and wide. Clippers passing way out to sea logged reports of seawater chocolate brown from horizon to horizon, and sharks feeding frenzied on drowned cattle, sheep, horses, and even human victims. They said the sharks didn't bother with the floating furniture, roof beams and such.

Thousands of 'dobe structures had just melted away like ice cream getting pissed on, but those rancheros who'd built on higher ground and used more whitewash hadn't got off unscathed once the sun came back out at last.

For they said it had stayed out, day after day, all through '63 and then '64 as if to make up for that one wet winter by not having any winter rains at all, and it never rained in summer out this way.

As if she'd read his mind, the old lady who doubtless recalled the events way better, said, "In God's truth, even though our *vacas*

206

had the river, low as it ran toward the end, they ate all the grass down to the roots a full day's grazing from our northmost tanks. *Los vaqueros* did what they could, cutting hay further out and hauling it closer to water. *Pero* was very dry hay after such a drought and in the end both ranchos lost more than how you say, three quarters?"

He nodded soberly and said, "They came out better than some, I hear."

She say, "*Es verdad.* Many *rancheros* lost all their *vacas* to the drought, and then came *las chapules*, I think you call them grasshoppers, no?"

He said, "Some call 'em locusts, when they come that awful."

She nodded and said, "They killed more livestock in the end than that long drought. They ate all the fodder livestock still had for to eat on the parched dry range, and then they ate things not even a goat could live on. *Chapules* will eat laundry off the clothesline if they get hungry enough and after two years with no rain these *chapules* were most hungry. Both ranchos, Don Carlos and Doña Felicidad were no even engaged yet, had to import baled hay by rail from the north end of the valley where the drought had not been as severe."

Longarm nodded and said, "Others have told me how expensive it can get, raising beef in these parts, even when you have a river and a rail spur handy. Didn't you used to have a cuss called Ramon as the *segundo*, here?"

She blinked, nodded, and said, "Si, Jesus Garcia took his place a few months ago. Some say he quit for to work for Miller Lux for more pay. Others say Doña Felicidad found him difficult for to handle once she had no husband for to back her. Jesus is all right, in his Anglo way. Nobody much younger than me recalls the old ways, when each guest room contained a bowl of gold and silver coins for any stranger who asked shelter for the night, as well as *ollas* of ice water, fresh Turkish towels, and the soap we made outselves from pure tallow and the ashes of oak, alone."

He'd heard all that, for all the good it might do him. He tried to get her back on more recent history. But she didn't remember that time her boss lady's worthless nephew had holed up there because she hadn't worked there half a dozen years back.

She droned on about her infernal Don Carlos being descended from one of those fancy first fourteen, as if she recalled Jose Roberto Carillo personal, and described fancy Carillo kin all over the infernal state before she narrowed it down to the ones she'd been born to serve as a mixture of mission Indian and poor relation.

He knew how a Mex hacienda worked. She still carried on about ships from far Cathay bringing candied ginger and genuine Oolong tea to serve French dressmakers to measure Doña Carillo for her gowns of silk brocade, or the tailors and bootmakers all the way from London or Boston town who spent months there rigging the men of the house like proper dudes in Harris tweed, Hindu whipcord, and such. He got out his pocket watch to stare at it pointedly as he feigned a yawn and said it was all mighty interesting, but . . .

"*Ay pendejo*! What must you think of us?" she cut in, adding, "We had just remarked on it being time for *la Siesta* when we heard you riding in. And here it is so late afternoon! You must think we have become barbarians after a mere generation under your red white and blue! Would you like me to carry some of that to your *sala* for you?"

He said he was stuffed as he rose with her, hoping she meant it when she mentioned a room in the singular sense.

She had. The guest room she led him to was mighty nice in a spare Spanish way. There was a big clay *olla* of water on the oaken washstand, albeit no chests of money. A disturbingly realistic crucifix on the stucco wall above the bed kept the hospitality as Hispanic as Miss Felix could likely afford, rich as she might be by sensible standards.

The oaken bedstead was made up inviting with more quilts than the local climate called for. The old housekeeper told him they'd serve him some more food and drink around four, if he felt up to it, and left him to his own devices.

He flopped on the bed lest she be listening outside the thick door. Then he forced himself to light a cheroot and smoke it all to give everyone time to settle down. With any luck those chores old Soose had mentioned while excusing himself involved some time in another bed with somebody prettier.

By the time he'd snubbed out his smoked-down cheroot and slid over to the door for a listen, the rambling ranch house seemed quiet as a tomb.

It wasn't the tomb he'd come all this way to investigate. So he cracked open the door and, seeing the hallway outside deserted, scooted along it silent as a cockroach to find his way out a side entrance. From there it was a hop, skip, and some jumping to the cover of a grape arbor leading him to a deserted herb garden with more fruit trees beyond. He circled by way of the shady side, ducked under the trees, and headed east, swearing he'd eat any damned dog who gave him away, this time.

None of them cared to. They'd doubtless accepted him as a smell that belonged on the spread by now. So he worked his way through trees he knew and some he didn't 'til, out in a secluded clearing ahead, he spied a sort of Greek temple about the size of a Cape Cod cottage. The Ortega family tomb had been decribed to him as being built that way, out of the same sandstone. So he nodded at the greenish copper door set deeper in the thick stone front betwixt two pillasters to murmur, "All right, Baker. Here I come, ready or not."

But as he stepped out in the sunlight that green door opened and Soose Garcia stepped out to greet him with a ten-gauge held at port and a .41 double-action on each hip.

A million years passed slowly by. Then Garcia said, "Doña Felicidad said she was worried you'd disturb her dead. I assured her by return wire that you wouldn't."

Longarm said, "I only want to disturb one of 'em, Soose."

To which the segundo replied as soberly, "One would be one too many. Don't make us kill you, *amigo mio*."

Before Longarm could ask how come the man barring his way seemed to be speaking in the plural sense he heard someone cock yet another gun behind him, as he'd no doubt been meant to. So he smiled thinly and declared, "Killing me would be the least of your problems, Soose. I've done some wiring my ownself and my boss really wants me to make sure Tomas Ortega Baker was the cuss you all have stored away in that tomb."

Garcia shrugged and replied, "*My* boss ordered me not to let you. I know your rep, Longarm. I still have to try."

Longarm sighed and said, "That makes the both of us and who can say? I hope you know that whether you stop me or not you ain't about to stop the government I ride for. They'll just keep sending deputies and if you think I sound unreasonable just wait 'til the team we call Smiley and Dutch shows up."

Garcia didn't answer. Another million years went by and then Longarm decided, "You can step aside or try and stop me. Either way, I got my job to do."

Garcia tensed up, too, and it seemed about to go either way when a familiar she-male voice called out, "*Basta!*" and continued in the same Spanish, "Blood is blood, water is water, and that disgrace to the family has caused enough trouble for everyone while he was still alive!"

Garcia said, quietly, "I think we could have, Doña Felicidad."

To which the imperious patrona replied in a resigned tone, in English, "There's little sense and no hope, fighting progress, Soose. We have to get along with them. Those who have not have gone under and there is no glory in dying landless in a *Yanqui* prison."

She stepped into view from the shade behind Longarm to join them as both men tugged politely at their hat brims. She still wore the same black riding habit. Her Spanish hat was as dusty from her long ride from the county seat. It was likely fatigue and the cruel sun that made her look that much older than him as he softly told her, "I ain't looking forward to what I just got to do, ma'am. I got me some authenticated photographs of your late nephew, here. So do we just open the lid a crack . . ."

She made a retching sound and told her *segundo*, "See that he disturbs none of the others, Soose. I'll be back at the *casa grande* when it's over. Make certain everything is put back exactly as it was."

Then she turned on one heel and marched off, spine stiff, as she slapped her dusty skirts silly with her riding crop.

Longarm spotted the vaqueros covering him from either side of the shady path through the orchard at about the same time. Garcia yelled at them to see their patrona safely back, judging from the way they puppy-dogged after the redhead with their rifles.

Turning back to Garcia, Longarm asked with a puzzled frown, "Was that Gypsy you just yelled, *amigo*? No offense, but you made no sense in any Spanish or English this child's ever heard."

Garcia cradled his scattergun in one elbow and reached in his pants as he replied, "Mission Indian, to the extent it's a language at all. Most of the help we have left are mighty uneducated. I'd be riding for Miller Lux or Tevis by now if the boss lady hadn't made me her boss vaquero. Lloyd Tevis runs most of his stock right here in Kern County and offers even higher wages than Miller Lux. I got the key to yonder doghouse, here. Let's get it over with."

As Longarm followed the somewhat older Californio over to that corroded copper door he decided, "You must have grown up close to here if you savvy the local Mission talk, Soose."

Garcia snorted, "I cannot tell a lie. I'm really a British spy. Of course I was born and raised in these parts. Look at my greaser face. Would you feel better about me if I wore a big straw sombrero and belched mescal at you?"

Longarm chuckled and said he'd noticed Californios had been U.S. citizens since '48. As Garcia fumbled the old-time lock of the tomb Longarm observed, "You must have gone to school with Anglo kids to talk so natural. Might you have known that schoolmarm the boy inside was accused of attacking?"

Garcia got the lock open and shoved hard as he growled, "The mean little shit wasn't accused of attacking her. He raped her after school in her very own classroom. I forget her name. She was after my time. I had close to twenty years on the kid. Come on, I'll show you where they shoved him after the services were over."

That turned out to be a slate shelf in the gloomy depths of the windowless chamber. By the light streaming in from the doorway you could still make out more than some might want to. There were better than a dozen coffins brooding on other shelves all around. Longarm idly wondered how it felt to say adios to someone in such a place, knowing one of those empty slate shelves left had been provided for your own inevitable future.

It wouldn't have been polite to bring it up in front of an Americanized Californio but Spanish-speaking folk could sure act casual about death. He'd once chased a suspect all over Mexico City on that holiday they called the Day of the Dead and the little kids had been eating sugar candy made to look like skulls and bones.

He tried to tell himself skulls and bones were with us all the time, in life and death, just under our goose-bumped hides, as he and Garcia slid the silver handled casket of thick shellacked oak partway out of its niche. Garcia warned, "Don't try to pry the lid up. Here, I have a screw driver blade on my jackknife."

Longarm did as well. But he watched with polite impatience as the Californio took his damned sweet time removing more damned brass screws than you'd think they'd need to hold a dead man down.

At last Garcia seemed finished. For he straightened up and said, "Have a good time. I'm going outside for a smoke or something while you and the little shit get acquainted. He's been rotting in there for months."

211

Garcia left. As he found himself alone with the unpleasant chore Longarm took out one of those enlarged photographs and a half dozen wax-stemmed matches. He put them on the empty slate shelf just above the unfastened coffin lid, got a grip on that with both hands, and took a deep breath before he lifted it.

Then he gasped, "What the fuck?"

For the fucking coffin was empty.

Chapter 23

Fresno Kid's Tia Felicidad was so upset by the news she had to see for herself, with a coal oil lantern from the house. As the three of them stood near the back of the tomb, staring down at the white sateen lining of the empty coffin, the ashen faced redhead said, "You're right. It's as if Tomas had never died. But, damn his twisted soul, we held his funeral for him with him lying dead in that very box and . . . He really was dead, wasn't he, Soose?"

Garcia soberly replied, "He looked mighty dead to me, and Padre Moreno was standing even closer."

Longarm felt no call to mention certain stains on the coffin lining as he assured them both, "There was a dead body in that there box for at least a little while. I'm sure all of you thought it was Tomas Ortega Baker and there's no way, now, to prove it wasn't. But try her this way. We were told by a former cellmate he planned to pull something mighty slick out this way. So my boss sent me out this way and at least two sets of killers have been doing their best to . . . Prevent me from doing what I just done?"

Garcia said, "They didn't do such a good job. Nobody sent me after young Tom and even I can see how he's slickered us all."

Felicidad demanded, "How? I mean, of course I see why my twisted nephew would want to make everyone think he was dead. But the body we entombed here was certainly dead, whether it was his or someone else's."

Longarm and Garcia exchanged glances. The *segundo* told her, gently, "It had to be someone else, ma'am. I know we all thought they'd sent young Tomas back from the Nogales Morgue. I was

213

there and it sure fooled me. But Long, here, meant to compare the remains with a true likeness and, well, a more detached attitude. They tried to keep him from doing that and then, when they saw they couldn't . . . They must have moved mighty recent, right?"

Longarm nodded grimly and said, "Last night was the last time anyone tried to kill me. Somebody mentioned a telegraph set somewhere on the premises, Soose."

Garcia shook his head and said, "In my room. I'm the only one here who knows Morse, unless one of our Mission vaqueros or old Simona have been holding out on us."

Felicidad was the one who got her *segundo* off that hook. She asked who'd tried to kill him, where, and when Longarm brought them both up to date on the attempt to blow him through a tin roof, leaving out the juicy parts with Aura Lee in 'em, Felicidad said, "We're only spliced in to the railroad telegraph running past us between Visalia and that mining camp. It can be awfully complicated, patching into the cross-country Western Union web and wouldn't anyone wiring Soose, here, need the use of a railroad telegrapher's set at one end or the other?"

Longarm nodded and said, "Yep. Even if they sent a coded message to start playing musical coffins, there'd be a record of a message sent from the Blue Dog end. Did you get message one from there last night, Soose?"

When the Californio said he hadn't, Longarm chuckled and said, "There you go, then. We call that an alibi in legal circles. The body you-all stored here must have been moved Lord knows where by Lord knows who for Lord knows what reason if that dynamite under my bed last night wasn't it."

Felicidad glanced around, wide eyed, to ask, "What if it was all just the mischief of some ghoul and . . . Oh, my God! What if they've stolen the bodies of my parents, my sister, the mother of Tomas or . . ."

"Easy, now," Longarm soothed as she covered her pretty face with her hands and began to really carry on. They both got her back outside as Longarm soothed, "Ain't none of your other kin wanted by the law, Miss Felix. There'd be no call for anyone to confuse the issue about any other deceased kith or kin."

Garcia murmured, in Spanish, "He is right. Why don't you both wait for me at the house. I can put things back in order and lock up, here."

The wistful widow didn't argue so Longarm led her off with an arm around her waist, platonic as he could manage, once he'd noticed her figure was all natural. They'd have told him about any kids she'd ever had. He could see why a lady with at least one homicidal lunatic in the family might have hesitated. It would have been forward to ask her how. Gals who knew how to read and write could find out how, if they really wanted to know.

So they talked about more proper matters as he escorted her back to the ranch house. He asked if he'd missed any angles your average crook might exploit for fun and profit. She said he was so right about the future in these parts lying with irrigated crops instead of the few black Moorish longhorns she still grazed sort of dry. But when he perked up to ask whether anyone had been trying to buy her out she shook her dusty red curls to reply, "Not the land. We never sell the land unless we're really desperate and, thanks to the foresight of my poor Carlos, I'd be able to hang on to our combined grants with or without the cooperation of Señores Haggin and Hearst."

Longarm whistled softly and marveled, "Senator George Hearst, the big mining mogul, is interested in this spread, ma'am?"

She smiled softly and explained, "Only as a financial backer of Big Jim Haggin's Kern River project. My husband was securing our own riperian rights under *Yanqui* law when he suffered that fatal heart attack at his desk, poor dear. He left me with iron-bound water rights, much as I miss him. So this is one ignorant greaser they won't take advantage of!"

As they entered her imposing *casa grande* via a side door Longarm chuckled and said, "I know how rapacious my kind has treated your kind, ma'am. Forgetting the land rents the Verdugo clan collects down around Pueblo de Los Angeles, ain't it true the Spanish-speaking firm of *Pioche y Bayerque* charges higher interest than most any other bank in California?"

She laughed and unpinned her Spanish hat inside as she confided, "Five percent, compounded monthly, and Carlos warned me never to do business with the Pico family either. They will sell land and livestock they never had title to, most often to gullible gringos."

In that same main room they were greeted by old Simona, who fussed at her younger patrona for not having bathed and changed, yet. When the redhead asked whether Longarm would be staying the night and he said he had to get it on down the road she told her

215

servant to fetch them some refreshments and let her worry about when she might or might not want some help with her boots.

As they sat down on that chesterfield to wait, the somewhat spoiled but reasonable-sounding widow said, "I don't mean to hold anyone up. I agree Joaquin Murieta overdid things back when I was wee. Thanks to my solid riperian rights nobody can gain full control of the upper Kern without my agreement in writing."

"Which is going to cost 'em a pretty penny," Longarm chuckled. It had been a statement rather than a question.

She shrugged and said, "I only expect what's fair. They're going to have to settle with Lloyd Tevis and smaller ranchers further downstream before they're through. I've agreed to settle for the highest bid on my own water rights."

"From who?" he demanded with a puzzled frown.

To which she replied, "Haggin Hearst or Miller Lux. They've both made grand plans for irrigating the San Joaquin Valley, at a good profit, of course, albeit all of us will come out ahead in the end."

That shy little *moza* scuttled in with yet another silver serving tray too heavy for her. His hostess waited 'til the girl had set it down before them and scuttled back out before she explained, "As a matter of fact I'm expecting some lawyers from both sides any time, now. That was why I was in such a hurry to get down here when first we met up in Visalia the other day. You're welcome to stay the night or as long as you like, if you'd like to question them about my water rights."

Longarm chuckled and replied, "Not hardly, ma'am. I've found few ladies fib about things so easy to check, even when I suspect them harder."

She dimpled and demanded to know what he suspected her of just a little, in that case. He flirted right back, if only for practice, and said, "I'll be switched with snakes if I know, ma'am. If you've been trying to cover for your wayward nephew you sure went about it odd, holding such a fancy public funeral for him. It has occurred to me an evil nephew might be out to inherit all this land and them water rights you just mentioned, if only there was some way a man wanted for murder and worse could appear in probate court to press his claims, as himself. It would make no sense for you to frame him for crimes we all know he committed, or murder him for a fortune you've already got the clear title to. Have you ever studied stage magic, ma'am?"

216

She poured for them both as she demurely replied, "Good heavens, no. Why would I want to do that?"

He said, "I reckon it's handier for a man in my line to know something about. This road show lady I used to know showed me some of the basic moves just in time for me to catch a troublemaking medicine man in the act of Wakan-Wastey. That's what they call good medicine, Wakan-Wastey. Stage magicians use what they call misdirection. That's getting you to look somewhere else whilst they stuff a rabbit in a hat, an extra lady behind a mirror or whatever."

She sliced them some ham, thinner than he might have, as she gently protested he was confusing her. So he said, "Someone's been trying to confuse me and, so far, they've done tolerable. I might have some notion what all this razzle dazzle was about if I had one sensible motive for a thing that's happened, so far."

She sighed and said, "Obviously someone doesn't want you to know whether my confusing nephew is really dead or alive. When do you think his body, or some other body, could have been shifted like that?"

He washed down some ham on sissy-bread with red wine and decided, "Most any time after you all left that tomb unguarded, remote from the nearest window. The more I study on that the less sense that motive makes. There was no sense trying to kill anyone to keep him from comparing a known likeness with a nobody at all, and, like I said, I figure there's been at least two sets of killers out to kill me for some other reason or reasons entire!

Chapter 24

Those other vaqueros who rode for the outfit straggled in late that afternoon, bone-weary and disgusted after following that cold trail the train robbers had left to the total confusion of an Anglo settlement where greasers weren't served at the bar.

Spanish-speaking folk supped later than most, after eating and drinking more all day, so Longarm said he just had to tear himself away, once Soose had let him put an all points out on the Fresno Kid with the rinky-dink telegraph in his combined office and quarters.

Longarm thought about what he'd just done as he rode out just before sundown, telling 'em all he meant to make the county seat by cooler night riding. It hardly seemed even a homicidal lunatic would climb out of his coffin unless he was really alive. After that it got harder to swallow. Longarm could see fooling everyone from Los Rurales to a family priest with spooky face makeup and damned fine breath control for a *few minutes*. After that a dead look-alike worked way better. But, damn it, why spoil it all by disposing of a substitute corpse good enough to fool folk who knew you, earlier, before it had had time to look less like you?

Longarm had been fibbing when he'd said he'd be riding direct to the county seat by moonlight. Once he was well clear of the old Ortega grant in the tricky gloaming light he crossed over the tracks to circle some through the high chaparral.

Old Simona had told him the old Carillo grant, just down the Kern, was only used for grazing, now, with riders only using the Carillo housing during inclement weather.

The sky above was clear and the fall nights were still comfortable for anyone dressed sensible. But of course an owlhoot rider who might not want to explain a camp fire could doubtless find use for even ancient 'dobe walls.

Longarm knew someone had built a fire to the southwest as he spotted smoke rising between him and the golden sunset. He rode a furlong further through the chaparral and dismounted to tether his hired roan to a scrub oak surrounded by wild anise, saying, "Enjoy yourself, Pard," as he drew his Winchester from its saddle boot.

Moving in on a strange camp called for more than one kind of care. He knew it was just as likely some simple vaqueros were brewing some damned old coffee on a handy hearth, ahead. So he didn't want to come in shooting.

At the same time, either honest men or outlaws were inclined to shoot at shadows creeping in on 'em. So the idea was to creep in good 'til you had a better handle on the situation.

Longarm crept good. He'd scouted mighty sneaky Indians in his time and while the chaparral was crackle-dry and the grass and forbs between crunched underfoot like cinders he managed pretty good 'til a damned pony nickered somewhere ahead.

Longarm hunkered low in a clump of scrub laurel and didn't bother to breathe for a spell as he strained his ears. The unseen pony who'd sensed him didn't seem to have further comments to make. Longarm still forced himself to count silently to a thousand, which usually did it, before he eased back up to move forward some more, even slower.

He could make out the old 'dobe walls now, their whitewash already stripped by the how-many years since old Chuck Carillo had married fancier. The roofless ruins still stood taller than a man, most places, and yep, there was a white man's fire burning inside the shell, judging from the glow bouncing off a far wall as the sky above got ever darker.

Longarm could see a narrow window cut through the thick 'dobe between him and the fire inside. He eased that way for a look-see, taking care where he put his feet. As he got closer the looming 'dobe cast an inky shadow across his intended path because of the sunset as well as the fire on the far side. So he hunkered down to stare at the dirt ahead with his eyes in the deep shade as well.

That was when someone shot his hat off. He whirled on his haunches to fire at the muzzle flash before it sunk in he'd just been gut shot from the side, if he'd still been walking.

His own target yipped like a kicked pup and spun away from the corner of the ruins like a drunken ballerina, flinging his own sixgun far and wide before crashing down in a clump of wild mustard.

Longarm let the moaning bastard lie as he dashed over to that window slit in time to spy a single spooked pony busting loose inside. As it tore out the far side of the ruins Longarm recalled where he'd seen its paint rump and one white stocking before. He'd passed on a pony with one pink hoof at the livery back in Visalia.

He knew it would take most of the night returning to its stall there, pausing hither and yon to graze as it took its own sweet time. So he set that concern aside and ambled over to see how the paint's more mysterious rider was doing.

There was just enough light left to make out the features of the poor soul staring wistfully up at him from the weeds. Longarm hunkered down, Winchester across his thighs, to remark conversationally, "Look on the bright side, Peewee. You said you just hated the notion of our hanging you and I feel sure I've hulled you fatal, you lying bastard."

The dying diabetic moaned, "You'd finish me now if you had an ounce of mercy, Longarm. For it sure hurts like fire to get shot smack through the paunch."

Longarm reached for some smokes as he replied, "I was only returning your intended favor. Lord only knows how bad you wounded my poor Stetson. Your lungs still seem sound and there may be time for you to enjoy a last cheroot as we discuss our more recent adventures."

Peewee said he didn't feel up to smoking and that he just wanted to die and get this over with.

Longarm lit one cheroot and put the other away as he said, "All in time you sneaky rascal. Let's start with who you've had gunning for me, well before you escaped from that Denver hospital."

Peewee sounded sincerely confused as he replied, "I didn't know you knew of this hidey-hole and I was hoping you might not guess I'd blue streak for old Tom Baker after I'd ratted on him back in Denver."

Longarm shrugged and said, "Well, Lord knows you were dumb enough to tether a livery pony loose. Let's try her another way. Where did you hide that body from the Ortega family tomb, and who's was it?"

Peewee Folsom was either telling the truth or a mighty good gutshot actor as he gasped, "I don't know nothing about no dead folk in these parts, but just stick around. How come you was ducking even before my bullet could leave my gun? Are you some sort of mind reader?"

Longarm sighed and said, "I wish I was. Let's try it another way. You're stupid as hell, but you just noticed, yourself, how risky it might be to rat on a cellmate and then join him at a secluded hidey-hole. So what if you were convinced as much as everyone else that Los Rurales had shot the right lad gone wrong? What if, in fact, you'd been the very one who betrayed him to bounty-hunting *rurales* after he'd told you about some he'd made a deal with and so . . . Shit, that won't add up to a piss-ant broke enough to rob general stores, will it?"

Folsom groaned, "Anything you say. I'd like to die, now, if it's all the same with you."

But Longarm growled, "I ain't done with you yet. Explain how come you knew about this old Carillo spread being deserted. The kid's Tia Felicidad hadn't married up with Chuck Carillo, yet, when she threw him out to graze with the rest of the black sheep."

Peewee said, "He used to get letters from her in prison. He laughed at her 'cause she kept fussing at him to go straight and all the time she was fussing she kept sending him money for tobacco and soap."

Peewee grimaced and added, "He spent lot's of it on sissy boys with soapy assholes. That's the only kind of whores they had in that prison and old Tom was sure a horny cuss. Used to go on and on about all the gals he'd had. Even said he'd almost had his Aunt Felix and meant to, someday, when it was safe to go home."

Longarm whistled softly and said, "Well, I doubt anything like that could be going on around here without the servants gossiping and the lady's a better fibber than you if she's gone in for incest with a bank robber this late in life."

He took a thoughtful drag on his smoke and let it slowly out before he decided, "Telegrams sent out from that *segundo's* private set have to be rerouted through the railroad and then Western Union to get anywhere important. Telegraphers just hate to gossip

221

about paid-for messages, but I have my methods and the best part is that I'll have two sets of records to compare."

Peewee didn't comment. He wasn't even breathing. Longarm gently closed the cadaver's eyes and said, "I ain't got time to tote you all about and it might be interesting to confuse someone else for a change. So I reckon I'll plant you shallow and mark your temporary repose in case any honest folk ever give a shit."

He strode back to where he'd tethered the roan and led it back to the ruins. He tethered it inside, saying, "That overdeveloped fire will burn sensible in a spell. Meanwhile there's something to be said for baking 'dobe walls before night sets in entire."

Then he broke out a folding camp spade he'd packed in one saddle bag a long time ago to bury the late Peewee Folsom by a dead fruit tree out back. Unlike the native vegetation, most fruits and nuts you planted out this way required fairly regular watering.

When he'd done he put his coat back on, having already found his hat, and rejoined his livery mount in the ruins to find the fire had died down to a bed of cheersome coals. That reminded him he'd missed supper. So he broke out a can of pork and beans to warm some before he et. But he'd no sooner opened the can and found it a flat place on the warm hearth when he heard someone coming, noisy enough to let him see they knew he was there and didn't want to spook him.

He still rose with his Winchester and rolled over a window sill to observe the proceedings from outside, where it was darker. After a proddy but not too long wait a couple of squatty vaqueros in white cotton and buckskin materialized on the far side of the shell. They'd left their own mounts somewhere else. But one held the reins of that paint livery mount Peewee Folsom had been riding.

Longarm saw neither seemed armed. They'd left any guns they'd brought along with their own ponies. So Longarm called out, "*Buenoches, amigos*," and showed himself, saddle gun pointed down as he rolled back inside.

They still seemed ready to bust out crying or bolt. Unlike the proud Felicidad or even old Simona, these kids looked pure Cañalino as most so-called Mission Indians had started out. Their Spanish was more basic than his and their English was nonexistent as they tried to explain what they were doing with his *caballo*.

He said he followed their drift about backtracking a runaway and since he didn't want to spook 'em with dead bodies he said

222

the paint was a spare mount from the same livery as yonder roan. This was the simple truth as soon as you studied on it.

As he tethered the paint by the roan, they seemed old pals, he invited the vaqueros to have some beans with him. So one tore back to their own saddle bags to return with some tortillas.

Longarm was glad, once the three of 'em were hunkered by the dying fire, stuffing their faces with rolled up tortillas stuffed with pork and beans. All three agreed it made for a new experience.

They thought his woman sure cooked frijoles sweet and swell. So he felt obliged to compliment their own homemade tortillas, and as a matter of fact these were a cut above the usual. They looked as much like undercooked flapjacks as most tortillas but something with more meat on its bones than bleached corn meal. But when he asked if it might be *Bellota* they didn't savvy. They had mayhaps a two hundred word vocabulary between 'em and that English language expert, Sir Richard Burton, said you needed about three hundred words of any lingo to get by in your average whorehouse.

But by backing and filling he was able to establish they rode for Doña Felicidad as he'd figured. They respected Jesus Garcia, thought old Simona a fuss, and knew *la patrona* about as well as your average English stock herder knew Queen Victoria. They said her black sheep nephew had been before their time and that Longarm was the only stranger they'd seen around these old ruins so far that year.

That didn't mean much. They'd never spotted Peewee Folsom, buried out back, and they might have missed everyone if that runaway pony hadn't tried to have supper with their own remuda. They're own line camp was a few *varas* off to the north, near a wind-pumped tank. They said Soose Garcia had told 'em to keep the stock moving from water to water lest they overgraze this late in the year. Longarm had figured Garcia for an old boy who knew which end of the cow the shit fell out of. These kids didn't seem to care and just did as they'd been told. Soose had said good help was starting to get expensive. Neither had heard a thing about bigger outfits bidding on Doña Felicidad's water rights. But they were sure they'd have noticed if there'd been any attempts to force her hand.

On the other hand, they hadn't known 'til just now that Peewee and Lord only knew how many others had been trespassing on her range.

Chapter 25

Longarm spread his bedroll in the middle of nowheres better than half the night and half the ride to Visalia and caught some short but safe shut-eye where nobody could try to dynamite him in his sleep.

He got back to the county seat before noon, settled up with the livery, stored his stuff, and picked up a pad of ruled lawyer's paper and some colored pencils before he buckled down to the sort of chores he just hated.

Billy Vail, back in Denver, hunted better on paper than most anyone. So one of the messages Longarm picked up from the home office via Western Union involved a disbarred lawyer called Undertaking Sam, last seen around Cheyenne, who'd once got a client off despite the coroner finding a hat pin way the hell up her husband's nose. Somebody as yet unknown had been wiring back and forth to Cheyenne in a code Billy Vail had found childishly simple. Smiley and Dutch had left for Cheyenne to bring Undertaking Sam back alive, if they knew what was good for 'em. The more subtle Deputy Guilfoyle, who could follow a suspect a whole hour without pistol-whipping him, had been assigned to stake out the Western Union in Denver.

He put all that down in red pencil and noted the less he knew about the killer who'd nailed that gal in Sacramento, and vice versa, in blue. He figured purple would do, for now, for the assholes playing with dynamite. They worked as well working for red or blue.

He was neatly putting all this down at a table in the reading room at the county hall of records when Miss Sylvia Moorehead of the *Fresno Observer* caught him in the act. She had a mess of old ledgers in her own hands as she joined him at the table, asking what they were looking up.

He smiled across at her to confide, "Nothing about that train robbery the other night, tempting as it felt to chase along partway with the boys paid to worry about such local matters. I got a can of worms of my own to sort out, and even with these fancy colored pencils it don't make any more sense on paper than I already had it in my head."

She said color coding different leads seemed awfully clever and asked it she might share the use of the same. He shoved the box out to the middle of the shellacked sugar pine and idly asked how she was doing with the Evans Sontag gang.

She said, "They got away clean with almost ten thousand and they might have been most anyone. Black Bart hasn't hit up around Fort Ross in quite a spell, they say."

Longarm shrugged and replied, "They say he's a poet, too, and I know that's a lie. Your mysterious Black Bart and his gang, if he has any gang, has yet to hit a train, north or south. Frank and Jesse have never yet stopped a stagecoach. Such gents seem creatures of habit as well as limited imagination. Kit Evans has declared war on the Southern Pacific and that Blue Dog line is an S.P. spur. So like the old Indian said, I have spoken."

She said, "Oh, pooh, you're no fun. My readers don't want to read of a local hero gunning helpless victims and tossing off speeding trains. I can't make mysterious Mexican raiders work. The posse tracked the train robbers to Anglo parts of the valley where nobody who never saw nobody would ever cover for Mexicans in the habit of murdering even a railroader of the Anglo persuasion."

He said he'd heard Joaquin Murieta had been dead a spell, if in fact he'd ever lived.

She said, "Black Bart is a sort of Robin Hood some might want to shield from the hired guns of the Octopus and, unlike our Chris Evans he's supposed to be a mean-eyed killer, so . . ."

"Back up," Longarm cut in with a laugh, adding, "Fair is fair and I've been following the sort of comical Black Bart's career since he started stopping stages back in '77. He almost always picks a Wells Fargo stage and to date he'd never harmed a hair on anyone's head."

She sighed and consulted her own smaller notebook, murmuring, "He appears alone in a flour sack and white travel duster where the stage slows down in rough parts of the trail, armed with a repeating rifle and shouting orders to his unseen confederates staked out all about."

Longarm shrugged and said, "Maybe. Nobody's ever seen any other members of his notorious gang, or cut the trail of more than one mount, after a stick-up. But do go on and tell me how in thunder stage robberies along the Russian tie in with train robberies betwixt the San Joaquin and Kern."

She saw how steamed he was, a mere man might not have noticed, and said, "Heavens, it's only a newspaper story. Why are you getting all upset about it if you don't even think it could have been Black Bart?"

He said, "We have to catch, try, and convict the Robin Hoods you and your kind only have to write about, Miss Sillie. That can be a chore when the public offers halfway intelligent help. Owlhoot riders such as Evans, Black Bart and your Fresno Kid are already doing all they can to confuse us. We don't really need more smoke in our eyes and I know the poor cuss stuck with tracking down Black Bart for Wells Fargo. His name's Jim Hume and he's a pretty good tracker. But it's hardly fair to have Jim searching for his man this far south. So what if I was to cut you into a better story?"

She beamed across at him to announce, "You're on. I can't reprint a poem that calls the owners of Wells Fargo a bunch of fine-haired sons of you-know-what in any case. What are we working on, ah, Pard?"

He said, "You missed the fun down to the old Ortega place. Miss Felix caught up with me just as I was fixing to open that tomb we were talking about."

She said, "Felix would never stand for that. I told you you'd never get at her nephew's body."

He smiled thinly and told her, "Somebody did. Before I go on, do I have your word you'll sit on everything I tell you 'til we work out the whole story, arrests and all?"

She said she followed his drift and didn't want to spoil a scoop by tipping off any crooks in advance. So he brought her up to date on most everything but Aura Lee since last they'd spoken. He made some thoughtful notes in red, blue, purple and, hell, green, as he tried to lay it all out sensible.

She found it as confusing, writing with the red pencil as she decided, "All right, you left Denver to follow up on a tip from one crook about another. Someone wired ahead about you before you could even get to Cheyenne."

He said, "That's all any color you want to try, before we know what I wasn't supposed to find out. So far all I've found out just has me more mixed up. So it's obvious I ain't found out enough."

He folded his pad over to write quickly but clearly in green as he muttered aloud, "I'll do better twisting telegraph wires to find out who might have wired whom in recent memory. You being a California newspaper gal who can even get at Black Bart's awful attempts as a poet, I'm putting down some questions for you to look up. Two heads may not be better than one but they can sure look up more facts and figures in the same amount of time."

He tore off her assigned research and slid it across to her as she mused, "Black Bart spells it Poe-8 and you're right about it being doggeral. What's this about Carlos Carillo having a heart attack, for heaven's sake?"

Longarm said, "Might help to know exactly where, when, with or without a doctor watching. His wife's nephew was a known killer whose whereabouts might have been unknown at the time. I'm still working on a suspect who's husband suffered a hat pin attack she almost passed off as a stroke."

Sillie blanched but sounded sure as she replied, "I wrote the obit for the Observer. About eighteen months ago without my notes. He suffered the classic symptoms at his desk on Montgomery Street in San Francisco. Felix was down at their ranch overseeing some new construction. Her Carlos, or Chuck, died in Saint Francis Hospital before she could reach his side and, oh dear, her nephew, Tomas, would have been in prison at the time, right?"

Longarm grimaced and said, "I can't even hang that one on Pee-wee Folsom so, right, the murder of Carlos Carillo can't be what even one mastermind wants to hide if the poor cuss died natural."

He made a note in purple and tried, "The cellmate of that black sheep nephew told me the randy rascal had incestuous yearnings for his pretty Tia Felicidad. Might she have confided anything like that, off the record, to a newspaper gal she was on confidential terms with?"

Sillie gasped, "My Lord, we hardly know one another that well and I, for one, would hesitate to tell a sister her child might be going insane that way, about my own flesh and blood!"

He soothed, "Incest is a felony. It ain't exactly insanity. Miss Cleopatra was encouraged to marry her own brother before she took up with all them Roman gents because her kind found incest the best way to keep crowns in the family. Her mom and pop had already been brother and sister and it didn't keep her from being nice-looking and smart."

Sillie said it still sounded disgusting.

He said, "I figure they passed all them laws against it because of how sticky things can turn out. When Miss Cleopatra decided she'd rather take up with all them Romans she had to have her husband killed and, him being her brother as well, it wound up way more sticky than average, so . . ."

"Felix Carillo has never mentioned anything like that," Sillie cut in, prim-lipped.

So he dropped it and tried, "His cellmate said she sent him money from time to time as well as good advice about his other disgusting notion. Your turn."

She shook her head and said, "You seem to have us down as old school chums. I'm only a newspaper reporter she's had friendly relations with. As you must know by now, Felix is friendly with most anyone who isn't trying to take advantage of her."

He nodded and said, "She was kind enough to me when she was making up her mind about a gunfight. But I doubt she'd cover for a lowlife who had the hots for her and laughed at her well-meant advice. There ought to be a record if she ever sent enough cash by mail or wire to finance his jail break. I'm betting I won't find any. I just can't come up with any use she'd have for him or any hold he might have on her. What can you tell me about those rascals bidding against one another for her riperian rights?"

Sillie looked so surprised he believed she hadn't heard a thing about that angle. So he swore her to secrecy, warning she could mess things up more than a tedious item on a back page could be worth, before he explained the rival would-be water lords trying to get the widowed redhead to sign with one or the other.

Sillie whistled softly and said, "Make that a rich widow indeed, by Old Californio standards! Granting riperian rights without ceding an acre of grant land ought to leave our Felix right up there with the Verdugos, Yerba-Irvines and their ilk!"

"Then we're talking pretty penny?" He insisted.

To which she replied, "Dollars. Oodles and oodles of dollars backed by Miller Lux beef and Haggin Hearst gold. You name a figure and the other will top it, for Big Jim Haggin plays for keeps and Hank Miller is one stubborn Dutchman."

It was Longarm's turn to whistle, louder, and decide, "I wish I owned many a mile of rancho grande along a year 'round river. I'd make 'em irrigate me as part of the deal and once I had all my purebred white faces browsing timothy and lucerne in the shade of all them fruit trees I'd never get up Monday mornings at all. What was that about Miller being a Dutchman?"

She shrugged and said, "Everyone knows that. He came out here from one of those German states as a Heinrich Müller, way back when. Does that mean anything to you, Custis?"

He made note of the name but said, "Likely not. Tom Baker's daddy started out with a German name and the Sontags have yet to give their's up. But we all got to come from somebody and a heap of Irish Americans have yet to ride with Billy The Kid. I know Senator Hearst to be hard as nails but above hired assassins. I hear Miller Lux have been hiring hands away from rival spreads. Have they ever been accused of more direct methods?"

She shook her head and said, "Not involving gunplay. Like Haggin and Hearst they've outgrown that stage of development. They can just about set the price of California beef already. If they beat Haggin and Hearst out of controlling the headwaters of the San Joaquin and Kern, the Kern being the key to irrigating the whole south end of the big valley, folk back east will pay what Miller, Lux and the railroad barons decide they ought to pay for California fruit and produce, too!"

Longarm shrugged and said, "That's the American way and Queen Housewife ain't so helpless in the end. Longhorn beef was good enough for her mamma but range stock's being bred up mighty prissy since that last business depression wound down. Didn't I hear something about a rival valley beef spread run by a cuss called Tevis?"

She nodded and said, "Lloyd Tevis and a handful of other ranchers are in the same swell position as our Felix. They stand to get rich quick letting others dam or not dam the waters running by their home spreads. Why would Tevis or any other rancher, big or small, want to start a range war at a time like this?"

Longarm made a note and decided, "It would be stupid. On the other hand the prisons across our great land ain't filled with wise old owls and Louis Napoleon could have quit whilst he was ahead if he'd had a lick of sense. The trouble with that line of reasoning is that it don't lead nowheres. Felicidad Carillo nee Ortega holds unclouded title to them water rights all by her pure self. Nobody could get 'em by killing her unless they married her first. Her only heir is already wanted for murder, whether he's dead or alive, so . . . How would we go about finding out whether someone I don't know about has been courting a no-longer-young but mighty pretty widow woman?"

Sillie said, "Leave that to me and the girls I gossip with from time to time. As of this moment I haven't heard anything like that, though. If we do learn of such a swain, how might that incriminate him in other ways, Custis?"

Longarm sighed and said, "It only gives me some infernal body to *consider*. There ain't no federal or even local statute forbidding the courting of widow women, even rich ones. But as of now I haven't one suspect I can tie to Miss Felix, her black sheep nephew, her firm but apparently fair *segundo* or . . . Say, could you scout up more than just names and dates on that Miss Ruth, the schoolmarm the Fresno Kid got so fresh with before he became the Fresno Kid?"

Sillie said, "That case was before my time on the paper but I'm sure we have all we printed about it in our morgue. I guess you know how delicately such crimes tend to be recorded, though?"

He explained, "I don't want any delicate details. I can likely imagine more than that poor schoolmarm would want me to. I was told she busted up with her true love and departed for points unknown to live down her disgrace. I'd like to make sure that was the whole story. Folk have been known to go loco for way less cause and someone's been acting mighty loco around here!"

Sillie frowned thoughtfully at him and demanded, "But why might even a certified lunatic or even her outraged true love even think of taking it out on you, Custis? You don't resemble Tom Baker in any way and if ever I'd been wronged by such a moral monster the last man I'd consider harming would have to be a lawman trying to hunt him down for me!"

Longarm shrugged and said, "Nobody said you were *loco en la cabeza*. A lunatic, by definition, don't think like the rest of us and I only work for Marshal Billy Vail and the Denver District Court. So how do you like a madwoman who steals dead bodies and hauls them all about with her like that spooky Spanish queen, what's her name?"

"Juana la Loca," Sillie surprised him by knowing, then adding, "She suffered what the doctors call necrophilia and it was her dead husband, not a villain who'd wronged her, she kept about the house. A woman would have to be even crazier than Juana la Loca to steal what I saw in that coffin with these very eyes to . . . My God, what?"

He shrugged and said, "Stick pins in, smother with kisses, do I look like a crazy woman? I know it's a long shot, Miss Sillie. I know that schoolmarm the boy wronged years ago could be most anywhere, now, and I can see her teaching school some more before I can see her coming back to seek some wild revenge on the wrong cuss entire. But its what we call elimination in my line. When you got a can of worms to take out one worm at a time, setting each likely innocent one aside, 'til after a spell you only have one or more mighty suspicious worms left."

She said she followed his drift. He said, "Bueno. Like I said, I'll eliminate worms on this list whilst you eliminate worms on *your* list and I promise you an exclusive when I get them, or they get me. It happens."

She smiled knowingly and said, "I'm betting on you. I've been doing a little background on you and I'm just dying to hear more about the time you saved the Divine Sarah Bernhardt from all those assassins! Was she really as, you know, as some say?"

He smiled fondly and replied, "I found her a nice little gal and if you're asking what I suspect everyone would like to know, she kissed me, sisterly, for saving her life that time. I never slept with her, in or out of that notorious coffin she's supposed to spend her nights in. It ain't for me to say who might."

The curious newspaper gal smiled sort of wicked and said, "I'll see what I can dig up about the personal habits of these less glamorous mortals. When and where do you want me to meet you later on?"

Longarm hesitated, then said, "I hadn't thought of that. I should have before I shot my mouth off. I've been awesomely hard on some of the hotels I've checked into, recent. Somebody still at large on your list or mine keeps trying to disturb my rest."

Sillie glanced about to assure herself they were alone in that reading room before she leaned forward to softly confide, "Few if any could know we're in cahoots here in Visalia. I'm barely

231

known here and I'm not registered at any hotel. An old school chum who has some recently inherited property for sale lent me the key to the one cabin that's still half furnished. So that's where my baggage is right now and if we picked up some stove wood and staples we could even avoid eating in public together. I may not be Sarah Bernhardt but I'm not a bad cook."

Longarm said he was sure she was. So she started to write down the address for him. Then she laughed sort of wild and demanded, "Lord have mercy, what am I doing? We barely know one another and . . . You didn't think I was talking about, ah, shacking up, did you?"

"Perish the thought!" he gallantly replied, even as he idly wondered what in thunder she did have in mind.

Chapter 26

There was grudging cooperation and then there was genuine enthusiasm. Your average telegrapher had been pestered now and again by lawmen and knew which side of his bread the butter was on. So, not wanting rough estimates or pure bull, Longarm decided to track down the district manager here in the county seat.

They were willing to tell him how at the Western Union near the depot. His office was right upstairs, only you had to back out the front and around to the side where an open stairway ran up one side of their frame building.

That sounded fair. So he ducked out and around, where he found a trio of obvious cowhands had backed a more peculiar-looking cowhand under the stairs with barrel staves and broom handles, which failed to strike Longarm fair at all.

Their intended victim, holding a length of two-by-four but staring at Longarm with desperate resignation, was a Chinaman dressed up as if to play cowboy. His Stetson had been knocked off, making it even easier to notice his American haircut and Oriental features. One of the other hands grinned at Longarm to declare, "Seeing you're one of us, grab a weapon and help us larn this Ching Chong Chinaman a lesson!"

Longarm let his frock coat open wider to display his .44-40 as he hauled out his wallet and badge, saying, "I already got a weapon and I ain't one of anybody. I'm the law."

He could see they didn't cotton much to that notion, but since it seemed easier to catch flies with honey than vinegar he frowned at the Oriental kid they'd backed under the stairs to continue, "Get on out here and let's have a look at you, boy. What's this son of Han been up to, gents?"

The self-appointed leader of the trio, a peculiar-looking cow hand in his own right, said, "Just look at him! High heeled boots and gun barrel chaps, for Gawd's sake! When we asked him where his tong might be holding their wild West show he confessed right out he was looking for work as a cow hand in our valley! Said he knew how to ride and even knew a thing or two about roping!"

Another Anglo there snorted and decreed, "Everybody knows you never see a Chinaman on a horse because their private parts are different."

Longarm nodded soberly and told the tight-lipped young Oriental, "You'd best come along with me on suspicion of impersonation, boy. We'll sort out your wild claims down to the station house."

The Chinese insisted he hadn't done wrong. The cowhands wanted to come along and watch him hang. Longarm decided, "I got me more important business in an office upstairs. So here's what I'd best do with this misguided youth. I'd best carry him along with me as I go about more important chores. I doubt I need you boys to guard such a sickly-looking cuss for me. Of course, if you think one white man and a .44-40 can't handle one of these critters . . ."

The leader of the trio spat and said, "My baby sister could lick him and his whole tong. Come on, boys, let's go have that drink I promised you, once we'd brought this squint-eyed shit to justice!"

They headed the other way as Longarm herded the still-confused Oriental cowhand up those stairs. As they ducked inside at the top Longarm told him, "I'm sorry I had to mean-mouth you like that, old son. I wasn't as worried about them as I was another 1871."

The Oriental youth stared up at the taller Longarm thoughtfully as he decided, "You called me a son of Han, not a Chink. You are tall with dark hair and mustache and your eyes are the gray of twin gun muzzles. You seem stern but not unkind and so you must be the lawman they call Longarm!"

To which his rescuer could only reply, "Aw, mush. Let's talk about your story. No offense, but Chinese cowboys do seem a mite unusual and you may have just noticed how some others react to the notion."

The youth he'd rescued said, "I may not stand out as much with my big sombrero in place. It still lies in the dust, down there."

Longarm said, "It'll keep, 'til we figure out what's best for the rest of you. You were about to tell me who you might be and how you come up with such odd ambitions."

The youth smiled sheepishly and said, "Call me Lou Drake. Duck Low sounds sort of silly here in Gum Sahn. My honorable father came to Gum Sahn from Kwang Tung to prospect for color in your Motherlode. But he wound up cooking for cowboys up the other side of Yee Fou, excuse me, I meant Sacramento. After a while he had saved enough to send for my mother. So I was born on a western ranch, which is more than many a cowboy can say."

"What are you doing down this way, then?" asked Longarm.

Lou Drake made a wry face and said, "My father and mother pleased the people in the big house. Their hands treated me and the other cute little Chinks with kindness, I suppose. Some taught me one trick with a rope while others taught me another. I was allowed to ride all I wanted by an easy going head wrangler. In time it seemed natural for me to help with the branding and other chores. But then, one day, when I asked to be put on the payroll as a regular hand, everyone laughed."

Longarm nodded soberly and got out a couple of smokes as he said, "They laughed at me when I come out west after the war, and I was a white boy who'd just fought a war. Cowhand humor can be caustic. So you thought you'd try down this way, where nobody might be as likely to notice you didn't look exactly Anglo Saxon?"

Lou Drake said, "I know what I look like. I know how well I ride and rope. I heard they were hiring cowhands down this way. So I came to find out."

Longarm frowned thoughtfully and replied, "I've heard much the same and that's sort of odd as soon as you study on it. There was a time most all this valley south of the Sacramento Delta was considered cattle country. Better than a third has been fenced off for farming, now. Yet, like yourself, I heard the bigger outfits are hiring the best hands away from the smaller outfits by offering higher wages. Don't that make an old cowhand like you sort of wonder?"

The Chinese-American shrugged and suggested, "Beef prices are at an all time high, back east, and the newer breeds of more tender beef can't take care of themselves as well as the old Hispano-Moorish cows that go natural with dusty range."

Longarm decided, "Mebbe. We might not be having this interesting conversation up here if you'd been packing a gun. Those assholes you were having so much fun with didn't strike this child as hired guns, either. Was mention made of that sort of riding when you heard they were hiring down this way?"

Lou Drake seemed sincere as he gasped, "Hell, no! I just want to grow up to be a cowboy, not a hatchet man! My old country folk raised us Bai Hoi, or don't tangle with the Round Eyes, and that's one thing I can agree about with 'em. If I was damn fool enough to risk my neck for money I'd do better, as I said, fighting for one of one of our own Family Associations, or even a tong."

Longarm didn't ask the youth to elaborate. He had pals among the Six Families as well as a couple of tongs. So he knew the difference between a sort of Scotch clan and a sort of bandit gang better than most American lawmen of his time. He nodded and said, "I've been told none of the big cattle outfits in these parts settle range disputes Wyoming Style when they can plow rivals under with slick lawyers and political pull. Mayhaps it's what that fuss-and-feathers over to London Town, Karl Marx, describes as economical warfare. Mayhaps the big outfits are just plowing the profits of higher beef prices back into busting the smaller outfits. *Hable 'Spañol?*"

The Chinese-American blinked and managed, "*Hablo muy poco y comprendo menor. ¿Porque?*"

Longarm sighed and said, "You're right. Your Spanish is dreadful, no offense. If you spoke it better I'd suggest you try this one outfit I know of. They tell me Doña Felicidad of the Ortega-Carillo spread is hurting for hands. I doubt they're paying half as well as Muller Lux or Tevis and you'd surely have a time making yourself understood in the bunkhouse, but they might not laugh as hard at the notion of a Chinee cow hand. I read somewhere that our Indians all started out in Asia with the rest of you Orienticated folk."

Lou Drake said he just might try at the Ortega-Carillo ranch. So Longarm said, "Just follow the Blue Dog line as far as the Kern and turn left. The *segundo's* name is Jesus but you can call him Soose. Don't tell him I sent you if you want the job. We seem to have parted friendly but we met sort of tense and I ain't about to commend any roper I ain't seen roping to begin with."

The Chinese-American agreed that sounded fair. So once they'd made sure nobody seemed to be laying for him down below they shook on it and Longarm strode down the hall to the office he'd been after all this time.

The district manager riding herd on Western Union's operations in these parts was going to look just like one of those Egyptian mummies an hour after he died. But he seemed a friendly enough dried-up old coot 'til Longarm sat down across from him and handed him that list of questions recopied in plain pencil.

The Western Union man read silently, dry lips moving, then whistled sort of dusty and decided, "You sure seem blessed, or cursed, with a healthy curiosity, Deputy Long. We'd have no records for half of these questions and even if we did, company policy forbids . . ."

"Don't paint yourself in a corner 'til you hear the rest of my offer," Longarm cut in.

The telegraph company hadn't promoted the old coot to a position of authority because he was stupid, or even hasty. So he stared dry and unwinking for a spell before he asked, with a rustle of bat wings somewhere inside his parchment-covered skull, "Offer, Deputy Long? I see nothing but demands, a lot of demands, on these two pages of foolscap."

Longarm nodded but said, "I like to offer verbal when I ain't sure who might or might not approve, higher up. Like you keep saying, I'm only a deputy. Is it safe to say you get a bonus now and again when you save your company money? I mean real money?"

The old coot cautiously allowed he stood ever ready to save Western Union and its stockholders an honest nickel or dime. So Longarm told him, "I know that for reasons having nothing to do with you and your company my opposite numbers out this way ain't about to stir from their hideyholes without one damned good reason before that congressional hearing and of course this November's election blow over."

The old telegrapher nodded and said, "You're so right, but I see nothing about Mussel Slough, here."

Longarm explained, "I don't need nothing on Mussel Slough. I don't want nothing on Mussel Slough. It ain't my case, praise the Lord. If you look close you'll see I ain't asking you for the exact wording on any of them wires anyone might or might not have sent. I only need the exact times on the exact dates. I can guess a heap once I have the true sequences. For example I only want to know *if,* and how often, wires might have passed back and forth betwixt your Denver office and that private telegraph key on the old Ortega grant, see?"

The old man shook his head and said, "You're asking an awful lot. We'd have to wire all over creation, during all three shifts, in hopes of having no more in the end than a bare bones sequence of senders and receivers, as you suggest."

Longarm insisted, "You can do it, and in less than twenty-four full hours, I'd be betting."

The older man shrugged and said, "Seventeen hours, tops. You still haven't told me why we'd want to go to all that trouble."

Longarm said, "With federal, state and county law out of action or not caring, you, the railroads and the stage lines have to pay your own company security riding overtime, right?"

The old man nodded grimly and said, "That's no secret, and you infernal federal riders are supposed to secure our wires stretched through Indian country. Those bastard Sioux and Apache cut the wires before they lift the first scalp as a rule!"

Longarm nodded soothingly and said, "I've never scouted *Yakuts* on the warpath but I can see why you'd want private patrols out at what, a dollar a day per rider?"

"Plus expenses," the district manager grimly replied, adding, "The damned BIA can't tell anyone where their damned Indians ran off to and the damned army won't chase Indians 'til they've done something hostile. You know, of course, the first hostile move they'll make will involve our telegraph lines, Christ knows where or when!"

Longarm hesitated, then said, "I told you this might work best as an oral agreement betwixt gents of the old school. I've no call to cause trouble for nobody, needless."

The old coot snapped, "Get to the point. I'm a gentleman of a school too old for you to recall. What have you got for us?"

Longarm said, simply, "The solution to your Indian problem. I got your word we'll solve it my way, provided no telegraph lines or folk working for your telegraph company get cut by Indians?"

The older man said he had it signed in blood, so Longarm told him, "Ain't no Indians on the warpath in these parts. That reservation jump was inspired by a chance for self-improvement. Boys being boys and unguarded stock and clotheslines being tempting, the few petty instances of Yakuts savagery can be chalked up to just passing through."

"Passing through to where?" demanded the Western Union manager.

Longarm said, "Some of 'em, at least, went to work as ranch hands and likely house servants at a certain spread I know. The only real difference betwixt your average Mex vaquero and a wild Indian is his attitude and a pair of pants. Tortillas and hot tomales are Indian inventions. Aztec, when they're made of lye-bleached corn, but Yakuts, I'd say, when the *muk'elas* grind in plenty of acorn meal. I used the Spanish for the same when I asked about some tortillas and the Yakuts vaqueros I asked didn't know what I was talking about. I don't speak near as much Yakuts as they speak Spanish, though, so I reckon that was fair."

The Western Union man smiled incredulously and demanded, "Are you trying to tell me those quill Indians who have everyone all het up have simply run off to be cowboys?"

Longarm nodded and said, "Ain't trying. I'm telling. Lots of Indians run off to be cowboys. It's way more fun than being Indians. Most of your Californio hands were pure Indian to begin with. The king of old Spain gave you whole county-sized grants if you could pass for white. Who was that colored gent they made the governor in Monterey that time?"

The Western Union manager growled, "I'm not that old. You're telling us we can call in those extra gun hands we have guarding our usual maintenance crews? That's all I really care about your reservation jumpers."

Longarm nodded and soothed, "I'd stake my hide on it. I just did, camping alone on open range last night because I'm more worried about really dangerous white boys."

He pointed at the sheets of ruled notepaper between them with his chin and added, "One or more of the pests I've been playing blind man's buff could emerge from the mists if I had answers to those few questions, sir."

The older man cocked a whispy brow and declared, "I'd hate to see what you'd describe as a lot of questions. As I told you, give me at least seventeen hours."

Longarm asked, "What about this time or a mite earlier, tomorrow?" and the Western Union manager said that would be even better, but not to come back at all if one fucking wire went down overnight.

They shook on it and Longarm left to chase other shadows. He tried the telegraph office below some more on the off chance something might have come in from Denver or Sacramento. Nothing had. So he still had no idea where that murderous murky Maggie, if that had been her name, had been sticking pins in the map and up the noses of less fortunate lovers.

Neither federal nor local lawmen had taken part in that other case involving train robbers. But Longarm could afford to be more curious about local Robin Hoods in an election year. So he headed next for that office building near the rail depot. As he ambled along the shady side he saw a main line varnish was just pulling out to the south after dropping off any passengers or parcels meant for Visalia. So he didn't think much of the two travel-worn but well-dressed gents coming his way from the depot 'til, half way across the dirt paved street, one of them yelled, "It's a trap!" as he went for the gun under his checked coat, staring owl-eyed and outraged straight at the hitherto friendly Longarm.

There were plenty of times to act friendly. But this couldn't have been one of them, so Longarm stepped off the walk to crab suddenly behind a watering trough and drop to one knee as he drew.

There was no way one shootist could get off the first round after two whole professionals had slapped leather first. But the one in the checked coat, more rattled than anyone else there, spanged two rounds through the shop window behind Longarm instead of the smaller human head he had to be aiming for. So Longarm jackknifed him with a round of .44-40 just below his belly button before he could fire thrice.

His sidekick, a year or so older and dressed like a dusty raven bird, lobbed a more deadly round at Longarm's guts. But since that trough had been fresh filled to the brim that very morning he only managed a modest imitation of Old Faithful, up Yellowstone way, before Longarm had made bloody hash of his gun shoulder, aiming for his heart through the cascading spray.

Then Longarm was up and around the trough to kick dusty sixguns every which way and the shoulder-shot rascal in the head as he tried to sit up. Then the three of them had the middle of the street all to themselves a while as the dust settled and the gunsmoke drifted away.

240

Longarm was reloading over his softly blubbering victims with his badge glinting on one tweed lapel of his frock coat by the time four Visalia boys sporting bigger brass badges showed up.

The bearded country man in charge recognized Longarm's silvery hunting license for what it was and asked with a weary sigh, "What did they do, stake a claim too close to the tracks, Marshal?"

Longarm said, "I'm only a deputy and I ain't with that bunch of federal riders. Name's Custis Long and I work out of Denver for the firm but fair Marshal Billy Vail. I had to gun these mysterious strangers, just now, because it seemed they were fixing to gun me. I doubt this gutshot one will ever regain full conscience. This other one in the gloomier duds ain't hurt bad as he let's on. I sort of kicked him flatter than my one round left him. He ought to be coming out of it any time, now."

A couple of townsmen the local law knew better had edged forward by then for a better look. One of them backed Longarm's version, saying, "The one in the checkerboard coat yelled a warning, or a challenge, and then it was over quicker than you can put it in words. You should see that lawman in the brown duds move, Mary."

The male deputy with the oddly girlish name, or nickname, nodded soberly at Longarm and said, "They told us you were out our way. It's considered polite to call on other lawmen, formal, before you shoot anyone in their jurisdiction."

Longarm said, soothingly, "I did drop by your courthouse the last time I passed through. Talked to an older gent called Blinky."

The bearded one made a wry face and grumbled, "You talked to the county, then, not the township of Visalia. But who are we to argue with the famous Longarm. You shot 'em, so you bury 'em if you're so smart."

Longarm said, "Hold on, they just engaged in an attempted homicide, smack in the middle of your fair city. Don't you have no civic pride at all?"

The Visalia lawman chuckled sort of dirty and replied, "We do, and it costs good money to patch up or plant old boys laid low by the law, whether said law wanted 'em or not. We've never seen these poor shot-up strangers before. So, like I said, they're all yours!"

Chapter 27

Seeing he was stuck with the tab unless he could get his own office to pay it, Longarm and some helpful townsmen got the two he'd shot it out with to the nearby clinic of a Dr. Chalmers, who doubled when called upon to do so as one of the better embalmers of the big valley.

Despite his natural misgivings involving a possible conflict of interests, Longarm found the laconic old Scot with rusty sideburns a competent enough wound surgeon. As Longarm watched him probe for bullets and irrigate the messy boreholes with vinegar water the older man allowed he'd treated worse, for the North, at Sharpsburg and Cold Harbor. Longarm allowed any sawbones who'd seen that much blood and slaughter likely knew his scalpel from his cock.

The doc said he doubted the gutshot one would ever wake up and that he wouldn't get far if he did. So Longarm used his one set of handcuffs to fasten the shoulder-shot one to his brass bedstead by one ankle. As they waited for the patched up cuss to come back to his senses Longarm shared a window seat with the occasional corpse washer to discuss other suspects.

Doc Chalmers knew all about the funeral of the perhaps late Fresno Kid. The body had been embalmed in Mexico and shipped home by way of Visalia, there being no directer rail route. Another mortician with a Spanish last name had overseen the last lap of the morose journey and that had been their fancy casket Longarm had found in the Ortega tomb, so empty. But they'd asked Doc Chalmers to look the stiff over for 'em and, if need be, do something scientific to keep things from getting too disgusting

242

before they could put it away for keeps.

The doc said, "They did a pretty good job in Nogales, if you don't mind the discoloration you get with a strong solution of formalin and arsenic salts. I shot some more formalin mixed with carmine into him to see if that might help the color. It didn't."

Longarm grimaced and said, "Everyone who was there recalls how black he'd turned, save for his red hair, that is. So in sum it's safe to say he was really dead as he lay there in that fancy box."

It had been a statement but the doc still treated it like a mighty dumb question, answering, "Dead as a doornail and embalmed almost hard as pine. Why are we talking about dead outlaws, Deputy Long?"

Longarm said, "The two live ones across the room haven't told me nothing, yet," as he reached in his side pocket. He hauled out a print of Tomas Ortega Baker, in life, and asked the man who'd examined some damned cadaver how they matched up.

Doc Chalmers shrugged and said, "Younger men with regular features photograph much the same in black and white. If I had the cadaver in question here to compare ear patterns it would be a matter of utmost simplicity, but . . ."

Longarm took the picture back to put away without asking what the older man had meant about anyone's ears. That French forensic surgeon, Doc Bertillon, had explained all about ears in that famous book he'd written about measuring crooks so's they couldn't lie so much. The human face could change natural or on purpose quite a mite. But the human ear stayed about the same, save for size and earlobe, from infancy to old age. So all he needed was one fairly preserved ear of that missing cadaver to compare with known likenesses of the one true Fresno Kid and . . . What would it prove, whether the ornery cuss was really dead or alive?

The shoulder-shot shootist cuffed by the ankle, his Cheyenne library card said his name was Williams, stirred in his stupor and bitched about his leg being stuck in quicksand.

Longarm and the doc rose to rejoin him at bedside. Doc Chalmers gently suggested he take it easy and let the opiates wear off natural. Longarm shook the wounded man roughly by his good shoulder and said, "I ain't got time to wait. So here's the deal, chump. You don't seem wanted in these parts and I can forgive a harmless joke as long as nobody's on my list of wants. So how's about it, chump?

Are you wanted federal or ain't you been at it long enough? Talk to me, chump."

The wounded man's eyes flicked open. He still looked way off in another time and place as he licked his lips and said, "They said it would be easy because he wouldn't recognize us. Where's old Reb? I seen him get hit, right after he yelled like that."

Longarm confided, not unkindly, "He took one in the guts. I agree he was dumb to yell like that. You say they picked your ugly faces on account I had no call to recognize either? That means you both must have graduated recent to federal offenses so, right, we get to be pals after all."

Longarm reached for a smoke, decided it might not be such a grand notion with all the funny fumes up there, and continued, "I hope I just convinced you they never offered you enough for shooting it out with me. Are you convinced, chump?"

The one he'd mangled least with his return fire laughed bitterly and replied, "That's for certain. I wouldn't have throwed down on your back, had I known how swift you bounce all about! It was like aiming at spit on a hot stove, Longarm."

The man who'd shot him smiled thinly and decided, "It's good to know you knew who you were out to kill. Now I want you to tell me who sent you after me. Before you lie, it's up to me and me alone whether you just go on about your business once you're able or whether I dig a mite deeper into your doubtless misspent youth for some damned lawman, somewhere, who might feel your extradition back to wherever would be worth the trouble. Am I getting through to you at all, chump?"

The man who called himself Williams sighed and said, "I'll allow I was a chump to sign on for a lousy two hundred if you'll believe old Reb, there, was the one as made the deal."

Longarm shook his head and said, "You got to do better than that. Gents sharing a smoke with a whore say more than that about future plans, even when they ain't asking the whore to back 'em in a shoot-out."

Alias Williams tried, "Reb told me the middle man was a half-assed lawyer who'd got in bad trying to bribe the wrong judge back there in Cheyenne."

"Did they call him Undertaking Sam?" asked Longarm.

Alias Williams shrugged the one shoulder he could to reply, "If you say so. I never met the cheap bastard. Imagine offering us poor boys less'n five hundred, between us, to take on spit on a hot

244

stove! Reb said the shady middle man had been promised some political favor and had to pay us out of his own pocket because he'd failed the boys he was working for, earlier."

Longarm nodded grimly and said, "She said her name was Maggie and a shady lawyer would have been just what she'd need after shoving a hat pin up some poor soul's nose."

Doc Chalmers said that sounded interesting. Longarm told him he had to eat this damned apple a bite at a time and shook the man in the bed again to demand, "Name me some names, damn it. I can't connect anyone on my list of folk who'd ever even heard of Tomas Ortega Baker with Wyoming Territory!"

Alias Williams said, "Neither can I. Who's this Tomas whatever and how did he get mixed up with Wyoming lawyers who wanted you dead?"

Longarm growled, "I'm still working on that, damn your eyes. I see, now, why those killers she couldn't have been working with killed old Maggie in Sacramento, and vice versa. That's the bunch covering up for the Fresno Kid, unless, of course, they're covering up for some other sons of bitches entire!"

Chapter 28

By sundown it was too early to say whether Longarm and Sylvia Moorehead were shacked up. But her cooking had a heap going for it as they ate by candlelight in the half-furnished cottage on that otherwise deserted homestead just outside the city limits. Sillie, as she kept telling him to call her, had brought some answers along with a market basket of groceries back to their hidey-hole.

Longarm had picked up a jug of wine, a loaf of black bread and some fresh telegrams that had come in late that afternoon. She'd got the drop on him by arriving earlier to play house in a frilly fresh-bought apron, with her chestnut curls let down as if they'd moved in her chum's cottage more permanent. So they got to eat her baked spuds and pan-fried corn beef, with her fancy Frisco coffee, at least, whilst she ticked off answers to the questions he'd put down on her list. Longarm wasn't about to eat any deep-fried spinach greens no matter how good she said they were for him.

She said she'd double-checked her own sources with the Frisco as well as the Fresno coroner's offices, by wire, when he hadn't been looking. So there went anyone trying to cover Murder Most Foul by anyone else in the Fresno Kid's family. The kid's mamma, Doña Felicidad's older sister but not co-heiress to toad squat, had come down with the Cholera and died of the same after heaps of puking and less delicate sufferings in the company of doctors and nurses who'd have noticed if her kid sister or worthless son had been there to poison her with anything.

Sillie pointed out it wouldn't have done anyone any good to murder the late Concepcion Ortega Baker in any case because her family had disowned her long before she'd taken sick. When Longarm nodded and allowed some old Papist families could be like that, Sillie shook her head and said, "That wasn't it. The gringo she ran off with was a worthless mooncalf who couldn't hold on to the grocery money from one payday to the next. By then they'd noticed how their one boy was turning out as well. So they decided their more sensible Felicidad was the one who'd best manage what was left of a once larger grant."

He nodded, washed down some meat and potato, and said, "They decided smart. She was kind enough to dole out eating money to her more romantic-natured sister and smart enough to marry into another land grant family. She told me her husband, Carlos, had been the one to nail down their combined water rights, gringo style."

Sillie nodded and said, "They had a good marriage. There's not a shred of gossip even hinting at trouble between 'em and of course he stood by her when the others turned on her."

Longarm blinked in surprise and told her to go back over that a mite. So Sillie said, "About her nephew, Tomas, of course. All the other Ortegas and Carillos, near and kissing kin, were content to let the Anglos have the Fresno Kid as one of their own. They thought it was just disgusting of Felix to hire lawyers, send him money in prison and so on. They cut her at social gatherings and later they cut Carlos as well when he refused to act like a proper grandee. But he didn't seem to care. He said a man chose his wife, not his infernal cousins, and that none of the good old boys who called him Chuck seemed to blame him and Felix for a black sheep they just couldn't seem to straighten out."

Longarm decided, "He sounds like a decent cuss. I'm sure I'd have liked him."

Sillie said, "Everyone did, save for a few fussy relatives, and I imagine they were more embarrassed than spiteful. Spanish folk can be sort of proud of outlaws such as Murieta or Vasquez, as long as they confine their brutality to gringos of the male persuasion. But Ruth Cooper was popular with her Hispanic pupils as well and the mean thing served other women, Anglo, Mex and Indian, the same way."

Longarm nodded soberly. "He had no redeeming vices anyone I've talked to can recall. I asked you to see if you could track down Ruth Cooper, afterwards, right?"

Sillie nodded but said, "You can forget her. She's dead, too. She tried teaching school up along the Sacramento Delta. The story and rude things written on schoolhouse walls followed her. She fled to San Francisco where she was known for a time along the Barbary Coast, not teaching school. Nobody had seen her for a while until her body washed up on the North Beach mud flats last winter. There were no signs of any injuries, other than those left by the bay crabs, of course."

Longarm was glad they weren't having seafood. It was hard enough getting the corned beef down so he could say, "That'd be about the time Tom Baker was in the news again as . . . Hold it, Peewee Folsom said Baker was serving shorter time than he deserved under an assumed name. So how could a woman he'd wronged have known he was planning anything?"

She said she didn't see how and added, "A no-longer-young and once-pure spinster could have other reasons for drowning herself in the Frisco Bay, you know. To save my having to go back for more grim details, yes, it was really her that washed up on those mud flats. Aside from the laundry marks in her hardly schoolmarmish working costume more than one Barbary Coaster who'd known her in life, if not in the Biblical sense, came forward to help the harbor police sort things out. The crabs hadn't done that much to her once-pretty face."

Longarm shoved the rest of his plate away and washed the green aftertaste down with black coffee stunk up with chicory. Then he asked her permit and lit a smoke before he asked, "What happened to that hard-riding and hard-drinking cowhand she'd been holding hands with before the Fresno Kid grabbed her so rude?"

Sillie sighed and said, "He left the valley about the same time. Some say he was killed in a stampede down by San Diego. Others say he followed his true love to Frisco where some feel sure they saw them, hand in hand, along Columbus Avenue. That would put them a short walk from the Barbary Coast but could you see a man who'd fallen for a schoolmarm allowing her to become a you-know-what along the Barbary Coast?"

Longarm decided, "It works better if someone just saw look-alikes in tricky light after some time had flown under the bridge. In either case there goes a swell notion about women driven mad by shame and out for revenge on a fine old Californio family."

Sillie frowned and said, "Custis, they've been trying to hurt you. They haven't done a thing to hurt Felix or any of her kith and kin."

He said, "You should have been there when the body of her black-sheep nephew turned up missing, and leave us not forget they almost got me into a shoot-out with her vaqueros with all this razzle dazzle."

He took a thoughtful drag on his cheroot and mused aloud, "When you study on it, they haven't harmed a hair on my head, for all their attempts to turn it white overnight. Have you ever had the feeling you were staring right at something you'd misplaced, like that letter hid in plain view in that story by Edgar Allan Poe?"

She said she did that all the time with her notepad. He asked her what else she might have noted, once he'd asked her.

She said, "Jesus Garcia has no reputation as anything but a top hand cum trail boss or ranch foreman. He made it through the eighth grade, further up the valley, without even scaring his schoolmarms with garter snakes, albeit he did get a licking, once, for dipping a blond girl's pigtails in his inkwell."

Longarm blew a thoughtful smoke ring and decided, "They say the Lord protects the drunk and innocent fools. He gives a good imitation of a man who's stood his ground with a gun on occasion. What about those rascals bidding on those water rights?"

Sillie said, "You're right about them being rascals but I can't see either Henry Miller or Big Jim Haggin sending hired assassins after anybody but each other. I've been covering their open rivalry and that reminds me."

He thought she might mean water hogging reminded her of the store-bought marble cake she was slicing. But she went on to say, "Felix Carillo is holding a sort of water auction down at her place the day after tomorrow. Agents of both big outfits will be there along with most everyone else. I'm sure Felix would put us both up, tomorrow night, if you'd like to escort me down to watch the show."

He smiled wistfully and said, "It ain't as if I had prettier company in mind, Miss Sillie. But I was sent out here to find out whether the Fresno Kid was dead or alive, not to ride in circles, and where ever he might be, dead or alive, I've already looked for him at his aunt's spread."

She shoved a tin plate of cake his way as if she was sore at it as she said, "Oh. I suppose that means you were planning to get fresh with me sooner, assuming you were planning to get fresh at all."

He laughed uncertainly and replied, "I ain't sure how a gent ought to answer a question like that, ma'am. I could sound unflattersome either way. But to tell the pure truth I came here tonight with a lot of other worries on my mind. I'll know better after I get some answers out of Western Union what I might be planning next."

She poured more coffee for them both as she asked what on earth the telegraph company had to do with his intentions toward a respectable working girl who was only trying to help.

He assured her he hadn't asked Western Union any questions about her, told her some of the questions he had asked, and added he'd sent some fresh questions to his home office as well.

By the time he'd enjoyed two slices of marble cake she'd been brought up to date on those unfortunate gunslicks sent by the mysterious Undertaking Sam.

Longarm explained, "He keeps adding up to a shady lawyer who undertakes to fix things with the courts up Cheyenne way. He seems to have been wiring back and forth with someone as shady in Denver. It remains to be seen whether any of the fake names used in Cheyenne or Denver can be tied in with Nogales."

She asked, "Wouldn't any such messages be sent in code?"

He shrugged and said, "Depends on who sent what to whom. Peewee Folsom told us the Fresno Kid was hiding out down Mexico way, planning to fake his own death with the help of bribed Mex lawmen. So anything along them lines would likely be tough for anyone else to make out. On the other hand, a straight tip-off to Mex lawmen more interested in bounty money than bribes might have been sent in plain English, or Spanish."

Sillie's big brown eyes got bigger as she marveled, "What a nasty imagination you have! Would anyone but someone he trusted know he was planning . . . Whatever he was planning?"

Longarm nodded and agreed, "It'd be sort of nasty, I imagine. But it happens all the time along the owlhoot trail. Whoever made up that stuff about honor among thieves didn't know much about thieves. Peewee Folsom had betrayed Tom Baker to us, then tried to hide out where his cellmate had suggested. Makes one wonder just how well that fake shoot-out with Los Rurales might have really gone in Nogales."

He polished off the last of his coffee cup and added, "On the other hand, a really sneaky fugitive who'd staged his own death might have talked a former cellmate into triple-crossing us by telling lies that were really true and . . . Never mind, you know what I mean."

She said she wasn't sure and asked, "How can you just let those hired assassins you shot it out with this very afternoon go free as innocent tweety birds, Custis?"

He said, "I won, so in a way they *are* sort of innocent. The doc says neither will be going anywheres for quite a spell. The one who might recover in time will never have much of a gun arm again and in any case we have no use for either before we catch someone they can testify against. As things stand we can't pin anything on either worth more than a few months in jail for disturbing the peace with inept shooting. Might be more interesting to see who calls on whom in times to come. I got a Visalia lawman interested in possible bounties keeping an eye on all concerned."

He regathered the cheroot he'd set aside to consume all that cake and said he'd be proud to help her do the dishes. But she just laughed and said tin plates were meant to go out with the rest of the trash.

That store-bought cake had looked expensive, too. It was good to know she had a more generous expense account than he did. Billy Vail would have a fit if he listed at least four bits worth of tinwear, thrown away after using just once.

She suggested he finish his smoke out in the other room. So that was where they wound up, in what she declared a more comfortable position. Her pals who owned the property had left some bedding but no bedstead for the use of any sales agents or other pals while the property was being sold. So Sillie had made up a mattress on the floor, against one wall, as a sort of daybed with the sheets and quilting from the linen closet.

They half sat and half reclined with their backs to the wall as they face the candlestick she'd lit in the fireplace across the room. He allowed they could get by without a real fire, the night being tolerable indoors and there being no cordwood to spare from the kitchen if he wanted a warm breakfast. He put his hat aside and removed his gun rig to lay more handy at the head of the mattress. Then he pointed a pensive chin at the nearby side window to remark, "I see your pals took their roller shades with 'em. So, no offense, that candlelight, feeble as it may be, would be more use to someone lurking outside than it is to us, right now."

She gasped and moved closer, asking, "Who could know we were here, together?"

He said he hoped nobody did. Meanwhile, it might be a fine notion to make anyone looking for either of 'em work at it. Then he rolled over to the fireplace, snuffed out the candle, and rolled back as she marveled, "Ooh, it's so dark in here, now!"

He said, "Moon's coming up and our eyes will adjust. Were you, ah, planning to read yourself to sleep, Miss Sillie?"

She repressed a laugh and replied, "I'm not sure what I'd be doing at this hour, alone in bed with someone I knew much better. If we got under the covers together, could I trust you, Custis?"

He asked, "To do what? I left my own bedroll lashed to my saddle at that livery. But if there's other bedding in that linen closet you mentioned I might throw together a more chaste arrangement."

She said they had all the bedding on the premises under them at the moment. He flicked his burnt-down smoke into the fireplace across the way and muttered, "Why me, Lord? All right, as soon as the town outside settles down for the night I'll traipse in to get my own dumb bedding and we'll work some dumb something out."

She said, "I wouldn't have you think me old-fashioned. I've read what Virgina Woodhull and those other young moderns have to say about, well, modern times and the need to adjust to a changing world, but . . ."

"Spare me the fine print," he cut in with a weary sigh, adding, "I read, too. The trouble with you young moderns is that you're a lot like them Fabian Socialists or old Henry George and his single tax. The Fabians are all for sharing the wealth 'til their upstairs maid asks for a raise and I notice Henry George don't own much of that real estate he feels only landlords ought to pay that single tax of his on."

She didn't answer for a time. When she did she sounded something like a kid who'd been dared to climb a grain elevator and didn't know how to get out of it. She demanded, "Are you saying Miss Virgina Woodhull and me are all talk? I'll have you know she's been arrested for publishing pornography, more than once!"

He chuckled and said, "That's nothing. She ran for President one time on a ticket advocating free love and friendly divorce.

252

I've never spent enough time in the dark with her or her odd sister, Miss Tennessee, to say whether she means what she keeps saying or not. I have noticed some of her admirers seem unwilling to either put up or shut up, though."

The she-male reporter hissed, "Are you saying I have to let you abuse my body lest you accuse me of having no will of my own?"

He laughed less gently and said, "I ain't accusing you of having any will or won't, Miss Sillie. I wasn't sent all this way to find out whether you were modern or old-fashioned. I wouldn't be here with you or anyone if somebody didn't keep blowing up places I checked into more public. So you just be as modern or old-fashioned as you like and I'll just concentrate on staying alive 'til I can figure out who's so anxious to have me dead. I figure once I figure that, I'll be able to make 'em cut it out."

She protested that she hadn't done anything to deserve such a sardonic tone and started to snivel. He reached out in the dark to place a comforting hand on her thigh. It felt less platonic than he'd intended as she sniffed that he was implying she might be a tease.

He laughed and soothed, "I ain't implying, Miss Sillie. Teasing goes with being a gal. It's the nature of the beast to gussie up, cinch up and stink up to where they have men panting for 'em, just so's they can order men not to pant for 'em. Mean little boys can get a dog to pant and whimper by holding a soup bone out to 'em and then snatching it back. But boys outgrow such habits by the time they grow up."

She grabbed his wrist in the dark to slide it up her own thigh as she demanded, "Would you say I'm not fully developed?"

He hauled her to swap spit with her as he worked to get a better grasp on the question. She helped by hauling her skirts up out of their way with her other hand. He noticed she kissed mighty grown-up as well. But he still felt obliged to murmur, with his lips brushing hers, a few words of warning about tumbleweed men who'd likely be moving on in the cold gray dawn.

She murmured right back that she seldom seduced men so sudden when she expected 'em to be in town a spell. So they tore off the first howdy-do with most of their duds on and then got undressed to get down to really catching up with the changing times.

Chapter 29

The next morning they slept late. Or they stayed in bed, leastways.
He'd found out in the dark about her one inverted nipple and
he was only mildly surprised to discover by daylight that she
touched up her hair a mite. The hair on her head, he meant. Gals
never seemed to worry about other hair, left natural, giving the
show away.

They probably figured once a man was in position to know
what color hair they had, all over, he was in no position to care.
Longarm didn't mention pussy hair to Sillie and he'd found he
could get both her nipples to stand out perky just by keeping 'em
well kissed.

By noon they'd gotten around to eating as well as all the
positions most gals would go for the first few weeks of a new
romance. So when she said she was starting to feel chaffed and
suggested they save some for that night down at Felix Carillo's,
on a swell featherbed, Longarm washed off in the kitchen and got
dressed to see what else might be going on around Visalia. He'd
evaded the topic of Sillie's invite to the old Ortega grant. A man
had to think ahead before he said yes or no to a temptation.

At the Western Union he found they were still working on
some of those answers he'd asked them to look up for him. But
a wire from his home office had been laying in wait for him all
morning. Smiley and Dutch had caught up with Undertaking Sam
in Cheyenne. The disbarred lawyer had resisted arrest. But he'd
made a dying statement implicating yet another shady lawyer both
Billy Vail and Longarm recalled as a member in poor standing of
the Denver Courthouse Gang. Winslow Epworth had been held in

contempt, more than once, and thrown off a case entire by firm but fair Judge Dickerson of the Denver District Court. Deputy Guilfoyle had kicked in the door of Epworth's last known Denver address to no avail. But the wire said it was only a question of time and Vail wanted Longarm to come on home and help, seeing the Fresno Kid and the cellmate who'd informed on him both seemed to be accounted for as no longer at large.

Longarm wired back he had a few loose ends to tie up and headed next for a calmer interview with one or more of those bush league gunslicks sent his way by the late Undertaking Sam.

He got there just in time to be presented with the bill by an M.D. who also served the township of Visalia in a more morbid way. The doc cum mortician said he just couldn't say why both his patients had gone west in the wee small hours, but opined it might have been a relapse of some sort in the case of the shoulder-shot cuss.

Longarm said if they were billing the Justice Department he wanted to view the remains. The doc said they'd already been planted, economic as possible, in their potter's field on the far side of the tracks. When Longarm suggested digging the rascals up the doc mumbled something about needing an exhumation order. So Longarm growled, "Get one, unless you want me to get one from the goddamned Supreme Court, if I have to."

The doc said he doubted anyone would have to go that far and asked why on earth Longarm was so testy that afternoon.

Longarm said, "I ain't testy, Doc. I'm just not as trusting as some about tales of death and burial. I'm sure you've told me true and I'll be surprised as hell if you can't produce them dead sons of bitches who tried to kill me only yesterday. But I still want to view their remains official and I'll be back around four, with or without some answers to some other questions."

So he was, before four, as a matter of fact, with a sheaf of yellow Western Union forms stuffed in a side pocket and some questions inspired by the first answers already out on the wires.

He found the two gents he'd shot it out with the day before reposing on planks in the dirt floored celler of the clinic cum mortuary. He saw at a glance why the doc had been a mite hesitant to have them dug up again. Neither had been planted in a coffin or even a burial sheet. But someone had splashed enough well-water over their faces for Longarm to recognize them as the same sorry sons of bitches. So he said he was sorry and proved it by not bringing up any cash either cadaver might have had in its pockets.

As a general rule the township was allowed to recover burial expenses from the unclaimed estates of unknown stiffs, with any difference being recovered from anyone else they could stick with the bill. Longarm only got stuck, personal, now and again. Judge Isaac Parker, over to Fort Smith, was notorious for making his federal deputies pay in full for planting outlaws he'd told 'em to bring back alive. But Billy Vail was inclined to be a better sport, having planted a few himself in his ranger days and knowing how unplanned such occasions could be.

He'd promised he'd help Sillie get started that evening, at least whether he wanted to spend the coming night with her as a house guest of Felix Carillo or not. So Sillie was pleased as punch when he not only suggested a spunky buckskin for her at the livery but allowed he still liked that roan. As the hostlers were saddling both brutes for them Longarm told the newspaper gal, "We've drawn nothing but low cards from the direction of Cheyenne. My boss can't connect a pair of shady lawyers in any way with Tomas Ortega Baker or any of his possible friends or foes. Nogales, Mexico, and our present location of Visalia seem to out of the way for anyone in Denver or Cheyenne to wire all that much. Western Union managed me some funny-worded messages sent to dull-sounding folk in Fresno and back along my travels since first I left Denver. But they all add up to sneaks sent after me by the sneaky Undertaking Sam. He was what crooks call a fixer. At one time or another he'd likely fixed things for all sorts of sinister folk who owed him. Billy Vail figures, and I'm inclined to agree, a fixer called Epworth started out to fix me in Denver, doubtless for something I'd done around there. So it's dubious that bunch cared one way or the other about any Fresno Kid."

The hands brought their mounts out to them, hers of course with a sidesaddle hired for an extra dime a day. As he boosted her aboard for the short ride to the siding where they could still catch the Blue Dog combination, if they hurried, Sillie asked, "What about those horrid fiends who tried to blow you out of bed down the line ahead, and how come they never did, darling? You never have explained that part to me."

He said, "Let's get a move on, lest we have to get down to that featherbed the hard way. That was a different bunch entire. So the fixer in Cheyenne had no call to wire 'em. Me and Western

Union are still working on that bunch. Meanwhile it's a funny thing about that photography gal in Fresno telling me the Nogales law had asked her boss for pictures of a schoolboy called Tomas Ortega Baker."

Sillie asked, "Good heavens, are you suggesting she was in league with the Fresno Kid?"

He shook his head and replied, "She'd have never mentioned anything about Nogales if she hadn't been pure. The Nogales authorities who wired her boss seemed to be acting in good faith at the time as well. Nobody sent nothing sneaky and Western Union kept records of the dates. They had nothing logged as to when the photograph studio sent photographs by mail, but that cuts no ice. That nice gal said they got 'em and I'd say they did. They wired Fresno for a true likeness of Tom Baker a good two weeks before they wired his Tia Felicidad, by way of Visalia, they had her nephew on tap any time she wanted to send for his mortal remains."

By this time they'd made their way to the siding where the Blue Dog train was made up. A brakeman who saw them coming called out they were just in time if they got them damned broncs right over to the loading ramp. So they did and Sillie didn't get to follow up on the questions his answers had filled her pretty head with until they were back on the observation platform, seated on wicker and sipping steamer with the train already moving at a merry clip.

When she asked, Longarm agreed, "That's the way I see it. Those Mex rurales never would have asked for those photographs if they hadn't been tipped off about Tom Baker's scheme, well in advance."

Sillie said, "What horrid people you associate with. Someone the wayward youth trusted told those Mexicans his entire plan. But then dosen't that mean the real Fresno Kid is really dead, darling?"

Longarm shrugged and said, "Mebbe. It gets more wheels within wheels when you recall he'd told Peewee, at least, he'd fixed it with crooked Mex rurales, a redundancy if ever I heard one, to shoot someone else in his place and say they'd shot him."

"But, dear, if they sent all the way to Fresno for proof . . ." She began.

"Proof of what," he demanded, "they were real professionals who'd surely and sincerely shot the right outlaw? In either event

257

they'd want to convince gents like me and the ones paying bounties on the cuss that they'd shot the right cuss."

"They convinced *me* as well as Felix and others at an open casket funeral," she pointed out.

He said, "So I've been told. I'd be more convinced if he was still in that blamed casket. An old-timer who treats wounded transients with about the same skill as he buries 'em did remind me of a handy way to identify remains just a mite the worse for wear. One young cuss with regular features and odd-colored hair looks much the same as another who might have had different hair, in life, once either's been sort of mummified dark as his boots. But if only I could compare the ears of that cadaver with the one ear showing plain in Baker's old year book photograph, I'd know for certain."

She asked how he meant to do that without finding the missing remains of whoever she and all those others had seen with their very own eyes.

He sighed and said, "If I knew that I wouldn't have to find the dead pest. There are only two at all sensible motives anyone might have for playing the old shell game with that cadaver. They don't want us to know the Fresno Kid could still be alive or they don't want us to know he's really been dead all this time, like everyone but Peewee Folsom said."

She said he had a lot of faith in an established crook and added that it seemed to her the motives he mentioned were in direct conflict with one another.

To which he could only reply, "That's what I just said. I got things figured two opposite ways. Now all I have to find out is which way works. My boss would never forgive me if I just went by guess and by God to turn over the wrong shell!"

Chapter 30

The Evans Sontag gang didn't mess with the Blue Dog train that evening. So it let Longarm and the girl off near their regular Kern River pause for boiler water and the easy lope up the river to the old Ortega ranch house barely made their ponies sweat.

Felicidad followed her underlings out on the veranda to wave a cheerful greeting as the two of them reined in. Naturally a couple of hands loped over to take their reins and see to their mounts and baggage. Longarm was pleasantly surprised to see that young Chinese, Lou Drake, had managed to land a job as a wrangler down this way, at least. He saw no need to make a fuss about it and of course hired hands taking charge of a visitor's mount weren't supposed to slap them on the back or even shake with them.

Longarm shook with Soose Garcia instead as the gals who called one another Felix and Sillie kissed like sisters. The titian-haired widow seemed pleasantly surprised by Longarm's return visit. He noticed her eyebrows going up a tad as Sillie took her down the veranda a piece to explain a bit more to the older woman.

Then Felix acted as young and modern in her own right as she pasted on a gracious hostess smile and told Sillie she'd have a word about sleeping arrangements with her housekeeper.

Longarm figured she had, by suppertime, judging from the funny little smiles of the serving mozas and the way old Simona looked away sort of flustered every time their eyes almost met.

Spanish-speaking folk started supper late and et all night if it was up to them. They made up by such ravenous manners by

259

eating slow and talking at table more than most country folk Longarm was used to. Their hostess had sat Sillie and Longarm at either elbow, she at the head of the long oaken table with poor Soose down near the far end, but not the very end, lest folk get the wrong notion of his position in this household. Longarm had been raised not to mention such things as business or dead bodies in front of ladies nibbling light courses after courses. But Felix wanted to know whether he'd come up with any new ideas about her poor dead nephew.

It was Sillie who brightly popped a green pepper between her teeth, proving she was a California gal, and told their hostess her Custis was going to arrest the ones who'd stolen the body, any minute.

Longarm couldn't kick her under a table so wide. So he just nodded and modestly allowed, "I'd have to know whose body they'd moved, first. I doubt anyone would steal such an item to keep at home, no offense."

Sillie prattled on about their conversation aboard the train. The missing outlaw's pretty Tia Felicidad said she couldn't think of any reason a deep-dyed villain of any degree would have for upsetting her so. She said, "I'm sure my poor sister's unfortunate mistake was the one we all hoped we'd seen the last of when he did what was only right for him. But let's suppose, for the sake of argument, your suspicions of a dead imposter are correct."

She counted on her well-manicured fingers as she continued, "Numero uno, I doubt even Tomas would be stupid enough to cast even further doubt on a staged death if he was still alive. Can't you see that even if we did somehow entomb some other young man, it would be wiser for Tomas to simply leave well enough alone?"

Sillie said, brightly, "Custis says there's a way to identify a dead person even when they've gotten pretty . . . you know."

Felix repressed a grimace, sipped at her wine glass, and insisted, "I can't think of anything more bound to arouse suspicion than a stark and staring empty casket."

Turning to Longarm she continued, "Fess up, Custis, would you have been as bulldog sure something odd was going on out our way if you'd found anyone who looked at all like my nephew in that tomb the other day?"

He smiled sheepishly and replied, "They were dumb to try and kill me so often, too. Albeit it was lucky for me they did, at least once. I see what you mean about the mastermind behind all those small time gunslicks, Miss Felix. It does seem every time I ought to make my mind up one way somebody twists it around another. Stage magicians call that misdirection. I've got so misdirected my boss wants me to just come on back to Denver. He says he needs my help on crooks closer to home and I agree at least one set of gunslicks I've been brushing with couldn't know beans about your wayward nephew."

The widow at the head of the table tried, "Isn't it possible the other bunch have been worried about something other than poor Tomas?"

He said he failed to see what. So she suggested, "The Evans Sontag gang, or perhaps the mess at Mussel Slough that led to all the tension out our way, ever since. You surely know a lot of people up and down the valley suspected you might be investigating for that congressional committee."

Longarm nodded, absently, then stared more thoughtfully at her to declare, "Why, bless your smart never-mind, I think that could be it!"

She looked totally confused as she asked what on earth she'd just said. So he said, "It's on record I was once hauled before a congressional committee and given a clean bill of health. I've been called on to investigate more than one case of government corruption and just before I left Denver some pencil pusher from the land office stuck me with a distasteful eviction chore. I was asked to run, a surly Swede with a gun off a homestead he'd sworn to defend to the death."

"Just like at Mussel Slough!" marveled Sillie, and this time he felt no call to kick her as he nodded and said, "I suspicion things were supposed to turn out as ugly. I know for a fact that a heap of federal employees got transfered all over creation in the wake of the Mussel Slough disaster. Now all we got to do is backtrack that attempt to ensnare yours truly in the same sort of tar and if he's ever been anywhere's near a Denver fixer called Epworth he's surely going to have a lot of things to tell us and, come to study on it, that congressional committee!"

Sillie said she didn't understand. She was young as well as modern.

Her older friend, Felix, showed she was smarter by explaining, "Custis means some political hack, trying to whitewash Mussel Slough by smearing other marshals with the same sort of mess, must have felt sure Custis had been assigned to, ah, backtrack his own messy part in the California tragedy when Custis not only refused to follow the same rough and ready route but headed right for the scene of . . . What, a crime or just a mistake, Custis?"

Longarm said, "Either one could get a man fired from a fine civil service position. Whether he she or it was in the pay of them land grabbers or not, asking them shady fixers to clean my plow was a federal felony for certain. It won't take Marshal Billy Vail long to paper trail everyone involved, soon as I wire him. It has to be some court officer who could promise a contemptible and disbarred lawyer more consideration in the Denver federal courts and all the courts in Cheyenne, Wyoming being a federal territory as yet."

Everyone there who spoke English seemed to think he was smart as hell. So they ate dessert, three times, then they had brandy with their coffee and Felix finally took pity on Sillie, who'd been saying for some time she'd had a long day and needed some sleep if she was ever going to keep track of the big water auction the next day.

Longarm actually wanted to hear more about the business reps coming from all over to bid on the widow's river view. It sure sounded like easy money if they offered anything. But Sillie kept tugging at his sleeve, so he let her haul him off to the room a blushing Simona had fixed up for them.

Longarm had meant to let the rest of the household simmer down. So he might have heeded Sillie's suggestions about trying it upright with a good grip on the bed posts had not they both been startled by a gentle but insistent rapping on the heavy oaken door.

It was Lou Drake. When Longarm hauled the young Chinese-American inside at gunpoint, Drake whispered, "I was told to stand guard, down the hall, and tell that ramrod, Garcia, if you left this room for any reason. I don't think he could have known we were on better terms than that."

Longarm smiled thinly and said, "Neither do I. Did he tell you what I might be leaving this room to stick my nose into?"

Drake shook his head and said, "Nope. I have my own thoughts on that but I'd rather not say, in front of this lady."

Sillie said not to mind her and Longarm demanded, "How do you know Soose is that familiar with his employer, or could it possibly be old Simona he don't want anyone else to know about?"

The Chinese looked startled by the mental picture, then avoided Sillie's eyes as he confided, "I just got here, but the other help talks. A lot of 'em are new, like me. Mostly Indians as a matter of fact. But a couple of mozas who may feel left out say Doña Felicidad spends a lot of time in her *segundo's* quarters, late at night."

Longarm shrugged and said, "Well, she might just be using the telegraph set he keeps by his bed. I'd know better if Western Union had logged any messages from here to Mexico. Only they never, early enough to count. Nogales wired her they'd shot her infernal nephew and she wired them a money order to send him to her, preserved."

Sillie said, "Pooh, I could have told you poor Felix was innocent. If she'd wanted to confuse the law about young Tom she'd have simply let him rot, in Mexico."

"Or even here." He nodded, musing half to himself as he explained, "There'd have been no call for an open casket ceremony if he'd arrived more spoiled in warm weather. So, right, she was a good sport about letting everyone take a last look and . . . I got to try again and you'll lose this job if I'm caught, Lou. So how's about it?"

The Chinese-American held out a hand to say, "I'm not the only son of Han you've kept from losing blood, Longarm. So put her there and tell me what you want me to do."

Longarm told him. Sillie insisted on coming along. Longarm decided, "You'll likely be as safe with us as here alone, should things go sour. But I got to warn you it may not be so pleasant for a lady, Sillie."

She laughed and said, "Pooh, who are you calling a lady?" So Lou Drake made sure the coast was clear and the three of them slipped out of the house and through the inky shadows of the surrounding trees, with Sillie assigned the chore of packing the unlit candelabra from the guest room. They got there quicker, that time, since Longarm had explored the way to the tomb out back before.

Getting in was a mite tougher, this time. But Longarm had asked that Denver locksmith to rework his pocket knife with just such occasions in mind.

Once inside, Longarm almost shut the heavy copper door after the three of them but left a slit for their young Oriental pal to peer out of as he lit the five candles and set the silver base of the candelabra on a high shelf, muttering, "Mebbe you'd best change places as lookout with Lou, Honey. From here on things might get disgusting."

She insisted she was a reporter and that this was the most exciting story she'd ever covered, whatever in God's name might be going on, so he got to work with the screwdriver blade of his pocket knife as he explained, "If that body from Mexico's been moved out of here all the way we'll just be disturbing some doubtless disturbing sights. But you got to start sniffing at the last-sniffed parts of the trail."

She asked if he didn't consider it awfully stupid to hide a dead body from one coffin in another, on the very same premises. He told her he'd just said that, but added, "A street grifter shifting that sponge rubber pea under one shell or another hardly ever rolls it along the walk. Lou, yonder, says the help, here, gossips about folk just being natural. How far do you reckon you could carry a mummy with red hair before someone noticed?"

From his position near the door Lou Drake opined, "A party of two or three could manage easy enough, late at night with the river just a few yards south. That's the border of this homespread and once they were on the far side, on open range . . ."

"Oh my God!" gasped Sillie as Longarm slid one lid only partly out of the way, "That looks like Tom's poor mother, Connie, only why is she screaming like that, however silently?"

Longarm shoved the lid back in place and drove two screws deep enough to hold as he said, "She wasn't screaming. Jaw bones just fall open that way as the face rots away. That's how come you hear all them tales of premature burials. I asked you not to look, Honey."

But she was looking a few minutes later, when he cracked open the coffin of an older lady who'd been boxed with a Spanish comb in her iron gray hair. It was odd how neatly combed her hair still lay, considering the rest of her.

They found an old gent, or his mouldering skeleton, in a Spanish-style outfit, gone vomit-colored with some fungus or other. Longarm muttered he was sorry and shut the damned box. There was no saying just who'd been in an even older coffin, so old the screws just fell out and didn't have to be twisted. Sillie said that despite the mostly dry climate of the Sacramento Valley they did make up for it with a good six weeks of frog-and-toadstool dampness in the winter. He agreed the bones and fuzz spread over the bottom of that old box had been rained on more than once, likely through some leak in the stone roof you didn't notice in dry weather. As he closed the lid again he sighed and said, "Those others in the back look even older and soggier. Not as easy to get at, neither. I'd have picked this easy opening one had I been in a hurry to tuck an extra cadaver into, sudden."

Sillie sighed and said, "Well, he's obviously not there now and he'd certainly not get back in his own box after going to so much trouble to get out, would he?"

Longarm gasped, "Lord love you, Honey, you're so smart at times it scares me!"

She asked how come as he slid the original coffin he'd found so empty out of its niche enough to get at. The screws turned easier every time they were driven in or out. He said, "I may not have been the only one who ever admired Poe's story of the purloined letter. I'll tell you in a minute."

Then he opened the lid and all three of them gasped at the sight of a ghastly black face with bared teeth and titian hair grinning up at them in the candle light.

"The spy who didn't want 'em to find that important letter he'd lifted left it atop other papers in plain sight, atop his desk. The sneak who didn't want me to see this sight the last time simply shoved it in that other box for the time being, then put it back here where nobody but someone smart as us would expect to find it. Dried out as it is by now, it can't weigh much and ought to be simple enough to shift, being stiff as well as so light."

Then he got out one of those photo prints, reached for the candelabra, and compared the ghastly reality to the picture of a merely unpleasant young cuss as he decided, grudgingly, "Yep. These here are the mortal remains of the late Fresno Kid and I sort of wish it was more complicated. His plan was slick enough. But someone he trusted betrayed him and he walked right into an ambush to die like a dog."

Then Lou Drake hissed, "Company!" and Longarm blew out all the candles lest they give the show inside the tomb away.

It was already too late. The familiar voice of Soose Garcia called out, "We know you and the girl are in there, Longarm. We told you not to disturb Doña Felicidad's dead and this time you ain't getting off so easy."

Longarm quietly moved the Chinese-American out of his way so he could call back out, "Who's *we*, Soose? Could I have a word with the lady or has she already lit out after giving you such stupid orders?"

There was a thoughtful pause. Then the *segundo* called, "What are you blabbering about, now? She went back to the house, all upset, and who can blame her? Do you want to come out or do we have to smoke you out, you infernal ghouls?"

Longarm called back, "Aw, that ain't no way to talk about a newspaper lady and I'm more curious than ghoulish. We just found Tom Baker. He was here all the time, the more fool I. I know you had nothing to do with that, Soose. A grown man and a boy could have snuck what was left of him off the ranch entire. So let me ask you something else. Is the patrona you know as Doña Felicidad red-haired all over?"

A sixgun cleared its throat and three slugs spanged off the far side of the tick metal door while Garcia called Longarm names he refused to take personal.

Sillie whispered, "How did you know that? I thought your were with me, you brute!"

He muttered, "Lucky guess, based on other suspicions about the lady in question." Then he called out, "Soose? I hope you understand you're talking to the U.S. law and enjoy your more usual work. The game's up for that natural blonde but there are real Ortegas and Carillos all over the state. So the courts will surely sort out a legit heir and they'll still need a *segundo* who can handle Indians so well at, well, Indian wages."

Another bullet spanged off the metal between them.

Longarm soothed, "I know you're confounded, old son. That was the name of her game. She didn't give toad squat about anyone in this here tomb, dead or alive. She just wanted the law too worried about that Fresno Kid to pay much mind to her. Now I want you to pay her some mind, Soose. I want you to send one of your muchachos to fetch her and when they tell you she's lit out I want you to cut this foolishness out before you get yourself in real trouble."

Garcia called back, "You're the one who's in trouble! You've broke into private property without a proper permit and unwritten laws as old as the hills give La Patrona every right to have you dealt with as common burglars!"

Longarm swore softly and yelled, "I know the kind of orders she'd have given and I know a mite more than you about common law if you think a greaser can get away with gunning a gringa linda in *this* state! Use your head or, better yet, find out if that fake redhead is anywheres within a country mile right now!"

Garcia, despite his fussing, had likely sent someone back to the house as soon as Longarm had suggested it. For it didn't take as long as it might have, otherwise, for the *segundo* to call back in a mighty strangled tone, "You were right. She's gone. On Miss Moorehead's livery mount! I don't understand this at all!"

Longarm yelled, "I do. She's used that same livery many a time and I chose that buckskin for its frisky nature, earlier. I'm coming out after her, Soose. If you gun me I'll never speak to you again and they'll likely hang you as well."

So nobody shot at Longarm as he tore out of the tomb and through the *segundo* and his hands in a dead run for the stables. The overly polite stable hands had unbridled as well as unsaddled that otherwise fast roan. So Longarm lost more vital time getting ready to ride and then he was riding, faster than he really wanted to, through the moonlit chaparral. For he knew that livery pony would beeline for its usual haunts in Visalia, as livery nags were inclined to. The quick-thinking adventuress out ahead had doubtless counted on that extra speed you could count on, one way, from any healthy mount with an oat-flavored destination in mind. But it evened out when both riders were mounted on steeds from the same livery stable.

He knew he'd never overtake her, all things being equal save for her weighing a hell of a heap less. But with any luck he could track her down in Visalia before she could catch a train out, if that was her intention.

The trouble with really sneaky women was that you could never be sure of their intentions, and she owned property all over the damned place, or said she did.

But a man could only try. So he pushed on through the scrub oak and salt bush, standing in the stirrups in hopes of falling clear if they hit anything serious in the tricky light.

Then, out ahead, he heard the high-pitched scream of a pony in pain. So he slowed to listen and get his bearings before he clucked his own mount on, trending a mite to his left.

He found the buckskin and its rider sprawled about where they'd fallen when they'd hit a bobwire fence some son of a bitch had strung since last she'd ridden this way, most likely.

Her mount was torn open so bad and hobbling about so pitiful on three legs he just had to finish it off with a kindly Winchester round.

They didn't allow you to put busted up women out of their misery that kindly. Longarm hunkered down beside the moaning woman and struck a light, soothing, "Others ought to be along in a spell, Miss Ruth. I'd be lying if I said I thought there was anything a living soul could do for you, though. You sure did twist your back on that fence, didn't you."

The woman staring up at him from the dust sighed and said, "I didn't twist it. I broke it. I can't feel a damned thing from my breasts down and to tell the truth it seems more trouble than it's worth to breathe as much as I still can. How did you find out? I thought I'd been so clever."

The match had burned down to where he had to shake it out as he assured her, "You were, ma'am. We'll say no more about your life of sin after you were ruined by the spoiled brat of a proud old Californio family. I figured he'd turned to an old schoolmarm for solace after his Tia Felicidad spurned his incest notions."

She hissed, "A lot you know! He blubbered at me about the times his innocent Tia Felicidad had let him go so far and no farther, all the time he was ravaging me, the nasty little brute!"

Longarm nodded sagely and said, "I figured they'd always been sort of fond of one another and that you'd looked something like the real Felicidad, save for hair color and minor details gals find it easier to fix with powder, paint and face veils. You'd have never passed for the real Felicidad close up, to anyone who really knew her. But fate, family pride and blind loyalty conspired to offer you a crack at revenge and unjust compensation."

Ruth Cooper hissed, "I had as much right to the easy money they wanted to give the stuck-up bitch just for being born a greaser!"

Longarm shrugged and replied, "I figured you must have felt that way when you or one of your Barbary Coast pals noticed how few close relations turned up at her husband's funeral. Nobody but a likely kind and loving husband could abide her backing of a beloved sister's rotten kid. So his death left the real Felicidad up Frisco way, bereft of close kith and kin, about the same time you or one of your sisters in sin found out those would-be water lords were just dying to comfort her as soon as she was out of seclusion. I hope you see how easy it figures to be for state and

268

federal help to round up the others you had helping you. They'll be able to tell us whether you were paying them off in cash or, ah, trade."

"You'll never catch my friends," she sneered, adding, "You'd have never caught me if it hadn't been for that damned fence and . . . What are you doing to my privates, you pervert? It feels like an icicle where I've never felt anything half that cold before!"

He told her, not unkindly, "You're dying, ma'am. About the handful of henchmen left over . . . You recruited the help you needed to burst in on the widow Carillo alone, murder her any of a dozen ways that don't show, and bleach her natural titian hair to resemble your own natural shade. Then, with both your heads colored less natural you had your pals dress her in your, ah, working costume so they could find and identify her, as you, in Frisco Bay. I'm sure the San Francisco P.D. will be able to round up such civic-minded denizens of the Barbary Coast."

He reached for a cheroot as he continued, "All you had to do was sit tight in the real widow's Nob Hill seclusion. I'll let Frisco P.D. work out the details about any house servants up that way you had to get rid of, one way or another. Nobody pays much attention when a rich widow sprouts a new butler or cook. You and your gang only had to make sure a few lowly Chicanos who might have balked at your imitation of their real patrona weren't on the premises when you showed up just long enough to sell them water rights and vanish forever with the cash you must have figured your ass had been worth in your schoolmarm days."

She didn't answer. He said, "You didn't know the real Felicidad had been sending money to her precious Tomas, or that she was likely in on his plans to sort of die and go straight, he said, 'til you got into the private papers of the lady you were impersonating."

He continued with the cheroot gripped in his sardonic smile, "You didn't want a boy you already hated coming home to spoil your show. So you wrote anonymous to some Mex officials too high on the Nogales totem pole for the Fresno Kid to reach. After he'd been really surprised by the old boys he'd bribed to put someone else in the box, you saw a chance to grandstand in your new titian hair and heavy veil, inviting Anglo folk who'd known him way better than any of his real kin and, had you been content to let things go at brazen, you might have sold those water rights and been long gone with the money before anyone questioned your sheer gall. But you couldn't buy my own simple story at face value. So you tried to have me killed and when that didn't work you tricked me into chasing a dead man 'til I caught you. Ain't a guilty conscience a bitch?"

She still didn't answer. When he lit his cheroot he saw why. So he shut her glassy eyes for her and got back to his feet as, somewhere in the night, he heard hoofbeats and a familiar voice calling his name.

He flared another match and called back, "Over this way and watch out for bobwire in the dark, Miss Sillie."

She did. As she reined in nearby the perky newspaper gal told him, "That nice Chinese wrangler sure knows how to pick a girl a pony and that calmed down foreman is telegraphing far and wide for help. Who's that at your feet in the moonlight, darling?"

He said, "You knew her as the pleasantly aloof Widow Carillo and we won't need much help, now. I'll be surprised if old Billy Vail hasn't rounded up that other bunch by the time I get back to Denver, come to study on it."

She sounded as if she meant it when she announced, "You're not about to leave my side again, you naughty boy, before my readers and me have the whole story straight in our poor confused heads."

He said that sounded fair and so, what with one thing or another, he never did satisfy anyone in Denver about that extra weekend in a fancy Fresno hotel.

Watch for

LONGARM AND THE REBEL BRAND

165th novel in the bold LONGARM series

and

LONE STAR AND THE GUNRUNNERS

121st novel in the exciting LONE STAR series

Both Coming in September!

Fury knew something was wrong long before he saw the wagon train spread out, unmoving, across the plains in front of him.

From miles away, he had noticed the cloud of dust kicked up by the hooves of the mules and oxen pulling the wagons. Then he had seen that tan-colored pall stop and gradually be blown away by the ceaseless prairie wind.

It was the middle of the afternoon, much too early for a wagon train to be stopping for the day. Now, as Fury topped a small, grass-covered ridge and saw the motionless wagons about half a mile away, he wondered just what kind of damn fool was in charge of the train.

Stopping out in the open without even forming into a circle was like issuing an invitation to the Sioux, the Cheyenne, or the Pawnee. War parties roamed these plains all the time just looking for a situation as tempting as this one.

Fury reined in, leaned forward in his saddle, and thought about it. Nothing said he had to go help those pilgrims. They might not even want his help. But from the looks of things, they needed his help, whether they wanted it or not.

He heeled the rangy lineback dun into a trot toward the wagons. As he approached, he saw figures scurrying back and forth around the canvas-topped vehicles. Looked sort of like an anthill after someone stomped it.

Fury pulled the dun to a stop about twenty feet from the lead wagon. Near it a man was stretched out on the ground with so many men and women gathered around him that Fury could only catch a glimpse of him through the crowd. When some of the men turned to look at him, Fury said, "Howdy. Thought it looked like you were having trouble."

"Damn right, mister," one of the pilgrims snapped. "And if you're of a mind to give us more, I'd advise against it."

Fury crossed his hands on the saddlehorn and shifted in the saddle, easing his tired muscles. "I'm not looking to cause trouble for anybody," he said mildly.

He supposed he might appear a little threatening to a bunch of immigrants who until now had never been any farther west than the Mississippi. Several days had passed since his face had known the touch of the razor, and his rough-hewn features could be a little intimidating even without the beard stubble. Besides that, he was well armed with a Colt's Third Model Dragoon pistol holstered on his right hip, a Bowie knife sheathed on his left, and a Sharps carbine in the saddleboot under his right thigh. And he had the look of a man who knew how to use all three weapons.

A husky, broad-shouldered six-footer, John Fury's height was apparent even on horseback. He wore a broad-brimmed, flat-crowned black hat, a blue work shirt, and fringed buckskin pants that were tucked into high-topped black boots. As he swung down from the saddle, a man's voice, husky with strain, called out, "Who's that? Who are you?"

The crowd parted, and Fury got a better look at the figure on the ground. It was obvious that he was the one who had spoken. There was blood on the man's face, and from the twisted look of him as he lay on the ground, he was busted up badly inside.

Fury let the dun's reins trail on the ground, confident that the horse wouldn't go anywhere. He walked over to the injured man and crouched beside him. "Name's John Fury," he said.

The man's breath hissed between his teeth, whether in pain or surprise Fury couldn't have said. "Fury? I heard of you."

Fury just nodded. Quite a few people reacted that way when they heard his name.

"I'm . . . Leander Crofton. Wagonmaster of . . . this here train." The man struggled to speak. He appeared to be in his fifties and had a short, grizzled beard and the leathery skin of a man who had spent nearly his whole life outdoors. His pale blue eyes were narrowed in a permanent squint.

"What happened to you?" Fury asked.

"It was a terrible accident— " began one of the men standing

276

nearby, but he fell silent when Fury cast a hard glance at him. Fury had asked Crofton, and that was who he looked toward for the answer.

Crofton smiled a little, even though it cost him an effort. "Pulled a damn fool stunt," he said. "Horse nearly stepped on a rattler, and I let it rear up and get away from me. Never figured the critter'd spook so easy." The wagonmaster paused to draw a breath. The air rattled in his throat and chest. "Tossed me off and stomped all over me. Not the first time I been stepped on by a horse, but then a couple of the oxen pullin' the lead wagon got me, too, 'fore the driver could get 'em stopped."

"God forgive me, I . . . I am so sorry." The words came in a tortured voice from a small man with dark curly hair and a beard. He was looking down at Crofton with lines of misery etched onto his face.

"Wasn't your fault, Leo," Crofton said. "Just . . . bad luck."

Fury had seen men before who had been trampled by horses. Crofton was in a bad way, and Fury could tell by the look in the man's eyes that Crofton was well aware of it. The wagonmaster's chances were pretty slim.

"Mind if I look you over?" Fury asked. Maybe he could do something to make Crofton's passing a little easier, anyway.

One of the other men spoke before Crofton had a chance to answer. "Are you a doctor, sir?" he asked.

Fury glanced up at him, saw a slender, middle-aged man with iron-gray hair. "No, but I've patched up quite a few hurt men in my time."

"Well, I am a doctor," the gray-haired man said. "And I'd appreciate it if you wouldn't try to move or examine Mr. Crofton. I've already done that, and I've given him some laudanum to ease the pain."

Fury nodded. He had been about to suggest a shot of whiskey, but the laudanum would probably work better.

Crofton's voice was already slower and more drowsy from the drug as he said, "Fury . . ."

"Right here."

"I got to be sure about something . . . You said your name was . . . John Fury."

"That's right."

"The same John Fury who . . . rode with Fremont and Kit Carson?"

"I know them," Fury said simply.

"And had a run-in with Cougar Johnson in Santa Fe?"

"Yes."

"Traded slugs with Hemp Collier in San Antone last year?"

"He started the fight, didn't give me much choice but to finish it."

"Thought so." Crofton's hand lifted and clutched weakly at Fury's sleeve. "You got to . . . make me a promise."

Fury didn't like the sound of that. Promises made to dying men usually led to a hell of a lot of trouble.

Crofton went on, "You got to give me . . . your word . . . that you'll take these folks through . . . to where they're goin'."

"I'm no wagonmaster," Fury said.

"You know the frontier," Crofton insisted. Anger gave him strength, made him rally enough to lift his head from the ground and glare at Fury. "You can get 'em through. I know you can."

"Don't excite him," warned the gray-haired doctor.

"Why the hell not?" Fury snapped, glancing up at the physician. He noticed now that the man had his arm around the shoulders of a pretty red-headed girl in her teens, probably his daughter. He went on, "What harm's it going to do?"

The girl exclaimed, "Oh! How can you be so . . . so callous?"

Crofton said, "Fury's just bein' practical, Carrie. He knows we got to . . . got to hash this out now. Only chance we'll get." He looked at Fury again. "I can't make you promise, but it . . . it'd sure set my mind at ease while I'm passin' over if I knew you'd take care of these folks."

Fury sighed. It was rare for him to promise anything to anybody. Giving your word was a quick way of getting in over your head in somebody else's problems. But Crofton was dying, and even though they had never crossed paths before, Fury recognized in the old man a fellow Westerner.

"All right," he said.

A little shudder ran through Crofton's battered body, and he rested his head back against the grassy ground. "Thanks," he said, the word gusting out of him along with a ragged breath.

"Where are you headed?" Fury figured the immigrants could tell him, but he wanted to hear the destination from Crofton.

"Colorado Territory . . . Folks figure to start 'em a town . . . somewhere on the South Platte. Won't be hard for you to find . . . a good place."

278

No, it wouldn't, Fury thought. No wagon train journey could be called easy, but at least this one wouldn't have to deal with crossing mountains, just prairie. Prairie filled with savages and outlaws, that is.

A grim smile plucked at Fury's mouth as that thought crossed his mind. "Anything else you need to tell me?" he asked Crofton.

The wagonmaster shook his head and let his eyelids slide closed. "Nope. Figger I'll rest a spell now. We can talk again later."

"Sure," Fury said softly, knowing that in all likelihood, Leander Crofton would never wake up from this rest.

Less than a minute later, Crofton coughed suddenly, a wracking sound. His head twisted to the side, and blood welled for a few seconds from the corner of his mouth. Fury heard some of the women in the crowd cry out and turn away, and he suspected some of the men did, too.

"Well, that's all," he said, straightening easily from his kneeling position beside Crofton's body. He looked at the doctor. The red-headed teenager had her face pressed to the front of her father's shirt and her shoulders were shaking with sobs. She wasn't the only one crying, and even the ones who were dry-eyed still looked plenty grim.

"We'll have a funeral service as soon as a grave is dug," said the doctor. "Then I suppose we'll be moving on. You should know, Mr. . . . Fury, was it? You should know that none of us will hold you to that promise you made to Mr. Crofton."

Fury shrugged. "Didn't ask if you intended to or not. I'm the one who made the promise. Reckon I'll keep it."

He saw surprise on some of the faces watching him. All of these travelers had probably figured him for some sort of drifter. Well, that was fair enough. Drifting was what he did best.

But that didn't mean he was a man who ignored promises. He had given his word, and there was no way he could back out now.

He met the startled stare of the doctor and went on, "Who's the captain here? You?"

"No, I . . . You see, we hadn't gotten around to electing a captain yet. We only left Independence a couple of weeks ago, and we were all happy with the leadership of Mr. Crofton. We didn't see the need to select a captain."

Crofton should have insisted on it, Fury thought with a grimace.

You never could tell when trouble would pop up. Crofton's body lying on the ground was grisly proof of that.

Fury looked around at the crowd. From the number of people standing there, he figured most of the wagons in the train were at least represented in this gathering. Lifting his voice, he said, "You all heard what Crofton asked me to do. I gave him my word I'd take over this wagon train and get it on through to Colorado Territory. Anybody got any objection to that?"

His gaze moved over the faces of the men and women who were standing and looking silently back at him. The silence was awkward and heavy. No one was objecting, but Fury could tell they weren't too happy with this unexpected turn of events.

Well, he thought, when he had rolled out of his soogans that morning, he hadn't expected to be in charge of a wagon train full of strangers before the day was over.

The gray-haired doctor was the first one to find his voice. "We can't speak for everyone on the train, Mr. Fury," he said. "But I don't know you, sir, and I have some reservations about turning over the welfare of my daughter and myself to a total stranger."

Several others in the crowd nodded in agreement with the sentiment expressed by the physician.

"Crofton knew me."

"He knew you to have a reputation as some sort of gunman!"

Fury took a deep breath and wished to hell he had come along after Crofton was already dead. Then he wouldn't be saddled with a pledge to take care of these people.

"I'm not wanted by the law," he said. "That's more than a lot of men out here on the frontier can say, especially those who have been here for as long as I have. Like I said, I'm not looking to cause trouble. I was riding along and minding my own business when I came across you people. There's too many of you for me to fight. You want to start out toward Colorado on your own, I can't stop you. But you're going to have to learn a hell of a lot in a hurry."

"What do you mean by that?"

Fury smiled grimly. "For one thing, if you stop spread out like this, you're making a target of yourselves for every Indian in these parts who wants a few fresh scalps for his lodge." He looked pointedly at the long red hair of the doctor's daughter. Carrie— that was what Crofton had called her, Fury remembered.

Her father paled a little, and another man said, "I didn't think there was any Indians this far east." Other murmurs of concern came from the crowd.

Fury knew he had gotten through to them. But before any of them had a chance to say that he should honor his promise to Crofton and take over, the sound of hoofbeats made him turn quickly.

A man was riding hard toward the wagon train from the west, leaning over the neck of his horse and urging it on to greater speed. The brim of his hat was blown back by the wind of his passage, and Fury saw anxious, dark brown features underneath it. The newcomer galloped up to the crowd gathered next to the lead wagon, hauled his lathered mount to a halt, and dropped lithely from the saddle. His eyes went wide with shock when he saw Crofton's body on the ground, and then his gaze flicked to Fury.

"You son of a bitch!" he howled.

And his hand darted toward the gun holstered on his hip.

If you enjoyed this book, subscribe now and get...

TWO FREE

A $7.00 VALUE—